Kin

JULIE ROWBORY

First paperback edition November 2024

Copyright © 2024 by Julie Rowbory

Julie Rowbory asserts the moral right
to be identified as the author of this work
julierowbory.com

ISBN 978-1-7399145-3-0 (Kin Paperback)
978-1-7399145-4-7 (Kin Kindle)
978-1-7399145-5-4 (Kin Hardback)

Sequel to *Kith*

Design by David Rowbory
Cover art by Charlotte Kiesel
Maps by Melissa Nash
www.melissanashauthor.wordpress.com

Set in Baskerville 11pt
with accents from Minion Pro

For Anna Chiabuotu, Alanna Creighton,
Rachel Ellison, Charlotte Kiesel and Rosie Weston,
who lingered long in Oakdene

THANKS

I would like to extend my thanks to the many people who helped bring *Kīn* to completion. These included the following advance readers and proofreaders who gave invaluable feedback: Anne Alford, Naomi Baxter, Anna Bishop, Agnes Brough, Sari Cabrera, Jennie Campbell, Emma Copeland, Mari Craig, Blessing Gideon, Deanna Greaves, Gemma Herbertson, Sarah and Peace Joseph, Ann Magill, Isyaku Isa Mato, Louise Miscampbell, Katharine Norton, Charlotte and Will Parkinson, Cara Ritson, Bridget Rizama, Iris Sacson, Janneke Verhaar, Hannah Worth, Zach and Christy Yoder.

I am indebted to Anna Chiabuotu, Alanna Creighton, Rachel Ellison, Charlotte Kiesel and Rosie Weston whose comments throughout the writing process were indispensable as the plot and characters developed. Your reactions to different scenes were fundamental to me gauging whether my writing was having the impact I wanted it to have. Thanks to all of you for laughing and crying your way through *Kīn* with me. I am truly grateful.

Once again, let me thank Charlotte Kiesel for creating more beautiful artwork for the cover design, and Melissa Nash for producing the wonderful maps of Oakdene and ninth-century England.

And finally, none of this would have been possible without the ongoing support of my wonderful family: my husband, David, and our daughters, Rebekah, Elizabeth, Abigail and Helen. Thanks, Rebekah, for naming the characters, Leoba and Bald!

I am grateful to God for all of you.

SPEECHHOARD

	IPA	
Æ/æ	[æ]	short 'a', as in 'cat', eg. Æthelred, Rædwald
a	[ʌ]	mostly long, as 'bath' in south of England
c	[k]	hard, as 'k' in modern English, eg. Cynestan
ea	[ea]	two vowels 'ey-a' (**not** 'ee'), eg. Eanfrith is 'Ey-anfrith'
œ	[œ]	as 'ö' in German
wig	[wi]	'wee', eg. Eawig is 'Ey-a-wee'
y	[y]	mid-word as 'ü' in German; 'ee' with rounded lips, eg. fyrd

WORDHOARD

Æscesdun
Ashdown, unknown site in
Berkshire where battle was fought
on 8 January 871 (depicted in
'Swordbrothers' in *Kith*)

Ætheling
close relative or heir of the king

amber
about 4 bushels or 145 litres

barme-cloth
(Old English, *bearmcláþ*)
apron

bookskin (Old English, *bócfell*)
vellum for manuscripts

brock (Old English, *broc*)
badger

bruisewort
(Old English, *brysewyrt*)
common comfrey

Brynefæx
burning hair

cackhouse
(Old English, *cachus*)
latrine or privy

Candlemas
2 February, commemorates the
presentation of Jesus in the temple

Child (Old English, *cild*)
a title of dignity for a youth of
high social position

Childermas
28 December, commemorates
the slaughter of infants by King
Herod

day's-eye
(Old English, *dæges eage*)
daisy

ealdorman
a prestigious noble man, just
under royalty in rank

eggwort (Old English, *ægwyrt*)
dandelion

farrowing
when a sow is in labour

fyrd (pronounced *fürd*)
militia gathered from freemen

kirtle
an overdress

kith (Old English, *cýþþu*)
knowledge, friendship, kinsfolk,
native land, home

leech (Old English, *læce*)
doctor, healer

Loafmas
(Old English, *hlafmæsse*)
1 August (Lammas Day), when a service of thanksgiving was held to mark the firstfruits of harvest

Lundunwic
London

Meretun
battle was fought here on, 22 March 871, possibly near Wimborne Minster where Æthelred was buried

Michaelmas
29 September

minster (Old English, *mynster*)
monastery

moot (Old English, *mot*)
meeting, village court/council

morning-gift
(Old English, *morgengifu*)
gift from husband to wife the morning after the wedding, strictly for her as security in case of future trouble or widowhood

neep (Old English, *næp*)
turnip

Paternoster
the Lord's Prayer, from the first two Latin words 'Our father'

Readingum
Reading in Berkshire

seax (pronounced *sax*)
knife carried by every free person, symbol of freedom

thegn (pronounced *thane*)
minor aristocracy with duties to the king

throstle
a song thrush

Twelfth Eve
5 January, the day before Epiphany which commemorates the visit of the wise men to Jesus

Wiltun
Wilton in Wiltshire where battle was fought in May 871

Winburna
Wimborne Minster in Dorset

Wintanceaster
Winchester in Hampshire

Winter's Day
7 November, marking the beginning of winter

Witan
(more properly *Witenagemót*)
a national council

workreeve
(Old English, *weorcgerefa*)
overseer of workers/slaves, estate manager

writing-seax
(Old English, *writseax*)
stylus

wyn
Old English name for 'w', written ρ

iv

MAPS

NORTHUMBRIA

MERCIA

ENGLAND in 871

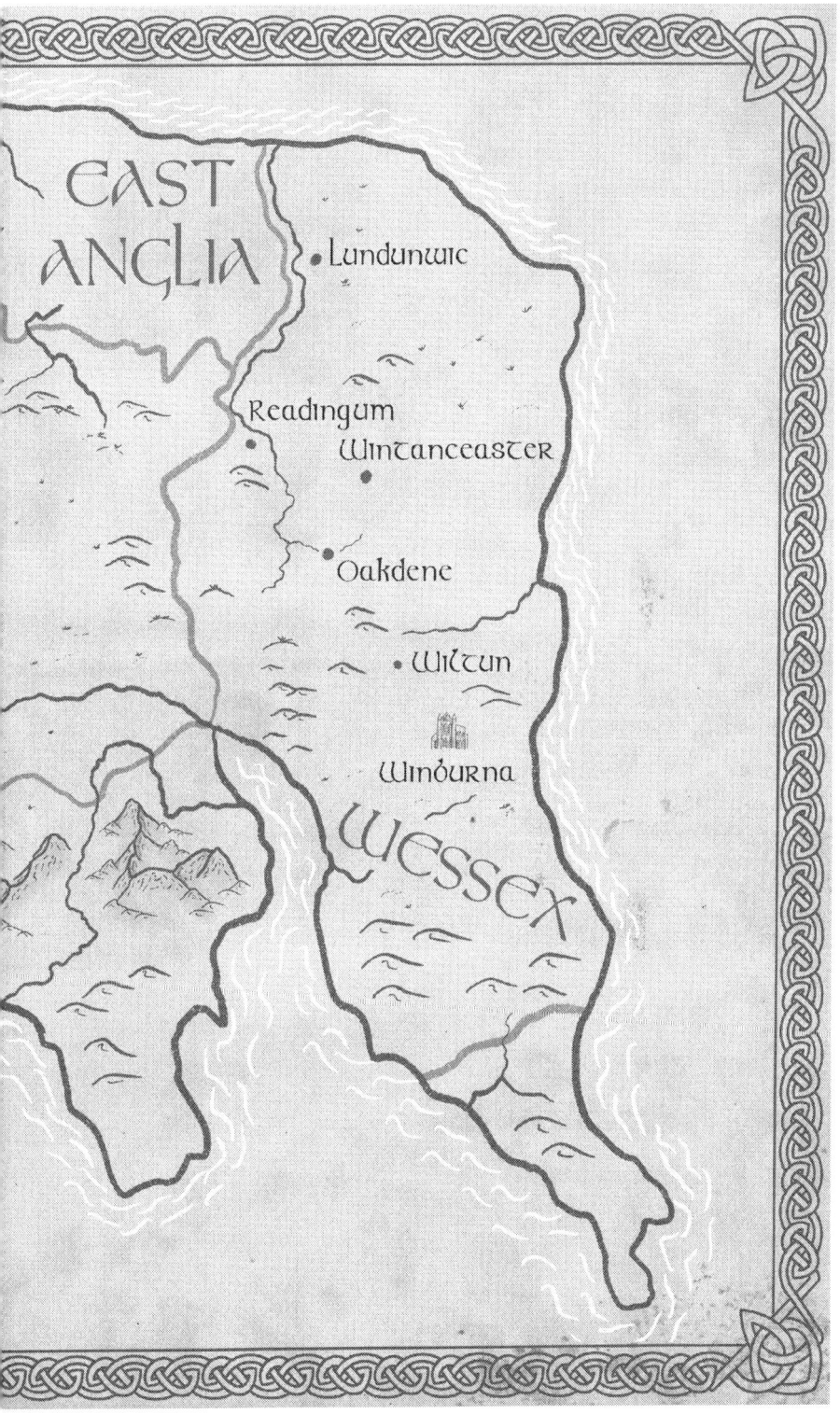

EAST ANGLIA

Lundunwic

Readingum

Wintanceaster

Oakdene

Wiltun

Windurna

WESSEX

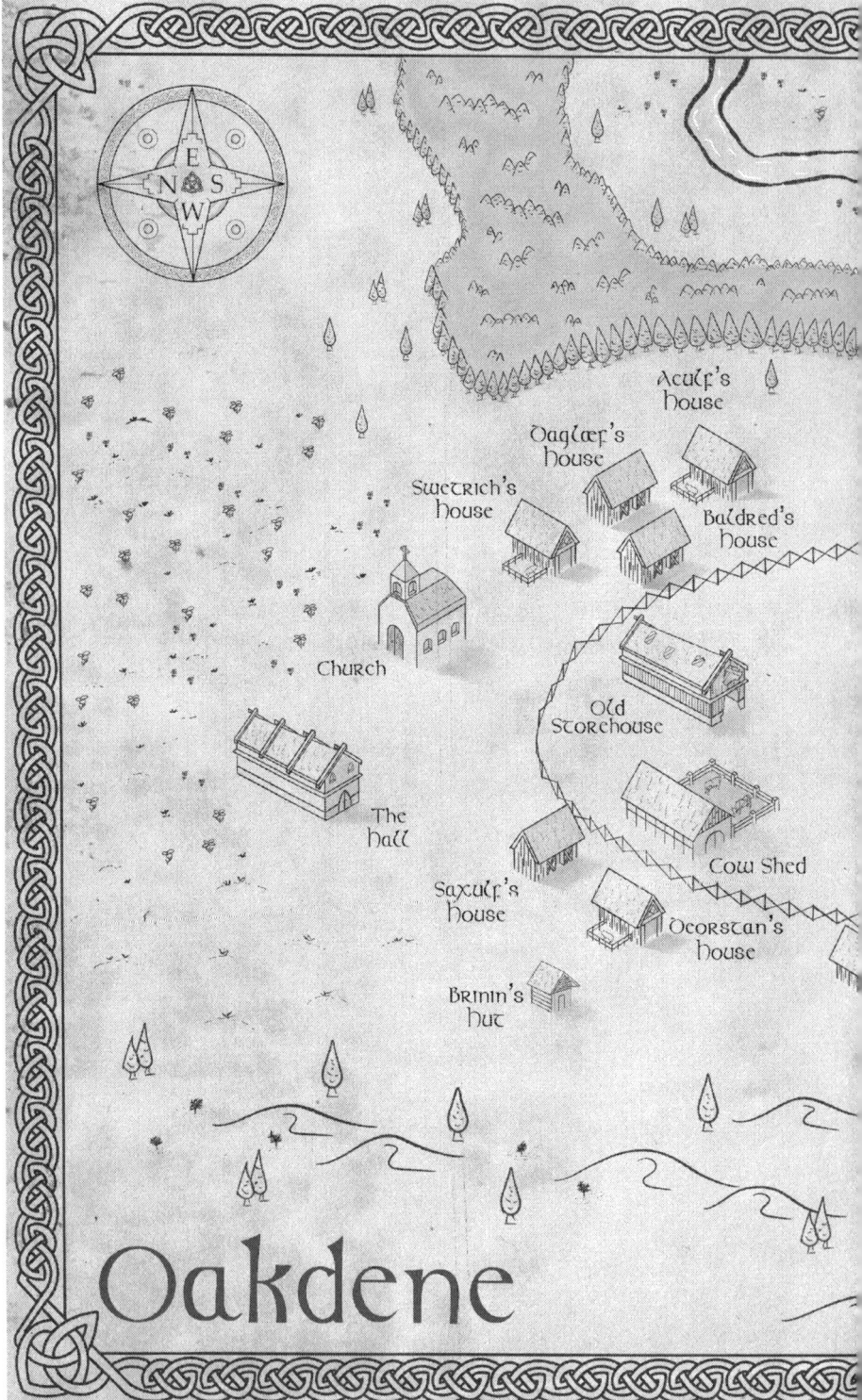

Aculf's
house

Daglæf's
house

Swetrich's
house

Baldred's
house

Church

Old
Storehouse

The
hall

Cow Shed

Saxulf's
House

Deorstan's
house

Brinin's
hut

Oakdene

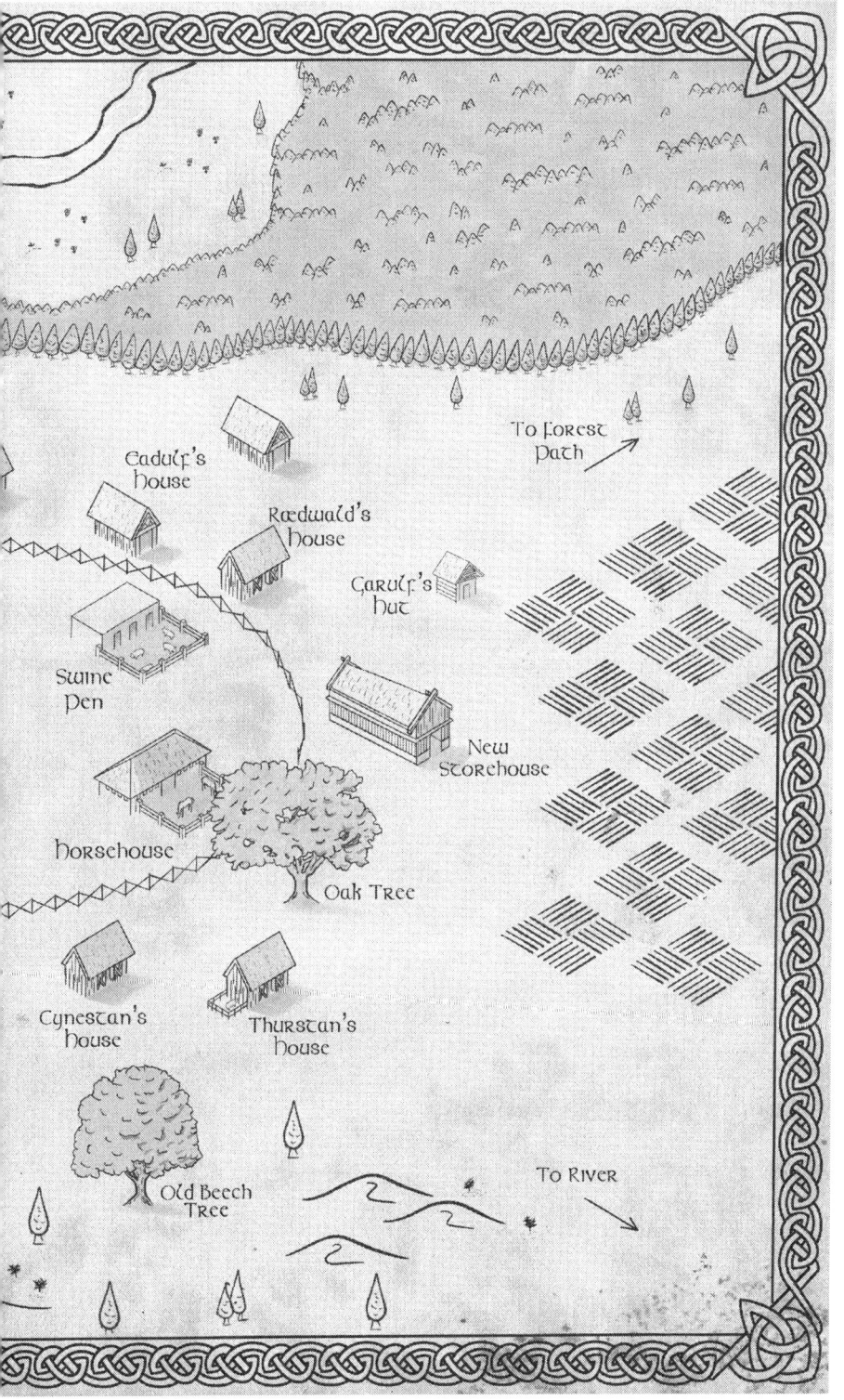

Eadulf's house

Rædwald's house

Garulf's hut

Swine Pen

New Storehouse

To Forest Path

Horsehouse

Oak Tree

Cynestan's house

Thurstan's house

Old Beech Tree

To River

FOLKHOARD

Edrich Thegn's Household in Oakdene

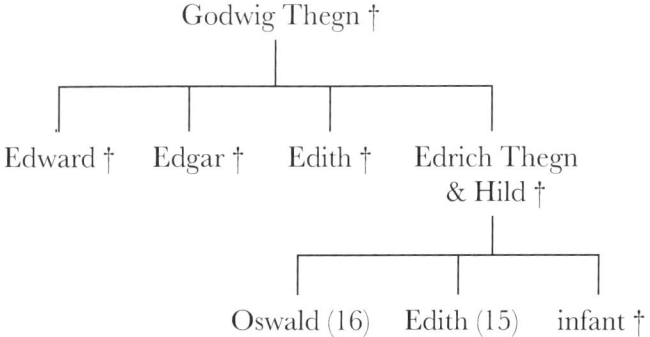

Godwig Thegn †

Edward †   Edgar †   Edith †   Edrich Thegn & Hild †

Oswald (16)   Edith (15)   infant †

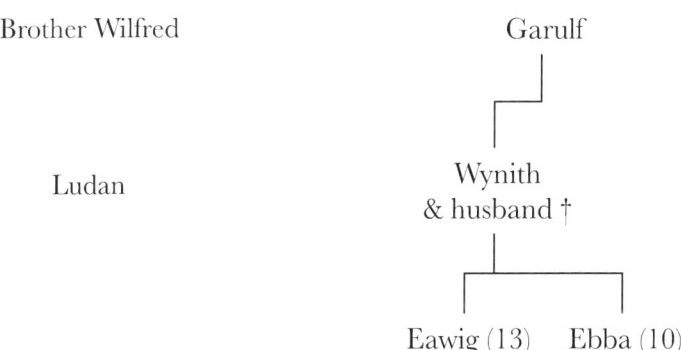

Brother Wilfred   Garulf

Ludan   Wynith & husband †

Eawig (13)   Ebba (10)

† indicates deceased by March 871
Numbers in brackets are ages of
children in March 871

KIN

Other Oakdene Households

Wulfstan †
& Hallveig †

Row † Gytha † Gyrich † Brinin (16)

Thurstan †
& Mildrith

Mærwyn (17) Cenwyn (15) Tidræd (12) Oswyn (8) Tidwine (5)

Cynestan
& Wynflæd

Leofwine † Leofgar (12) Leoflæd (5) other children

Byrnhelm

Daglæf ··········· *maternal cousins* ··········· Aculf
& Bægswyth   & Sægyth ·······························

Bealdwulf (11) Bealdwine (8)   Wulfrich (9) Ulf (6) two daughters

---

Households from Other Villages

Edrich's brother-in-law, ············· Hildræd ············· *cousins* ·········
Oswald's maternal uncle   & Ceolwyn ·······················

Alrich † daughter Aldred (13) Aldulf (9)

xii

FOLKHOARD

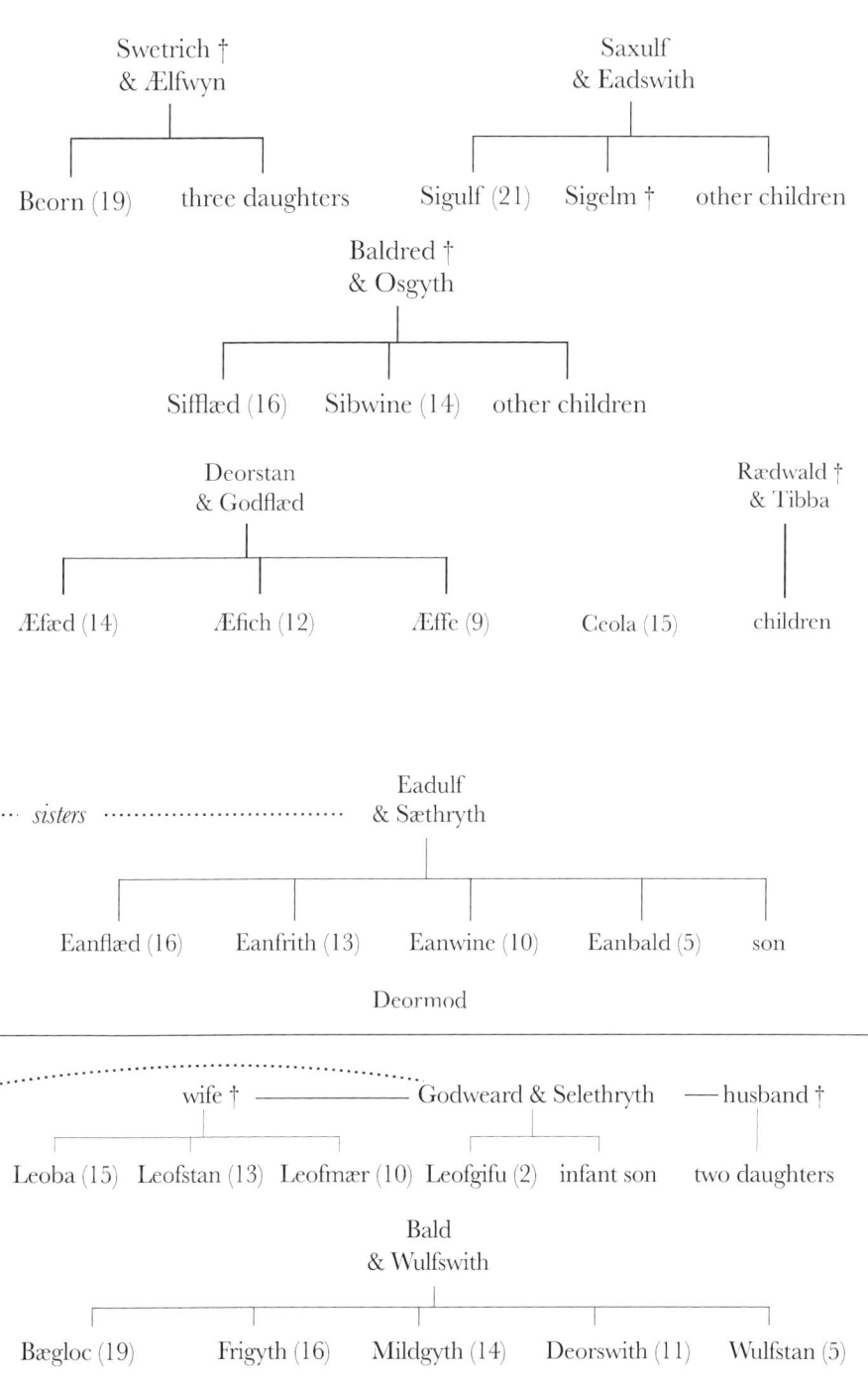

WESSEX, 22 MARCH 871

BLOOD

There was blood on his face as he roared towards Oswald, shieldless and fearless. High above his head, his sword quivered, ready to fall in biting death. Oswald stumbled away, hardly knowing or caring what he stood on. The sword missed him by an arrow's breadth, but the blood-faced foe swung it round again, sending a rattle of pain through Oswald's body as it struck his shield. Oswald thrust back with his own blade, but his foe's sword was everywhere and their weapons met, edge to edge. The man's hair was matted, sticking to his forehead, the blood dark around it. Was it his own blood? Oswald couldn't see the wound.

Leofwine was nearby, still fighting hard but kneeling before a foe who towered treelike over him and sent down blow after blow that Leofwine was barely blocking. His shield arm hung limp at his side, the shield already lost. Oswald couldn't go to him. There were too many men, too many sword-thrusts between them. He couldn't get away from his foe, couldn't kill him, couldn't turn left or right without his foe's weapon following him. Yet without him, Leofwine would die; Leofwine, whom he'd known all his life, would fall with no swordbrother to help him.

Friendship fed Oswald's weary sword with fresh strength. It bit his foe, wounding the empty shield arm. But still he came, roaring and screaming, more warlike with more wounds. He drove Oswald back, battering his uplifted shield with one-armed blows. A few more would be enough to bring Oswald down. He was stumbling and unsteady now; his shield was cracking. It was the end. He and Leofwine would both die on their knees in the mud, neither helping the other. There was no time left to feel the fear of it, only the cool knowledge that it was coming.

Oswald fell. He raised his shield above his head and thrust out blindly, hopelessly with his sword. One last wound before he died might spare the next man. His shield was braced, his whole body ready for pain and darkness. But there was only a sudden stillness. The foe sank before him—almost on top of him—a spear in his back, flung by some unknown hand. Oswald was spared, spared even as death was clutching at him.

He scrambled, breathless and shaking, to his feet, looking everywhere for Leofwine. But he was gone. Oswald stared round wildly, but he could see him nowhere in the battlethrong. That was when he felt the fear, or was it shame? Leofwine hadn't scrambled to *his* feet. Not with that foe standing over him; not with the wound that Oswald had seen. It was too late, too late for help or hope.

Somehow they drove them back, the King with his men and the Ætheling with his. Oswald didn't know how they did it. The Danes were so many in their two great bands and the fyrd too few. So many were falling that there was nowhere to look without the sight of them. Yet Wessex, few and weakening, held their ground and the Danes could not scatter them. Throughout the day, throughout the long rush of battle, they held it.

'Stand fast, stand fast!' The cry rang loud, passing from man to man. They gathered again behind the shield wall, ready to spring out at their foe like some small snarling hound rushing at a wolf.

The Danes were driven back, but not driven away. All was uproar and slaughter. Shields were raised against spears, and arrows tore where they fell. At Oswald's side, at his shoulder, a man he didn't know died at his feet. But no one could stop to think of—or look at—the dead. They could only ready their hearts to follow them.

The Danes turned in a wild rush, swarming forward to meet them eye to eye, overwhelming them with their many men. The shield wall was broken as they threw themselves upon them. Who was falling? Oswald only knew that he was yet to fall. And there was blood on his face, as there had been blood on his foe's. He felt it there but didn't know whose it was.

The ravens gathered, as below swords and axes readied a feast for them. Breathless, battleworn and battlebitten, foe fell on foe. Sword shattered shield, and no one knew how far the sun had passed through the sky. Oswald had long since lost his shield, snatching up another from among the dead. His sword dealt death to men with faces: the blue-eyed man; the one with an adderlike scar on his cheek; the foe with hair as burning and firelike as Brinin's. There was no shouting now to strengthen the thunder of battle. His throat was too dry for that. With each sword slash he only grunted like a beast.

The small snarling hound drove the wolf back, snapping at its throat and biting at its ankles. The Wessex bands came together again, ever tighter, ever smaller. It was too early for battle gladness though the sun was low in the sky. It was too early to rest when the wolf might still turn back to fling itself upon them again.

'Stand fast!' The Ætheling's bellow soared above the sounds of battle. 'We've held the field, but the battle is not over. One more rush and we will drive them away. Come together now and ready yourselves.'

They stood ready, but Oswald was alone among strangers. He stood, but Leofwine had fallen. In the throng he was without hearthfellows; Saxulf stood far off perhaps, but no one else. His sword was filthy and dark with blood as he waited for the war cry. And he couldn't see his father anywhere.

WORK

'What do you think, Cenwyn?' said Edith. 'I like the yellow better but I don't know if I can make two shirts from the brown.'

Two lengths of woollen cloth, soft and skilfully woven, were spread out over a bench as Edith stood looking down at it.

'Did you weave these yourself?' asked Cenwyn, rubbing the brown cloth between her fingers. 'You're better than I am.'

'I like weaving. It gives me time to sit and think.'

Or sit and not think. There had been too much dread and waiting that winter; too much wondering if she had watched her father and brother ride away for the last time. Likely that was why the cloth was well woven. She had kept her mind on her loom so that it wouldn't wander to the battlefield. The last of the winter frost had melted away now, but not the last of the waiting. Perhaps tomorrow she would start some more cloth. There was always something to do with it.

'Even in winter I'd rather be outside in the cold than sitting at a loom,' said Cenwyn. 'I can weave well enough—Mother has seen to that—but I've always liked to work with the beasts or in the field. And now...'

Now it was a good thing that Cenwyn did like it, with Thurstan dead and Tidræd still too young to work with a man's strength. It always fell to the women to do the men's work when their husbands, fathers and brothers went to war. But Cenwyn and her mother and sister weren't doing it only for a while. It was their work now, not their father's, and must be done alongside everything else.

'I want to make myself a new kirtle. This one's still good, but my blue one is worn at the back, so I'm going to give it to Wynith to make something for Ebba; hers is too short now. And I'll make two shirts with whatever is left. My father and Oswald will need new ones when they come back.' Better to say 'when' and not 'if'. 'But I don't know which to make the kirtle with and which to keep for the shirts. I like the yellow better, as I said, but the brown would go well with this.'

Edith unwound a long, thin band of red cloth, woven with waves of brown and white that twisted and crossed each other.

'Did you make this as well?' said Cenwyn wonderingly, as she took the band from Edith.

'No! I can't make anything like this. My father once bought it for me in Wintanceaster, and I've been keeping it until I knew what to do with it.'

'Make the kirtle from the brown then, and sew the band along the neck and edges of the sleeves, and even along the hem at the bottom. There'll still be enough left for one shirt, as well as any you make from the yellow.' Cenwyn laughed. 'I'm good at telling others what to do with their cloth, even if I don't like doing it myself! I'd be happy to leave all of that kind of thing to Mærwyn.'

Edith folded the cloth, and they sat down together on the bench.

'Mærwyn looked tired when I saw her earlier,' she said. 'Is she worrying about Leofwine?'

'She hasn't said so, but I know she is. When my father and Cynestan asked them to wait until after harvest for the wedding, none of us thought the Danes would come so soon. Now I think she wishes they hadn't waited. But I don't know how it would have been any better. Even if she was his wife, Leofwine would still be away and she would still be waiting.'

The waiting seemed to grow heavier, weighing them down a little more each day. There was no way to lighten it when the end was often so bitter. That was why Edith was always busy, wearying herself with whatever work she could find. How else could she keep herself from stumbling under the load? How else could she be sure of sleep when darkness came?

'Tidræd is our worry now,' Cenwyn went on, 'not Mærwyn, though Mother says he always was, when it wasn't me.'

'What's he done now?'

'What hasn't he done? He mostly heeds Mother but he always seems to do things that no one would think of forbidding. Yesterday he slipped from the house so early that no one was awake to stop him. He went hunting. I don't know what he thought he would find; he didn't come back with anything. It was almost dark when he got in, and he'd done no work all day. Mother was so angry, but Tidræd only said that Father sometimes went hunting and that she hadn't said he couldn't. Not that Mother listened to *that*! He likely won't do it again, but he'll think of something new instead. Father would keep him with him, you know, to teach him things and stop him from making trouble. He does things now he wouldn't have dared to do if… if Father had still been here. And he doesn't want to be always at his mother's or sisters' sides as he was with Father.'

'Aren't most boys troublesome at twelve winters? He's still young and he's always been bold.'

'You sound like someone's mother!' laughed Cenwyn. 'It wasn't so long ago that *we* were only twelve winters! Are we old and wise now? Besides, I don't remember Oswald being like Tidræd.'

'Not often, no. But that was Oswald. He never wanted to be troublesome, and my father can be very stern.'

Cenwyn dropped her head, her laughter spent. Why had they strayed into speaking of fathers when Cenwyn's was already gone and Edith's own soon might be? It had been easier to speak of the cloth.

'Do you know what I think?' said Cenwyn at length, and she too sounded older now, wearier if not wiser. 'I think Tidræd wishes he could somehow *be* Father. When… when we heard, he ran off and didn't come home for a long time. He's never let any of us see him weeping about it, though I've often seen from his eyes that he has been. He remembers all those tales Father told him of when he was a boy—things he did with your father—and Tidræd wants to do them to be more like him. But they're all the kind of thing my father and yours would have been so angry with Tidræd or Oswald for doing. Well, yours would have been angry; mine would only have seemed to be then laughed about it afterwards when he thought no one was looking. I saw him do that sometimes. Tidræd looks at Father's sword every day and talks about working on his warcraft to be ready for the Danes. But he forgets that Father did all the other work too, and that it still needs to be done even though the Danes have come.'

'What's your mother going to do about him?' asked Edith. Tidræd was a brother so unlike her own that it was hard to think what it might be like to be his sister. Oswald had always been so eager to know what he ought to do. Tidræd seemed to look for ways to do what he knew he oughtn't.

'She told him yesterday that he's to be in the field every morning by sunrise to plough, and that if he goes anywhere else without her leave he will soon wish he hadn't.'

'And will he heed her?'

'For now. Father always made him, and he knows he must. But once the ploughing is over, he'll think of new mischief.' Cenwyn stood up. 'I'd better go. I have work to do, and Mother won't like it if I sit here all day. She's always so tired now.'

They all had work to do. Edith watched Cenwyn go, then went back to her own work to shut out the dread that was gnawing at her. Perhaps they would know soon.

BEGINNINGS

B rinin laid aside his tools and stood back to look at his swine pen. He was happy with it. The fence was strong, and the shelter lay tight against the wall of his hut. It was small but big enough for one sow and, he hoped, her young. He had built it with his own hands for his own beast, and the knowledge of that was the best of all.

It seemed so long ago now, that day when Edrich Thegn told Brinin the field was his, but it had only been long enough for the hardness of winter to soften a little and the first fresh green to spring out everywhere on tree and shrub. He had gone to sleep that first night in wonder; free, a man with a field of his own. But in the cold of the next morning he had opened his eyes in worry. He was alone with no tools, no seed, no food, no kin; with nothing but the cold earth, an almost empty hut and the clothes he stood in. He had dreamt that night of making himself a plough but by sunrise he had known that it couldn't be done. How could he make a plough with no tools? Where were the oxen to pull it if he had one? And if tears had come readily to him he would have wept.

The sun hadn't been long up when Oswald had come with tools under his arms that he had dropped at Brinin's feet. They were from his father, he had said, because he couldn't free a man to starve for lack of work. There was a spade, a shovel, an axe, everything he might need. There were even tools for woodcraft—only Oswald would have thought of those. Later Edrich Thegn had called Brinin and told him to take his food from the hall until harvest and that he could pay for it with a little work now and then, though not too much as he had his own work to see to. And he had given him a gift of seed so that Brinin had almost all he needed to begin.

Weeks had passed since then, and he had begun. It was almost time for the sowing, and there were already some furrows in his field. The day after Oswald and Edrich Thegn had ridden away again to war, Thurstan's widow Mildrith had come to tell him that if he ploughed her land he could plough his own with her plough and oxen. Brinin didn't know if she had thought of it herself or if Oswald or Edrich Thegn had thought of it for her. It was a kindness, and without it his field might never have been ploughed. Even the sow was a kindness, too high a payment for a bench he didn't think Oswald needed. But Oswald had only said that it was for him to say if he needed a bench; and as the beast was his, a gift from his father, he could buy a bench with it if he liked. There had been so many kindnesses, and it was hard to turn them away. But there mustn't be too many. There must be no more after harvest. That's when he would know he was free and not only playing at it while eating another man's bread.

Brinin had just put away his tools, stacking them tidily in the hut, when he heard Eawig coming along with the sow.

'She's a good beast,' said Eawig, leaning against the pen once the sow was safely inside. 'Her mother's strong and gives good young.'

Eawig knew swine. He was better with beasts than with the plough, and at thirteen winters folk called him a swineherd.

'How would you like a swine of your own, Eawig?'

'I'd like it,' laughed Eawig, 'but I'm never likely to have one, am I?'

'It's not easy always to work alone,' said Brinin. 'Come and help me sometimes when no one needs you. I'll ask Cynestan if he'll spare you. And when the sow has her brood, you can choose whichever you like from among them.'

'You would give me one of your swine?'

'I wouldn't be *giving* it to you. You'd be earning it. But you can choose any of the brood, even the best of them.'

Eawig laughed again, this time in a kind of wondering disbelief.

'Well!' he said. 'I *will* come then, if Cynestan will let me, any time you like. A swine of my own! Who would have thought it?'

And who would have thought that Brinin would be the one offering it to him? There were some things that none of them could ever have foreseen.

The sun was low now, and it was time for Brinin to fetch his food, but his own swine in his own pen was another step nearer the time when he wouldn't need to. Eawig walked with him until he was called away by Cynestan. Cynestan was out of his bed now, but not fit for battle; he would likely never be fit for the fyrd again. There was never a good time to be a thrall, but perhaps it was a better time to be one of Edrich Thegn's now that Cynestan was workreeve. He was as unlike Aculf as a workreeve could be. Cynestan was mild and slow to anger. He smiled more than he frowned. In all those weeks of freedom Brinin had only seen one slave beaten, lifting his arm to shield his head from the blows; but it had been Eadulf's slave, Deormod, and not one of Edrich Thegn's. He had once heard Cynestan scolding Eawig for letting one of the swine out, but not more sternly than he might have scolded his own son. Eawig had listened to worse from his grandfather later by the hearth. Cynestan never went looking for misdeeds. There was no strutting or shouting with him. The only stick he had was to steady himself and give strength to his wounded leg.

Brinin went to Garulf's hut with his food. He often ate there now. Some days it was easier to sit by Garulf's hearth and listen to him talk than to sit alone with only the crackle of the fire to hear and the shadows to look at. Brinin heard Eawig before he reached the hut, telling the news of his unborn swine with swift eagerness.

'And I'll share it with you, Ebba,' Eawig was saying to his sister, as Brinin went through the door. 'It'll be your swine too!'

'But which end shall be mine?' asked Ebba. 'The head or the tail?'

Everyone laughed at this, but it wasn't laughter that Brinin saw in Garulf's eyes when he turned to him with a smile.

'You're a good lad, Brinin,' he said. 'I always said you were, but to offer the boy a swine...'

'I need his help from time to time,' said Brinin, 'and I've nothing else to offer him. There's nothing to stop a slave from having a beast so long as he comes by it through work and not theft.'

That night Brinin's hut seemed to lose a little of its emptiness. He was alone with the shadows when he lay down to sleep, but the firelight fell on his tools by the doorway and there was a gladness in knowing what he had built with them. And beside him, beyond the wall, he could hear his sow snuffling in her pen. She was his own sow, and perhaps the beginning of something better for Eawig too. It had been a good day.

10

TURNING

Hope was short-lived, and the Danes too strong. They held them off until the shadows were long, but they couldn't drive them away. Their swordbrothers sank with the sun, falling with the darkness, and the Danes scattered them. The fyrd turned and fled. The Danes took the field and gloated over it as though it were truly their own. They picked over the Wessex dead to take their swords and arm rings and left their bodies unburied for the ravens.

Oswald was scattered with the others. They stumbled away in the twilight. There was a shameful bitterness in it when they had all spoken so boldly that morning of putting the Danes to flight. It felt no better than running from his own house and leaving it to thieves. At the beginning of each new battle, the boasting rang ever more hollow. There was none of the fierce pride of that first morning, when he had roared at the foe with Saxulf and Thurstan on either side. The Danes were doing as they wished with Wessex and they could do little to stop them. It was like leaving his house to thieves, knowing that his kin and all he owned were still inside.

He was alone at first, not even asking where he went, running on heavy legs and hating himself for it. And when the battleglad shouts of the Danes were far off, he sank to his knees, weak and spent, breathing in heaving pants that could easily have become sobs had he let them. He sat on the cold ground with his head in his hands. The roar of battle still seemed to be all around him, that blood-faced foe still rushing towards him, Leofwine still struggling on his knees.

His father had been at his shoulder that morning as they had set out after the King and the Ætheling, but where was he now? Where were any of his hearthfellows? Was he alone left? Could his father still live without Oswald even glimpsing of him? It wasn't like the day when

Thurstan had come, sorrowbearing, to the minster—that had happened in another time. He had been spared long mourning then, but was ready for it now, ready every day for death or sorrow. But the fear that it had come at last was still as cold as the earth he sat on. If his father was slain and he was left, it would fall on him to ride home and tell Edith. If he alone had lived, he would have to bear the tidings from house to house.

Oswald was startled out of his gloom by voices borne towards him through the evening. He scrambled to his feet, ready to run again. But these men were not foes. They walked, talking as friends, speaking his own tongue. He turned to meet them as they came through the dusk, and he saw that one of them was Beorn. So he wasn't left alone then. One hearthfellow was enough to hearten him like a crowd.

'Beorn!' It was all Oswald could do not to fling his arms around him. 'I was worried I was the only one left.'

'It's good to see you, Oswald Child.' Beorn spoke warmly, a hand on Oswald's arm in friendship. 'I saw Saxulf too, not long before the end. I don't think he fell. This is Wulfmar. I didn't know him yesterday, but he helped me today when I most needed help. A man can become a swordbrother and a friend quickly in times like these.'

'Have... have you seen my father?' Oswald almost didn't dare to ask. What if Beorn had seen him lying dead on the ground?

'Not since morning.' Beorn frowned, so freshly fatherless himself that he couldn't misunderstand what Oswald was asking. 'But there are always so many men in a battle that it might not mean—'

'No,' said Oswald swiftly before Beorn could speak the fear aloud, but a little more hope slipped away. 'It might not mean that. I didn't see _you_ either, after all.'

'If we find what's left of the fyrd, Oswald Child, we may find him there among them.'

'We'd better keep walking then,' said Oswald grimly. He drew a deep breath. 'And Leofwine's dead. I saw him fall.'

They worked their eyes and ears hard to find their way in the darkness. They strained to see through the night, moonlit but cloudy and dim, listening all the time for the slightest whisper of the fyrd or what was left of it. Wulfmar became their leader. He had lived all his life near the battlefield and knew the land like he knew the way from his threshold to his hearth. Even in the darkness he could lead them back to where, still hopeful, they had left the camp that morning.

It was late, though still nearer to sunset than dawn, when they saw the light of a fire ahead and heard men talking. They weren't likely to be Danes—not here—but they were careful as they drew near, as soft as hunters after their prey.

They were fyrdmen, only six of them, too weary and broken to go any further that night. They sat wretchedly round their fire and spoke in heavy voices of what they had seen, of how the battle had gone, and of those among their swordbrothers cut down. Oswald knew none of them—though he half-remembered some of their faces from the camp— but two of them knew Wulfmar and asked them to sit with them by the fire.

'Did you hear about the King?' asked one man as Oswald and the others sat down.

'No,' said Wulfmar. 'I've heard nothing and seen no one but these two I'm with. He's not dead, is he?'

'Wounded,' said the man, 'and I don't know how badly. I saw them bear him away. He was alive then.'

That was another blow on this day of blows. Oswald was rather bruised by them all. If the King should die…

'Pray God it isn't badly,' said Wulfmar. 'This wouldn't be a good time for the King to die.'

'It would be the worst of times,' said one of the other men, 'with the Danes among us and the King's sons only children. Small children too. Even Æthelhelm, the older one, can't be much more than five winters.'

'The kingship needn't go to his son,' said Wulfmar. 'The Ætheling has been at the King's side all through this, as strong in battle as the King himself. If the King dies, the Ætheling should follow him. That's better than having a child for a king, and the Ætheling is fit for kingship.'

'He may be fit for kingship,' said the first man, 'but could the Witan pass over two living sons and give the kingship to his brother?'

'Let's not bury the King before he's dead!' said a man from the other side of the fire. 'He's wounded, not already fallen. Wounded men sometimes live—I was wounded at Readingum and fought again today.

And besides, when the time comes for the Witan to make a new king, no one is going to come to any of us seeking wisdom!'

And that was all that could be said. Oswald stared into the fire without speaking a word, not even to Beorn. He had lived through another battle, but what was he left with? Little hope, shameful defeat, a fallen friend, a wounded king. A father? He was ready for the worst. Likely the morning would bring news of it.

BIRDSONG

They spent a sleepless night and rose with the sun. By some wonder, they found the camp as they had left it—the tents and the horses—but the fyrd was broken and thin. They crept back ashamed, like whipped hounds, to learn who had lived and what was to be done against such a foe.

The King was on everyone's lips. Men they had not shared a word with before stopped them to ask if they had heard. The King was wounded. Some said his wounds were heavy; some said they were only slight. No one said that the King was whole. It was a bright morning, fresh with birdsong and new life, but a chill hung over the camp as bleak as winter.

Saxulf was the first of their hearthfellows whom Oswald and Beorn saw, with Sigulf not far off. Four then. Could a friend be welcomed with gladness? What news might they bear?

'It's good to see more of us still standing,' said Beorn as they reached Saxulf and Sigulf. Sigulf, white and ill-looking, had a dark patch of sticky blood on his shirt, but he was still on his feet. Oswald was glad to have Beorn at his side; he had a way of keeping hold of himself even on the worst of days. 'Have you seen Edrich Thegn?'

'No. We got here not long ago,' said Saxulf. He turned to Oswald with a frown. 'You haven't seen your father?'

'Not since… since sometime before the end. I can't remember when. Everything was so…' But the words faded away. They had all been there. They knew.

'Among so many it can be hard to see anyone,' said Saxulf, but Oswald saw the quick look he shared with Beorn and Sigulf; a grim look that stung like a sword's edge. It was going to fall on him to tell Edith.

'Baldred is badly wounded,' Saxulf went on. 'I hardly know how we got him here. He was wandering in his mind, speaking strangely, before we even reached the camp. Likely the fever was already setting in. He may not live.'

'Leofwine's dead,' said Beorn. 'Oswald Child saw him fall.'

'Cynestan will take that hard. It's a bitter thing to lose a son,' said Saxulf heavily, his own son's grave still too freshly dug.

The birds burst into song again, warbling, joyful and swelling as they called to one another. But it was anger that swelled inside Oswald. How could they dare to sing so boldly on a morning like this?

'Come, Oswald Child,' said Saxulf. 'Your father's well known. Someone will know where he is. We might find Rædwald too. I haven't seen him either. Did you hear about the King?'

Everyone had heard about the King. The word about him had spread among them even more swiftly than the fyrd had fled the Danes. But they didn't see any other Oakdene men, and Oswald's hope ebbed low; a word from one who had seen his father's end was all he wanted now. His eyes swept through the crowd, passing from man to man. At last he saw a welcome face: Hildræd his uncle, filthy from the battlefield and looking as weary as Oswald felt. Forgetting the others, Oswald rushed forward, pushing past men in his haste.

'Oswald, my boy!' Hildræd grasped Oswald's arm warmly. 'I'm glad to see you still with breath in your body! I was afraid—'

'My father, sir…' said Oswald breathlessly. 'Is he… have you…?'

'Wounded, but alive and likely to mend,' said Hildræd. That was all Oswald needed. The birds could sing now if they liked. 'And the sight of you will do more for him than any leech. He was worried… but come, come. Let me take you to him.'

His father was lying in their tent, grey-faced and ill. He began to sit up when Oswald ducked inside, Hildræd not far behind him, but he gave up on it and sank back weakly. Oswald knelt by his side with a thankfulness that felt near to prayer. He had been spared mourning yet again; he wouldn't have to tell Edith.

'Oswald, I thought perhaps… I feared…'

'Yes, Father.' No need to say more than that. They both knew what the other had feared. 'You… you're wounded.'

'My shield arm and one of my legs, but don't worry too much. All my bones are sound. Oh, and my shoulder too, but the leather of my sword strap stopped the arrow from going in too deep. Is what I can see your only wound?'

'Wound? What *can* you see, sir?'

'On your forehead.'

'I didn't know.' Oswald lifted his hand to his forehead, feeling where the blood had already dried and hardened. 'I don't know how I got it. I don't think I have any other wounds, Father.'

No more wounds. Not torn, only bruised and aching. The bruises were throbbing a little now that the fear had been lifted from his mind.

'Do you know anything of the Oakdene men, Oswald? Have you seen any of them?'

'Yes, sir. Saxulf, Sigulf and Beorn are all alive. I haven't seen Baldred, but Saxulf says he's very bad and feverish. He has little hope for him. And... and Leofwine is dead. I saw him wounded and about to fall. I haven't seen Rædwald.'

'He's dead,' said Edrich dully. Was Rædwald in his mind, stuck there as Leofwine was in Oswald's? 'You'll have to go to Oakdene—you and another man—once I know if you can be spared from here. They've heard nothing for weeks. It won't be for long, only to go with word and come back again. I'd go myself, but... You can go on my behalf. Not yet. In a day or two when we know more of what will come of all this. The King... I heard about the King. It was a shameful day, a shameful day. Let me sleep now.'

Edrich shut his eyes with such a heavy sigh it was almost a groan. Oswald, too tired for speech or even the tears that suddenly felt so near, curled up on his bed of leaves and dry grass and listened to his father breathe. It would fall to him to tell Leofwine and Rædwald's kin. The birds were still singing outside the tent.

SONS

Ploughing began early, before the sun had time to scatter the shadows. In the evening Brinin, with aching, heavy limbs, would almost fall onto his fleece to sleep. But he liked it that way. It was better to be too weary to think; better to shut his eyes swiftly and sleep too deeply for dreams to ensnare him in the night. His field and Mildrith's were well furrowed now, more than half-done. Mildrith sent Tidræd to drive the oxen, and that was good too. Tidræd talked so much that there was little time for Brinin's mind to wander to Row and the days when they had ploughed together.

Then one day Tidræd hadn't come. Brinin had waited for a long time before he went to look for him, leaving the oxen tethered fast to a stake in the ground. He hadn't found Tidræd, only his mother, more than unhappy to learn that her son was not where he ought to be. Brinin didn't want to bring trouble on a boy he liked—and he saw in Mildrith's eyes what kind of welcome Tidræd would meet with when he came back from wherever he had hidden—but what else could be done? The fields needed to be ploughed and Brinin couldn't drive both plough and oxen alone. And if ever there was a boy who earned his trouble it was Tidræd. They didn't find him, and no ploughing was done that day.

In the morning Mildrith had marched Tidræd down to the field herself. The boy had stood awkwardly—half-ashamed, half-sullen—while his mother told Brinin that if there was ever a day when Tidræd wasn't in the field by sunrise, he was to come and find her at once. Tidræd had been gloomy all day and had barely said a word. But that had been yesterday. His gloom and sullenness had melted away in the night and now he worked at Brinin's side as cheerfully as before.

'Your father's dead, isn't he?' said Tidræd when they stopped to water the oxen. That seemed to be the way with Tidræd; he rushed from thought to thought with little warning of where he might go next.

'Yes.'

'He died a long time ago?'

'When I was only four winters.'

Tidræd said no more about it until they were cutting their way through the earth again.

'Did he die suddenly in battle?' he said at length.

'No.' At least not from the kind of battle Tidræd meant. He had died slowly, sick and weary, worn out by years of hard work.

'So you didn't much have a father. That must be why I don't remember anything about him. I know everything about everyone in the village!'

'I had a brother. You remember him, I know.' Their speech was taking a somewhat painful turn that Brinin would never have chosen, but now that they were on that path it might be worth keeping on it for a while. 'My brother wasn't much older than you are now when our father died, but he became like a father to me.'

'How can a brother be like a father?'

'He taught me what our father had taught him.'

'What? Not warcraft—you were slaves.'

'Is warcraft the only thing to learn? How to kindle a fire, to plough, to work with a sickle or scythe.' Was it sly to drive their speech along like this? But Mildrith had been kind to him, and he had thought of a way to be kind to her. 'And that I must never go off to play when there was work to be done.'

Though Brinin had meant to say it softly, hiding it among the other things that Row had taught him, the shadow of a scowl crept over Tidræd's face.

'*You* never did that!' he said.

'I did, but only once,' said Brinin.

'Did your brother beat you for it?'

'No, but he told me why I couldn't do it.'

'Why?'

'Because I was a slave, and slaves never have time to play.'

'*I'm* not a slave,' Tidræd muttered.

'Your brother will be like me,' said Brinin. 'When he's older he'll hardly remember your father, but he'll learn from you how to work and fight and do all the things that your father taught you.'

Tidræd seemed to like the thought of that. It pulled him back from falling into sullenness again, and his chatter went on cheerfully until it was time to unyoke the oxen.

～

Thoughts of fathers and sons stayed with Brinin throughout the day: Tidræd's bold father; his own shadowy father, barely remembered; the brother who had been almost like a father. They stood by as he shovelled away his sow's dung. They walked with him as he took the bucket of dung down to his field and watched as he spread it on the land as yet unploughed.

He was on his way back to his hut, walking behind the horsehouse, when he heard men talking on the other side of it where he couldn't see them. He only half-heard them until one of them said something that drove the other thoughts away.

'Does he plough Edrich Thegn's land? I've only seen him ploughing Thurstan's.'

'I don't think so,' said another man. 'He ploughs for Mildrith, and she lets him have her team for his own field.'

'His *own* field! Without owing Edrich Thegn any work for it? That doesn't seem right to me, when I pay in ploughing and harvesting for leave to till my field. Why should a freedman have better than that? His father was a slave too, and not even from Oakdene. Why should…?'

Brinin walked on. What good would it do him to listen to any more? He knew long before he reached his hut that someone was there; a little dark shape flitted behind it before he could see who it was. He was almost at the door before he saw Wulfrich, Aculf's older son, peeking round at him from the swine pen. Wulfrich was almost the last boy Brinin would have thought he might find there, less likely even than Aculf himself.

'What are you doing here?' he asked. He didn't mean to sound unfriendly, but the words came out gruffly and he softened them a little. 'Did you come to look at the sow?'

'No, only to sit here. I always came here when you were gone because Fa… no one would think of looking for me here.' Wulfrich was stiff and wary, his brow furrowed with worry. 'You aren't angry, are you?'

'No. Likely you're doing no harm.'

Wulfrich watched Brinin as he went into the pen to tend to the sow, filling up the water and feeding troughs. He didn't smile and didn't speak, but he didn't leave either.

'Do you like swine?' said Brinin at length.

'Yes,' said Wulfrich, and his wariness seemed to lift a little. 'When I'm bigger I'm going to have a whole herd of them and make them all fat and then I'll sell them and take the money and go to Wintanceaster.'

'What will you do when you get there?'

'I don't know. What *do* folk do in Wintanceaster?'

'I can't say I know myself.'

Brinin patted his sow on the back and left the pen, fastening the gate behind him. Wulfrich was still watching him thoughtfully, still not smiling.

'I don't know why my father doesn't like you,' he said suddenly.

Brinin hadn't been ready for that. It seemed to come from nowhere. Wulfrich looked much like his father, or how his father might look if he scowled less. But he wasn't going to talk about Aculf to his son. Besides, he had no answers to offer.

'You were kind to my brother once,' Wulfrich went on.

'Was I?'

'My brother took some flesh my father was going to eat, and my father thought it was you and beat you for it, and you didn't tell him it was my brother. I was watching from behind the cowshed. Perhaps you've forgotten about it.'

'I haven't,' said Brinin, and Wulfrich's watchful face brightened a little.

'My father would have beaten him if you'd told him.'

And what would he do if he were to pass by and find Wulfrich talking to Brinin, whom he loathed?

'Your father might not like you coming here to talk to me.'

Wulfrich wriggled uneasily and glanced down towards the fields.

'He wouldn't,' he frowned, then leaned towards Brinin with a whisper. 'But he hasn't *said* I can't come here and he doesn't much come to this side of the village. He won't know unless someone tells him. Are you going to tell him?'

'No.'

'I like you!' Wulfrich smiled suddenly. That was an odd sight on a face so much like Aculf's. 'I'm hungry now. I'm going to see if my mother has any food for me. Can I come back another time?'

'I don't mind,' said Brinin.

Wulfrich said no more but dashed away to find his mother, leaving Brinin alone with his thoughts of fathers and their sons.

∿

'Can't you leave us alone? We don't want you following us.'

Brinin knew that voice. He couldn't see the speaker, with Deorstan's house standing between them, but he knew it was Tidræd, bold, loud and too ready to speak his mind. Brinin glanced up from his swine pen where he knelt at work and saw Wulfrich, unsure and wavering, standing with his back to him.

'Yes, go away!' said another unseen boy. 'You're too small, and even if you were bigger we wouldn't want you.'

It wasn't for Brinin to step between those who were foes one day and friends the next. Boys and their fleeting battles had nothing to do with him. Yet was this a fleeting battle? He couldn't think of a time when he had seen Wulfrich playing with the other boys. He always seemed to be on his own. Wulfrich jumped to the side as something flew past him. Not a stone; a clod of earth, more likely. Brinin stood up. Once, long ago, he had been the one the other boys had thrown the earth at.

Even Wulfrich didn't see Brinin coming round Deorstan's house. He stumbled backwards as two more clods hurtled towards him, missing him narrowly.

'Now go away!' That was Tidræd again.

Brinin stepped round the corner of the house, just in time for another clod to hit him hard in the chest. He looked at the five boys whom Wulfrich had so much wanted to be part of. They looked back at him. Then they scattered, all but Tidræd. He stood staring at Brinin with a warlike scowl, the clod he had been about to throw still in his hand.

'Wulfrich is smaller than you,' said Brinin. 'And there were five of you and only one of him.'

'You'd better take me to my mother then,' said Tidræd, much as the fyrd might dare the foe to fight them. This boy wouldn't be swift to flee.

'Wulfrich,' said Brinin, turning back to the boy behind him. 'Wait for me at my hut. I'm strengthening the sow's pen, and you can help me with it, if you like.'

'Well, *are* you going to take me to my mother?' said Tidræd, still glowering stubbornly. 'I'm not running away. You won't have to catch me. Do you want to tell her, so she'll beat me for it? I don't care! It won't hurt—not much anyway.'

'Why would I tell your mother?' asked Brinin.

'You did before, when I didn't come to plough. Tell her if you like!'

Tidræd almost seemed to want to goad Brinin into telling Mildrith, to be set on finding trouble if he could. He didn't back away even an inch. It wasn't because he was sorry—Brinin could see that. But anything was better than running scared like the others, and he wasn't above a little taunting.

'You're like your father,' said Brinin. He'd seen Thurstan stand his ground and he'd seen him goad those he didn't like.

'Am I?' Tidræd stayed unshifting, though the scowl softened.

'Once Aculf wanted your father to help him catch me. Your father wouldn't. He said he didn't care that I was a slave. I haven't forgotten that.'

'I remember that!' Tidræd brightened at once. 'You called Aculf a fool, and he locked you in the cowshed. My father said you were wiser than half the men in the village.'

Brinin didn't doubt it. But so much sorrow had sprung up from that day and perhaps Brinin's words had sown the seeds of it, words with far more truth in them than wisdom. Thurstan, bold and too truthful like his son, would have been glad to hear them said. But he hadn't cared that Brinin was a slave.

'You want to be like him, don't you?' said Brinin. 'You already are. You're bold, and the other boys follow your lead. Well, you won't be like him if you lead them to throw dirt at a boy who has no other friends.'

The brightness on Tidræd's face clouded over. He stared at Brinin, clutching the clod of dirt as though he would like to throw it at him as he had thrown others at Wulfrich. But he didn't. He flung it to the ground, then turned and ran.

Wulfrich was standing forlornly by the pen when Brinin reached his hut.

'Did they hurt you with the dirt?' he asked, eyeing the muddy patch on Brinin's shirt.

'No,' said Brinin. 'Nothing to worry about.'

'I don't know why they never let me go with them.' Wulfrich kicked half-heartedly at a tuft of grass. 'They always send me away when I follow them.'

'Why do you keep following?'

Wulfrich shrugged his shoulders unhappily.

'I don't know. It's better than doing nothing all day.'

'Don't your father and mother have any work for you? You're a bit big to do nothing all day.'

'If I stay near the house Father does give me work, but I never do it right and then he gets angry and…' Another sigh, full of meaning that Brinin could grasp only too readily. 'He isn't always angry if I keep away. Sometimes he forgets to be. But he is when I do the work wrong, and I always do it wrong. It's better to keep away because he might not be angry when I get home.'

Brinin couldn't fault the boy's wisdom; anger that might be forgotten was always better than the sure kind. Wulfrich was rather like Oswald, a little too ready to share all that was in his mind, but without Oswald's easy warmth. He stood watching Brinin awkwardly, as he had awkwardly followed the other boys. Why had Brinin been chosen to hear all his thoughts? He hadn't meant to befriend the boy. He would never have driven him away from his hut, yet surely offering him friendship could do him no good; not this boy, not with the father he had. Yet there might be more harm in withholding it.

'Perhaps I shouldn't always follow them,' said Wulfrich sadly. 'They all have wooden swords, and it's no good asking my father for one.'

'I only had sticks, but they make good swords,' said Brinin. Wulfrich *would* have a wooden sword before many days had passed. 'Now, I have work to do and if you want to stay here, you'll have to help me with it. Hand me that bundle of withies. I'm going to weave them into the side of the pen here, and after you've watched me do a few, you can weave one in yourself.'

～

Brinin didn't know how Tidræd would be in the morning. Would everything be forgotten? Would he come sullen and warlike to work in scowling gloom? Would he risk his mother's wrath and stay away altogether? With Tidræd there was never any saying what he might do.

But he did come, and Brinin didn't even have to wait long for him. He held up his head, walking with long strides as he drove the oxen ahead of him. Although he said nothing as they yoked them to the plough, he met Brinin's eye; and if there was any lingering shame from the day before—if indeed there had ever been any shame—he didn't show it. Perhaps keeping away, like running away, was too akin to fear.

They worked without speaking for a long time, Brinin's arms and back tight as he strained to keep the plough steady. Back and forth they went, driving the earth apart, ready to take in the seeds. It was only when they stopped to water the oxen that Tidræd had anything to say.

'When you called Aculf a fool, my father didn't only say that he wouldn't help him catch you,' Tidræd began as if no time had passed since they had last spoken of it, as if there had been no night, no sleep and no anger in between. 'He did something else too. I can't remember if it was the same night or not, but after he thought we were all asleep, he told my mother that he'd warned Aculf to leave you alone. I wasn't asleep. I heard everything. My father was even better than you thought he was!'

Little wonder that Oswald's sorrow for Thurstan had been so bitter, or that his son might ache to be like him. Aculf's blows *had* stopped for a time and when they fell again, they had not been so many, heavy or often as before. They should never have run away from Oakdene. Thurstan had been a better man than Brinin had known.

'I didn't know that,' he said.

'I *will* be like my father one day!' Tidræd said rather fiercely, but Brinin knew that it was as near to saying he was sorry as the boy would let himself come.

It was the next day that Brinin knew that he had cut a straight furrow and that the seeds had been well sown. He was near the meadow in the evening, when the day was cool but the light not yet too dim. He saw Tidræd there with his bow, standing behind a smaller boy to teach him how to draw it. And the other boy was Wulfrich.

STRENGTH

Oswald and Beorn reached Oakdene late in the afternoon. Fear and dread were in the eyes of everyone they saw. Likely neither of them looked like men who came with any gladness, only two when they had left with more. It took strength to ride out weaponed against the foe, another kind to ride back with word of the dead. As Oswald drew up near the horsehouse, the riding back felt almost as hard.

'Oswald Child,' said Beorn as they slid from their horses. 'It's no easy thing to tell a man's kin that he has fallen. Why take on all the burden of it yourself? Let me go to one house, and you to the other.'

'No,' said Oswald, wishing he *could* do as Beorn asked. 'My father would have come himself if he hadn't been wounded. He means me to do the telling. Besides, we're only here for one night. Go home to your mother. Who knows if either of us will ever see our kin again after tomorrow? We can't make it through many more battles like that one.'

Edith was standing stiffly in the doorway, white and still, when Oswald reached the hall. She didn't say a word, but her eyes asked everything.

'I left Father well enough,' said Oswald quickly, and Edith drew in a little quivering gasp, as though she hadn't dared to breathe before. 'He's wounded, but not badly. They beat us. There were so many of them. Sigulf's slightly wounded but he'll mend. Baldred's worse. He was feverish when I left, and he might not live. And the King's wounded. I don't know how badly. I heard they were taking him to a minster.'

'You're wounded,' said Edith, looking at his forehead.

'That? That's not a wound, not like…' But Edith didn't need to know what a wound was like. Why put thoughts like those into her mind? 'Rædwald's dead, Edith, and… and Leofwine.'

'Not Leofwine!'

Why was Leofwine's death the harder blow? Because they had been boys together? Because Oswald had seen his last kneeling fight? Because he now had to tell his father and mother that they had lost their son?

'That's why Father sent me back. To tell their kin. He couldn't come himself. And we have to ride back again tomorrow.'

'So soon?'

'We don't know when we'll have to fight them again. I can't linger here.' And lingering was the only thing Oswald wanted to do. He was so tired.

'Come and eat something, Oswald,' said Edith, taking his arm. 'How long were you on the road?'

'Since first light, but I'll only drink now and eat later. I'd rather go to Cynestan and Rædwald's houses quickly. I've been dreading it all day.'

When Oswald reached Cynestan's house he found him there, by some mercy alone with Wynflæd, his wife, but all the children out. Cynestan met him with only half of his warm smile. Oswald was too fresh from battle and Cynestan too wise in it for overglad welcome.

'Well now, Oswald Child,' he said. 'Have you come with word of the Danes? Will we drive them out?'

'Cynestan, I…' How could he say it? How could he say that Leofwine had fallen almost at his side, yet out of reach and without his help?

'Leofwine?' Knowledge burst onto Cynestan's face, sparing Oswald the need to say it aloud. But the wounding anguish in his voice was worse.

'I'm sorry. My father sent me to tell you.'

And when the worst news came it was Wynflæd who had all the strength and Cynestan little of it. She stood, one hand on the roof-post, her eyes all sorrow but her voice steady as she asked what she needed to know. Perhaps she had learned how to do this as a child while Cynestan had learned to wield a sword; she had waited for news of her father, her brother, her husband, her son. Cynestan crumpled onto a stool and wept without shame, without strength to speak or even lift his head.

'When did he fall?' asked Wynflæd.

'Five days ago.'

'Where?'

'Meretun, near Winburna. We did battle with them for the whole day. He... he fought bravely'

'And put them to flight?'

Would it be easier for her to think that her son had fallen winning a great victory, than one of many fallen in defeat?

'We held them off all day, but they were too strong for us. There were too many of them.'

'Where is he buried?' Wynflæd's words were still so strong, so quiet, coming so swiftly.

'I'm so sorry.' Oswald couldn't speak as steadily as she could. She hadn't seen as he had that the dead were too many for any friend to be found; that with the Danes holding the field they couldn't even reach them. 'We... we couldn't find him.'

'Then how do you know he's dead and not taken like Edrich Thegn was?'

'I saw him.' And he had seen him more than once since when he shut his eyes to sleep. 'He was near me and... and wounded but still fighting. I couldn't get to him until it was too late.'

Oswald couldn't say more than that and prayed that Wynflæd wouldn't ask. He couldn't look her in the eye and tell her that her son had died shieldless on his knees.

'Were there others?' she said at length, still strong though not so steady now. 'Or was he the only one among our men to die?'

'Rædwald died too,' said Oswald. 'And Baldred is so wounded he's not likely to live long. No more from Oakdene, but so many fell. Even the King is wounded.'

After that there was nothing more for Wynflæd to ask or Oswald to say, and perhaps her strength was waning. Cynestan was still weeping on his stool. Oswald only had to leave them to their sorrow and do it all again at Rædwald's house. When he left, he found Mærwyn outside the door listening, white as death.

Brinin waited for Oswald that evening in the dark stillness of his hut while the fire crackled and cast about its dim glow. When Oswald came at last, ducking through the doorway, it was with a weariness that even the shadows couldn't hide.

'It isn't good, then?' asked Brinin, pushing a stool towards him.

Oswald sat down with a sigh. He tossed a bow and a quiver of arrows onto the floor beside him.

'Leofwine's dead,' he said. 'And Rædwald, and likely Baldred soon will be.'

Oswald, his head in his hands, sat slumped and wordless for a long time. Had he spent all his strength on the battlefield? Brinin understood now, as he hadn't before. He had been among the Danes; had heard the far-off roar of battle; had seen the wounded, the dead and the dying. It was enough to drive strength from the heart of even the most fyrdlike of men.

'There are so many of them!' said Oswald at last. 'Every time we go against them, we seem to be fewer. We held them off the whole day, drove them back, and they still turned somehow and defeated us. However many we kill, however hard we fight, they seem to grow stronger every day. And it isn't only battles. They're everywhere, taking whatever they want. It's a wonder they haven't been here yet. We can't withstand them for much longer.'

What would that mean? Death and loss? New lords? A weak king who did their bidding? Folk talked of all those things and it was hard to sift out the truth from among the fears.

'Did many fall?' asked Brinin, throwing another stick onto the fire.

'So many, Danes too. Even the King is wounded. It was worse than Readingum. I… I don't even know how I'm still alive myself.' Oswald reached down and lifted the bow lying at his feet. 'I've brought you this. You should learn how to wield it. I wish I could show you but I have to be gone again in the morning.'

Brinin took the bow, running his hand along the smoothness of the wood.

'My father was a bowman.' Could a man's kin bequeath him their skill like they gave him their eyes or their hair, or was it all learned? And was he too old to learn it? 'You're not giving me this for hunting, are you?'

'It's the only weapon I can spare you. I have another bow. There's no one left here who can fight. Cynestan and Daglæf are both too wounded, and Daglæf's father is too old. Some of the boys can handle weapons, but they know nothing of battle. They only think they do. If the Danes come here… They will come, Brinin; we can't hold them back! If the Danes come here then a bow is better than no weapon at all. One of your tools might also do; an axe would be good—men wield axes in war—or a shovel, anything. But be ready for them to come.'

Fear chilled Brinin then. He'd never felt much fear about things unseen or waited for. His fear had almost always been when the trouble was before his eyes. But he'd been among the Danes and had chosen which side to die with when he'd walked out of Readingum.

'You don't think it's too late for me to learn?' he asked.

'You *must* learn. Listen, Brinin, Wessex can't win. We haven't defeated them in two months. We're fighting because we have to, but we can't drive them out now. I can't tell Edith that. I haven't said it to anyone and I'm only telling you because I know you'll keep your mouth shut. There are too many of them and too few of us. When we first fought them, nine of us from Oakdene went into battle together; and Rædwald and Beorn were here, and my father was with the Danes. That makes twelve. Now there are five. There will be fewer next time, and still fewer after that. They'll overrun us as they've overrun everywhere else.'

'What will that mean?'

'I don't know. But there will be few fighting men alive to see it. I don't know what will become of anyone else. That's the hardest thing, knowing we'll all likely fall and thinking of those left behind, thinking of Edith—' Oswald reached out and gripped Brinin's hand, a strong grip of friendship like the one they had shared before Brinin and Row fled to the minster. 'I'm glad you're free and that you have a field and a beast. And I hope you have a good harvest, many good harvests, and more beasts too. I'm… I'm glad I lived long enough to see it. There was a time when I didn't think I would. I'll pray they won't come here and that you'll live to see all the good of what you have now.'

When Oswald rose to leave, Brinin rose with him and stood beside him in the doorway. It felt like a parting, an ending, the time for last words and tokens of friendship and fellowship. But beyond meeting Oswald's grip with his own strong hand, Brinin didn't know how to part. He had none of Oswald's ready words and no strength to find them.

'I keep thinking of how it was to be a child, playing at battle or fighting dragons,' said Oswald. 'Boys don't know what they wish for.'

And that was the end. Oswald left, walking away into the darkness. Back to war, with no hope of victory and little hope of life. Brinin stood in the doorway long after Oswald had melted away into the night.

CLOUDS

The bitterness of winter was over, but it was chilly when Oswald and Beorn took leave of their kin the next morning. It was barely light, but the time for lingering had been lost when the Danes had come to Wessex. When he left Edith, Oswald knew he said too little for fear of saying too much; and afterwards he couldn't remember what he *had* said. Beorn's mother and sisters also stood there to watch them ride away, but Oswald didn't listen to their farewells. These things were between a man and his household and not for other ears.

Oswald had slept—it was hard not to after a day on the road—but somehow sorrowing households, dying friends and white-faced, worried kin had fought their way into his dreams so that he couldn't feel whatever good a night in his own bed might have done him. Now as their horses thundered along—no time to stop, no time to rest, no time to linger—the road seemed to blend with other downcast journeys in his mind. That first sorrowful ride to the minster when every jolt of his horse had throbbed through his still aching back. Those wretched grey days when he had ridden to Oakdene with Thurstan, believing his father to be dead yet forbidding himself to weep. That overwhelming first ride to battle when he had had to be lord of his men yet felt himself nothing more than a frightened boy. These last days had left him so weary that his thoughts were being pulled into dark places. Better to look at the new leaves and budding blooms. Better to smell the spring and feel the morning sunshine. Better to watch the clouds drifting above them in a pale blue sky. It was a lovely morning, all buds and birds and sky and clouds. And the sun would still shine and light burst out of winter long after these fearful days were forgotten. Long after he was forgotten too.

By the time they stopped to eat and rest the horses, Oswald had settled on not speaking of the Danes or of battles or even of their dead and wounded, of not even thinking of them if he could. Let them be free of all that for one morning, and if Beorn spoke to him of war he would answer him swiftly and turn their speech elsewhere. War mustn't cloud and darken the day. He was tired of it.

'Did you find your mother and sisters well?' asked Oswald as they sat eating while their horses grazed and the first little day's-eyes of the year peeked up at them from the grass.

'Well enough. My mother worried over my clothes and made me sit by the fire in my undershirt while she patched up a few tears. And she had my sisters running around so much fetching me things I didn't need that I was almost afraid they'd be glad to be rid of me this morning. And I mended one or two small things in the house that had gone awry. It was good to be home. If my mother hadn't killed a chicken—though I told her there was no need for that—it would have been like I'd never been away. It's not every day we eat chicken in our house. But what of your sister, Oswald Child? Is she well?'

'As far as I know. She keeps busy, I think. She was always like that, ever since we were small children. I was always the one who was scolded for idling. Never Edith.'

'Likely that hung on whether your father or mother was doing the scolding. My father was always sterner with me, and my mother with the girls. That's always the way of it and likely always will be. But it's better for her to be busy. My mother's the same and keeps the girls busy too, and I'm glad of it. She's wise that way. And now she knows that Baldred isn't likely to live she'll be watching out for Osgyth too. They've been friends since they were girls.' Beorn lay down and stretched himself out on the grass, watching the sky as he spoke. 'Did you know Leofwine and Mærwyn had been hoping to wed?'

'No!' But now Oswald understood Mærwyn's white face and why she had been listening outside Cynestan's door. And he had wounded her.

'Leofwine was born only three days before me, so our mothers always told us. And you know, Oswald Child, I had—have—a girl I want to wed too.'

'Who's that then?'

'Ah now, Oswald Child, how can I tell you that when I haven't spoken about it yet to her mother and father, or to my mother, or even much to the girl herself? Though I think she may have understood my thoughts on the thing, and not disliked them either.' A cloud overhead darkened Beorn's face in fleeting shadow. 'I mind the day I settled myself to it. I was in the swine pen, shovelling up the muck, and I stopped and leaned on the shovel and said to myself, "Now it's no good lingering over this. You need to speak." And as I was standing there the word came that the Danes had killed my father, and yours too, though with yours things took a turn we couldn't have foreseen then. So I said nothing that day and have said nothing since. Did you ever think of such things yourself, Oswald Child? Of taking a wife?'

'You forget I'm younger than you, Beorn. I haven't had time. I was a boy and then had to lead Oakdene against the Danes.' And so Oswald broke his word to himself and strayed too near the battlefield. He ought to have shifted their talk as soon as Leofwine's name was uttered. It was hard to keep away from war, however hard he tried. It drifted over them unheard and, cloudlike, was upon them before they knew it was there. 'Perhaps I'll think of it once all this is over. My father was only a little older than I am when he wed my mother. Perhaps I'll think of it then.'

'Perhaps,' said Beorn. 'I had settled on it, but I'm glad now that I didn't speak. Better to see how things will be first.'

There was a steadiness about Beorn. He never seemed to let his mind wander off into wild, dark or hopeless thoughts. Or if he did, he kept the thoughts well hidden. If Oswald lived long enough to follow his father as lord of Oakdene, Beorn was the kind of man he'd trust, that he'd want to have at his side, as Beorn's father had once ridden by Oswald's father's side and had fallen there. Perhaps Beorn was much like Swetrich had been. Perhaps he'd been raised to be steady.

'See there to the north, Oswald Child,' said Beorn, his eyes still on the sky. 'The clouds are darkening. We'll have rain later, or someone will.'

'We'd better be on our way, then,' said Oswald. 'Let's see if we can outride them.'

Edith wept for a long time that morning. She waited until Oswald and Beorn had ridden so far out of the village that there was nothing left of them to see; until she had shared one painful glance with Beorn's mother, Ælfwyn; until she had found herself a hidden place among the shrubs on the hillside, all green with new leaves.

The first few tears seemed to let loose a whole flood that had been swelling for weeks. When it ebbed at last to a trickle she didn't feel any better, only wearier with an aching head. Above her, clouds were gathering, threatening rain. The Danes were gathering, threatening... Edith had seen the hopeless truth on Oswald's face and the way his eyes hadn't fully met her own, like some misbehaving child lying to keep out of trouble. But he hadn't been lying. He had only been trying to shield her and had done it badly.

But what were they to do? The clouds would gather. The Danes would gather, and such a downpour of fear would burst upon them that they might all be swept away. How could Oakdene hope to be spared if Wessex drowned? They had been ready in the winter. Were they still ready now that spring had come?

It was well into the morning before Edith went back down to the village. She found Cenwyn behind Mildrith's house, flushed and hot, with a heap of split logs at her feet and an axe still in her hand.

'I've never felt so much like hewing wood in my life!' she said as Edith reached her. 'Mother was going to have Tidræd do it when he came up from the field, but I wanted to. I'm so angry, and if I could have ridden away with Oswald and Beorn this morning...'

'How's Mærwyn?' Edith ached for Mærwyn as much as for Cynestan and Wynflæd, or for Rædwald and Baldred's kin. The thing had been between Mærwyn and Leofwine, between her father and mother and his, settled though not yet done, and little spoken of. But Mærwyn had lost what she had longed for before she ever got to have it.

'She looks ill,' said Cenwyn grimly. 'She's sat at the loom all morning, barely saying a word, and doesn't want to see anyone. We knew this might happen, but we all hoped... Folk are saying this morning that Wessex can't win, that the Danes are too strong for us. Did Oswald tell you that?'

'No, but I think that's what he believes. We shouldn't talk about it too much. We don't want to frighten everyone.'

'Where have you been this morning, Edith? It's too late for that. Everyone *is* talking about it, and they're already frightened. If they're too strong and they win, what are we going to do?'

'I don't know,' said Edith. 'I don't know what they want.'

'My father once said that they came to take anything they could bear away with them. Will they go when they have all they want?'

'They must want more than that. I think they want us all to be frightened.'

'Then they've already won! We *are* frightened. I am, when I'm not angry with them. I didn't think I could hate them any more than I did already, but I do today. If the Danes wanted fear then they've already won.'

'My father said that the Mercians paid the Danes to make them leave. I wonder if the King will do that, if they become too strong for us.'

'I heard that too, but wouldn't it be a shameful thing to do?'

'It might be a wise thing to do.' But wouldn't the business of kings be done without two girls to say if it was wisdom or shame? 'Cenwyn, do you all have somewhere to hide if they come here? I'm worried that folk have forgotten to be ready.'

'Tidræd has found at least a score of places. He says he'll help us hide but that *he'll* be needed to fight off the Danes—he's a man now at twelve winters, you know, when Mother isn't scolding him for being a wilful child! Don't worry about folk forgetting, Edith. If they had forgotten, this morning they have remembered again.'

'When Tidræd is done with his work today, send him to talk to me. I want to know where all these hiding places are, and make sure that no one has forgotten.' That might be better than a loom to keep her mind away from the battlefield, and if the Danes did come what good would cloth be anyway? If only her head didn't ache so much.

SEEDS

ear hung over the village like a stench, unseen but everywhere. Brinin felt it as soon as he left his hut the next morning. He knew Oswald had said little, but Beorn might have said more. And another two—perhaps three—were dead. It only took the truth to be spoken aloud at one hearthside for everyone to swiftly learn it. By morning all Oakdene knew: the Danes were too many; the fyrd too few; the hope too small to cling to.

It was only later in the morning that Brinin himself grew a little uneasy. He was ploughing in Mildrith's field, with Tidræd driving the oxen as they cut the last furrows before the sowing. Tidræd had always been talkative before, bold and full of speech. But now he worked without a word; he even seemed shy, seldom lifting his head. It couldn't only be a fear of the Danes that stopped his tongue, not in a boy like Tidræd, keen to do battle and not yet wise enough to know what he wished for.

'When you fled,' said Tidræd at length, 'folk said you'd gone to the Danes and that Oswald Child had helped you do it. I said that to my father, and he told me that a fool will say anything and believe anything, but that if he heard *me* say it again he'd thrash me for it. So I didn't say it again.'

This was new, though Brinin had sometimes wondered if much more had happened then than anyone had ever said. But why should Tidræd tell him now, his friendly chatter all forgotten? It seemed to spring out of a fresh worry.

'*Did* you go to the Danes?' asked Tidræd, still not looking up.

'No,' said Brinin. 'I went to a minster.'

'But you went to the Danes later, when Edrich Thegn was taken?'

'Yes.'

'*After* you heard they'd taken him? Not before?'

'After.'

'And you only went to find him?'

'Yes.'

Tidræd looked up at him then as though seeking the truth on Brinin's face.

'Likely it's all only fool's talk then, like my father said,' he said. 'He was mostly right about things like that.'

Tidræd seemed to forget about it then and talked as he always did, but Brinin couldn't forget. The seed of a warning had been planted in his mind and it sprouted and grew throughout the morning. When he left the plough, his eyes were sharper than they had been. Had he been blind before? Or had there been nothing to see?

There was whispering as well as work that day, men speaking to one another in low voices. Once or twice he thought he saw them turn towards him as they talked. A child hid behind her mother as Brinin walked past, and he thought she was hiding from him. Then Cynestan came to ask him about helping to mend a door, and Mildrith thanked him so cheerfully for the ploughing that he knew he must be wrong about everything else. Why should he take a boy's worries and make them his own? He hadn't forgotten the last time the Danes had come or how it had been for his mother then. But he wasn't his mother. He had been born here. Folk here had known him all his life. They had known his father. They knew he was no threat to them. They knew he had risked his life to save their lord. Everyone was frightened—little wonder they whispered—but he needn't make a fool of himself and see what wasn't there.

Brinin had put it from his mind by the evening. He fetched his food from the hall and walked with Garulf to his hut, meaning to eat with him as he often did. But Garulf seemed uneasy, frowning as he walked and unwilling to reach his hearth too quickly.

'How was your work today, lad?' he asked.

'Good,' said Brinin. 'Mildrith's ploughing will likely be done tomorrow, and the last of my own in a few days.'

'That's good, lad,' said Garulf, still not smiling much. 'You've done well. No trouble today then?'

'No. Why would there be any trouble?'

Garulf didn't answer. He stood by the door of his hut, looking hard at Brinin. It was another seed to shoot up beside the others. Perhaps Brinin had better eat at his own hearth after all, where he could think in the stillness. Besides, if there was going to be trouble, he needn't share it with Garulf.

But there was no stillness at his hut either. Wulfrich was there waiting for him, sitting up on the pen as he watched the sow, and so hungry for a little of that friendship he seldom found elsewhere that Brinin had no heart to send him away. They sat together as the sun set, and Brinin shared his food with him. The thinking would have to wait until later.

'Are you a Dane?' asked Wulfrich suddenly. Were the Danes all that anyone could think of that day? 'My father says you are.'

'I've heard him say so.'

'But *are* you?'

'My mother was a Dane.'

'Does that make you one too? My father says you speak their tongue.'

'I *can*. My father was a Wessex man, and I can speak his tongue too. What does that make me?'

Wulfrich had no answer to that. He sat, deep in thought, as though Brinin had told him a riddle and he was trying to untangle it.

'Why are you asking me this, Wulfrich?' said Brinin at length. And why had Tidræd asked about him going to the Danes? And why had Garulf wondered if there had been trouble? All put together, something more than the fear of war seemed to be stirring in Oakdene.

'I heard some men talking about it earlier. One of them said you were a Dane, and my father says so too.'

All the seeds had sprouted now, sprung up too high to overlook. His folly hadn't been in watching for what wasn't there; it had been in telling himself that there was nothing to see.

'I don't think you're a Dane,' said Wulfrich before he left. 'The Danes are fearsome. Everyone says they are. But you aren't fearsome at all.'

WOMEN

Edith's head ached the whole day, and she was weary by the time Tidræd, more than keen, came to see her. He had so much to tell her and said it all so quickly that she could hardly follow him. When she crawled into her bed at last, so many thoughts were rushing about and ramming into each other that it was a long time before she slept. One thing she did know: Tidræd had thought of enough hiding places for at least half the village, and no one need be without.

But knowledge found her in the night, and she woke with a clear mind. Why go from house to house when the sight of her unsmiling on the thresholds would only make everything worse? They had all seen Oswald and Beorn ride weary and hopeless into the village. Word of the Danes' unstoppable strength had swiftly spread. As far as they all knew Oswald and Beorn had ridden away to die. If she—*she*, Oswald's sister—went to folk suddenly asking them where they would hide, they would all think that Oswald had told her something worse than they already knew. Yet they must all be ready to hide.

None of that was the answer. The women were. She'd often thought that the women were the quickest to see how things were in the village. They sat on stools outside their houses, side by side with their neighbours. It was easy to talk while they were combing wool or spinning it or making the food. They heard what the children were saying, and any talk reached them first. The men talked too, but it was harder to give the time to it while sweating in the fields.

Edith was up before first light, getting the work for the day started so it could quickly be done without her. She found Cenwyn at the milking. Her bucket was almost full, the creamy milk rippling gently as her deft hands worked the udders.

'We have work to do, Cenwyn,' said Edith.

'Don't we always?' laughed Cenwyn. She stood up and patted the cow on the back. 'That's all for today, I think.'

'I don't mean that kind of work. I mean work making sure that everyone knows what to do if the Danes come.'

'Oh! Are you still thinking about that? Likely you're right. If something *can* be done, we ought to do it. Let me take this in to Mother, and then you can tell me about it.'

'I'll come with you,' said Edith. 'I want to talk to your mother too.'

When they reached the house, they came upon some slight scuffle, dying down now but still smouldering a little. Tidræd was outside, glowering and sullen, while Mildrith stood stern in the doorway.

'And if I ever see you at anything like that again, you'll get worse! Do you hear me?' Mildrith was saying. 'Now, go and tend to the swine!'

What had Tidræd done this time? Edith glanced at Cenwyn, but perhaps she had been Tidræd's sister for too long to even wonder any more. She only smiled back wryly. Tidræd trudged away crossly, kicking at the grass and muttering something under his breath.

'Here's the milk, Mother,' said Cenwyn cheerfully, setting down her bucket. 'Edith wants to talk to you.'

'Come in then and sit down for a while,' said Mildrith, with one last worried frown at Tidræd's back before the neighbouring house hid him from their sight.

Mærwyn was by the fire, Tidwine at her side. She was holding up a shirt against his shoulders. It was too long for him—and by the look of it, too small for Tidræd now—but Mærwyn's needle and yarn were in her lap, ready to get to work on it.

'The shirt can wait until later.' Mildrith handed Tidwine a basket. 'Go and see if the hens have laid and when you've done that, fetch some more sticks for the fire.'

There was always work to do, and Mildrith made sure that they did it. The death of a husband or father was not enough to leave it undone. Mourning was for the darkness when the beasts were stalled, fields ploughed, seeds sown, cloth woven, food cooked, children seen to. Perhaps other tears fell when no one was watching. Mildrith steadied Edith somehow. She'd been watching her for all these months, learning how she should be if—when—her own time came for mourning. Mærwyn had already learned it. She was white, even by the firelight. But she had sat at her loom all of the day before, and now her needle was already in her hand.

'Have folk forgotten where to hide?' asked Edith as soon as Tidwine was gone. 'Everyone was ready in the winter, but are they ready now?'

'I know what I'll do,' said Mildrith. 'I would hope everyone has thought about it. But it's easy to talk and to say we'll do this or that. It might be harder when the time comes and we're all frightened.'

'I know, but with my father and brother both gone, isn't it down to me to make sure everyone is ready? But if I go from house to house asking them—'

'Oh no! No need to do that! It might do more harm than good. Don't take too much on yourself. Your brother's warned us all to be ready, your father too. If some forget, you can't blame yourself for that. Thurstan always said that you can't make a man wise. Didn't he, girls?'

'Yes, Mother,' said Cenwyn. 'What he always said was: "You can talk wisdom to a man all night, but he might still be a fool in the morning."'

'I don't put it like that myself, perhaps,' said Mildrith, with a half-smile, 'but it is the truth of it. Be ready yourself and make sure those in your household are ready. Likely no one will forget, not now we know how… how bad things have become.'

Mærwyn sat with her head down, fingering the needle in her lap. It felt like an unkindness to come and speak of such things with her sitting there to hear them. And for all Mildrith's wisdom, it wasn't enough. It wasn't enough to wait and hope for the best. Edith *had* to be busy, busy doing something—anything—that might help. She'd go mad otherwise.

'It's easy to start folk talking,' said Mærwyn, looking up from her needle. 'If you choose well who you say something to, you can have the whole village speaking about it before long. All we need to do is talk to those who can't keep a still tongue. There's no need for you to go from house to house.'

'Yes! That's what I was thinking!' It had felt like wisdom when Edith woke that morning, more so now that she had heard it come freely from another's lips, without her having to coax it out of them. 'That's what I meant when I said we had work to do, Cenwyn.'

'Well, there's no harm in that,' said Mildrith. 'A word here and there might bring it to mind again for folks.'

～

Later, in the afternoon, Edith was at her loom when Cenwyn strode into the hall, a somewhat ragged shirt in her arms.

'Can you leave the weaving until later?' she said. 'Fetch your sewing, and we'll pull a bench outside where the light is better.'

'When have *you* ever asked me to sit and sew with you?' Edith stood up. She'd mostly been staring at the loom and had woven little. 'I can if you like, though.'

'Oh, I don't *want* to! But I've been at work talking, or getting ready to talk at least. Mother sent me with something for Sæthryth. I asked her if she could spare Eanflæd to come and sew with us. She said she could as soon as she'd swept the house. She'll be here soon.' Cenwyn held up the shirt with a sigh. 'I don't know how Tidræd gets his clothes like this—the other shirt isn't much better. I doubt I'll do this one any good. Likely Mærwyn will pick it all out and mend it better later.'

Edith had already cut the brown cloth for her father's new shirt. The pieces lay beside her, folded neatly on top of a chest. Now was as good a time as any to begin the sewing.

'It was clever to think of Eanflæd,' she said. 'She talks a lot!'

'I know! That's why I chose her. And everything we talk about, she'll tell again at home. And if she tells her father, so much the better. All his neighbours will hear of it by tomorrow! Eadulf talks a lot too!'

They hadn't been sitting for long when Eanflæd came swiftly along with her basket. Wisps of fair hair had slipped out from under her headcloth and brushed against her plump, cheerful face. She laughed breathlessly as she sat down.

'I thought I would never get away! You saved me, Cenwyn! Mother hasn't let me sit down for two breaths together since dawn. I could almost lie down here and sleep! But better not.' She sighed and lifted a green shirt, half-made, from her basket. 'If I have nothing to show Mother when I get home, she'll scold me for idling. I like that brown cloth you have there, my lady Edith. What are you making with it?'

'A shirt for my father. I thought he'd need a new one when—' Edith didn't say 'if' and tried not to think it—'when all this is over and he comes home again.'

'Indeed, my lady Edith, and we all hope he *does* come home and others with him. But have you heard what they're saying? Of course you have! You must know everything. Everyone's saying the Danes are too strong. Did your brother tell you that, my lady Edith? Does he still think Wessex can drive them all out?'

'He didn't talk about it much, and I didn't ask. I don't think anyone knows.'

'Isn't war always like that?' asked Cenwyn, as though she alone among them was a warrior with many battles behind her, who could speak with true knowledge. 'Whatever happens, we'll be ready for them coming here! Tidræd has found us at least a score of hiding places, and I'm sure everyone else has done the same. Surely you remember Oswald Child telling us to do that in the winter?'

'Yes,' said Eanflæd slowly. 'I think my father knows where we should go. Yes, I'm sure he does, only I can't remember what it was he said. I'll ask him later, though I don't like asking him about the Danes. They make him so angry! And I must ask Sifflæd if *she* knows where she is going to hide. She forgets what she's doing from one day to the next. Mother says she'd remember soon enough if she were *her* daughter! But you're right, Cenwyn. We must be ready. We can't be too careful and we mustn't *tell* anyone where we're going to hide. It's so easy to talk too much and say things we shouldn't—Mother's *always* scolding me for that—but we mustn't. Not when there's one among us who might hear and who might help the Danes if they *do* come.'

Cenwyn shot Edith a gloating look of battle well-planned, well-fought and swiftly won, but Edith couldn't share in it. There was something in what Eanflæd had said—something awful—that chilled her to the bone.

'What did you mean by that, Eanflæd?' she said, her voice as cold as she suddenly felt.

'Mean by what, my lady Edith? Oh! About there being a Dane among us? Isn't Brinin, your father's slave, a Dane? That's what everyone says. His mother was one. My father would never let me talk to her. He says you can't trust any of them. I forgot once, and he saw me and didn't he slap me for it!' Eanflæd laughed uneasily, as though becoming aware that she was straying onto forbidden land. 'Oh, I like him well enough! He's handsome for a slave, isn't he? Though he isn't a slave any more—I forgot. And last week he helped me gather up some firewood when I dropped the basket. Mother had told me to hurry and she would have skinned me if I'd got back to the house any later. So it's a good thing he did help me, and a good thing my father didn't see me letting him. There's not much harm he can do *now* when there's only one of him. I like him well enough. But if the Danes do come, he's bound to help them. They're his own kind, after all! So we should be careful and—'

'Can't you hold your tongue, Eanflæd?' groaned Cenwyn, throwing a frowning glance at Edith.

Edith was on her feet, sickened suddenly. Was that what they all thought? She had never, not even once, thought of Brinin as a Dane. He was her brother's friend, and he had been among them for as long as she could remember. She had known his mother was a Dane, but she hadn't cared. She had liked his mother and his brother. They had all belonged to her father's household. Brinin was one of them, had always been one of them. And now this! After what they all knew he had done for her father!

'If he wanted to help them so much, why didn't he stay with them?' Edith could hear her words quivering a little as she spoke. She could almost have wept with anger, could have flung her father's shirt at Eanflæd for being so foolish and for saying such a thing aloud. But it wasn't only Eanflæd; it was the whole village. Eanflæd alone couldn't be blamed for all their folly. 'Why didn't he stay, instead of risking his life to get my father away from them?'

'My lady Edith!' stammered Eanflæd. 'I didn't mean… I know he did! I only meant that—'

'Eanflæd! Stop talking!' snapped Cenwyn.

Edith walked away. As she crossed the threshold into the hall, she heard Eanflæd behind her, in a whisper still loud enough to reach Edith's ears:

'Oh! I think I said all the wrong things!'

ARROWS

The ploughing was done, and the seeds were in the ground. The peas and beans were already creeping out and unfolding themselves, fresh and green but still little, helpless and easily broken. Brinin looked at them each day, watchful as a father with his children and always ready for any weeds that might spring up to overwhelm them. They were his peas, his beans, the first crops he had ever grown. Nothing must harm them. In the darkness of the earth lay the kernels of wheat, while that hidden wonder made them into something new. Brinin had never understood how. Soon they would shoot out sharp and arrowlike all over his field, and in time—let him trust God that it would be so—in time he would have a harvest.

Oswald's bow had lain too long unhandled in his hut. He had wanted Brinin to learn, and Brinin had all but given him his word; unspoken, but a word nonetheless. With the ploughing done, he had time for such things. There was a fellowship in doing what his father had once done, besides the wisdom of the thing. Often now when he shut his eyes to sleep, Brinin wondered if shouts and weapons and death would come before dawn. Dread by night. Every night at the minster, the monks had sung something about that before they slept. Brinin had once seen it written on Oswald's waxboard—not the Latin, but the meaning. He had written some of it onto his own waxboard and had meant to learn it but then he had left both the minster and the waxboard behind. He wished he could remember it now. There had been something about arrows too.

The meadow was empty when Brinin reached it, and he went to the far end where few would see him. He cast his eye round for something to shoot at and settled on a little shrub far enough away to be worthwhile. He plucked at the bowstring and that was when he was stung by another kind of arrow, stabbing him deep inside.

It had been one of those last days before he had suddenly been left kinless. No one was following them, and they were far away where they could stop to rest for longer. Row had taken the bow that Oswald had given them for the road and had shown Brinin what their father had once taught him long ago.

'Do you see how I'm holding it, Bruni? Let me see if I can still do it. Look how these fingers go on either side of the arrow.'

Brinin took out an arrow and fumbled with it as he fitted it somewhat clumsily to the bow. He seemed to hear Row—could almost see him—as he did it. He held it as Row had done, or as near to that as he could remember.

'Now, you lift it and look along the arrow like this,' came the voice of Row from all those months before.

Brinin lifted the bow. The end of the arrow brushed ticklish against his cheek as he gazed along its shaft towards the shrub. He drew the string tight, tighter…

'What will I aim at?' Row had said. 'That tree over there, I think. You keep it steady, then shoot!'

Brinin's arrow flew from him, strong, swiftly. It missed the shrub and fell a little to the right.

'You forgot about the wind. You should have aimed to your left a bit more.'

Behind him stood Tidræd, watching Brinin with a keen eye.

'I didn't know you could shoot,' said Tidræd.

'I can't.'

'I'll teach you then!' said Tidræd cheerfully. 'I'm the best in the village. Among the boys anyway. Some of the men might be as good as me.'

'I'm sure they'd be glad to hear you speak so well of them.'

Tidræd grinned and shrugged his shoulders.

'Well, I *am* one of the best. Why should I lie? I'll fetch your arrow so you can try again. You held it steady. You'll soon learn the way of it.'

Tidræd, for all his overbold youth, was a good teacher. He said what he meant, a little too readily for some perhaps, but Brinin didn't mind. Thurstan had taught Tidræd well, and his son had forgotten none of it.

He was more than happy to share everything he knew. One evening wasn't long enough for that, but by the time the meadow began to darken Brinin could hit the shrub almost without fail, wind or not. There would be other days to grow better still, and it was bittersweet that his father's skill should be within his grasp.

As he walked back home through the dusk, he saw Row in his mind as he had seen him that last time. He saw him as he lay with Oswald's bow and arrows and knife at his side, waiting for Brinin to hide him with earth and stones. Brinin hadn't known if it was right to bury those things with his brother or if perhaps it was forbidden to handle the dead like that. But he had wanted Row to look like a hunter in death and not like a thrall, to give him a last gift when he could do nothing else. Now, somehow, bows and arrows had become all tangled up with his father and brother in his mind. And the sight of an arrow could be as biting as its tip was.

'Well, my boy,' said Brother Wilfred, coming towards Brinin as he neared the church. 'Are you learning to be a bowman?'

'Oswald Child asked me to, sir, with times being as they are.'

'Sad to say, there's wisdom in that. Our times are evil ones indeed. But come, it's been long since we have spoken. Whenever I've seen you you've been hard at work. Are your seeds all in now? Why not sit with me for a while and tell me how it goes with you?'

By the flickering light of one candle they sat and talked, while beyond its small glow the church sank into darkness and shadow. They spoke of seeds and swine, work and woodcraft. Brother Wilfred was so friendly, so fatherlike, eager to know everything.

'And what of the things you learned at the minster, the reading? Have you forgotten it now that all these months have passed?'

'I don't think so, sir, though I've nothing to read. The waxboard was the prior's, and I left it at the minster. The reading wasn't hard, sir, once I understood the way of it.' Brinin looked down at his hands, rough with work. 'It was the writing that was hard. I could never do it well enough for Brother Deor. He wanted all the words to be small, none taller than the others. But he was happy with my reading, and I liked doing that.'

'I'll find you a waxboard and write something on it for you. Don't you think it would be a shame if you forgot?'

'Yes, sir,' said Brinin. Wasn't that the way of it? The good was often too easily forgotten, while the bad broke into his mind unwelcomed, settled down and couldn't be shifted. Yet he had never hoped that Brother Wilfred would offer to do for him even a little of what he had done for Oswald. 'I've been trying to remember something the brothers sang each night before they slept, sir. Oswald Child showed me the meaning once, something about arrows and dread by night.'

Brother Wilfred broke into song, that slow speechlike song of the minster, well-known but not understood, with the meaningful words scattered among the rest: *Dei, dicet Domino, Deus meus.* He sang as the monks had sung, his one voice rising like their many.

'This is the one you mean, I think,' said Wilfred, when the last sung words had died away. 'I'll write it for you. I learned it as a boy and, since childhood, I too have said or sung it every night before sleep. Let me fetch a waxboard.'

Brinin watched as Brother Wilfred walked away with the candle and left him in the gloom. When he came back he sat down on the bench with the candle at his side. He bent over the waxboard, muttering the Latin softly to himself, stopping to think, then scratching the words into the wax. They were all so small, so straight. Brinin didn't know how anyone could write like that.

'This will be enough for now,' said Brother Wilfred at last. 'It isn't the whole psalm, only the first half. Why don't you write it out where I have left the waxboard empty? Don't worry about making the words small—you aren't trying to become a scribe. Read it, write it, learn it, and when you know it so well that you don't even need to look at the waxboard to say it, come back to me and I will give you some more.'

Brinin took the waxboard and ran his eye slowly and haltingly along the words, mumbling them under his breath much as Brother Wilfred had done. He *hadn't* forgotten how to read, and this was what he had seen on Oswald's waxboard.

'"You will not fear the dread by night, nor the arrow flying by day,"' he read. 'Sir, what does this mean? Were there raiders even then, when this was first written?'

'There have been such things for as long as men have known how to be evil, and will be until all things are made new. It may speak of raiders but it need not only speak of that. There are many things in this world to frighten us; many dreadful things, both seen and unseen, that come by night. But here we learn that the one who hides himself in the Lord need not fear them. What does the psalm say? "He will shade you with his shoulders, you will hope beneath his feathers; his truth will be a shield all around you.""

Later Brinin sat by his hearth, his bowl half-full, but his mind overflowing with psalms and kind friends, arrows and lost kin. He had wandered so far from his hut that Daglæf startled him as he greeted from the doorway. But Brinin welcomed him in and offered him a stool. Brinin saw Daglæf glance down at the waxboard, but he didn't ask about it. As he spoke to Brinin of work and the weather, it wasn't the waxboard his eye kept falling on. It was the bow.

'You're learning to shoot,' said Daglæf at last.

'Oswald Child asked me to.'

'And I'm sure he thought no harm would come of it, but be careful who sees you do it. Folk can be foolish at times and—'

'And they're saying that I'm a Dane who wants to stand with other Danes against them.' Brinin knew that his words were somewhat arrowlike, sharper than Daglæf had earned. Hadn't he come in friendship to warn him? 'They think I've got myself a weapon to turn against them.'

'Don't take much heed of it. Folk can be foolish, as I say. But take care.' Daglæf glanced down at the bow again. 'Likely you are wise to learn with times as they are. Let me show you somewhere where no one will see you. I can even teach you the way of it and help you learn, not that I can do much now with an arm like this.'

Daglæf's wounded shield arm still hung limp, not much good for work and less for battle. There was little he could do in his field or with his beasts without the help of his young sons, working like men before their time. Brinin seldom saw them playing with the other boys now. For Daglæf to offer Brinin his time, when all his work was heavy and slow, was a greater deed of friendship than even the warning had been.

'What do you say?' said Daglæf. 'Why don't I come and find you tomorrow?'

'Thank you, yes.'

'Good! I'll come and find you when my work is done. And don't pay too much heed to them.'

MENDING

Edith found Wynith by the new storehouse, skimming the milk for butter-making. Ebba sat on a stool beside her mother, the butter churn tightly wedged between her feet as she thrust the churn-staff up and down. It would be ready soon. Ebba was straining a little as the butter thickened. New butter, made from good spring milk. Edith's tongue remembered the taste. She would have some later, on bread still warm from the baking.

'Don't stop,' she said, as Ebba began to stand. 'I can talk to you both as you work.'

Edith shook out her blue kirtle, its soft folds tumbling down to the grass.

'Ebba needs something new to wear,' she said. 'Do you think you can make her something with this? The cloth's a little worn at the back, but most of it's still good.'

'Thank you, my lady,' said Wynith, wiping her milky hands on her barme-cloth and lifting the hem of the kirtle to rub between her fingers. 'She grew that much this winter. And this is lovely cloth, my lady, and good of you to give it to her. I mind you weaving this. You're that skilled with your loom, my lady. Thank the lady Edith, Ebba.'

'Thank you, my lady Edith,' said Ebba biddably, half-rising again, then turned to her mother with a whisper loud enough for any passer-by to hear: 'But, Mother, can't we make something for Brinin instead? His clothes are much worse, and I don't mind mine being short.'

'Ebba!' Wynith reached over and slapped her daughter sharply on the arm. 'It's not for you to say what's to be done when the lady Edith has been so good as to make you a gift. I'm sorry, my lady. That girl needs to learn to hold her tongue! I'm ashamed of her for speaking so boldly!'

Ebba, blinking back tears and flushing a deep red, dropped her head so low that her forehead almost touched the churn-staff. Edith felt her own cheeks burning, but not only from pity. She ought to have seen what Ebba had seen but she had been too caught up in her own cares. And now Ebba had been scolded for speaking the truth when it was she, Edith, who should have been ashamed.

'Don't scold her any more,' she said, 'and don't be ashamed of her. She's right. Brinin *does* need something new. Take this and make something for Ebba with it, and I'll see what can be done about Brinin.'

Edith thrust the kirtle into Wynith's lap and walked away swiftly towards Brinin's field, hoping to glimpse him as he worked. She hadn't gone far before she met him coming from his hut, a bucket of dung in one hand and a hoe in the other. He passed her quickly, with only a slight softening of his face, a half-nod and almost a smile as greeting. But he didn't pass by too quickly for Edith's ready eyes to take in everything.

He was working barefoot. That didn't worry her—most did now that the weather was getting warmer. His breeches were turned up to the knee to keep them out of the mud, but they were so worn and threadbare that it was hard to say what the cloth had once been like. His shirt was well patched though frayed and torn round the bottom, and there was a dark stain on the chest, the sight of which hit her like a blow. She knew what it was. Her father and Oswald had both told her that Brinin had been wounded by a Dane in Readingum; a slight wound, they had said, but she could see that he had bled enough for the stain to linger. He had risked his life to save her father, had walked in among the Danes, had been wounded, had bled, and she had left him with nothing but a torn, blood-stained shirt while she wove fine cloth for herself. It wasn't Ebba who ought to be weeping and bowing her head in shame.

It was too late to mend the shirt, but she could mend herself. Edith turned back to the hall. Could she go to Brinin with a bundle of clothes and tell him she'd seen his rags and wanted him to have better? No, such talk would be a wound and not a gift. He was much too proud for that. Whatever she did must be half-hidden and not so giftlike. Her father and Oswald had thought of almost everything:

tools, food, Mildrith's oxen for Brinin's field. But they hadn't thought of clothes. Why would they? They had little to do with the making of them.

In the hall, she slipped past her father's curtain and knelt by his clothes chest. Deep down, underneath the best of what he had, lay the oldest shirts and breeches kept only for harvest or other unthegnlike work. It was no good giving Brinin anything better—he would know straightaway where it had come from—so she had to choose the oldest, the plainest and the least often seen of everything her father owned. And only her father's clothes would do. Oswald was slim and swift, Brinin broad-shouldered and strong. Brinin was tall, but at least her father could match him in breadth.

Two pairs of breeches, old but not ragged; two linen undershirts, mended only a little here and there; one good shirt, grey-blue and unfaded, but a little worn now. No one would remember who had once worn these clothes, least of all Brinin. What time had he ever had to think about what his lord was wearing? The leg bindings could come from Oswald. She'd made him some new ones not long ago.

Edith sat down on her father's bed to fold the clothes. The new brown shirt she was making for her father was almost done, all but the twisted threads she had wanted to sew around the neck. Brinin could have it, and she would make her father another. It wasn't right for only her father and brother to give their clothes, while she kept all she had. Her new kirtle could wait.

Beside her own bed, Edith laid all the clothes in a small chest she had. The lid was broken and needed to be mended. Didn't Brinin often mend things now that he knew how to turn his hand to woodcraft? He could mend the chest and keep the clothes as payment. And he need never know she had left them there.

The shadows were long and dusk falling when Brinin got back to his hut, his whole body heavy from work. He sat down on the grass by his sow's pen—he liked to be near her—and leaned against the fence with his legs stretched before him as he ate his food. The air was cool and the grass damp, but it was good to sit there as the sun slipped away and listen to the throstles at their evening song. There was barely a wind and across the village the smoke rose straight from the hearths, through the roofs and into the darkening sky.

At last—somewhat unwillingly—Brinin dragged up his weary limbs and trudged into his hut to kindle a fire. When the sticks were crackling and the leaping flames warming the dim hut, he caught sight of something in the corner that hadn't been there that morning. It was a little chest, its lid broken and half-hanging off, and on the stool beside it, neatly folded, lay a small bundle of clothes.

Frowning a little, he brought them nearer to the fire to see them better. Who would leave these things here, and why? There were two good shirts—both better than any shirt he'd ever had—and breeches. Even undershirts and leg bindings which he'd never worn in his life. But what were they for? He glanced down at the broken chest and laughed in disbelief. Surely it wasn't an offer of work? Mend the chest and keep the clothes? Yet what else could it be but a little hidden friendship towards the Dane in their midst, done stealthily so that no one knew about it? And whoever had left them knew nothing of woodcraft or the worth of shirts and breeches, or they would have known that even one shirt was too high a price for work like that.

Yet he needed a new shirt and breeches too. Had he ever looked more like a beggar, now that there was no careful lord to dole out clothing to his thrall? He needed them but he couldn't cheat this well-meaning friend. One pair of breeches or one shirt and no more—even that was too much for such a little thing. It had better be the breeches then; only a fool could happily wear such a shirt with the tatters he had for breeches. It had been a kind thought, but the rest of the clothes could go in the chest when he had mended it, and back to whoever had left it here. A well-meaning, kind, though fearful friend. Who could it have been?

WEAPONS

It took Brinin some days to find the best wood for Wulfrich's sword, a bough the right width and straight enough to be easily shaped. And then the time had to be found to work on it, little shavings of time snatched here and there. In the evenings, sitting on a stool by his hearth, he strained his eyes to work in the dim glow of the flames. He shaped the sword, smoothed the wood and learned Brother Wilfred's psalm at the same time.

He has freed me from the hunter's snare. Brinin almost knew the psalm now. He had marked the words out in the dirt with a stick, had scratched them on a bit of birchbark, had written them on his waxboard, not well but better than he had hoped. *You will hope under his feathers.* When he worked in his field, the words buzzed around in his head like bees in a hive. And now he mumbled them to himself as he twisted twine round and round the hilt, crossing it over until it was strong. *You will not fear the dread by night, nor the arrow flying by day.* He almost knew the psalm now, and the sword was done.

Brinin stood up, thrusting and swishing the sword around in the darkness. It was a good sword, strong but not too heavy for a boy. Together Brinin and his weapon made fyrdlike shadows on the walls. What would he have given for a sword like this when *he* was a boy! Wulfrich's foes had better take care. They would go home bruised if they weren't swift enough to block his thrusts. That was a thought. Didn't all fyrdmen have shields to stand behind, 'a shield all around them', as Brother Wilfred's psalm said? He hadn't seen many of the boys with shields, but why shouldn't Wulfrich have one? He would hide the sword away until both were ready. Wulfrich would like a shield.

By the doorway sat the little chest, its lid newly mended. All the clothes were packed inside it again, all but one pair of breeches that lay on a stool. He would wear the breeches in the morning for his unknown friend to see and know that the chest was ready. There wasn't much life left in his old breeches, and he hadn't liked the thought of going barelegged like a small boy, though he had feared it would come to that. Now he could keep the old breeches for the dirtiest work only, though he might spare some cloth from the end to twist into straps for Wulfrich's shield. He'd need some way of holding it.

Brinin hadn't worn the clothes—Edith had been watching him for days—and it had saddened her. Short of speaking to him, which would likely be a blow to his pride, she didn't know what to do. And then she saw him, early when the air was still chill and the grass damp. He was holding an axe and a basket and making his way along the meadow. He was wearing the same old shirt, but the breeches were new. But why wait for days then wear them now, and why wear only the breeches and not the rest? Unless it was a word that he had done the work and was taking his payment. How else could he let her know?

She swiftly walked to Brinin's hut, taking care not to be seen. The chest was on the floor, just inside the door. Edith didn't stop to look at it beyond a quick glance to see that it *had* been mended. Then she snatched it up and dashed back to the hall.

It was only when she was sitting on her bed, hidden behind her curtain, that she opened the chest; and she almost groaned aloud at what she saw there. All the clothes were still inside, all but that one pair of breeches. Edith shut the lid crossly. Hadn't he understood that *all* the clothes were meant for him? She would make him understand!

She was almost at the door when she was struck by another thought. Perhaps he hadn't misunderstood. Perhaps he was telling her something. Not even the whole chest would be enough to pay for so many clothes, let alone the little time it must have taken him to mend the lid. In her eagerness, Edith had forgotten that. But Brinin was proud and stubborn and seldom ready to take a gift. She had sometimes wondered if he wanted to *prove* to himself that he was truly free. Likely he knew what the clothes were worth and was unwilling to take them for nothing. Let him think what he liked. *She* knew how to deal with that!

Edith cast her eyes round the hall for something else—anything else—that might need to be mended. But there was nothing. Nothing stayed broken for long; her father had always seen to that. Then her eye fell on a little stool that Wynith sometimes sat on when she was working by the hearth. It was strong—wholly sound—but the legs were long and thin. It would be easy to break them. It wouldn't be sound for long.

Behind her curtain again, Edith laid the stool on its side and put her foot on one of the legs. Harder and harder, she bore down on it until the leg snapped, the splinters sticking up sharp and spearlike. It broke so suddenly that she hit her ankle on the wood and gasped in pain. Surely if anyone could have seen her now they would have thought she was mad! Then she turned the stool and did the same with another leg. That was enough.

Edith scooped up the broken stool and the clothes, all the clothes. This new work wouldn't be so easy. Brinin was stubborn, but she was dogged. That was her weapon. She would hack away at his pride until he had done what she wanted.

Brinin found the wood for Wulfrich's shield with unforeseen ease. His feet lead him to a fallen tree, half-hidden among the leaves and long grass. He stumbled over it and when he had picked himself up again he saw straightaway that it was what he wanted. He cut off a chunk and headed back to his hut. It wouldn't take long to shave and smooth the wood into shape. He would do that today instead of working on his bowmanship.

The door of his hut was slightly ajar when he reached it, creaking a little in the morning breeze. Inside, the chest was gone as he had hoped it might be, but where he had left it lay a broken stool and the same bundle of clothes. Hadn't this unknown friend understood that he was giving the clothes back? Or perhaps the clothes were payment for mending the stool.

Brinin turned the stool over in his hands. It was hard to see how it had even come to be broken unless someone had wilfully smashed it. But then, some folk were careless. Had this friend gathered all their broken things together to bring to him one by one? Perhaps that was it.

Perhaps she was one of the new widows among them. Ælfwyn or Mildrith or Osgyth or Tibba. No, not Mildrith. She would have come to him herself, straightforwardly, and asked him for whatever she wanted. Yet it might be one of the others, with no husband left to do the mending, no time to learn to do it herself, and men's clothes sitting at home that her husband would never wear again. He would mend it, then, and keep a shirt as payment. But not today. Wulfrich's shield was first.

It was in the evening, when the shadows were long, the light warm but the breeze cool, that Brinin saw Wulfrich coming round Deorstan's house. Brinin was on a stool outside his hut with the shield in his lap. The straps were already fastened to the back, and he was smoothing a few last rough spots on the front. It wasn't beautiful, but enough like a shield to do. Wulfrich held back at first—he was always a little shy to begin with—but Brinin could see him eyeing the shield and drawing nearer inch by inch.

'Go into the hut and fetch out what you find on the stool by the hearth,' said Brinin, not looking up from his work.

He heard the creak of the door and the sound of Wulfrich's feet on the wood, then a gasp and a scuffle as Wulfrich burst out again, all his awkwardness gone.

'It's a sword! Did you make it?'

'Yes.'

'What's it for?'

'You'll have to tell me that. It's for you. What are you going to do with it? Fight dragons? Or rush into battle?'

'For me? But it's a wonderful sword! It's the best I've ever seen! None of the other boys has a sword as good as this!'

And Wulfrich leapt forward, thrusting and slashing, cutting down unseen foes on all sides, much as Brinin had done in the darkness of his hut, much as he had done with sticks as a boy, when no one was nearby to see him taking a little time away from work to play.

'Is that a shield?' asked Wulfrich when the last of his foes had fallen.

'Yes, and that's for you too,' said Brinin, handing it over, with a sudden uneasiness that for *him* to befriend this boy of all boys was an unkindness and not a help. Yet Wulfrich was so happy, and it was good to see him smile.

There was more fighting then, crouching, blocking, more battle to be done. But then, without warning, Wulfrich's face fell and he lowered his weapons.

'I can't take these home,' he said sadly, a little quiver in his voice much like a sob not yet fully grown. 'I'd have to tell my father where I got them—he'd *make* me tell him! I don't want him to put them on the fire. I had a stick as a sword once, but I didn't see him coming and swung it too near him and… and afterwards he put it on the fire.'

'Don't take them home then,' said Brinin. It wouldn't do for Aculf to learn where his son had got these new weapons. 'Is there nowhere else you can keep them?'

Wulfrich stood frowning and still for a long time before his face brightened again.

'I'll ask Tidræd to keep them for me,' he said. 'Tidræd likes me now. I don't know why. He never did before.'

'Better give them to him quickly, then, before it gets too dark and you have to go home.'

Wulfrich, a fyrdman once more, dashed away, but before he was out of sight he stopped and turned back.

'They're the best sword and shield I've *ever* seen!' he called.

Wulfrich came back the next evening, as Brinin was filling his sow's watertrough. He had tucked his sword into his belt and had found some string somewhere and fastened it to the shield so he could wear it across his back and leave his arms free. He came up to the swine pen without even a shadow of awkwardness and leaned cheerfully on the fence.

'Tidræd showed me somewhere to hide them,' he said. 'He knows so many places. And he thought they were the best sword and shield *he'd* ever seen too. He has a *real* sword! It was his father's, and he showed it to me and even let me lift it. It's heavy. It's too heavy for Tidræd too, but he can lift it higher than I can. Then his mother came back and sent us out. He wants you to show him how to make a shield like mine and he's going to look for wood. He wants to make it himself if you'll show him what to do. Would you?'

'I don't mind,' said Brinin. 'Now, as you're here, can you go into my hut and fetch me my shovel? I forgot it.'

Wulfrich walked away, fingering his sword hilt as he went, and was swiftly back with the shovel. He handed it to Brinin.

'What's that thing in your hut, on the stool?' he asked, as Brinin bent down to scrape the dung into the bucket. 'The small thing with marks scratched on it?'

'It's a waxboard.'

'What's it scratched for?'

'The scratching is writing.'

'Is that what Brother Wilfred taught Oswald Child to do? My father says it's best left to monks.'

'But if one man can write,' said Brinin, 'and another can read then they can speak to each other without even being together.'

'How?' Wulfrich eyed Brinin doubtfully.

Brinin lowered the dungbucket over the side of the pen then swung himself over after it.

'Come, and I'll show you.'

Brinin went to his hut and fetched out the waxboard and a stick from the woodpile. He sat down on the grass where the light was good, and Wulfrich squatted beside him, still with one hand on his sword.

'When you want to say something,' began Brinin, 'a sound comes out of your mouth like this: "sword". Then if you know how to write you can take the word and turn it into writing like this.'

There was a patch of brown earth beside them, where the grass had been worn away by his feet. Brinin took the stick and scratched the word into the earth, while Wulfrich watched, somewhat baffled.

'But it doesn't look like a sword,' he said.

'No,' said Brinin. 'A wise man long ago thought of a way to take all the sounds our mouths make and turn them into marks. Look here. This mark is wyn. Wuh. Wyn. You need it to write "sword" but you need it for other words too. Here's another one. It looks like a weapon, doesn't it, an axe? Wuh. Weapon. And wuh. Wintanceaster. And wuh. Wolf. And wuh. Wulfrich. Why don't you try to write it?'

Wulfrich took the stick and, biting his tongue, scratched another wyn in the earth beside Brinin's, then handed Brinin back the stick.

'This one does look like a weapon, but it doesn't look like Wintanceaster or a wolf and it doesn't look like me,' he said. 'And that doesn't look like a sword. What's it for? No one knows what the marks mean. Only Brother Wilfred, and if you want to say something to him you can go and find him.'

'In the minster Oswald Child and I went to, they had old books. The monks could still read them even though the men who wrote them are dead.'

Wulfrich's eyes grew wide. 'I don't want to know what dead men are saying! I'd be frightened.'

'They weren't dead when they wrote them.' Brinin tossed the stick aside.

Wulfrich glanced up at the hillside where the sun was getting low.

'I need to hide my weapons before I go home. I'm only going to play with them on this side of the village, away from the house.' He looked down at the writing in the dirt again. 'That one *does* look like a weapon.'

SWINE

Eawig had knowledge that Brinin had never learned, knowledge about beasts and their ways handed on by a grandfather full of wisdom. Brinin had spent his whole life gathering only scraps of it. The days he had worked at Garulf's side had been feast days when he had greedily swallowed more in a morning than in all the weeks before. He had always been taller than most and had grown stronger by the year until he was taller than Row, taller than the other slaves, taller than most men in the village. And with growing strength had come the slowest, heaviest, dirtiest work that needed little thought and less skill. Eawig was slight and swift-footed, stronger than he looked but not much good for the heavy work. Perhaps that was why he had first been put to work with the swine, and even Aculf had seen that the boy had a way with them. Now he knew more about swine than anyone else in Oakdene, and Brinin could bear a heavy load but needed to be taught how to care for his own beast.

In a few short weeks Eawig's knowledge had more than earned him his unborn swine. He had shown Brinin how to handle his sow, where to graze her, where to find good fodder for her trough. And when Brinin had been beset by worries that she had eaten too much or too little, or done something new that he hadn't seen before, it had been Eawig who had soothed the worries with tales of other such sows he had known.

All these thoughts were in Brinin's mind as he spent yet another evening by Garulf's hearth. He had never minded being by himself—had longed for it at times—but now that he always worked alone, rested alone, slept alone, Garulf's friendship had become very welcome. In these last months Brinin had wondered if perhaps men had not been made always to be alone, had not been made to eat alone. A meal tasted better when he could eat it while others talked, even if he said little himself.

'I've been thinking about beasts, Grandfather,' said Eawig, scraping out the last mouthfuls from his bowl.

'There's seldom a day when you don't, lad,' said Garulf. 'What is it this time?'

'Brinin should breed his sow soon.'

'So will you?' said Garulf, turning to Brinin. 'You'd be wise to, as the lad says. Then she'd have her brood before the weather turns cold.'

'Oswald Child said I could take her to one of his father's boars, and I've already spoken to Cynestan about it. And Cynestan's offered one of his too.'

'That's what I was thinking about,' said Eawig. He set his bowl down on the floor, then sat with his chin in his hands, frowning a little in thought and leaning towards the fire. 'I look like Mother, always have, but Ebba doesn't.'

'I'm like Father,' said Ebba. 'That's what you say, isn't it, Mother?'

'It's your eyes, and the way your hair curls,' said Wynith. 'His was the same.'

'It must be that way with beasts too,' said Eawig. 'The boar gives something to the young and not only the sow. I don't think you should take the sow to one of Edrich Thegn's boars, or Cynestan's either. They're good enough beasts but they aren't the best. I've been looking at the other boars in the village too.'

'Do you know all the swine in this village?' laughed his mother.

'Almost all,' grinned Eawig. 'Not Eadulf's. I had a look once, but he smacked my head and sent me away. But listen, you know that big boar that Thurstan bought last year, the one with the black spot on his back? That's the best boar in the village.'

'It is a fine beast, that one,' said Garulf.

'I'd give a horse for a boar like that!' Eawig was speaking more warmly, more swiftly, the more he thought of the boar. 'If I had a boar even half as good as that one I'd—'

'You don't have a horse,' said Ebba, 'or even an ass!'

'Brinin's sow is a good one, and I think her young will be good too,' went on Eawig, with a scornful glance but no answer for his sister. 'But I want them to be the *best*. Then you'll get good money if you sell any.'

'Well, what about it, Brinin lad?' said Garulf. 'The boy talks wisdom. Will you ask Mildrith if you can take your sow to her boar?'

'I'll think about it,' said Brinin slowly. 'Mildrith has been kind.'

'More than kind, lad. She isn't likely to mind a little thing like that after all you've done for her with the ploughing.'

'She's already paid me for the ploughing with her oxen and plough. My field wouldn't have been ploughed without her. But I'll think about it.'

Brinin did think about it, later that evening as he leaned against the sow's pen, stroking her back in the darkness. He liked her rough skin and her short, bristling hair with a little fire in it like his own, though it was too dark now to see it. Perhaps her hair wasn't quite like his own. His was brighter, while hers was rusty like an old tool left to sit too long in the rain.

Brinin wasn't one to love a beast as a man loves a friend. A friend was a friend, and a beast a beast, for work or meat only. He remembered how, years before, Oswald had wept when one of his father's old hounds had died, a hound Oswald had loved and sought out when he was unhappy. He had wept over it like a lost friend, then had never spoken of it again and never befriended another in the same way. But Brinin's sow was only a beast. He liked how her back felt, and the way she let him rub it. She knew him now.

Likely there was no harm in asking Mildrith. Brinin was learning to take offered kindnesses, learning that there were more of them in the world than he had thought. It was harder to ask for what had not been offered, too awkward to think of. It almost seemed like begging and that was something he had never learned to do. Yet Mildrith was kind and more than likely to give him what he asked for. Let him do it for Eawig, so that his unborn swine would be the offspring of the best boar in the village. Eawig would like that.

'Why would I mind a little thing like that?' laughed Mildrith when Brinin clumsily found the words to ask her. 'You've more than earned it. You've been such a help to me.'

'You already lent me the plough and—'

'Oh, I don't only mean the ploughing! You're welcome to the boar, and I hope you get a good brood from him. And you're welcome to anything else you need too. Thurstan was proud of that boar, and he liked you and would have been glad to lend him to you. And I know you've been good for my boy too. You've steadied him a bit—don't think I haven't seen that. You be sure you ask me for anything you need, anytime at all!'

And Brinin left Mildrith with the bewildered feeling that she thought *he* was doing her a kindness and not the other way.

Eawig kept on earning his swine. He was the one who told Brinin when it was time to take the sow to the boar and he was the one who eased his mind later.

'There's no need to watch her all the time,' he said one evening, with a half-smile that made Brinin feel a little foolish. Was he growing too fond of this beast? She was only a beast, after all. 'There'll be nothing to see for a long while yet. She won't have her brood until after the harvest has begun—some weeks in, I should think—so put it from your mind until then.'

'So there's nothing I need to do?'

'You could make her pen a little bigger. There'll be time enough for that after the haymaking. And you'll want to keep all the straw from your wheat for her. That's all. You'll know when her time's coming. And if you don't, I'll tell you. To think my swine will be the offspring of that fine boar!'

Eawig went cheerfully home and left Brinin with his sow, her rough back and her bristly ears. Perhaps he might spare Eawig two of the brood.

SWARMS

More came. More than Oswald had ever thought *could* come. Throngs of Danes flooded in from somewhere to overwhelm them. The word seemed to have spread that there were easy pickings in Wessex, good weather to get there, a kingdom ripe for the taking. While the King lay wounded they swarmed in, and Oswald's last dim hopes were snuffed out with the news. He knew what the end would be now.

Oswald's father was on his feet again too soon. He could walk and wield a sword, and that was enough for him. But Oswald saw pain on his face every day; the too-tight jaw, the long breaths, the few words. He wondered at him and the strength of mind and body that drove him. He asked himself if he had strength of his own to match it. And he feared what the end of it all might be.

It wasn't all pitched battle. There were skirmishes here and there, news of raids, ambushes and spreading fear. Oswald's father had known seventeen winters before he ever saw war. He had crushed the Danes at Aclea and lost both his brothers in one day. The headstrong lastborn son who would never be lord became the only son—the only child—left alive, then rode home with his father to forget he had ever been a boy. And he had forgotten so thoroughly that it often seemed to Oswald that his father had never been a boy at all. Now Oswald, who had not yet seen his seventeenth winter, had lived through five battles. And so many others—better, older and stronger men than he—had fallen. Would he too forget what he had been before?

They were camped near Readingum again, and he sat by the fire one night with Beorn when both of them should have been sleeping. Oswald hated Readingum now, with those wretched heaps of earth the Danes could hide behind like bees swarming in their hive, while more and more joined them every day. He sometimes wished the earth would open up and swallow Readingum and all the Danes with it.

There was talk in the camp that the King was dying or already dead, though no one seemed to know the truth of the thing. And they were likely going to fight the Danes again in the morning. There was talk of that too. Perhaps that was why Oswald and Beorn sat up late. It might be the last time they could sit by a fire in the darkness, all smoke and sparks and moths and stars.

'Do you ever ask yourself what it will be like when all this is over?' asked Oswald as he stared into the flames.

'At the beginning I did,' said Beorn. 'I was angry with you, Oswald Child—I don't mind telling you now—for making me stay behind in Oakdene. I wanted to make them pay for my father's blood, and then I was left behind. I almost wanted them to come to the village so I could kill a few of them myself. And once we'd killed some and driven the rest away, I thought everything could be as it was before. I thought we would all be at home again doing the work that sometimes seemed so dull but which I'd give anything to be doing now. But I never think about that any more. I've been to war. I've killed a few Danes—though we haven't driven them away—but now I never think beyond tomorrow. It's better that way.'

'I didn't mean what it would be like if we all went home. I don't think I ever thought it could be the same again, not after my first battle. That was the day I became a man, I think. I meant what it would be like if the Danes never leave. We can't go on like this for ever. What do they even want? To settle on our lands? That's what they've done in Northumbria. And if the King *is* dead or dying, what then? I don't see how his son *could* be king. It'll have to be the Ætheling, with the Danes swarming round us like this. He's a good leader—I wish he were here now—but is there even anything he can do? Yet it will have to end somehow.'

'That's why I won't think beyond tomorrow, Oswald Child,' said Beorn. 'How can I, the only man left of my kin, with a widowed mother and three young sisters at home? I'll get up tomorrow, fight this battle they're talking about and do my best to live through it. And if I do live and reach sunset with breath still in my body and my right wits, then and only then will I think about the next day. It's the only way. Think further ahead than that and we'll drive ourselves mad.'

It was like all the other times. The march and the waiting that sickened the gut, while all the little things Oswald saw seemed to grow big. The world was awash with new life. Buttercups and eggwort were scattered yellow throughout the grass, little knowing it was the last day they would see the sun.

It was like all the other times. The mud and the gore, the wild rushing, the roaring and shouting, the baffling uproar, the unstopping, endless strain, when they gave breath and blood and sweat and got back only shame and bloody defeat.

It was like all the other times and unlike any of them. More than ever before, Oswald stared death in the face. His foe was young, not any older than himself. They were evenly matched, and there was no true hatred in his eyes, only the knowledge that he must kill or die himself. His shirt was new. Perhaps he was one of the fresh bees swarming about the hive.

And it all went wrong. Oswald didn't know how. His shield cracked under a heavy blow. It fell from his arm and in the shock he lost his footing and stumbled. He fell, not even to his knees. To his back like some writhing weevil about to be trampled underfoot. No way to get up. His foe bearing down on him and only a sword to block him. No hope. No tomorrow.

A sudden tangled web of limbs as someone sprang on the Dane from amid the roaring throng of men; sprang as fiercely as a hound on his prey and brought him down in death. Beorn.

He grabbed Oswald's arm and pulled him as he scrambled to his feet. Oswald snatched up the fallen Dane's shield but too late for it to be much good. 'Fall back! Fall back!'. No hope of winning, not enough men to risk losing any more. Shame and bloody defeat. They ran, stumbling through the dead with the bays and gloating shouts of the Danes at their backs, and a few flung spears to boot. Shame and bloody defeat. Why couldn't the earth open up and swallow these howling Danes whole?

When, beaten and breathless, they slowed enough to speak, Oswald grasped Beorn's hand.

'You saved me!' he gasped. 'You saved my life. If there's ever anything I can do, anything…'

'I always think of my father when I kill a Dane,' said Beorn, with that slow way of his. 'But as you once said to me, lord before kin. And you're almost my lord, Oswald Child, and were for a short time. But let's not speak of "anything" just yet. Let's get to sunset and think about tomorrow first. No further ahead than that.'

DRAGONS

Brinin was learning the best places to find wood now that he had more woodcraft to turn his hand to. Some he found himself; others Daglæf, in his neighbourly way, told him about. He was on his way back from the forest one afternoon when he walked near Aculf's house. He had almost passed it when a yell—a boy's yell—sounded through the half-shut doorway. It was swiftly followed by others. Brinin stopped walking. Another yell, mostly a sob this time. As a slave, he had known so many little ways to stand between Aculf and the smaller ones. But now he was free, free from Aculf and his blows and free to stand helpless because he couldn't walk into another man's house and put himself between him and his son. And it felt like shame to walk away because he couldn't bear to hear any more.

Later, when his work was done, Brinin went to see his sow. He liked to lean on the pen and watch her and know that she was his own. But as he came towards his hut, he heard a little whimpering sniffle, not made by any beast. Wulfrich leapt up from where he had been crouching by the pen, wiping his eyes fiercely with a grubby hand.

'I wasn't weeping! I was only sitting here.'

Perhaps there were other ways than weeping for a boy to make his face as dirty and tear-stained as Wulfrich's was, but Brinin didn't know them. He didn't need to see at the tears if Wulfrich didn't want him to. The boy didn't know that Brinin had heard the beginning of them.

'It's good to watch a beast,' said Brinin, keeping his eyes carefully on the sow and not on the boy. 'She'll be a fine sow once she's grown a little bigger.'

Wulfrich kicked the pen half-heartedly.

'I didn't lose his shovel!' he said, still fierce and wiping his eyes again. 'I never even had it. And he saw me with my sword and shield and almost took them away, but Tidræd said they were his and he didn't. But he said it too boldly and my father smacked his head and said he didn't care whose son he was, he'd better not talk to him like that again. And then he said I took the shovel, but I didn't! He likely set it down somewhere and forgot. And later when he finds it he'll remember that he put it there himself, but he still won't be sorry that he beat me for nothing!'

Wulfrich ended his speech with another harder kick, a little helpless fight in a boy who could do nothing else. It was the same old tale, but worse because Aculf was lord under his own thatch with nothing to hold him back.

'If I ran away to Wintanceaster, do you think I could find work there?' he asked hopefully.

'No,' said Brinin. 'I think you'd have to steal or beg for your bread, if you ever got there at all. You're still a little small to run away to Wintanceaster.'

'Perhaps I'll wait then,' sighed Wulfrich. 'But I *am* going to go there some day, as soon as I can!'

'Do you like to listen to tales?' asked Brinin. A sad, sore little boy with no way out of his troubles. That came so near—so painfully near—that the long-ago, hearthside sagas flooded Brinin's mind. 'I know a good one. Come and sit here and I'll tell it to you.'

Brinin pulled two stools out of the hut. They were old now, those stools, and had heard many a tale when his mother had still been alive to tell them. While Wulfrich, still sniffing a little, settled down beside him, Brinin searched for the words to begin. He could almost hear them, an unforgotten whisper spoken behind him, past the threshold in the dimness of the hut. But they had been spoken in another tongue and with an easy readiness that he had never had. Yet a tale told awkwardly was better than none at all.

'Far away from here,' he began, 'away to the east and north, lies a great mountain. It's covered in dark trees that never lose their leaves, even in the cold. Its top reaches high into the heavens and, long ago, it was always hidden by cloud. At least, it looked like cloud but it was smoke, for what do you think lived at the top of the mountain?'

'I don't know,' mumbled Wulfrich, shrugging his shoulders. Brinin, well-taught in tales for as long as he could remember, had always known the answer. He had always been ready for dragons or trolls or other fearsome beasts, for battles or danger. But perhaps Wulfrich had not heard enough tales to learn all that. 'Had someone built a fire? Was it an ironsmith?'

'No, it was a dragon, a big one with great yellow eyes that seemed to turn all ways at once. It could knock down ten men with one swipe of its tail and with one fiery breath could burn down a whole village. No one in that land ever knew when it would come and they were always afraid. One by one all their fighting men had climbed the mountain to fight the dragon and none had ever come back.'

The words were stiff, limping a little, but Brinin saw Wulfrich's eyes grow wide as his own had once done. In his mother's tale, it had always been Bruni who climbed the mountain to fight the dragon; Bruni, that name he never heard spoken any more. But today Bruni must step aside. A tall, fiery-haired man with a Danish name would never do for Wulfrich.

'There *was* still a man left who was bolder than all his neighbours thought. He was better than bold too; he was wise and did nothing without thinking. His name was Wulfrich'—a little start from the boy at Brinin's side—'and he thought about the dragon for a long time before he did anything. Then he went to the ironsmith and asked him to work a great iron shield, for wood was no good against a dragon. And when it was ready he took the shield and his sword and spear and began the long climb up the mountain.

'He stopped before sunset and hid among the trees. When the dragon had flown out to kill and burn, it had always come at night and had always been gone before daylight. Wulfrich thought that the dragon worked by night and slept by day, like owls and foxes and brocks. Surely it was better to come upon it stealthily as it slept. Throughout the long night he sat awake, listening and watching, as still as the trees. And from time to time he heard a sound far above him, the sound of some great beast moving slowly about.'

Wulfrich had stopped sniffing now. He was leaning towards Brinin eagerly, as Brinin had once waited hungrily for his mother's words. Those tales had never taken his troubles away—not truly—but they had hidden them for a time. They had let him forget until the delight faded and he remembered everything.

'Early in the morning, before the sun was up, Wulfrich crept out from among the trees and up to where the great dragon lay. He smelt it first, a foul stench that stung his eyes. Then he heard the dragon's breath, swelling and fading like a snoring man.

'Then he saw it, a grey-green worm curled up and twisted as it slept, its dark batlike wings spread over it like a cloak. But it wasn't the dragon, fearsome though it was, that stopped Wulfrich's breath. Behind it lay the greatest hoard—gold and silver and bright stones—that he had ever seen, more than he had even dreamed of. Wulfrich gripped his spear and stood staring while the loathsome beast slept.

'But he couldn't reach it. The sound of his feet on the dragon's hoard would wake it long before he could get near enough to kill it. He could see that others had tried before him and failed; their bones and blackened weapons lay where they had fallen. One wrong step and he would soon lie among them.'

'But…but won't it kill him too, like all the others?' whispered Wulfrich, his voice low and breathless. 'Perhaps he should creep away before it wakes up.'

'But then who would kill it?' smiled Brinin.

'I don't want him to die! I'd be frightened.'

'Likely he was too, but he didn't creep away. He watched the sleeping dragon for a long time. Its face was turned away from him. Even if it opened its eyes, it wouldn't see him straightaway, hidden as he was behind one of the rocks that lay scattered around the dragon's lair. At last Wulfrich knew what he would do. If the dragon would only stand up so he could see its soft belly; if only it would keep looking the other way…

'Softly and hardly taking his eyes off the dragon, Wulfrich reached down and lifted a stone that lay at his feet. He raised his arm and threw. The stone flew up, up, up. It soared over the dragon, far beyond it, up to the top of the great hoard where in the light of dawn the gold and silver and bright stones sparkled like stars. Then it fell.

'With a clatter, the stone landed on a golden cup. The cup knocked against a silver bowl and it all began to slip. A golden arm ring rolled down the shining heap and landed on the dragon's back. The beast lifted its head. Wulfrich crouched low behind the rock, his spear held tightly in one hand, the iron shield heavy on his other arm. The dragon didn't move. It stared at the top of its hoard to see who had dared to come to steal its gold, but it kept its back to Wulfrich. Then with something like a growl and a hiss, it clambered to its two great feet.'

Brinin hadn't known that he could do it. How could his slow lips tell such a tale? But Wulfrich was leaning so far forward on his stool that he almost tipped it and had to fling himself back to steady it again. The words that had begun so sluggishly seemed to gather a little of his mother's skill as he spoke them, even if they were in the wrong tongue. Again he almost heard her whispering behind him, just inside the doorway: 'And then Bruni ran.'

'And then Wulfrich ran,' said Brinin, 'as swiftly as he could, ready to thrust his spear into the dragon. He could see its white belly. He almost reached it. The spear tip was just beginning to scratch the soft flesh. Then he stumbled. He fell'—a gasp from Wulfrich—'the spear flew from his hand, and the dragon turned round.'

'He's going to die! The dragon will kill him!'

'Wulfrich snatched his sword from its sheath and slashed at the beast looming over him. He heard it hiss as the sword struck home and saw the dark blood trickling from the wound. But it wasn't a deathwound. All he had done was anger the dragon.

'And it *was* angry. It spread its wings and soared far above Wulfrich. One of its claws caught the sword and sent it flying from Wulfrich's hand, out of reach. Wulfrich saw the light in the dragon's yellow eyes and the smoke rising from its nostrils; he knew the fire was coming. And he ran.

'Even as he ran he felt the heat on his back but did not dare look behind him. He slipped and fell again, rolling and sliding, and only stopped between two rocks when he could slide no further. What a fool! What a fool! He hid behind his shield, trapped.'

The unforgotten words whispered to Brinin from long ago: 'Death if he went out, death if he kept hidden.'

'Death now whatever he did,' said Brinin. 'Even as he thought it, a burst of flame struck the shield, licking round the side and scorching his shield arm and leg. He crept back further, cowering away from the fire. There was no hope now. His hand touched something in the dirt, something hard and cold. He looked down. Beside him, almost hidden, lay a long iron spear, left behind by one of those bold men who had died before him. One last weapon and one last hope.

'Round the side of his shield he saw the dragon, its head raised, its open mouth ready to gush out another burst of fire. Wulfrich grasped the spear. The dragon swooped down. Just as it reached him, Wulfrich flung his shield aside and thrust the spear through the flames into the dragon's mouth, and deep, deep into its throat. The beast rose high into the sky with a long hissing screech, the fire spluttered and died away and the dragon crashed to the ground and lay dead at Wulfrich's feet.'

'It's dead! He killed it!' Wulfrich had left his stool and was kneeling at Brinin's feet. 'And then what did he do?'

'He went home. It took him a long time because the dragon had burned him and he was weak, but he did reach home. Everyone loved him because he had slain the dragon, and he became the wealthiest man in the land because of the dragon's hoard. But he loved the old iron spear more than all the gold. It had saved his life, and he hung it up in his house and looked at it every day.'

'Until his deathday,' whispered the voice in Brinin's head, 'he was thankful for that old iron spear.'

'That's what I would do!' said Wulfrich, springing to his feet and snatching up a stick. He swung it back and forth. 'If I ever kill a dragon, I'll hang up the weapon in my house too.'

'Your father's still in his field,' said Brinin. 'I saw him there when I was leaving mine. Why not go back to your mother now and eat and sit with her before he comes? Likely she's wondering where you are.'

Brinin watched as Wulfrich left him, swinging his stick swordlike to slay a dragon. He patted his sow fondly on the back and turned to go into the hut. But he stood for a long time on the threshold, leaning with his hands against the lintel. If only life could be like the tales, where one bold man and one bold deed drove all the trouble away. Wulfrich would swing his sword all the way home, but there would be no boldness when the sun set and his trouble was beside him at the hearth. Brinin kicked a nearby stool, sending it flying across the hut. Then he went inside to kindle a fire.

FOLLY

'Come quick!' gasped Tidræd, running to meet Brinin as he clambered down the hillside with a bundle of firewood under each arm. 'Your sow's broken out and is running all over the village. Eawig's gone after her. There'll be trouble if she gets into anyone's wheat and that was where she was heading.'

Brinin dropped the wood and ran after Tidræd. That pen had been strong. He'd looked over it for weaknesses again and again. How could she have broken out, unless... No time to think of that now, not until she was safely where she should be.

Eawig, rope in hand, was coaxing her to him. Brinin saw him ahead, bending low, beckoning her with something—likely some good thing she'd want to eat. Then as she came a little nearer, he dived and made a grab at her, but she slipped away from him and Eawig stumbled and fell headlong after her. Someone was shouting now, and the sow squealed. Had something hit her? That gave a little more speed to Brinin's wearying feet. Another shout. He was almost there now, but he could see where the sow was going and his heart sank. Why there? Of all the wheat in the fields, why must she run there? Then, too swiftly for Brinin to see it done, Eawig caught her just as Aculf, still shouting, reached boy and beast. He rushed at Eawig, slapping at his head and back, but Eawig wasn't letting go now that he had the sow in his grip. He held her as she squealed and writhed and Aculf's blows fell on him like so many leaves and nothing more. Wulfrich, wide-eyed and fearful, stood a little way off and did not dare to come any nearer.

'Can't you keep those filthy beasts in hand?' bellowed Aculf. 'You've been shirking your work, you idle hound. Cynestan will hear of it, and I'll make sure he deals with you. I'd have had the skin off your back!'

'Leave him alone!' panted Brinin with the little breath he had left. His chest was bursting from the strain of the run. He grabbed Aculf's arm to pull him away. 'It's my beast.'

'Get your hands off me!' Aculf shoved Brinin away and kicked at Eawig, narrowly missing him as the boy struggled to his feet, his rope now fast round the still unhappy beast's neck. 'Did you drive that swine here to wreck my crop? If I see it anywhere near my field again, believe me, you'll be sorry! Get it away from here!'

Brinin's breath was coming back to him now, but he wouldn't waste it on Aculf. Now Brinin could walk away from him if he liked. Besides, he wasn't going to squabble with his neighbours, not even with a fool of a neighbour, and not with Wulfrich watching. Aculf could splutter and yell all he liked. The beast hadn't got into his field—thanks to Eawig earning those unborn swine yet again—and his threats meant nothing. Without another word, Brinin turned away and followed Eawig and the sow, leaving Aculf still shouting after him. But he wasn't gone quickly enough to miss hearing a curse, a sharp smack and a yelp.

'What are you staring at?' barked Aculf at Wulfrich this time. 'Didn't you hear me tell you to fetch the rake? Get it now before I take a stick to you!'

Wulfrich dashed away. Brinin saw him out of the corner of his eye. Perhaps he should have stayed to squabble—he half-wished he had. That would have kept Aculf's thoughts away from his son a little longer. Would there ever come a day when he would learn to look at Aculf without loathing him?

Garulf was at the swine pen when Brinin and Eawig reached it, frowning as he looked over the fence.

'It must have been very weak for the beast to break out like that, lad,' he said, 'though the rest of it seems strong enough.'

'It was *all* strong enough,' said Brinin.

Eawig led the sow into the pen and tethered her to a post. Brinin knelt by the fence to see what harm had been done to it. One post was so shattered that it lay flat like a felled tree, splinters and the withies he had woven in so carefully scattered about the grass. It was well broken, but not by his sow; not without a hand to wield an axe or a booted foot to kick with.

'The beast couldn't have broken out unless there was a weakness,' said Garulf.

Brinin said nothing. What was there to say? That he trusted in his own handiwork so much that he could more readily believe that one of his neighbours had smashed his pen when no one was watching? That sounded like folly, like the words of a madman who seeks foes where there are none. But the fence *had* been strong. Garulf seemed to understand at least some of Brinin's thoughts. He shook his head.

'Come, lad, surely you don't think that! No one could have…' he began, before tailing off and leaving the folly unsaid.

'I don't think,' said Brinin. 'I know.'

'But who would do such a thing?' Garulf was still unbelieving. Was it easier for him to think that Brinin had been a careless workman, that he'd left his pen half-done? 'Even if there are those who don't much like you, lad, there's no need to think like that. Who among them would go so far? And in daylight, when anyone might see them at it! No, there must have been a weakness in the fence. It's easy to overlook a small thing like that.'

'It *was* strong, Grandfather,' said Eawig, giving the sow's rope one last tug to tighten the knot that held it to the post. 'I've been here almost every day. I'd have seen if it was weak.'

'But who?' said Garulf again.

Brinin shrugged his shoulders. It hadn't been Aculf. That much he knew. Aculf had been too sure that Eawig had been shirking his work. Brinin went inside for his axe. The pen would have to be mended before nightfall and he had to fetch the wood to do it.

'Is she tethered fast enough, Eawig?' he said. 'You should go. Cynestan will be looking for you.'

'Should I tell him about the pen? He already knows she got out.'

'No,' said Brinin. 'What good would that do?'

Then he left them—Garulf frowning, Eawig unhappy—and went to fetch more wood.

NEIGHBOURS

'You have an eye for it, and no mistake,' said Daglæf one morning, lying sprawled on the grass as Brinin sent arrow after arrow to the mark without even one going astray. 'Some men take years before they learn to line up an arrow like that. Others seem to be born with the skill. You're one of that kind, I think.'

Brinin lowered his bow, tightened and loosened his shoulders—they were stiff as they learned this new work—then drew another arrow. He hardly knew whether the knowledge that he could shoot made him want to laugh or weep. Daglæf had been true to his word. Brinin had barely known him before, but now he was something a little more than a good neighbour.

'Not that skill is always enough in battle,' Daglæf went on. 'No, then you need a swift mind even more than a sharp eye. If you wait a little too long, the foe cuts you down. How do you think I got this arm? I held back—for less time than it takes me to tell you—but it was too long. You have the makings of a skilled bowman, but do you have a quick mind? That's what you need most.'

'I don't know,' said Brinin. He drew back his bow, eyeing the target along the shaft of the arrow, then let the arrow fly. It landed not an inch from where he wanted it.

'Must be quick enough, surely, to have got Edrich Thegn out of Readingum!'

'No, I thought about that for more than a day before I did anything.' The blow to Skorri's face had been the only swift thing about their flight, that and the running at the end. He'd always been wary of thoughts that were too quick. They so often led to folly. His swiftest thought had been choosing to call Aculf a fool, and look how well that had turned out! 'I'm never likely to go into battle anyway.'

'With the days as they are, who would know? Who would know?' Daglæf stretched and rose to his feet. 'That's enough for today. I have to work out how to mend a broken fence with one arm. My father's eyes are too old and his hands too unsteady for it, and the boys are too young to do it well, though perhaps I can talk them through it. They're good lads and they need to learn.'

'I'll do it for you, if you like, and help teach the boys too,' said Brinin. Wouldn't that be a small thing between one neighbour and another? 'That's one thing I *can* do swiftly.'

'If you can spare the time, I'd be glad of your help,' said Daglæf, smiling broadly, 'and glad to pay you for it too.'

'No need for that. If I can spare the time to shoot, I can spare the time to mend your fence.'

'Well then, let's be about it! But I'm not taking your work for free. Gather in a harvest or two before you work for your neighbours out of kindness alone. And don't look at me like that! I reckon I'm as stubborn as you are. You'll let me pay you or you're not helping me at all!'

They were still at the fence when the sound of oncoming horses broke through the still of the afternoon. Word came that Edrich Thegn, Oswald and two others had ridden into the village. Nothing would have kept Daglæf at his fence then. Brinin had seen Daglæf's hunger for the battle he would never taste again; he ate his fill of fresh news instead. Brinin stayed with Daglæf's sons and kept working. Any word of the Danes would find its way to him sooner or later. Besides, Edrich Thegn and Oswald were alive. That was enough for now.

But the news didn't linger. Daglæf was back as swiftly as he had gone, almost bursting with what he had to tell. He called over the few neighbours who were within earshot. Brinin, crouched low with the fence between him and the others, stopped his work, and Daglæf's two sons stood and listened wide-eyed to their father.

'The King's dead! And already buried. They buried him at Winburna, at the minster there.'

'What's that about the King?' asked Daglæf's father, Byrnhelm, leaning forward on his stool.

'The King's dead, Father,' said Daglæf, a little louder.

'What's to be done now?' Brinin couldn't see him from where he sat, but he knew Eadulf's sharp, warlike bark. 'Aren't his sons only small boys still? They can't lead the fyrd against those filthy Danes!'

Filthy Danes. Likely Brinin had been wise to keep out of sight. Yet wasn't Eadulf right? How could a small boy lead a kingdom at war? It was a bad time to lose the King.

'They've passed over his sons and given the kingship to the Ætheling! Perhaps the King settled it with his brother before he died. Who knows?' Daglæf turned to his father again with that loud, slow voice: 'They've made the Ætheling King, Father!'

'Ælfred the King, eh?' said Daglæf's father. 'I thought the King had sons.'

'Æthelred was a good king. He was God-fearing and died as a king should,' went on Daglæf, 'and Ælfred will be a good king too. He can lead the fyrd. If you'd only seen him at Æscesdun—not that I saw him myself with this arm, but I heard about it from those who did. He rushed ahead of the fyrd, wholly fearless, and ran right up at the Danes, though they held the higher ground. He'll be a good king.'

'Heaven knows we need—' Eadulf broke off sharply and when he began again it was with more roar than talk. 'What are you standing idle for?'

From where Brinin squatted he could see Deormod, Eadulf's slave, not idle, not standing at all but staggering under the weight of two heavy buckets of dung. At Eadulf's roar, he broke into a stumbling run and the sight of the helpless, hopeless fear on his face sickened Brinin's gut.

Eadulf rushed at Deormod, grabbed him by the hair and shook him. Deormod, with something between a gasp and a yelp, started and dropped the buckets, spilling the dung onto the grass. This angered Eadulf still more. He shoved Deormod to the ground, with curses and a few kicks to drive the wrath home.

Brinin was on his feet now. They looked on awkwardly: Daglæf and his sons, Baldred's son, Sibwine and Eadulf's own son, Eanfrith. There was the slightest shadow of scorn on Daglæf's face, but Eanfrith's face was tight, flushed and utterly ashamed. He dropped his head and did not meet his neighbours' eyes.

No one said a word. No one asked Eadulf where this rage had come from when Deormod had done nothing amiss. Brinin said nothing either—he couldn't think of *what* to say—and there was shame in that too. Eadulf had caught up a stick from somewhere and now he was raining down blows on Deormod. Deormod didn't scramble away. He only groaned softly and held his arms up round the back of his head to shield it as the blows fell wildly wherever the stick landed. Brinin saw Eanfrith clenching his fists.

'Is Eadulf beating that slave again?' Daglæf's father suddenly spoke up in the too-loud voice of an old man who is years beyond caring what he says or who may hear it. 'He'd get more work out of him if he beat him less and fed him more. Go and tell him, Daglæf! I don't want to listen to it any more!'

The old man spoke too loudly for there to be any need for Daglæf to say anything. Eadulf swung round angrily, but he lowered his stick long enough for Deormod to put a few swift feet between himself and his lord.

'Likely we all have work to do,' said Daglæf coldly. He nodded to his boys, who scuttled away. The others seemed only too glad to follow them. Even Eadulf, flinging a last curse at Deormod, tossed his stick aside and left, muttering as he went.

Brinin was left alone with Daglæf and his father. He watched as Deormod scraped the dung back into the buckets. He wasn't groaning now and he didn't weep. Eanfrith, glancing round warily to be sure that his father was out of sight, knelt beside him to help, a hand on Deormod's shoulder as he whispered to him. But Deormod looked utterly wretched as he trudged away, and Eanfrith still ashamed as he followed.

'He did nothing!' said Brinin. 'Eadulf's worse than Aculf!'

'There are some men who should never have a slave,' sighed Daglæf. 'Eadulf only has him because of the wergild his father got when a man wounded him in a fight. Some of us thought the money could have been better spent, but they *would* have a slave. Pity the slave. But it is what it is, and what can his neighbours do about it?'

Brinin took the long way back to his hut, behind the church and the hall and across the near end of the meadow. Now that the whole village was doubtless talking about the new king and whether he could drive away the Danes, it likely wouldn't be good for him to be seen striding through the midst of them with a bow. 'Those filthy Danes,' Eadulf had said. What a loathsome man he was, one of those worse men that Row had once warned him of. It would be better to be almost anything else than the thrall of a man like that. He wasn't even rich, like Edrich Thegn, only a small farmer without land of his own, who wielded all the little ugly power he had against Deormod because he could, while his neighbours watched and said nothing.

'Where have you been? I was looking for you?'

Oswald was standing by the church, dusty from the road and with a weary darkness under his eyes.

'I was helping Daglæf with a fence,' said Brinin. 'We heard we have a new king.'

'Pray that he doesn't fall quickly like his brother. Though the Æth… I mean the King knows how to fight. I've seen him.' Oswald nodded to Brinin's bow. 'You've been working on your bowmanship?'

Brinin ran his hand along the bow. He liked how smooth the wood felt. 'Daglæf's been helping me. And Tidræd from time to time. *He's* the best bowman in the village, or so he says himself!'

'He should be, given the father he had. But what about you? Are you any good?'

Brinin shrugged. 'I don't know, but the arrow always seems to go where I want it to.'

'You *are* good then. Didn't you say your father was a bowman? Perhaps it's in your blood.' Oswald ran his hands through his hair and sighed. 'I'm so hungry! I haven't even had so much as a cup of ale since we got home. There have been too many folk to see. Let me go and eat and then I'll come and find you. We're only here until the morning.'

Back at his hut, Brinin hung up his bow and quiver. Perhaps that was one more thing that he could share with his shadowy father, a skill that could bind them across the empty years. Likely he would have taught him as Thurstan had Tidræd, if his father had only lived and their lot had not been thraldom.

He left his hut and went to see his sow, but was hit by a stench too strong for a pen he had cleaned out only that morning. The sow lay sleeping… no, not sleeping! What swine slept in its own dung? Too-watery, stinking dung was spread everywhere. She lay open-eyed, open-mouthed, unmoving. And Brinin's heart, the breeze, the birds, the earth around him all seemed to stop at the sight of her. He gripped the pen. She was dead.

HOME

In the hall, a smell from the pot on the hearth left Oswald's tongue tingling in readiness. And Edith had cheese on the table, and honeybutter and eggs and ale and bread still warm from the oven. His father was already eating, and Oswald sank onto the bench eager to take his time and taste each bite to the full. He was home, and everything smelt right, looked right, sounded right and felt right. The thought of leaving again in the morning was like a kind of ache sitting beside the hunger.

He'd barely begun eating, barely let the cheese linger in his mouth, when Edith came from somewhere in the hall with a bundle of cloth in her arms. Shaking it out, she held up a brown shirt.

'I thought you'd both need new shirts after being away for so long,' she said. 'This one's for you, Father; and this yellow one, Oswald, is yours. I don't know if you want to take them away with you now or leave them here until… until another time.'

'I'll take it now, Edith,' said Edrich between bites. 'They're both fine shirts. I'll gladly wear mine tomorrow. It will be good to have something new on my back.'

Oswald, following his father's lead, praised the shirts. He too would wear his in the morning, but he knew it would go no further than that. He would wear it once and then pack it away to wear again if he ever rode home. Why take a shirt so new, so clean and bright and fresh and befoul it with the gore of battle? But Edith didn't need to know that. She was watching their father carefully. Was she looking for that wound she knew of? But he was hiding it with more skill than ever.

Edith sat down beside them and poured herself a cup of ale but she didn't drink it. She shifted it from hand to hand and didn't even raise it to her lips.

'Father,' she began at last, 'perhaps I ought to have asked your leave but… Brinin's clothes were very bad. His breeches were little more than rags and his shirt not much better. I took some old clothes from the bottom of your chest, only a few that you hadn't worn for a long time. I didn't want to give him anything that looked too new, because then he might not have wanted to wear them for work. And I didn't want to make a gift of them. I thought… well, a slave is fed and clothed by his lord, but a free man has to feed and clothe himself. I wonder if he wants to *feel* as free as he is. So I found some things for him to mend—a chest and a stool—and left them in his hut with the clothes, so he would think he was earning them with his woodcraft. He doesn't know it was me. But I hope, Father, that you don't mind that I didn't ask you first.'

'You did right, my dear,' said Edrich. 'While I'm away you're right to follow your own wisdom and that of those you ask to help you. There's no need to wait for me. Do as you think best. And this shirt is worth more than any old ones I might have had. I don't think I could have even told you what was at the bottom of my chest. I won't miss them, Brinin will have what he needs, and you have spared his pride. You did right, my dear.'

Edith had a way with folk. Oswald saw that more and more as they both grew older. She'd always been good at seeing small things that others—that he—missed. Perhaps she also had some inner wisdom that told her what Brinin, or others, might think of this or that. Oswald knew she was right. He'd almost had to browbeat Brinin into taking a swine for a bench they both knew Oswald didn't need. It had been hard to shift him. But Edith had got her way without any browbeating and without Brinin even knowing she was the giver. Oswald couldn't call to mind what Brinin had been wearing or what his clothes had been like before. When had he ever thought about Brinin's clothes, or anyone else's either? But Edith was good at seeing small things.

'There's something else, Father,' Edith went on. 'I'm worried about how frightened everyone is. Something changed the last time Oswald came. Oh, I know you said very little about the Danes then, Oswald, but since then—I don't know how to say it—sometimes I can almost *feel* the fear. And I don't know what to do about it.'

'A little fear can be wise,' said Edrich. 'If we fear getting burned, we don't go too near the fire. The Danes are among us—I don't want to frighten *you*, Edith, but you are not unaware of our danger here in Wessex—and we don't know what the end of all this will be. If fear keeps folk ready for whatever may come, then perhaps it is no bad thing.'

'Yes, Father,' said Edith. 'After Oswald left I made sure that folk hadn't forgotten where to hide. And I still have men watching. We haven't stopped that for so much as a night in all these months.'

Edith's voice was so steady, but as she spoke Oswald saw how tight her face was, how weary her eyes and that she still wasn't drinking the ale. And as suddenly as he had seen it, anger seemed to spring on him from nowhere. Why couldn't these wretched Danes have kept to their own lands? There was something praiseworthy for the fyrd to keep fighting against all hope. There was glory in emboldening their hearts as their strength dwindled, in falling in battle, in dying well; though Oswald wondered if the glory was much good to those left behind. What did Edith get? What did all those left in Oakdene get? Fear, long waiting and mostly loss at the end of it.

'Father,' said Edith. 'Do you think when folk are fearful, they might believe what isn't true or do foolish things?'

Edrich answered Edith, in a low voice as steady as her own, but Oswald had stopped listening. His eyes wandered round the hall, settling first on one thing, then another. The shields fastened to the roof beams, brightly painted and no two alike. His grandfather's spear hanging on one of the posts. His mother's seat, empty now but still there to look at; he'd never seen Edith sit on it. The long strip of sunshine that streamed over the threshold and far across the floor. The dark corners that lay beyond its reach. The benches around the edge of the hall where slaves or guests slept. The thick curtain that hid his bed. Wynith straightening up from where she bent with a broom to say a few words to Ebba. Ebba dashing away. Edith's loom by the doorway, half in shadow, half in light, some new cloth hanging on it, waiting for her swift fingers. It was home, and the tale of his whole life was here.

His hand rested on three deep cuts in the bench where he sat, and he ran his fingers along them. He remembered making the cuts as a small boy and his mother catching him at it; and how glad he had felt as she scolded him that she'd been the one to find him and not his father. And likely his father, sitting now at his elbow, still knew nothing of them. The hall was full of little things like that, each with its own tale to tell. Some could still make him smile; others he wished he could forget. His whole life had been here, all but these last months at the minster, on the battlefield, on the road, sleeping here and there. He longed to be home and yet hated it, because each time he crossed the threshold and left home behind, he knew it might be for the last time, for himself or his father or both. It was easier to have one last time, not many. Perhaps they would have been better not to come.

'Now, Edith.' Oswald's father's voice brought his thoughts back to his kin at his side. 'We have one night here. Let's speak of happier things. Tell me about the wheat and the barley. Tell me what news there is, what babies have been born.'

One day. One night. Why not spend it as if he were staying at home for ever? Oswald took his leave and went to find Brinin.

YEW

She was dead. Dead without warning or any time to help her, and so much hope struck down with her. Brinin was sitting slumped on a stool outside his hut, his head in his hands, when Oswald came. He saw Oswald frown slightly as he drew near.

'She's dead,' said Brinin dully. 'The sow. Dead before she even gave me any young.'

'What?' Oswald sounded aghast, almost unbelieving. 'What do you mean she's dead?'

'There was nothing wrong with her this morning, and when I got back I found her dead in the pen.'

'There must have been something wrong with her! Are you sure she wasn't sick?'

'Yes! There was nothing wrong with her at all.'

'I want to see her. There must have been something wrong!'

Oswald strode behind the hut to where the sow lay dead on the straw, Brinin following wretchedly behind. But they weren't the first to reach her. Wulfrich was there, gripping the fence and staring wide-eyed at the dead beast. He backed away fearfully when he saw them.

'I… I didn't know she would die!' he stammered. 'I didn't know there was anything wrong with it. I didn't want her to die. I only did what I was told. I had to or he…'

Then he dashed away before either of them could stop him or ask him any more. Oswald looked grimly at Brinin, then swung himself into the pen. He dug about in the feeding trough, still half-full of food. Brinin watched him without a word, already dreading, already knowing what he might find. Wulfrich's frightened outburst was like a fist in his gut or a knifewound.

'I know you've never had a sow before, but you're not such a fool as to feed a beast yew leaves!' Oswald handed Brinin a little shoot of yew, the needle-like leaves still dark green, fresh from the tree. 'These aren't the only ones. They're all through the fodder. Someone put them there to kill your sow, and I think we know who.'

The truth had been on Wulfrich's white face. Who else hated him so much that he couldn't bear to let him have even one beast to call his own? Who else would send a child to do the work for him?

Oswald scrambled back over the fence, flushed and angry.

'I'm going to my father! I'll have Aculf before the Moot for this. My father will call it before sunset. We've seen enough to know Aculf is guilty. You were working with Daglæf all afternoon. Aculf must have seen you there and sent his boy while you were nowhere near your hut. My father will make him pay you every penny for that sow. His boy's already said enough to prove it, and if someone spoke to him sternly enough he'd tell more too. What kind of man sends his son to kill another man's beast? The village will soon know what Aculf is. I'll make sure they know! I'm taking that shoot to my father. Come with me. Aculf will be sorry for this!'

Someone would be sorry if it went before the Moot, sorry to bear Edrich Thegn's anger—and he *would* be angry—sorry when the money was handed over, sorry as the whole village stood by and watched it all happen. But it wouldn't be Aculf.

'Wait,' said Brinin. 'If this goes before the Moot, Aculf won't be sorry. He'll be angry.'

'I don't care, and since when were *you* worried about that? Let him be angry! What can he do to you if he is? You have no more beasts for him to kill.'

'That's not what I meant. You saw how frightened Wulfrich was.'

'Little wonder! Who isn't frightened when their wrongdoing is found out? He knew we'd see the yew and find out what he'd done. Brinin, you can't let Aculf kill your sow and do nothing about it. Because you pity his son? Why? He's troublesome enough, from what I hear!'

'I don't think he knew anything about the yew leaves, and he isn't troublesome.'

'Everyone says he is.'

'How do they know? Have you ever seen him do anything you would call troublesome? I haven't. He's no worse than any other boy; less trouble than most, if anything. I've heard Aculf grumble about him often enough, but when was his word anything to go by? You didn't believe it so readily when he was grumbling about me.'

'But, Brinin, even if all that's true, you still have to do something. Men can't kill their neighbour's beasts and get away with it. If my father knew—'

'If this goes before the Moot, more harm than good will come of it. I'll have the money or another beast, but Aculf will be angry and he'll make someone smart for it.'

'Wulfrich, you mean?'

'Aculf beats him.'

'Whose father doesn't? Mine beat me, and his father beat him. That's got nothing to do with it!'

'Not like Aculf he didn't, too often and with little to earn it. Aculf always has to find someone to blame for... I don't know what! First it was me, then Eawig while I was at the minster. Now it's Wulfrich. It's easy to tell a man he's no longer workreeve, but you can't tell him he's no longer a father because he isn't fit to be one. We only thought of Aculf because of what Wulfrich said. What's Aculf going to do if that comes out at the Moot? Even if we could prove it another way, it would still be worse for Wulfrich. I know what Aculf's like. But there's no way to prove it unless we tell everyone what Wulfrich said, and I'm not doing that.'

'I know how he was with you, but Wulfrich is his son. You can't know how—'

'I *do* know,' said Brinin. 'Wulfrich comes and sits here sometimes and talks to me.'

Brinin could see Oswald struggling with himself, kindness pulling him one way and anger the other. He kicked at the grass and prowled about, simmering with rage but wavering nonetheless.

'You amaze me sometimes,' said Oswald at last. 'You're not going to let me do anything about this! It was the only beast you had.'

'I'd sooner lose the sow. I could come back here every night and forget about Aculf until morning. Wulfrich can't even do that. Who stands between a man and his son?'

'Well, if you're set on it…' sighed Oswald. 'I shouldn't listen to you. I should go to my father now whether you like it or not! But likely Wulfrich would be the only one to suffer. Come on. I'd better help you get rid of the sow, if you'll let me do that much. It can't be eaten. Not at this time of year and given how it died.'

When the wretched work was done and Oswald had gone, Brinin stood for a long time leaning on the pen. How could the loss of a beast smart so much? He'd thought it was only the beginning of something better: dung for his field, flesh to eat, more beasts to sell or keep. He had never thought that beasts were anything more than that. But this one had been his. He hadn't even known he loved her until it was too late. And it stung all the more because he had no way to keep his word to Eawig now. It was hard to do nothing, but doing anything would mean doing more than he wanted to.

Brinin bent down and picked up the sprig of yew leaves. He wouldn't knowingly harm Wulfrich with this knowledge, but was there a way to help him with it? That might be something to think about. It was a thought to sleep with until morning. He needed time to see if there was any wisdom in it. Could he bring about a little good from a dead sow?

THREATS

Thurstan gave Brinin the answer in the night. *You want me to help you beat a boy who has spoken truth to you?* Brinin woke with Thurstan's scornful words sounding in his head. They hadn't helped much at the time. Aculf's wrath that day was so seared into Brinin's mind that he could almost still feel the blows. But Thurstan hadn't stopped with scornful words. Tidræd had said that he had warned Aculf off, and Brinin knew Aculf had heeded him for a time. What had that warning been like? Words had always been too slippery for Brinin to think of them easily. What would Aculf fear? Shame? Loss of power? Thurstan telling Edrich Thegn what his workreeve truly was? Could such a threat—no, that was too strong—such a warning help Wulfrich? Would Aculf be a little kinder to him if Brinin said nothing about the sow? He needn't tell Aculf how he had learned his guilt. Thurstan had understood Aculf well. Why not follow his lead?

As soon as the sun was up, he found Aculf alone in his field. He met Brinin with no great welcome.

'What do you want?' snapped Aculf. 'I have too much work to waste my time on you!'

'My sow died,' said Brinin. No need for empty greetings with a man like Aculf. Better to say what had to be said and be gone.

'So? What's that to do with me?' Aculf was better at this than Brinin had thought he would be. His words came as near to a cool, unblinking lie as anything Brinin had ever seen. 'What do I care if you can't even keep your own beast alive?'

'You sent your son with fodder for my sow, and I found these in the trough,' said Brinin, holding out a handful of yew shoots.

'Did that boy go and—'

'Nothing to do with the boy,' cut in Brinin quickly. Wulfrich's fearful stammerings had helped them, but likely the truth would have come out sooner or later. 'You know how it is: there's always someone to overhear or see.'

'How dare you come here like this? What do I care for your beast? Why should the likes of you even have a beast? You take Oswald Child's friendship—foolish friendship—and make yourself greater than you ought to be. Even slavery was too good for you!' Aculf shoved Brinin aside and turned to leave. 'When I see that boy—'

'It's nothing to do with the boy!' said Brinin again. Wulfrich must be kept out of it. 'Oswald Child found it out and told me. He was ready to ask Edrich Thegn to take you before the Moot to make you pay me.'

Aculf swung round with such anger that Brinin thought he might strike him. But he seemed to think better of that. Perhaps even he knew that it wasn't wise to kill a man's beast one day, then strike him the next.

'I asked him to say nothing about it,' said Brinin.

Aculf stood in speechless rage, but Brinin was without a doubt now. Strange how much truth there could be on the face of a man who seldom had it on his lips.

'I thought it was better to overlook it… this time.'

'This time!' Aculf almost spat the words at Brinin. 'Get out of my field before I drive you out! Take it before the Moot if you like!'

'You won't think that when you're cooler. I know you killed her and I'm going to overlook it,' said Brinin. Aculf wasn't even trying to lie about it any more. That opened a path for the warning. 'One more thing: you're too harsh with the boy. You shouldn't beat him so much.'

'Do you dare to tell me how to raise my son? Get out of my field!'

'I've been kind to you, Aculf, though I've lost what you owe me by doing it. You'll lose nothing by being a little kinder to the boy.'

'You're threatening me! You're threatening to go to Edrich Thegn if I don't do what you want!'

Warning. Threat. They were near kin, after all. And threats and anger were Aculf's own tongue. He knew nothing else. He heard Brinin's words as he himself would have meant them. Let him misunderstand. Brinin didn't need thanks or meekness from him. There was only one thing he wanted.

'Be kinder to your son,' he said, then walked away.

~

Late in the afternoon, Brinin sat outside his hut mending the broken stool his unknown friend had left. Too many days had gone by with no time to work on it, and he didn't want its owner to think he had forgotten about it. He'd need to find more work like this now, from Daglæf or anyone else who would give it to him. How else would he ever earn enough for another sow?

The angry squeal of a swine lifted his eyes from his work. Wulfrich was coming towards the hut, dragging a young sow along by a rope. He kept his head down, but Brinin could still see his tears. There was none of his fierce wiping; he was too wretched even to try. For the first time that morning the smallest shadow of doubt clouded Brinin's resolve. Yet Thurstan had warned Aculf, and Aculf had listened.

'My father... said... I was to give you this sow,' Wulfrich stood stiffly, still not lifting his head, his words barely a whisper. And Brinin saw suddenly that these tears weren't only Aculf's work. Wulfrich thought that a dead sow meant a dead friendship. That was a heavy blow for a boy whom other children seldom even seemed to see.

'I know you didn't mean to kill the sow, Wulfrich,' he said, not as steadily as he would have liked. 'Stay here, and when I come back I'll show you how to mend a broken stool.'

Brinin took the rope from Wulfrich and strode back across the village to Aculf's house, the sow following behind even more unhappily than before. Brinin might have kept the beast if he could think it had been sent in friendship or sorrow or the slightest knowledge of wrongdoing. But he knew Aculf too well for that. It was no gift. Aculf wanted to be sure that he had nothing to fear and nothing to be thankful for. Cool speech and forbearance were meaningless to him, and Brinin was too angry now to offer any more.

Aculf was outside his house speaking to some of his near neighbours. He reddened as he saw Brinin coming. He likely hadn't thought he would see his sow again so soon.

'What is it now?' he growled.

'I've brought your sow back,' said Brinin.

'I sent the boy to give it to you.'

'I know you did. I don't want your beast, Aculf. I already told you what I want.'

'You *are* threatening me! I warned you about that this morning.'

The other men were looking on a little bewildered and would likely ask what it was all about. Let them. Aculf would have something to say, and Brinin didn't care what it was. Brinin tossed the rope at Aculf's feet. If the sow ran off Aculf could go after her himself.

'I wasn't, but if that's all you'll understand perhaps I should. Keep your sow and be kinder to your son.'

Brinin turned to Daglæf as he left.

'The next time you hear him beating that boy,' he said, 'tell me.'

Wulfrich was still where Brinin had left him, squatting unhappily with his back against the wall of the hut. Brinin went inside and fetched out another stool for him, then sat beside him and took up his work again.

'Look how the leg is broken on this stool,' he said, handing Wulfrich the broken leg. 'Now I'm going to put in a new one.'

Brinin showed Wulfrich the new leg and how he was shaping it to fit the hole left by the old one. He had Wulfrich hold his tools and did nothing without telling him why. But Wulfrich didn't answer with anything more than a nod or a sniffle. He watched Brinin with heavy eyes that barely seemed to see. After a time, even the nods and sniffles became too much, and he put his head down on his knees and wept. There was no more woodcraft after that. Brinin put the stool aside, and they sat together without work or words until the sun was low in the sky.

FELLOWSHIP

Brinin was kneeling on the ground, pulling up weeds from among the little pea shoots he was growing near the pen when, without warning, Eawig came round the side of the hut and stopped dead.

'Where's the sow?'

'Dead.' Brinin grasped a weed and tugged it a little too hard. It almost pulled a pea shoot up with it. He would have to be more careful. He'd been dreading talking to Eawig—as he had seldom dreaded anything—and a few, gruff words were all he could gather.

'She can't be dead!' It was like talking to Oswald all over again, but this time Brinin knew the truth and didn't want Eawig to know it too. 'I was here two days ago, and there was nothing wrong with her. When did she die?'

'The day before yesterday.'

'But I was here! I saw her in the morning!'

'She died in the afternoon.' Another tug, more careful this time, but still too hard. Brinin stood up. Better see to the weeding later. It wouldn't do to lose his peas as well.

'But there was nothing wrong with her in the morning!' Eawig was dogged, not easily drawn aside. 'I saw her. Why would she be dead by the afternoon? How was she when you found her?'

'Dead!'

'You know I didn't mean that! How did she look? Did she look like she was sick?'

'She looked dead.'

'Was there any spewing or dung? How were her eyes? How was she lying?' Eawig shot the words at him like so many arrows, each

96

one so swiftly following the last that there was barely a breath between them.

'I don't know. There was dung, watery dung. Her eyes were open. I'm sorry. I know you were waiting for one of her brood and I wanted you to have it. As soon as I have enough to buy—'

'It'll take you a long time to gather enough for another sow! Don't you know how much men buy them for at market? I'm not worried about the swine. I've never had one and I can live without. But that sow wasn't sick. She must have eaten something she shouldn't. What did you put in her trough?'

'What I always have.' But this was straying too near to the truth. If Eawig kept going the way he was, he would walk right into it. 'I have to go to my field now, but I *will* still give you a swine one day if I can.'

Brinin lifted his tools and walked away quickly. He didn't look back but he heard Eawig shouting after him.

'That sow wasn't sick!'

Brinin ate his bread alone that morning, out of sight, but Garulf still found him. Brinin's heart sank when he saw him walking slowly towards him, coming to talk to him, to ask him what he didn't want to answer. It was fellowship that brought him, just as Eawig had shouted at him in friendship. Brinin knew what it was and loved them for it. He couldn't lie to them and couldn't tell them the truth either. The fewer who knew—the fewer who even asked anything about it—the better. But he couldn't keep his mouth shut and walk away. Not from Garulf. Saving Wulfrich from his father's sins was proving harder than he had feared.

'Eawig told me about your sow, lad,' said Garulf, easing himself down beside Brinin and looking a little too old to do it. Brinin offered him a chunk of bread, but Garulf shook his head. 'He says the sow wasn't sick, and the lad knows swine better than anyone.'

'I hadn't thought she was sick either.' It was a step to the side in the hope that Garulf might think Brinin had made a mistake. It was the truth—she hadn't been sick—but it felt near to a lie to say it as he had.

'Eawig's sure she wasn't.' Garulf frowned a little, tightening his lips. 'When your sow got out you said you knew the pen was strong and you thought someone else had broken it. And now she's died so sudden, and Eawig says you didn't think you'd put anything in the trough that would make her sick. But think about it, lad. All your life you've had someone else to tell you what work to do and how to do it. All you had to do was heed them. You didn't have to think too much about it. And you always worked well, lad. I'm not saying you didn't. But all this is new to you. You have to do all the work yourself, with no one to tell you what you should and shouldn't do. And you're still young, and some of it you've never done before. No one will blame you if you make mistakes at first. We all forget things at times or we miss something or we're careless. I'm old now and I do it myself. Only yesterday I forgot about something Cynestan had asked me to do. It went right out of my mind until he spoke to me about it again. Perhaps now I even forget more than I did before. We all make mistakes. But learn from them, lad. Learn from them and take better care.'

Brinin could have winced at this if he hadn't spent years teaching himself not to, but it was better than where he had feared Garulf was taking him. Better to be thought a fool who couldn't keep his own beast alive than for folk to learn what he had sworn to himself they wouldn't. He wasn't worried about the men who had seen him give Aculf's sow back. Aculf was bound to have had a tale or two ready. But Brinin didn't know what to say to Garulf, so he said nothing. Garulf seemed to take his wordlessness for shame and put his hand on his shoulder.

'Don't be too disheartened, lad,' he said, then leaned on Brinin's shoulder heavily to get himself to his feet again. 'Eawig says you're worried that you can't give him his swine now. Don't think about it too much. He can live without it, and we know you meant to. Perhaps you'll have another sow one day. Keep working hard and take better care.'

In the evening, Brinin sat outside and watched the shadows grow long over the thatch of Oakdene. He had learned something about himself that day. It was far easier to be called a fool or a hound or a filthy Dane by men that he cared nothing for—men like Aculf or Eadulf—than to be thought careless by a friend. And the kind chiding and well-meant wisdom stung too much to eat by Garulf's hearth and perhaps listen to more.

Ludan was one of the last men Brinin would have thought to see walking towards his hut. He liked Ludan—he always had. There was an unspoken fellowship between those who had smarted under Aculf's blustering, strutting anger. They understood each other. But their work seldom brought them together, and Ludan wasn't one to seek someone out for speech and friendship alone. He walked slowly—he had never been a man for needless speed—and he had something tucked under his arm. Brinin couldn't make out what it was; it wasn't a chest though it was shaped a little like one.

Ludan reached the hut and sat down on the grass. Brinin offered to go inside and fetch him a stool, but he shook his head and wouldn't take any share of Brinin's food.

'I'll have mine later,' said Ludan. He set the chestlike thing before Brinin on the ground. 'Now with this new woodcraft of yours, have you ever worked on a lock?'

'No,' said Brinin, understanding only now what Ludan had brought with him. 'Stools and benches and the like.'

'Well, never mind. You can look at it all the same. Oswald Child broke it the night you left Oakdene—likely you know all about that. Aculf had it mended at the time, but whoever he asked made poor work of it. It's never been the same since and it's worried me. So this evening I say that to Cynestan. And he took it off the door and I think to myself, "Perhaps young Brinin would like work like this." You see, I'd heard from Garulf that your sow was dead and I thought you'd be wanting to earn something to put by for another. So I say to him, "Shall I take it to Brinin, sir, and see if he can mend it?" Cynestan's a man you *can* speak to before you're asked, and he won't strike you for it or curse you. So he says, "Yes," and I was to say you'd be paid for it. And I was glad to be sent, for I wanted to speak to you myself. I knew he'd send me and not come himself. I could see he'd been too long on that leg of his today and was feeling it and wanted to be by his hearth.'

'I'll see what I can do,' said Brinin. Why *did* Ludan want to speak to him, when neither of them was much given to idle chatter? 'It was good of you to think of me.'

'Show it to Daglæf, or better still to his father if he can see it well enough. Old Byrnhelm was always good with locks. Daglæf too. Neither of them can do much of that kind of work now, but they could tell you what to do. I don't think it will be hard to mend. The front keeps coming loose.' Ludan settled himself down a bit more, leaning on his elbow. 'Now let me tell you this. I said nothing to Garulf when he told me about your sow. I wanted to think on it a bit. The day before yesterday I saw Aculf's boy crossing the meadow behind the hall. Odd to go the long way with a bucket he could barely lift, I thought. And I called to him and asked if he wanted any help. But he only looked frightened and said his father said he wasn't to talk to anyone. And on he went. I saw him running back the way he came a little later, and the bucket was empty, for he could lift it easily. But I thought no more about it.'

Brinin listened without a word. Why speak and perhaps help Ludan go where he didn't want him to? And likely there was little he could say to hinder him. Ludan was making his way there slowly, but so steadily that it would be hard to stop him. Better let him talk and then work out what needed to be said.

'Then yesterday I saw Aculf's boy again, leading a sow behind him. I spoke to him, but he didn't answer, and I could see he was weeping. "He's been scolded for some wrongdoing," I think to myself, "or beaten more likely, given the father he has." And then I saw *you* with what looked like the same beast. That seemed odd too. I only understood when Garulf told me about your sow.' Ludan leaned towards Brinin and jabbed at the ground with his finger to strengthen his words. 'Your beast is dead, and Aculf had something to do with it. Didn't Eawig say she hadn't been sick? That boy was taking the bucket towards your hut. Why would Aculf send his boy there—he's no friend of yours—and tell him not to speak to anyone? I think there was something in that bucket that killed your beast. I can't see how you did it yourself, whatever Garulf might think. When were you ever careless about anything? I said nothing to Garulf but I had a mind to go to Cynestan straightaway. The word of a slave isn't worth anything much, but I thought Cynestan might look about and ask others what they'd seen. But I couldn't make out what his boy was doing with that sow, nor you neither. I couldn't make it out. Unless perhaps Aculf knew he'd gone too far or it was a mistake and he didn't want word of it getting out. But why would you take the beast back to him? I didn't understand it and, after all, I didn't *see* the boy with your sow. I think to myself, "There may be more to this than I know so better hold my tongue until I've spoken to Brinin himself." So here I am.'

'Don't speak to Cynestan, Ludan,' said Brinin. 'Who knows the truth? And as you say, you didn't *see* Wulfrich at my hut. If folk start asking if Aculf killed my beast and he's shamed before the village that won't do his boy any good. And as you say, few will listen to the word of a slave. Best say nothing about it, though it was good of you to come.'

'A little shame might not do Aculf any harm!' muttered Ludan. 'I can see you know more of this than you're saying. I dare say he *would* find some way to blame the boy, but likely he'll blame him for something sooner or later anyway, if not for this for something else. He's the boy's father and there's naught you nor I can do about that, though we might not think he's much of a father. Why not let me speak to Cynestan? And soon before folk forget what they saw and before the haymaking is on us and we're all too busy for such things. You can ill afford to be without your beast, and Cynestan might learn something and make sure Aculf pays you for it. And if it turns out I'm wrong, and Aculf had naught to do with it, what will you lose? Though I still can't make out why I saw you with that young sow, and I can see you aren't going to tell me.'

'I'll think about it. But say nothing to Cynestan yourself, nor to anyone else. It's no good talk like this getting about if it doesn't need to. And tell him I'll try to be quick with this lock. It might be easier for Daglæf and his father to show me how to make a new one.'

'Which is as much as to say that you won't speak to Cynestan.' Ludan rose to leave, a shadow standing over Brinin in the nightgloom. 'I dare say you know your own mind even if *I* can't understand it. I came as a friend—and leave as one too—so I've done what I ought. Perhaps I should have gone to Cynestan first.'

LOCKS

In the morning, when the shadows still stretched long, Brinin went to find Daglæf. He was kneeling by his herbs, pulling up the weeds he found among them. Byrnhelm, his father, sat on a bench by the doorway, throwing his wisdom at his son from time to time, but mostly watching the morning.

'Well then,' said Daglæf, looking up from his work as Brinin reached the house. 'It can't be bowmanship you've come for this morning. You've left your bow behind, and I'm not sure what you *do* have.'

'It's the lock to the horsehouse door. It's weak, and Cynestan wants me to mend it. I'm told your father is good with locks and I know almost nothing about them.'

'There was none better when his eyes were younger.' Daglæf stood up and, one-handed, brushed the dirt from his knees. 'Father, here's young Brinin with a lock for you to look at.'

'Brinin? Who's Brinin again?' said Byrnhelm, squinting up at them. 'Come into the light, lad. How can I see you there in the shade of the house? Ah, now I mind you. You're the one with the fiery hair. Little wonder they call you Brinin! You were here a few days back.'

'You remember Brinin helped us with the fence, Father, the day we heard the King had died.'

'Ah yes. That's when it was. I *do* mind you now. You're the one with the Danish mother, aren't you?'

Daglæf frowned and opened his mouth to speak, but his father brushed any words aside with a snort and a wave of his hand.

'Come now, Daglæf! I'm not telling the boy anything he didn't already know! You knew your own mother, didn't you, lad? So she was a Dane. What of it? Is it their women that are troubling us in Wessex? I've fought the Danes three times—when I was younger, you understand, lad—and I didn't see a woman among them! Likely there's no more harm in their women than there is in any of ours. And you've been reared here and haven't been taught the Danish ways, and are likely as much a Christian as I am—I hope you are, lad. I said as much to… to—I can't rightly mind who it was I said it to. No need to be ashamed of having a Danish mother. I hope you aren't—I'd think the less of you for it if you were. No boy should be ashamed of his mother unless she's wicked, and I've never heard anyone say she was wicked, only that she was a Dane. But there are a great many fools in the world, lad, and more by the year. More by the year.'

Daglæf glanced rather ruefully at Brinin, a wordless plea for forgiveness that his father was striding so boldly into such a forbidden place. But Brinin hardly minded. How could he mind a man who told him he mustn't be ashamed of his mother?

'Well now, Father, shall we take a look at this—'

'And here's another thing, lad,' said Byrnhelm, with another wave of his hand. 'Folk all say that the Danes are our foes, and so they are. I've fought them too, as I said. But they forget the Mercians! My father died in battle against the Mercians when I was younger than you, not yet a man though almost one. And I went to battle against them myself with Edrich Thegn's grandfather. That was long before you were born, back in Ecgbert the King's day. Folk say now that the Mercians are our friends with these weddings and peacemaking and I don't know what! And now we're to stand with them against the Danes. I don't mind fighting the Danes, but are the Mercians our friends because we share the same foe? Not if we're wise they aren't! Folk forget these things too quickly. Never trust a Mercian, lad!'

'Now, Father, Brinin doesn't want to hear about the Mercians or your old battles!' said Daglæf, taking the lock from Brinin and thrusting it into his father's hands. 'Why don't you see to the lock now? He can't stand here all day waiting for you!'

'If he doesn't like it, he has a tongue in his head to let me know! And before you tell me what I should be saying you'd do well to remember that I'm still your father, for all you're a grown man with sons of your own. I'm no less your father for all that!' Chiding done, Byrnhelm held out the lock at arm's length and turned it over in his hands. 'How can I see it with you standing in my light, lad? The sun doesn't shine through you! Come here and sit on the bench. That's better.'

Byrnhelm put his hand inside the back of the lock and slid the pegs back and forth. Daglæf shrugged his shoulders and, with a wry look at Brinin, went back to his herbs.

'Did someone try to mend this before, lad?' asked Byrnhelm.

'I think so, sir,' said Brinin.

'They made poor work of it, whoever it was! I can see they knew little about wood and less about locks!'

'Would I be better to make a new box, sir?'

'Nothing else you *can* do. But keep the pegs for the new one. Go inside and ask Bægswyth to give you my tools—the small ones, tell her. Bring all of them. That's easier than telling you which of them I want. And don't think I'm going to do the work for you. My hands aren't steady enough for that kind of work now, nor are my eyes what they once were. Your eyes will worry you when you get to be as old as me, if you live that long, which most don't. But I'll talk you through taking this one apart and tell you what to do to make a new one. And I'll look at the new one when you're done and tell you if it's strong enough. Now don't stand there, lad! Go and get the tools! And tell Bægswyth I'm thirsty and ask her to send you out with a cup of ale too.'

It was hard to be swift to heed a man who kept talking as he sent you away. Daglæf might be a man with a wife and sons of his own, but it was easy to see that it was Byrnhelm who was lord in this house, and they all likely ran to do his bidding. Yet who could dislike such a man, whose wits were sharper than his eyes and whose wisdom was steadier than his hands? Perhaps some were too proud to bear the sting of his tongue, but Brinin had been stung by too many other, sharper things to mind such well-meant pricks as these.

When he came out again, struggling not to spill the ale while bearing an armful of tools, he caught sight of a little child learning to walk, as she waddled round Aculf's house nearby. She tottered unsteadily for a few more steps before sitting down on the grass with a bump. Before she had time to think about what had happened to her or whether she wanted to wail about it, Wulfrich bolted into sight. He lifted her to her feet with soft words that Brinin couldn't hear. He held her hands and walked behind her, bending low to whisper something heartening to help her along.

As Brinin handed Byrnhelm the ale, Wulfrich saw him. Brinin smiled, but Wulfrich only stiffened and looked over his shoulder fearfully. Was he too near the danger to acknowledge any friendship? Brinin set the tools before Byrnhelm on the grass, just as he heard Aculf bellowing for Wulfrich from somewhere nearby. Wulfrich started and dashed away, leaving his sister to walk alone. She took another step, then sat down again and this time she did wail.

'Daglæf!' called Byrnhelm, setting down his cup on the bench beside him. 'When you see Aculf, tell him I'm tired of listening to him shouting. His boy's not deaf and neither am I—not when folk speak up and remember not to mumble, anyhow. Sit here then, lad. Take this and prise the front off. You can have any tool you like for it—I'll tell you if it's the wrong one. It should come away easily enough, and then we can save the pegs. That's it.'

Byrnhelm took another draught of ale and sighed happily. He leaned back against the house and stretched out his legs before him.

'Now that I think of it, lad, Daglæf tells me that Aculf wanted to sell you a beast, and you wouldn't take it. Very wise. You'll likely get a better beast for less elsewhere. Aculf is cunning. His father was the same. I never liked him, though he did wed my wife's sister.'

Aculf's tale was even flimsier than Brinin had thought it would be. Who would believe it? No one who knew much about either of them or how things had been between them. It looked strong enough, like the lock, but would break easily with the right tools.

'So don't buy any beasts from Aculf. That's all I'm saying to you, lad. But likely you're sharp enough to know that. I know you're sharp. Daglæf tells me you're the one who got Edrich Thegn away from the Danes. Good thing you did have a Danish mother!' Byrnhelm chuckled and slapped his leg. 'That was one of the best tales I've heard in years! I wish I'd been there to see Edrich Thegn walking into the camp when we all thought him dead! But they won't let me go to war now, though I've been doing battle since before any of them were born. Perhaps they're right—I *am* old now. But if the Danes come here, I still have my sword and I haven't forgotten how to wield it either!'

Wulfrich's little sister was still wailing on the grass. At last Aculf's wife, Sægyth, came hindered by another daughter, not more than three winters old. The girl clung fretfully to her mother's kirtle and had a tear-stained and snotty face. Sægyth stooped and lifted her child then stood with her in her arms. Brinin saw her watching him, but her face said nothing. There was neither anger nor friendship on it, neither hatred nor welcome. Brinin had never seen a face he could understand less. All her thoughts seemed to be locked away, shut up fast where no one could catch even a glimpse of them. She watched him without a word, then walked away and was hidden by the house.

'Well done, lad!' said Byrnhelm, dragging Brinin's thoughts back to his work. 'I can see you have a way with wood. Now tell me how you will set about making a new box.'

SCYTHES

little river wound its way between reedy banks. The hill sloped
down to it then rose again on the other side, and the knee-
high grass rippled and swayed under a light breeze. Oswald
sat and watched the shifting light as it fell on the river. Beorn lay on his
back, almost hidden by the grass. Behind them lay their camp, where
the fyrd was waiting to learn when their new king would lead them out
against the Danes.

'They'll be getting ready for the haymaking at home,' said Oswald,
waving away a fly that kept buzzing too near his nose.

'They'll begin within the week, I should think,' said Beorn drowsily.
Sleep could ensnare a man easily here, creeping up unseen among the
meadow flowers.

'It will be good hay this year if the weather holds and the Oakdene
meadow is anything like this one.'

'Likely will,' said Beorn, sitting up. 'But there'll be no haymaking
here, Oswald Child. Didn't you see the village when we passed it the
other day?'

'No. I didn't look.'

'All the houses but two were burnt to the ground. The wheat was
growing well, but there wasn't a man nor woman nor beast to be seen
anywhere.'

'No one at all?'

'Only a dog—one dog. That was all.'

Oswald saw the river with new eyes. The meadow suddenly seemed
like a wilderness. What kind of raid had driven them away so utterly,
homes and harvests never to be rebuilt or reaped? The grass would
grow tall, the wheat would ripen and it would all rot throughout the

winter. Where had they all gone? How could they live? The thought of it thrust him into speechlessness for a long time.

'I'm not much good with a scythe,' said Oswald at length, as much to keep the empty village from his mind as to speak of hay.

'You have little need to be, Oswald Child. Your father has men to do such work for him, and likely so will you. But it's easy enough once you have the way of it. Look.'

Beorn sprung to his feet and swung his arms and body as though he were slicing through the grass with his scythe. Oswald couldn't help laughing at the sight of him twisting and swaying with nothing in his hands.

'If anyone's watching from the camp, they'll wonder what you're about!'

'Mowing! What else?' grinned Beorn as he sat down again.

'I tried it one haymaking but the only thing I cut was my own leg! It wasn't much more than a week before my mother died.' Oswald could still see that day as though it were happening as he spoke, as though no sorrow, winters or war had shoved themselves between. There were days like that, the ones that never seemed to fade in his mind. 'I almost didn't want the wound to heal as it was the last she ever tended for me. I still have the scar—it looks a little like an adder. It was almost time for the baby to be born, and she couldn't bend. I had to sit on the table while she bound it up, and while she was doing it my father spoke to me very sternly about how I would never have cut myself at all if I had been with Brother Wilfred learning my Latin, where I ought to have been.'

'I don't think I would much like being spoken to sternly by your father. I heard him at it once and mind being glad that he wasn't speaking to me. My own father was never much given to stern talking. My mother's the talker in our house. My father always *did* more than he said: a quick clout when he thought I needed it, but seldom more than that.'

'You wouldn't like it! I always dreaded the talking the most, even when I knew there was worse coming when he had said all he wanted. But now I think that was mostly because I didn't understand my father very well. We understand each other better now.'

'It's hard not to when you've fought side by side, nor when you thought you'd lost him then got him back again,' said Beorn. 'If you'll forgive me for speaking of it, Oswald Child, it seemed to me that there must have been some misunderstanding at the bottom of that bad business last harvest. My father thought the same. But perhaps you don't like talking about all that now.'

'I don't.'

'So will you forgive me if I ask you something, Oswald Child?'

'What's that?'

'*Did* you know where your father's slaves had gone?'

'Yes. I sent them there.'

'Well! After that, it's little wonder that Brinin went after your father; after what you did for him, I mean. We learn who our friends are when times are hard. And if you'll forgive me for this too, Oswald Child: you're more stubborn than you look!'

The grass was ready for mowing within a week, tall and rippling with flowers that sprouted up among the blades. And within a week they stood in a meadow on the southern bank of a reed-lined river. The grass was ready for mowing, but they had no scythes, only spears in their hands and swords in their sheathes. There would be no haymaking here either. The grass would be trampled underfoot and men would be cut down, scattered to lie under the sun like hay.

Oswald saw his father a few men away to his right. Hildræd his uncle was at his father's side and they spoke together in low voices. Oswald couldn't hear what they were saying. Oswald didn't think his father had slept. He had slept fitfully himself and each time he had opened his eyes he had seen the dark shape of his father in the gloom of the tent, always sitting, never lying down. Once or twice he had thought he heard him praying in heartfelt whispers. And now it was morning.

Saxulf and Sigulf stood behind him and Beorn was at his shoulder, hearthfellows and all that were left from Oakdene. Swetrich and Sigelm were dead. Thurstan was dead. Godræd was dead. Leofwine was dead. Rædwald and Baldred were dead. All dead. Who would still stand by sunset?

'I overheard my father talking to some other thegns last night,' whispered Oswald to Beorn. 'They said that if we lose this, we lose Wessex. It's our last hope.'

Beorn looked behind him, turning his head as his eyes took in the fyrd on all sides.

'Then I wish there were more of us,' he said. 'Do you think they spoke the truth?'

'Look at the King. If you lean a little towards me you'll see him.'

They saw the King between the shoulders of the men in front. He stood with his back to them, among his ealdormen, all older than he was. He was restless, shifting about, often glancing from side to side, and each time he turned his head they saw his face. They saw how tight his jaw was. They saw his shut lips, his deep frown. They saw how grim and white and ill he looked.

'It *is* the truth,' said Beorn. 'May God help us.'

And then they came. A host of them, a great seething throng, twice, three times as many as the fyrd. No, more than that even. Too many to speak of. Too many to withstand. They came, the taunts and jeers and banging of shields already beginning. They stood and roared at them across the field. Oswald's mouth was too dry to roar back.

Libera nos a malo. The words sprang into his mind. Free us from evil. Save us from evil, from foes, from utter loss, from shameful fear if not from death.

'*Libera nos a malo. Libera nos a malo*,' he said. He didn't mean to speak the words aloud, but they were out of his mouth before he could stop them. He saw Beorn staring at him in bewilderment. 'It's from the Paternoster; you know, the prayer. It means "save us from evil."'

'Amen,' said Beorn. 'Amen.'

Between the fyrd and the Danes, the grass and meadow flowers rippled in the wind, ready for the haymaking, ready for the scythes to slice through and cut them down. Oswald's eyes met his father's, and he saw for the first time how like Edith's they were. Ahead of them, the King seemed to draw himself up a little taller. Beorn put his hand on Oswald's shoulder.

'One last hope then, Oswald Child,' he said. 'And may God indeed save us from evil.'

A stillness, sudden and short. The song of a lone bird, high, warbling, beautiful. The charge.

HAY

It was only the first day of the haymaking and already the meadow was stubbly like a man with shorn hair. Edith stood behind the hall and watched as the scattered mowers swung their scythes. Others bent low, their rakes stretching from their hands like snakes whose gaping mouths and wooden teeth snatched the fallen grass and pulled it into long rows to dry in the sun and wind. And the smell was everywhere, fresh and damp and sweet. It made Edith want to sneeze. On a morning like this, it was hard to believe that there was any wrong in the world, that everything wasn't the same as it had always been. So they made the hay ready for winter, as they had done every year, though none of them knew what winter would bring. They didn't even know what summer would bring. Edith loved the smell. It was easier to think about that and not the unknown shadowy fear hanging over them.

'My lady Edith!'

Ludan's voice pulled her thoughts back to Oakdene like the rakes shifting the grass. Why was he running? When did he do anything swiftly? She had even heard Cynestan, who seldom scolded his own children, chide him for being slow, though on a day when—Edith knew—Cynestan's leg was aching and making his tongue sharp. Yet here was Ludan, running and breathless.

'What's wrong?'

'My lady Edith!' gasped Ludan. 'Cynestan's asking for you, my lady. Old Garulf's took ill.'

'Ill? What kind of illness? Where is he?'

'I'll take you there, my lady,' said Ludan, as Edith followed him. 'I don't rightly know what's wrong, my lady. He's not retching or aught

111

like that, but he was swinging his scythe and before any of us knew it he was lying on the ground, all aswoon.'

Garulf wasn't lying when they reached him. He sat in the long grass at the eastern side of the meadow. Eawig knelt beside him, and Cynestan stood over them both, talking in a low voice. When Garulf saw Edith coming he muttered something to his grandson, who took his arm and helped him to his feet before Edith was near enough to stop him. He stood leaning heavily on Eawig. Edith could see his hands trembling.

'Forgive me, my lady Edith!' Garulf spoke breathlessly as though it had been he and not Edith who had been running. More than that, he was flustered or even afraid. Did he think she would be angry and leave no room for weakness? 'Forgive me. I'll be back to my work now.'

'Now then, Garulf,' said Cynestan. 'We needn't be too swift about that.'

'What happened?' said Edith. 'Are you feverish?'

'No, my lady,' said Garulf. 'I was a little shaky, that's all, and I swooned. Perhaps I was too long in the sun. I'll be better now.'

'Perhaps you should take a drink,' said Edith. How could he have been too long in the sun, so early in the day? The sun was still low and the shadows long, and they stood where he had fallen in the shade of the trees.

'Young Tidræd fetched me,' said Cynestan, 'and I sent him for some ale. He'll be back soon.'

'You mustn't work any more today, Garulf,' said Edith. 'Rest today, and tomorrow we'll see if you're better.'

Garulf said nothing but he bowed his head as if she were scolding him, though she knew she had spoken as kindly as she could. Edith felt her own cheeks flush. Here was an old man standing before her and not even speaking unless she asked him to, while she was the one who said what must be done. They both knew it must be this way. This was how their lives had fallen, and they must both live and work in the places that had been given to them, she as a thegn's daughter and he as a slave. How else was it to be? But this morning it seemed upside-down. Garulf was so old, and she felt—all the time, these days—so very young.

'That's what I said, my lady,' said Cynestan. 'I don't like his hue and I don't want him working and perhaps swooning again. Ah, here's Tidræd now.'

Tidræd was like a hound after a hare, turning swiftly as he ran so he wouldn't bump into anyone. Yet he was barely breathless when he reached them and handed the flask to Garulf.

'There was no one in the hall,' he said, 'so I had to get this from my mother.'

The flask shook as Garulf raised it unsteadily to his lips and some of the ale spilt onto his shirt. Eawig, watching his grandfather almost fearfully, seemed near to tears. Enough of this standing about! Edith turned to Cynestan but before she even opened her mouth, he nodded.

'Take your grandfather home, Eawig,' he said, 'and see him settled before you come back.'

Edith watched as they left, Garulf leaning on his grandson and Eawig helping him along and walking as slowly as he needed. A mother couldn't have shown more care to an ailing child.

'By your leave, my lady Edith, I'd like him to rest for longer,' said Cynestan. 'At least, there is some work he *can* likely do, but not haymaking. He's been a strong and hardworking man all his life and is as skilled with a scythe as anyone I've ever seen, but he's old. You wouldn't think it to look at him, but I believe he's even older than Byrnhelm who sits outside his house all day and watches others work. Too old for work like this. If you'll let me, my lady, I'll put him to other work, but that will leave us with a new worry to think out.'

'Worry?'

'Your father already has two slaves fewer than the last haymaking, with Row dead and Brinin free. I'd already been asking myself if we'd make all the hay we need while this weather lasts. There are those freemen who hold land from your father, but I don't like to ask more from them than they owe. None of the other slaves can put their full time to it, not without leaving something else undone—they're mostly watching the beasts. Garulf knows all this as well as I do. I think that's why he was so fearful, my lady. And it's a frightening thing for a man to learn that his strength is leaving him and he can't do what he always did before. I saw it in my father and I've learned it myself these last months.'

'So what should we do?'

'Well, my lady, we *must* make the hay. How would this be? Young Brinin has no need as yet to make much hay for himself. He had a sow, but I heard it took sick and died. How would it be, my lady, if we hired him to make hay instead of Garulf? Your father said I could ask him to do a little work now and then to pay for the food he takes—though I think your father was likely sparing the lad's pride as much as anything. But this is more work than your father had in mind, so it's only right that he's paid for it. How would that be, my lady?'

'I know where he is!' piped up Tidræd before Edith could answer. She had forgotten he was even there. 'He's helping Daglæf's boys; not *doing* it for them, only standing by and telling them when they're going wrong. Daglæf said the boys were to do it. Brinin could easily come and do the work for you.'

'Now then, Tidræd,' said Cynestan sternly, 'is it fitting for you to listen to the speech of your elders and offer them your thoughts unasked? You'd do well to hold your tongue until you're spoken to.'

'The lady Edith isn't *much* my elder!' said Tidræd cheerfully. Was scolding something he ever felt? 'Shall I fetch him for you?'

'Yes, but you're only to say that the lady Edith and I want to speak to him, and nothing more,' said Cynestan. 'Then get on with your own work. Do you want to have to tell your mother that there's no hay for her beasts this winter because you spent all your time listening to folk talk and didn't make any?'

Tidræd grinned then dashed away, and Cynestan turned back, smiling, to Edith.

'He's too bold for his own good, that one!' he said. 'My Leofgar would willingly follow him into mischief if I didn't keep a sharp eye on him. Mind you, my lady, I followed his father into it often enough myself—and your father did too—though we almost always wished we hadn't afterwards. But he's a good lad nonetheless.'

Tidræd was swift, and it wasn't long before they saw Brinin coming towards them. If he wondered why he had been called, he didn't show it.

'Will you ask him, my lady, or shall I?' whispered Cynestan.

'You,' said Edith.

'Can you help us with a little work, Brinin?' said Cynestan, wasting no time. 'Garulf took ill this morning.'

Still Brinin said nothing, but his eyes said everything. Edith saw a sudden spark of fear in them, much like she had seen in Eawig's. And she knew then that, to Brinin, Garulf was much more than a man he'd been enslaved with.

'Now, there's no need to worry,' said Cynestan. 'He needs a little rest, though perhaps he is getting too old for this kind of work. But Edrich Thegn's hay needs to be made, and we don't have enough hands for it now. There are few we can ask, so the lady Edith would like to hire you for it.'

Brinin looked from Cynestan to Edith, then back to Cynestan again.

'Where is Garulf?' he said.

'Back in his hut, resting. He walked there on his own feet. As I said, there's no need to worry.'

'I'll do his work for him. I can spare the time. No need to speak of hiring me or anything like that.'

'Well now, lad, it's no small undertaking, as I'm sure you know. It's not something the lady Edith can ask you to do for nothing.'

'Edrich Thegn said I was to work a little to pay for the food I eat. And Garulf's been good to me. I'm happy to do it.'

'But *I'm* not happy,' said Edith, cutting in suddenly. 'My father said you were to do a *little* work. This is more than that. And Cynestan and I are the ones who will have to answer to him when he comes back and learns that we have asked you to do more than he wished. I can't overlook his bidding. He wouldn't like it. If you won't be *hired*, you can't do the work at all. There isn't anyone else, is there, Cynestan? Do you think *I* could learn to handle a scythe? I know Cenwyn can.'

Brinin had never had ready answers on his tongue, and Edith knew it. She could be swift.

'I'm going to see Garulf now and speak to Wynith,' she said. 'I'm sure Brinin will help us, Cynestan, and be paid for it. But if he won't, send someone to find me, and I'll learn how to do it myself.'

Then she left them to work out the rest of it between themselves. But she looked back once, before the church hid them from her sight. The scythe was already in Brinin's hand.

PATERNOSTER

The last hope took a long time to die. Each time Oswald thought it had breathed its last, it struggled to its feet, gasping but still fighting. He was gasping himself, his sword growing so heavy that it was almost too much for his aching arms. Short-lived glory, false wiles, and the hope was struck down for the last time. They lost their ground and their good name. Oswald was driven back, not eye to eye with a foe, but between the shoulders of the broken fyrd. They were driven from the battlefield, from the hill, the river, the town and the abbey. The Danes held them all, and hope didn't follow them as they fled. Among so many dead, how could they even know where its body lay?

It left Oswald cold. He couldn't stop shivering though sweat trickled down his face and neck. What now? What now for Wessex? For the King? For Oakdene? For Edith? Was it better now to be among the dead? Who *were* the dead? He was driven along among swordbrothers, but nameless ones he barely saw. Not walking, not running, only staggering blindly, aching and shivering, he went where the men around him went and neither knew nor cared where that was.

He stumbled and almost fell as his foot caught on something which, in his blindness, he hadn't seen. It was only then that he saw anything. It was a leg, its owner—likely one of the many dead—lying half-hidden by a little shrub. Oswald didn't know why he looked. He didn't need his eyes to tell him what war did to a man, or how he died. Too many such sights were in his mind, and his gut was already battling with itself as it had seldom done for months, not since the beginning. But he did look and understood with a wretched, sickening knowledge. He fell to his knees beside the man who lay there, a spear with a broken shaft jutting from his side. Beorn. With a strangled cry that sounded too beastlike to have come from his own lips, Oswald grasped Beorn's hand and touched his deathly face.

'Beorn!'

Beorn's face and hands were not utterly without life. Oswald saw understanding in his eyes, felt Beorn's hand gripping his own.

'Quick!' said Oswald, putting his arm under Beorn to lift him a little. 'We have to get you away from here. Can't anyone help me?'

No one of them stopped. But Beorn gripped his hand tighter, his eyes fastened on Oswald's, his lips moving but no words reaching Oswald's ears. Oswald pulled him up, cradling him like a child, and bent as near as he could.

'Too… late… go…' Beorn gasped for each word like a drowning man, each breath a struggle. Was this what a spear did to a man? Yet there was barely even any blood coming from the wound.

'I'm going nowhere! If I can't take you with me, I'm staying here until—' Oswald couldn't say the rest, but Beorn's grip on his hand grew tighter.

So Oswald knelt, still aching, still shivering, and held Beorn while he fought for breath, a last battle that he couldn't win. And all that was left of the fyrd fled in shame, while the Danes flung taunts and jeers and even weapons at their backs. Beorn shuddered—Oswald felt it in his own body—and lifted his hand to Oswald's head. He pulled his head down until his ear almost touched Beorn's mouth.

'My… mother…' The gasps were little more than whispers now.

'She'll have everything she needs! If I get out of this alive, I swear to you that she'll want for nothing, even if I have to work her field with my own hands. Remember "lord before kin"? Forget "lord". Kin. Brother. Do you hear that, my brother? I'll do all I can for your mother and your sisters, as much as if they were my own. Can you hear me? Do you understand?'

Beorn squeezed Oswald's hand, but not so tightly now, his last strength needed to snatch whatever breath he could. Oswald saw tears on his face, but he didn't know if they were Beorn's or his own, fallen there as he bent over him. He lifted him a little higher. Would he breathe better that way? Was there no way to bring ease to a dying man? And why must it be so slow? Beorn's whole body stiffened. He coughed, and blood spattered from his mouth onto Oswald's arm. His lips moved again: 'mother' or 'brother'. Oswald couldn't hear which it was.

'Listen, my brother,' Oswald put his mouth to Beorn's ear now. 'I'm staying with you. Remember the Paternoster? I'll pray it now for both of us and I'll say the English too. I don't think that's wrong. Brother Wilfred taught me the meaning.'

He didn't know why he was so cold, nor why his head was spinning. Was it even clear enough to remember all he had once learned? May God bring it to his mind!

'*Pater noster, qui es in coelis...* Our Father, you who are in heaven... *sanctificetur nomen tuum...* Let your name be holy... and let your kingdom come and your will be done on earth as in heaven.' Another shudder, another cough, more blood. Oswald held Beorn tighter. 'Give us our daily loaf today and forgive us our guilt as we forgive those guilty against us. And don't lead us into temptation but save us from evil. Remember that, Beorn? Save us from evil.'

Beorn's eyes were still open, still looking up at him, but he didn't seem to see Oswald any more. He could barely feel Beorn's breath now, though his chest still heaved, and his face was whiter, as ashen as a dead man. Even his lips had lost their hue. And still the Danes roared, and the fyrd fled. Beside them, the grass had been trampled down, beyond all mowing, crushed into the mud.

'I'm still here, brother,' said Oswald. 'I'm still here.'

He gripped Beorn's hand again, but there was no strength left in it now. And because Oswald didn't know what else to do or what else to say, he prayed again from the beginning.

'*Pater noster, qui es in coelis, sanctificetur nomen tuum.*'

Oswald didn't see Beorn die, but he knew suddenly that he was gone. He ought to have left him then and fled like the others, but he was too cold, too weak and too broken to do anything but kneel there and weep, still cradling Beorn in his arms.

'Oswald! Quick! You can't stay here!'

Someone grabbed him, pulling him to his feet. Beorn slipped from his arms onto the grass. Oswald turned and saw Hildræd his uncle, filthy and wild-eyed.

'He's dead,' said Oswald. 'He died in my arms.'

'Come! They're shooting and flinging their spears at us. We can't linger!'

Oswald stood looking down at Beorn, but he couldn't see him well and couldn't seem to steady his feet or bid them to run.

'Come, Oswald!'

Sudden fire seared into his shoulder. He heard his uncle cry out and saw him lunge towards him. And there was falling. And darkness.

HEARTHSIDE

With heavy limbs Brinin made his way through the lengthening shadows to Garulf's hut that evening. He was weary as only summerlong days could make him. He hadn't seen Garulf all day, only Eawig who had said that his grandfather was resting and felt a little better. But Eawig's words weren't enough to ease Brinin's mind, and the thought of Garulf too ill to work—this man who had been more than a friend to him—gnawed away at him all day. It was a bad time to be sick, when few could be spared from the meadow, yet a good time all the same. A better time than a year before when Aculf was workreeve. Garulf's grey hair had shielded him from the worst of Aculf's ways, but he would still have been driven hard, sick or not. There would have been no room for weakness nor weariness, no stopping to rest a little, only sweat and struggle. How often did Brinin thank God for Cynestan that day? These were new times indeed.

Garulf was alone when Brinin ducked through the doorway. He wasn't lying down, sick or feverish as Brinin had feared. He sat on a stool by the hearth, a little white perhaps, but beyond that there was nothing of this sudden sickness to see. He greeted Brinin with a smile which, though weary, was as warm as the fire he sat by.

'Well, lad,' he said, 'it's been some days since I last saw you. I was even wondering if I'd spoken too freely to you about the sow, and you were keeping away. You mustn't mind me, lad. You know that anything I say to you is kindly meant. Come and sit with me for a while. It's too still in here with the rest of them out.'

'Oh, you can talk to me as you like,' said Brinin as he sat beside Garulf. Yet he *had* kept away; perhaps not knowingly, though he had somehow found other things to fill his time and now he hardly knew why. 'I heard you took sick this morning.'

'It was an odd thing that. My heart was pounding like I'd been running and the next thing I knew I was on the ground with Eawig kneeling beside me. I must have swooned, though I don't mind it. I'm well enough now—only a little tired—so likely there's not much wrong. I'm old, that's all, and not as strong as I was. I could have worked today, after a drink and a short rest, but Cynestan and the lady Edith wouldn't hear of it. And there's to be no more mowing tomorrow, nor the day after that, they say. Cynestan was here not long ago to tell me. Eawig says they've hired you for the haymaking.'

'I'm happy to do the work, but there's no need for them to pay me for it when I'm still eating Edrich Thegn's bread. I don't like earning from your sickness.'

'We don't need any talk like that, lad! If they won't let me mow they're going to have to hire someone, and I'd sooner it was you than anyone else. You taking on the work didn't make me sick and being paid for it won't make me worse. Why wouldn't you take paid work that's offered to you? You're a free man now and can't work for nothing. Earn what you can and put it by for such times as you need it. Take the work, lad, and know that I'm happy for you to have it!'

'I have taken it,' said Brinin. Was he being foolish, after all? Didn't he need to gather something he could put by for another beast? All his life Garulf had given him wisdom and friendship, and these days Brinin often felt like a stranger in a new land. Was Garulf to show him how to be free, as he had once shown him how to be a slave? 'The lady Edith wouldn't let me do anything else. While I was thinking of an answer, she told Cynestan that I'd do it then left before I could say anything.'

'Have you met someone more stubborn than yourself?' laughed Garulf, and he looked less sick with the laughter. 'Come, lad, you can't say that you aren't stubborn, and I dare say that's sometimes been a help to you. But there's no good in being *too* stubborn, least of all when there's no need to be. Where's the wisdom in that? A wise man won't turn down lawful work when it's offered to him. If you mean what you say about me talking freely to you, then let me tell you to have a little wisdom, lad. As for the lady Edith, folk say she's like her mother, and no doubt she is. But Wynith says she grows more like her father every day, all the more the longer he's away. You may be a free man, but Edrich Thegn is still lord here and the lady Edith is in his stead. If she's asked you to work for her, you'll need to do it her way or not at all. It's a kindness for her and Cynestan to think of you at all.'

Brinin didn't know how to answer this, or even if Garulf wanted him to. If anyone in Oakdene was to chide him, tell him he was wrong and share his wisdom, Garulf had more right to do it than most. He'd earned it with many winters and grey hair and with all his small kindnesses. Why *had* Brinin kept away? If Garulf was waiting for an answer there was no time to give it. Before Brinin could speak, Ebba came in, walking slowly and holding a bowl. There was a cloth over it, but the steam still found its way out under the edges and brought some good smell with it.

'The lady Edith sent this broth for you, Grandfather,' she said. She sniffed the bowl. 'I don't know what's in it, but it smells good. I was worried I'd spill it. Mother warned me not to, and I've been walking so carefully.'

'Good girl!' said Garulf, taking the bowl. 'You haven't spilt a drop. Now, lad, you're going to eat here with us this evening, and I won't hear "no" from you. Who else will eat by our hearthside if not you? Ebba will fetch your food for you. And I'm glad they've hired you. I still think I could have done the work myself, but as they won't let me, who better to do it than you? It's just what you need, lad, just what you need.'

GUILT

Before mid-morning, Sigulf rode into the village with a stranger. Edith was months beyond hoping that every sound of horses' hooves might be her father and brother coming back, never to leave again; months beyond hoping that any word from the battlefield could be anything but bad. She had no hope left, only a little fluttering sickness in her gut. Why Sigulf? He'd never been sent before. And who was the man with him? Edith didn't stop to ask if it was beneath a thegn's daughter to drop her basket and run. She was months beyond caring about that too.

'What news, Sigulf?' she panted, reaching him before his feet had even touched the ground.

Sigulf slid from his horse and fumbled with a bundle strapped to its back. He wasn't looking at her, like a guilty child who knew he'd been misbehaving and was afraid to meet his mother's eye.

'Your father sent me, my lady Edith,' he said, gazing over her head at some unknown thing behind her. Why wouldn't he look at her? 'We were with a kinsman of your uncle. This is one of his men. I'm to go to Ælfwyn. Beorn fell a few days back, and I'm to tell her and give her his sword and seax.'

He'd already begun to walk towards Ælfwyn's house before Edith had time to feel the weight of his news, but he stopped and turned back to her after a few steps.

'Oh, and the word is the King is making peace with the Danes,' he said.

'Is that good?' said Edith. 'Does that mean it will be over and that my father and brother and everyone—everyone who's left—can come home?'

And there was the guilt again, clouding his face as though she were blaming him for some shameful misdeed.

'I can't say I know as much as all that, my lady,' he mumbled and walked away.

Edith turned to the man Sigulf had come with, but he had already gone, likely off somewhere to tend to his horse. She looked back at Sigulf uneasily, watching him as he walked. Was he hiding something? Or only tired from the road and dreading being the bearer of such tidings to Ælfwyn?

Ælfwyn was outside her house. Edith could see her from where she stood. She saw Sigulf stop and stand before her, saw Ælfwyn lift her hand and lean against the house. One of Ælfwyn's daughters ran through the doorway to her mother. Sigulf held out his bundle to them—it must be Beorn's sword and seax—but Ælfwyn didn't take it, and he gave it to her daughter instead. She saw Osgyth, Baldred's widow and Ælfwyn's nearest neighbour, run from her own house. Osgyth took Ælfwyn in both her arms and led her inside. Sigulf dropped his head and stood outside the house alone before walking away. Then Edith's eyes became too clouded to see any more. Hiding something from her? Wasn't what he hadn't hidden bad enough? Wasn't it bad enough for Ælfwyn to lose a husband and an only son between midwinter and midsummer? When would it end? When would it all be over?

Edith ran her hand across her eyes to wipe away the cloudy tears. She would have to go to Ælfwyn and sorrow with her, even though she didn't know what it was to have a husband or a son, let alone to lose them. But not yet. Let Ælfwyn weep with her daughters and friend first. And let Edith go somewhere alone to strengthen herself for the sorrowing. When would it end?

She fetched her forsaken basket and went to the forest. The strawberries would be ripening. Mildrith loved them but seldom had time to find any. She had been such a wise and steady friend and so motherlike that Edith wanted her to know that she felt all the good she had given her. And the forest would be dark and still and she might find strength there.

She had barely reached the trees when she heard someone running behind her.

'My lady Edith! My lady Edith!' It was Eanflæd, stumbling over her kirtle as she ran after her, a basket in her hand too. Edith's heart sank a little. There would be no dark stillness with Eanflæd. 'Can I come with you? What are you looking for?'

'Strawberries.'

'That will do well enough. Oh, my lady Edith, what a morning it's been! Two swine got out and Father and Eanfrith and Deormod had such a time getting them back in again. And Father's so angry with Deormod now that I can't bear to stay at home to watch. And I don't think Deormod *did* let them out as he's always so careful and he knows what Father would do, and I saw Eanbald climbing on the gate earlier though he's nowhere to be seen now. I told him to get down. But it's no good telling Father that, not when he's angry. Eanfrith asked him to stop once, and it only made things worse. And Father took the whip to him once he was done with Deormod, to teach him to hold his tongue and mind his own business. I did tell Eanfrith afterwards that he would have been wiser to say nothing, but he only said… Well, perhaps I shouldn't tell you what he said as it wasn't kind, and he likely didn't mean it. He was angry when he said it and he might be ashamed of it now, though he hasn't said so. I wish he would listen to me, for I *am* older, but he doesn't. Does your brother listen to you, my lady Edith?'

'Sometimes,' said Edith, giving up all hope of any stillness that morning, with a pang of guilt for wishing her away. How could she blame Eanflæd? 'Not always, though.'

'Likely that's the way of things with brothers then. I thought perhaps it was only *my* brothers. Oh, and my lady Edith, please don't think that my father always has a whip in his hand. Far from it! He seldom beats anyone but Deormod. He isn't harsh with his children! Only sometimes when he needs to be, but aren't all fathers harsh from time to time?' Eanflæd sighed. 'I don't see much good in having a slave if it only makes you angry. I'd rather do all the work myself and be happy. Wouldn't you, my lady Edith? I don't mind working, but when folk are angry it makes me cold all over. Oh, my lady Edith! Look at those strawberries! There are so many and some so big! How did you learn of this place? My mother *will* be pleased if I get a good basketful!'

After that even Eanflæd stopped talking for a while and they both moved from plant to plant, turning over the leaves to find the hidden berries beneath them. Eanflæd kept going long after Edith was done, eating almost as many as she dropped into her basket. Edith sat under a tree and scrabbled about for the right words to say to Ælfwyn.

'That will be enough,' said Eanflæd at last, sitting down beside her. 'Mother *will* be happy. We haven't had any strawberries yet this year. And you're so good, my lady Edith! I don't believe you've eaten even one. If I see a strawberry or any other sweet thing like that, I can't stop myself from eating it straightaway!'

'I never eat them,' said Edith. And why not tell Eanflæd why? Even if half the village learned of it, it wasn't something she was ashamed of. 'I was picking strawberries the day my mother died. I thought she'd like them but by the time I got home, it was already too late. I've hated even the smell of them ever since.'

'Oh, my lady Edith! You had such a lovely mother! She was always so kind, and I think you're very like her.' Not as like her as she ought to be. Not kind enough to be happy for Eanflæd to follow her. And now Eanflæd was stroking her arm like she was soothing a weeping child, though Edith hadn't shed a tear. Eanflæd would be a good mother some day, talking cheerfully, wiping away tears and not letting anyone be too angry or unkind in her house. 'But why did you come, if you don't even like the smell? The smell's everywhere here. What do you want them for?'

'For Mildrith. She's been good to me.'

'Mildrith *is* good. My mother says she doesn't know how she gets by with five children and no husband. And Tidræd is… is, well, lively. I like a lively child—don't you, my lady Edith—but Tidræd is livelier than most and it can't be easy to be his mother. I don't think my own brothers would dare! My father wouldn't like it, nor my mother either. I like him, though he is lively. I was a bit frightened of Thurstan, may God rest him, though he was a good man and that's the truth of it. It's so hard for Mildrith.' And Eanflæd did look truly sad and even sat without speaking before turning to Edith again. 'I thought I saw Sigulf riding into the village this morning, but it was when I was trying to get away from the house and then I forgot about it until now. Did you see him, my lady Edith? Did he have any news?'

'Yes. Beorn's dead, and he came to tell Ælfwyn.'

'Oh! And her husband not long dead! It's too much!' Tears filled Eanflæd's eyes and easily spilled over, and Edith's own stung at the sight of them. 'I hate all this. I wish it was over, and we could go back to how things were before.'

'I have to go and see her. I haven't been yet. She was with Osgyth, and I wanted to give her some time before I went.'

'Oh, you must go, my lady Edith!' Eanflæd was on her feet at once. 'You mustn't let me keep you here. We ought to go back at once. My mother will want me back, and… and everything else will be over by now.'

The nearer they got to the village the less talkative Eanflæd became, frowning as they walked along. Before they stepped out from the shade of the trees she stopped Edith, a hand on her arm.

'My lady,' she whispered as though she didn't want the trees to hear her. The village was in sight, but no one was near them. 'I feel dreadfully guilty that I said nothing to my father about the gate this morning, but you see how it is. Eanfrith has tried, and it doesn't do any good. I wonder if I should find Deormod and give him some strawberries before I go back to Mother—she won't miss them. My father wouldn't like it, and it might not make Deormod feel any better, but *I'd* want to know that there was at least someone who wasn't angry with me, wouldn't you? What do you think, my lady Edith?'

'I think you're very kind and that you should give him some whether your father would like it or not. Isn't it better to do something small than nothing at all?'

'Thank you, my lady Edith. I will do it then and I'll take good care that my father doesn't see me, nor my mother. And thank you for letting me come with you. I was half-afraid you wouldn't want me.'

Edith felt warm towards Eanflæd as she dashed away. All that endless talking hid the better, kinder Eanflæd underneath. Edith hadn't seen her before because she hadn't stopped long enough to look, but she would never think of her the same way again. She glanced towards Ælfwyn's house and sighed. Now to get rid of her basket and go there to sit and weep. She didn't know if she had found the strength for it.

DREAMS

It was dark. Someone was weeping, softly, almost unheard. But Oswald heard. It must be Ælfwyn, weeping for her son. Yet how could it be? He hadn't seen her yet to tell her. He ought to have done it before he went to bed. He had to tell her quickly. He couldn't remember going to bed. His shield arm was resting on his chest, but he couldn't lift it. He tried to sit, gasping as burning pain shot from his shoulder, and hands pushed him down onto the bed again.

'No! Don't sit up. Lie still now.'

That sounded like his father. Where was Ælfwyn? Perhaps he had dreamt the weeping. He would tell her in the morning. He still couldn't lift his arm, only his fingers.

There was shuffling nearby. Oswald opened his eyes. It wasn't so dark as he had thought. In the candlelight he saw the shadow of a man sitting near his bed. The candle was on a table behind him, and Oswald couldn't see the man's face. The shape was like his father, but surely his father should be asleep. They were all so weary. He wanted to say it, but how does a son tell his father to go to bed? It was too hard to think it out, and his lips were too sluggish for speech. He could only hope that his father might understand his thoughts. His eyes were heavy. They shut by themselves without Oswald bidding them to. He heard a sigh but didn't know if it came from his father or himself. Perhaps the sigh was a dream too, like the weeping. Perhaps it was all a dream. It would be morning soon.

∾

The Danes were roaring, and the last hope of saving Wessex was trampled into the mud. Beorn lay dying in Oswald's arms, spattering

128

drops of blood as he coughed. He reached up and held Oswald's neck, drawing his head low to whisper some last words in his ear. Oswald felt his hand there. No, not Beorn's hand. This hand wasn't pulling his head down; it was lifting it and made his shoulder throb. Someone was holding a bitter drink to his mouth. He knew the smell. He'd drunk it before but didn't know when. He didn't want to drink it but he couldn't say that with the cup already at his lips. It was easier to swallow it. It made him cough; only a little spluttering cough, not a bloody, deathly one like Beorn's.

The hand laid him down again and turned him onto his side. He felt it on his cheek, on his forehead. It was a rough hand but it touched him softly.

'I think he's cooler now, my lord. A little warm, but not so hot as before.' A woman was speaking. Oswald didn't know who it was. 'I don't think the wound is foul. It's some other fever.'

Someone—a man—answered the woman in a low voice, but Oswald couldn't hear what he was saying.

'I will, my lord,' said the woman, 'later when the light is better. But I'm not so worried this morning as I was. I never thought it was woundfever. But since the priest came he is a little better. I don't know if it was the priest or the herbs which helped him, or if the fever is lifting by itself as some fevers do. If you feel him yourself, my lord, you'll see that he isn't so hot, and he isn't shivering like before.'

Another hand was laid on his forehead, a bigger, heavier hand. It rested there longer than the first one and stroked his hair as a mother might her child's. Oswald wanted to open his eyes but he was too tired. Was the bitter drink making him sleepy? He was ill and wounded. He had understood enough of the woman's speech to know that.

'Forgive me for speaking so boldly, my lord,' said the woman, 'but won't you rest now for a while? You have barely slept for days, and perhaps now we may have a little hope.'

The man answered her, his voice floating further and further away as Oswald drifted into stillness.

≈

Oswald lay face down on the bed. His back was cold, and hands were working at his shoulder. It ached. Brother Wilfred had come to put salve on his back. There was honey in it, and Oswald could smell it. He had thought all that was over; that the Moot had been many months ago in that lost time before the Danes had come. But now he was somehow back there, smarting again.

He hadn't forgotten any of it. He had pushed his forehead against the roof-post and shifted his feet to steady them and strengthen himself for what was coming. He had shut his eyes so he wouldn't see the men around him, as though that would somehow shield him from the knowledge that they were all there watching. And as the whip had torn and burned, he had shifted his feet again, had leaned harder against the roof-post, had shut his eyes tighter, had shut his mouth to stifle his groans so he wouldn't shame himself by being too loud. But his legs had shaken and wouldn't be steadied. His whole body had shaken and fallen. And he was in his bed, and Brother Wilfred was with him with the sweet-smelling, stinging salve, healing and hurting.

Oswald opened his eyes. It was daylight, but all he could see were folds of cloth—dirt green—falling before his eyes. This wasn't the clothing of a monk; it was the clothing of a woman. Brother Wilfred wasn't tending to him, and Oswald didn't know where he was. The Moot *was* long over, after all. There was no fire across his whole back now, only a deep throbbing in one shoulder.

But he could still smell honey.

The water was cold, swallowing him and pulling him down. His father had told him not to come here, had warned him of the danger, had uttered stern threats should he fail to heed him. And now he was sinking, rising and gasping for breath, sinking again. A shout. A branch. Wild grasping. He lay on the unshifting grass, spluttering and drinking in clean, dry breaths.

The eyes of a friend watched him fearfully. Oswald hadn't known until that day that they *were* the eyes of a friend, nor that neither of them would ever look at each other in the same way again.

There was sunshine in those days and only small fears. And the Danes had not yet come.

'Well done!' said Thurstan, slapping Oswald on the back. 'You're well on your way to becoming a fine bowman. Stand still, Tidræd; you'll have your turn soon enough! Now, Oswald, fetch your spear. That'll be what you'll want if the Danes ever come.'

But it was too late. The Danes had already come, and all Oswald's spears were broken. He couldn't lift his shield; his arm was fastened to his chest and wouldn't shift. Some of the Danes lay dead before him. Their faces, old and young, stared up at him with unseeing eyes. But there were more coming, more and more as far as he could see. He turned to run, but they were behind him too, around him on every side. And Thurstan was dead. Tidræd was dead too young. Alrich was dead. Beorn was dead. His father was dead. *Pater noster qui es in coelis… libera nos a malo. Libera nos a malo.* He was dying himself, sinking under a sea of Danish spears. *Libera nos a malo. Libera nos a malo.*

'He's talking in his sleep.'

The words shot arrowlike, flew spearlike into his dreams, and light came with them. The Danes and the spears and the dead melted away. He wasn't at home. The bed was too wide. Oswald opened his eyes.

The roof beams were low, with the shadowy thatch above them. He turned his head. Light flooded through the doorway and brightened the room. His father and Hildræd his uncle sat nearby on a bench, watching him. His father, ashen-faced and with uncombed hair, shut his lips tightly as his eyes met Oswald's.

A man Oswald didn't know was standing behind his uncle, but there was no woman anywhere. Oswald thought there had been a woman, but perhaps she had been a dream. There had been so many dreams, bewildering and frightening. A dreadful ride through darkness and bitter cold. Loud voices and running feet. Strong hands that pressed him to the bed and wouldn't let him flee from the fire that burnt his shoulder. The sweet smell of honey. Whispered words he couldn't understand. Bitter drink after bitter drink. And always the endless shaking.

A jug was sitting on a little table. Its sides were round and smooth, and a long curved shadow stretched away from it. Oswald's lips were very dry, and he wondered what was in the jug. He looked back at his father again.

'I'm thirsty,' he said hoarsely.

FOE

Cries in the night, pounding, heavy footsteps, a hand in the darkness snatched Edith from her sleep and dragged her bewildered to her feet. Screaming outside, running and shouting, wailing and deadly fear.

'They're coming, my lady! Almost here. Quick!'

It was Ludan, panting and breathless. No time for a cloak or kirtle, a headcloth or shoes. She ran with him in her smock and bare feet. A glint in the firelight, a spear tip, her grandfather's spear hanging on the roof-post. She stopped to lift it down.

'No time, my lady Edith! Run and hide.'

She grabbed the spear and ran, stumbling out into the night. All was uproar, men and beasts bellowing alike. Hounds barked; shrieking children were borne along in their mothers' arms. They all scattered everywhere. Men and boys rushed weaponed with axes, shovels and forks.

'Run! Run!' Edith couldn't shout loudly enough as she stumbled along. Her voice was thin, coming out almost soundless as in a nightmare.

A thunder of horsemen from the north, bright torches drawing nearer, too sickening and dreadful to be true. And there was no time.

'Run! Run!'

She saw Ludan on the threshold of the hall, a dark shadow against the dim glow, standing ready with a fork in his hand.

～

Dread by night. Brinin didn't need a neighbour to bang on his door to warn him, and none of his neighbours had. The cries outside told him everything. He himself felt no fear. He tried to as he tucked an axe into his belt. Would he meet death that night, death, swift and bloody? He strapped a quiver of arrows to his back and lifted down Oswald's bow, but he could feel nothing. Dread by night, dreamlike now it had come. Why *was* he taking the bow? It was too dark to shoot, and by daylight he might be dead. But Oswald had wanted him to have it.

He stepped outside into the fearful uproar and shut the door behind him. He didn't know why he did that either; it wouldn't stop anyone from going inside. Out of the darkness, someone charged straight into him, almost knocking him from his feet.

'My… my grandfather…' Eawig, out of breath, clutched Brinin's arm. 'He sent me to see if you were awake.'

That was when the fear wrenched Brinin's gut. Who would save these unweaponed slaves, these kinlike friends who had slowed their own flight to help him with his? He opened the door again and took out a shovel and a fork from where they leaned against the wall by the threshold.

'Take these,' he said, thrusting them into Eawig's arms. 'Do you know where to hide?'

'In the forest. Grandfather knows somewhere.'

'Then get your mother and sister and your grandfather there quickly. And don't leave them too soon. Run. Get away from here.'

He shoved Eawig, and the boy stumbled into the night. Not too soon. The Danes had come. Dread by night. They were here, and Brinin didn't know what to do.

Someone came upon Edith from behind. She screamed, but it was so smothered by fear that the scream died on her lips. Struggling, she fought with the unseen hand that tugged at her.

'Edith, stop! It's only me.'

No foe, only Cenwyn, with little Tidwine clinging half-stunned to her back.

'Mother said you're to come with us.'

Edith hardly knew what they stood on as they scrambled up the hillside. Nettles, brambles, twigs and briars. She felt none of them, bare-footed though she was. Tidræd was shouting behind them, driving his mother and sisters ahead of him, shepherdlike with his sheep.

By the time they stopped, breathless among the shrubs, Oswyn and Tidwine were both weeping, and Edith near to it. Below them in the blackness of the village, she saw the light of the Danish torches. One, two, three. How many? Six? Were there six of them, and no more? They were near now, almost at the church. Shouting, far off now, reached them even where they sat.

Tidræd was shifting around in the darkness, shadowy, handing something to his mother.

'It's Father's sword,' he said. 'You'd better take it, Mother. It's still too heavy for me. I have my bow and an axe, and I don't want them to get the sword.'

'What do you mean?' snapped Mildrith. 'You're frightening the little ones with talk like that. Sit down and hold your tongue. It's not too dark for me to beat you if you need it!'

But Edith could already hear Tidræd scrambling away from them. Surely he wasn't going to fight the Danes!

'Tidræd! Tidræd!' shouted Mildrith. 'Come back here now! Do you hear me, Tidræd?'

'I can't, Mother!' Tidræd called back, already making his way down the hill. 'Oswald Child said we had to be ready for them, every boy over twelve winters. Have you forgotten?'

'Tidræd!' Mildrith started after him, but her youngest children were weeping and clinging to her.

'Stop that, Tidwine,' said Cenwyn. 'Be still now and come over here to me. You take Oswyn, Mærwyn. Mother, Oswald Child *did* say that.'

'When I get hold of that boy…' But the words seemed to choke Mildrith. She didn't follow him.

Something was choking Edith too. When would Mildrith get hold of Tidræd? Where would he be in the morning? Would any of them even see the morning?

Brinin didn't know what to do. What could he do, with no warcraft and few weapons? He stood still, finding his nighteyes and listening. The Danish torches came round the church. Where was Brother Wilfred? *Shade him with your shoulders. Be a shield all around him.* They were off their horses now, walking swiftly, perhaps not many of them. Could the men of Oakdene, standing as one, drive them away? With no leader and little skill? Couldn't Cynestan or Daglæf lead them? Had everyone scattered to save his own kin? Brinin had no kin to save, and yet… He left his hut and ran.

South between the houses, keeping in the shadows, he passed Deorstan's house, passed Cynestan's. Cynestan stood shadowy by the doorway, with three spears in his hand.

'I can't run at them,' said Cynestan grimly, 'but I haven't forgotten how to throw a spear, and they're like walking candles, easy to see. Once they're near enough… and if they get *too* near I have an axe.'

'Have Mildrith and her children gone?' asked Brinin. Mildrith wasn't his kin, but his field would have been unploughed without her, and Thurstan had once been kind to him.

'Up into the hills and the lady Edith with them.'

Edith too. There was nothing for him to do here. *Be a shield all around them.* He crept round Mildrith's house and looked east across to the village. They were nearer now. Where? By the cowshed? Too near. There were no houses between him and Garulf's hut, nowhere to hide. But if he was swift—he knew he could be—if he was swift he could reach the oak tree. Beyond their torches all would be deep blackness. They were near, but he ran.

He stopped with his back to the tree, hiding behind it.

'Ivar, we'll look for the beasts.' A shout sounded in that well-known tongue, lost to him now, never on his lips, never heard but always unforgotten. 'Go with Sigurd to the longhouse. That's where the wealth will be.'

'I don't know where Sigurd is,' called back another voice. Ivar's? How many were they?

'He was behind us,' shouted back the first man. 'I'll come when I've found a few swine. It'll be easy work tonight. They've all fled.'

Swine? Wealth? Easy work? Was that what they wanted, swift and easy takings? Herjolf had given him roasted swine flesh in Readingum. The takings of a raid like this? And *had* everyone fled, or were others hiding as he was in the shadows, ready to rush out at them? Mildrith had fled, Edith, Garulf, all safe with their kin he trusted. *Shade them with your shoulders.* Wulfrich? Surely he was gone by now with his mother and father. Aculf wouldn't linger long and risk death. But knowing was better than hoping. Another dash through the darkness and Brinin was round the house that had once been Rædwald's.

In the shadows he ran straight into something no higher than his knees. He fell tumbling and rolled over on the grass. The bow flew from his hand and the axe dug into him as he landed on it, nicking his side. No time to think of that now. He felt for the bow. He dared not go on until he had it or he would never find it. What *had* he fallen over? His hand touched the bow on the grass, and he snatched it up. A hound? Then it whimpered. That was no beast. It was a child! Brinin got onto his knees and crawled back towards the whimpering.

'Who is it?' he whispered. 'Where's your mother?'

A louder whimper. Brinin reached out and touched the child, who was shaking with fear and shrinking from him against the wall of the house.

'Don't be scared,' he whispered again. 'It's me, Brinin. Where's your mother? Who are you?'

'Ulf.'

Where was Aculf, that his little son should be alone in the dark? Where was Sægyth? Brinin scooped the boy up and crept through the shadows towards Aculf's house. Surely they hadn't all left to hide without him.

Between the buildings in front of him, Brinin made out the shape of a woman, moving slowly, turning all ways as she strained to see. She stretched out her hands before her, sometimes kneeling. Brinin had no doubt who she was. Who else could it be but Sægyth, looking for a lost son? Brinin tried to warn her that he was coming, but his whisper didn't reach her. She stifled a scream as she saw him suddenly before her, but Brinin hushed her and thrust her son into her arms.

'I found him by Rædwald's house,' he whispered, as Sægyth clutched Ulf with a breathless sob. 'Where are the other children?'

'With Aculf in the forest, but we lost Ulf. I thought he was with Aculf... he thought he was with me, but—'

'Better get away quickly. They may come this way.'

Sægyth turned back once as Brinin watched her melt away into the night. He heard her whispered thanks, then she was gone with Ulf still in her arms. Ulf was too big now to be carried, but he was too frightened to walk, and his mother too frightened to let him.

Brinin crept back to the beasthouse fence and squatted low behind it. The Danes still held their torches. Could he shoot at the fire and wound or kill one of them? Did he even have the skill? Should he take his axe and run at one of them? That would mean death, whether or not he brought one down with him. Would it be a bold death or only a foolish one? Or a little of both? He would be no good to anyone dead, however boldly he fell. Better keep a bold death until there was nothing else he could do. There was no harm in trying the bow.

One Dane stood still. The torchlight fell on his arm and head, leaving the rest of him in darkness. His head seemed to float, bodyless. Brinin slid an arrow from the quiver and took aim. He kept his eye on the floating head, drawing the string tight, readying the shot, but too slow, too unsure to let the arrow fly; a wavering, faltering fool.

Sudden barking and shouting. The bright head jerked and fell into darkness. The torch lay on the ground. Brinin saw it burning there. More shouts, a scream, swift shadows, rushing torchlight. What now?

$\sim$

It was cold. Not bitter like winter, but only a smock and no shoes were not enough against the chill. Now that they sat still in the darkness, Edith felt every sting and scratch of the nettles and brambles they had fled through. She had hardly felt them when she had been running.

After a while Tidwine, tiring of his sister, clambered onto her lap and fell asleep. She was glad of the heat of his body. They would warm each other, and it was good that he slept. Better that he knew little of this dreadful night. Tidræd didn't come back.

They sat wordless, listening to the far-off shouts—fewer now than before—and to the hounds barking and to other sounds that Edith could not name. She shut her eyes, though she couldn't have said why. There was little to see in the darkness, and shutting them didn't muffle the sounds around her. Above them somewhere an owl shrieked, then as though it had sounded a warning Edith heard another shriek—a scream—near enough to be sickening. She gripped Tidwine a little too tightly and he whimpered in his uneasy sleep. The scream was followed by stillness, but that was almost worse. Who? Why? Why had they stopped?

The scream was still sounding in Edith's head when Cenwyn grabbed her arm.

'Look!' she whispered.

Edith opened her eyes. The village below them was no longer in darkness. It was aglow with bright flames. A building was burning. The six torches were doing their work.

FIRE

Someone lay dead by the cowshed. Fire leapt high from its roof and lit the body, a dark shape crumpled on the ground. The shouts and wild rushing had died away, all but the rushing inside Brinin's head. Dane called to Dane, but he only heard scattered words. In the light of the flames, Brinin could see everything now. A man walked from the horsehouse, leading a horse by its bridle. He reached up and held his torch to the thatch as coolly as another man might shut a door.

Was now the time to run at one of them with his axe in that last deed of valour or folly? Others had, and it had done no good. The Danes were still among them. There was no time for long thinking, yet all he could do was waver, too slow for a fyrdman, thinking too long, taught only in work and not in war. Long careful thought was wisdom by his hearth but folly now.

The fire was sweeping too swiftly from building to building, warming him like his own hearthside. Whether he ran out to die or crept away to hide, he must do it quickly. No more wavering. That was when he heard the weeping, gasping sobs and whispering from inside the swine pen.

'Find us a few swine to fill our bellies with,' called one of the raiders.

A man with a torch was walking towards the pen. And the fire was growing, too bright, shining on everything. The Danes were coming. They would find the hidden weeper.

'There's nothing here. I've already looked.' Brinin heard himself shouting almost before he knew what he was saying. 'Is Ivar still in the longhouse?'

As the Dane turned away, Brinin scrambled over the fence and into the swine pen, his heart pounding. Careful thought. Careful but swift thought. No more wavering.

'Who's in here?' he whispered.

Even as he said it, the glow of the flames lit their faces. It was Baldred's son, Sibwine and his sister, Sifflæd. And it was too bright for them to stay there.

'I came out to fight them.' Sibwine was almost old enough for the fyrd and doubtless keen to fight on behalf of his fallen father. 'But my sister lost our mother in the dark and I hid her in here. She doesn't want me to leave her, and I don't know if I can get her out now.'

'You must. They're looking for beasts and they'll find you. Get out and run. Get to the forest quickly.'

Sifflæd was shaking and weeping, but her brother and Brinin dragged her from the pen and over the fence. Then they ran. Sibwine pulled his sister along by the arm, Brinin running behind them. There was no stumbling in the dark now as the village blazed brighter. They passed the last house, heading for the forest.

'Look! Over there!'

A shout from behind them. No time to look back. Sibwine and Sifflæd were lost to Brinin now, hidden by the trees. He could hear twigs breaking under their feet. Brinin pulled himself up into the nearest tree.

Then he looked back. There *was* one coming after them, a shadow against the glow of the village. He was coming straight towards the tree, coming swiftly. Let him come. Brinin was ready for him. He grasped his axe. No more wavering. He would fall on him, fall to bold, foolish death if he must. This night would have to end somehow.

The flames leapt and spread, house after house alight, scattered throughout the village: one here to the south, another two on the eastern side. Then Edith's breath seemed to leave her. Another fire, two buildings burning side by side. One of them was the church—it could be nothing else—and the other, the flames sweeping across it so swiftly that its roof was almost swallowed up already, was the hall.

It would be gone. Nothing would be left but ashes. The fire was too hungry now to stop, lighting the village like lamps in a dark room. She could even see the shadowy shapes of men moving about. The hall would be gone. It was almost gone already. And she wept.

'Oh, Edith! Do you see it?' whispered Cenwyn.

But Edith didn't answer. She couldn't. Her tears fell silently onto Tidwine's sleeping head as he lay against her shoulder. Her home was gone and all her clothes but the smock she sat in, but those could be rebuilt or woven anew. Her father's wealth was hidden—all but the land—and where it was the flames couldn't reach it. But her mother's seat was gone, and the curtain her skilful needle had made lovely. Edith hadn't thought to hide a seat or a curtain. She had only thought of theft and not of fire. Her mother's ring and breastpin were hidden with the rest of the wealth but Edith hardly cared about those. Her mother had made that curtain and soon it would be dust, and so would all the other little worthless things that had been her mother's and which Edith had kept and loved. They would all be lost.

Her father would come back—if he ever came back—and his home would be ashes. It had been his wife's home, his father's and mother's home, his brothers' and sister's, all dead. It was lost, and all that was left of them with it.

There was more shouting. Brinin could hear it. More fighting and death. Who would they find still alive in the morning? Perhaps no one would find *him* alive. The Dane was near now, almost below him, only a few steps away. Brinin shifted a little on the bough he sat on, steadying himself with one hand, grasping the axe with the other. Then he dropped.

The fall was jarring, boneshaking, but true. The Dane yelled as Brinin landed on him and they both tumbled to the ground. Brinin's axe was raised. He brought it down, but the Dane was struggling fiercely and rolled to the side. The axe missed its mark, only grazing the Dane's shoulder and digging into the soft earth beside them.

There was nothing fyrdlike about their fight, not any more than if they had been two boys wrestling in the dirt. They grunted and gasped, their weapons all but forgotten and no good to either of them. Brinin was strong, but the Dane was too once the first shock of Brinin's fall had passed. There wasn't much between them. They matched grip for grip, wrench for wrench. But whichever of them could stay strong for longer would be the one who would live.

The sky brightened as they struggled, but not with the cool light of early morning. Warm and flickering, roaring and crackling, the fire gorged itself on Oakdene. Brinin tasted the smoke now, even by trees.

And that fleeting fear was a weakening. Too swift to stop, the Dane was on top of Brinin, pinning him to the ground. Brinin had long since lost his axe and he couldn't reach the seax. It was the end. Dread by night. Death in the darkness. Others had already died that night. He would only be another among the many fallen throughout Wessex, on battlefields and in scattered villages. And no one needed him to live.

That dreadful flickering warmth lit up the Dane's face. And Brinin saw then that he hadn't fallen on a stranger to kill him in the dark. He hadn't been grappling with an unknown foe. He had been wrestling with a man he knew. It was Skorri.

'It's you!' Knowledge flooded Skorri's face, but he didn't shift or loosen his grip. 'I knew I should have cut your throat that night we first met. I *told* them all afterwards that I should never have listened to Herjolf. What are you doing here?'

Would he answer Skorri who had come in the night to kill and burn and ride away with what was not his? What was *he* doing there?

'Herjolf welcomed you,' said Skorri, drawing his knife. It shone, golden and alive in the firelight. Not long to the end now. 'He was my kinsman and he was kind to you, and you lied to him.'

'I didn't lie to him. My mother *was* a Dane. How else do you think I learned to speak like this? And I've had little kindness from the Saxons. But the man I was with that night, his son is like a brother to me. Was I to see his father in your camp and leave him there? Some ties are as strong as kinship.'

Skorri raised his knife. Its blade burned, firelike and gleaming. Brinin shut his eyes. *You will not fear the dread by night.* The fear would pass. It was fluttering inside him now like a bird trapped in the rafters. It would pass, flying away as his life did.

'I should have killed you that first night,' said Skorri. Then he struck. The knife slashed along Brinin's arm, searing like a brand. Brinin cried out as it tore into his flesh. Skorri didn't strike again. He stood up and shoved Brinin away from him with his foot.

Brinin staggered to his feet, gasping with pain and clutching his arm with the other hand. Warm blood trickled between his fingers.

'That's for the bloody nose you gave me, Bruni Hallveigson,' said Skorri. 'But you spared me then, so I'll spare you now. If we meet a third time, I'll kill you.'

Skorri began to walk away, but he stopped after a few steps.

'Herjolf's dead,' he said. 'He died that day you left the camp, never came back with the others.'

Then he left. Brinin stood and watched him, a dark shape that broke into a run, heading back to that frightful, roaring blaze that had once been Oakdene.

ASHES

Flames lit the sky, brightening it with such a dreadful glow that it was hard for Brinin to see the beginnings of dawn. He sat with set teeth just inside the forest, pressing handfuls of moss against his wounded arm to stop the blood. Now that it was over, now that he *thought* it was over, he felt sick. He was weak and shaky. They were gone now—he had heard the thunder of their horses riding away—but he did not dare to go back into the village, not when he didn't know what he would find there, not when he didn't know what was left to find.

Others were the first to come out of hiding. Brinin heard them calling to one another in the grey morning. He staggered to his feet, his hand still on the wound, and began the slow walk towards the shouting and everything he feared to see. The smell of burning wood and thatch hung everywhere, the smoke rising dark into the sky.

The hall was almost gone, a fallen heap still burning. Folk were running to it with buckets, drenching it with water but there was little left to save. All that was left of the church was a little smouldering wood, blackened and broken. The horsehouse was the same. Other buildings were still burning as everywhere men and women rushed to quench the flames. There was a wind that morning, a slight one but enough to fear.

Daglæf was where the cowshed had been, kneeling with his father dead in his arms. It must have been his body that Brinin had seen there in the night. Daglæf's back was to Brinin; he couldn't see his face. But he saw how Daglæf's wife and sons wept as they stood around him. He saw how Daglæf leaned forward, bent low, cradling his father's body as a mother might her child. They had sat together once, Brinin and Byrnhelm. Old and sharp-tongued, yet not unkind, he had been alive

144

at dusk and dead by dawn. Surely he ought to have been hiding while younger, stronger men fought them. And now Daglæf, who had been kinder even than his father, was weeping. There was something tight in Brinin's chest: sorrow, unshifting.

'Look! Look!'

A quivering hand clutched Brinin's arm. Tidræd, red-eyed and white-faced, was beside him, pointing at two bodies nearby. It was Ludan, lying dead with a fallen Dane at his side, their bodies so tangled it was hard to tell one from the other.

'I saw him. I saw Ludan fall.' Tidræd's voice quivered as his hand did, his words coming much too swiftly and breathlessly. 'He ran at that Dane with a fork. Look, it's still there. He ran so quickly and he got him, but the Dane had an axe and brought him down as he fell. I tried to shoot the Dane, but it was too dark for that. But… but Ludan got him. He ran with the fork like it was a spear.'

Tidræd grew more like his father every day, fearless and ready for battle, but wouldn't it have been better for his eyes to have been a little older before they saw men die like that?

'Where's your mother, Tidræd?'

'Hiding. I left her and my sisters and brother, and the lady Edith, up on the hillside when the Danes came.'

'Don't you think she'll want to know that you're still alive? Better find her again quickly.'

Brinin could barely bring himself to look at Ludan, but he knelt and pushed the Dane away from him a little. There was a spear with a broken shaft still in the Dane's shoulder. Where had that come from? Was it one of Cynestan's? Brinin had no hope of finding Ludan alive, not with those wounds, but it was right that someone should kneel in sorrow beside him. Who would have thought that Ludan would die like that; that Ludan, slow-speaking and slow-moving, would die rushing warlike at a foe? Who would have thought that a slave, forbidden to bear a weapon, would die so boldly like the best of the fyrd?

A shadow, long in the morning light, shrouded Ludan in darkness. Brinin looked up and saw Garulf standing over him, his face streaming with tears he didn't try to hide. Tears felt near to Brinin then too; he grew hot, the ache inside worse than his wounded arm. It wasn't only because Garulf and Daglæf were weeping, or even because Ludan lay lifeless on the ground. It was all too raw, too much like another time when he'd knelt helpless by the dead.

'Where is my daughter? Have any of you seen Eanflæd?' Sæthryth, Eadulf's wife, was running everywhere, wild-eyed and fearful.

Brinin stood up with one last look at Ludan and one glance of shared sorrow with Garulf. He couldn't stay kneeling when there was so much work to be done, and he couldn't work until he found someone to tend to his arm. A heartrending cry nearby told him that yet another had been found slain.

$\sim$

As Edith watched the black billows of smoke, there was a rustling of leaves and snapping of twigs as someone came running up the hill. Mildrith and Cenwyn, not burdened by sleeping children as Edith and Mærwyn were, sprang to their feet. Edith reached out for her grandfather's spear that had lain all night at her side.

'Mother! Mother! They've gone!' a voice called breathlessly from nearby, and Tidræd stumbled towards them.

Mildrith, scolding and almost weeping, met her son with a blend of slaps and kisses, shakes and hugs, all of which Tidræd bore without a word. He stood, still and meek, and let his mother mete out her feelings at the sight of him whole after the night he had given her. It was only when all Mildrith's anger and tearful gladness were spent that he spoke.

'They've gone,' he said again. 'All but one, but he's dead, and I think I shot one. I didn't kill him, but I might have wounded him. And our house isn't burning, Mother, but… but…'

He glanced at Edith almost guiltily, as though bringing her word of the hall was the same as telling her that he'd put a torch to it himself.

'We know,' said Cenwyn. 'We could see it from here.'

Oswyn had been woken by her mother's scolding, but they had to set Tidwine, whimpering and still half-asleep, onto his feet and make him walk. As they set off down the hill, Tidræd turned to his mother again, biting his lip and blinking too much, his boldness suddenly gone.

'Let me show you the best way to the house, Mother,' he said in a small, quavering voice. 'Some… some folk are dead, and it would be better for the little ones not to see them.'

It was only when they were near Mildrith's house, the smoke stinging her throat and eyes, that Edith felt how unclothed she was in only a smock; how unfit she was to be seen, a thegn's daughter walking about almost naked for all to see. There was nothing she could do about it. Everything was gone. She couldn't hide away. It was for her to go round the village, to see who had fallen and say what was to be done. Yet how could she go like this?

'What am I going to do, Cenwyn?' she whispered. 'I need to see everyone, but this smock is all I have left to wear!'

'Oh, don't worry about that! Why are you even thinking about that? Mærwyn and I between us will have something for you, won't we, Mærwyn? Only be thankful that our house is still standing and we *have* something left for you to wear! And you'll have to sleep with us. Mother won't hear of you sleeping anywhere else. I know she won't. Now come inside quickly, and we'll find you something.'

Mærwyn and Cenwyn were both a little taller than Edith and the kirtle they found her was slightly too long, but it did well enough when, hands trembling, she had fastened a belt around it and tucked the cloth up. She didn't ask them for shoes, only a headcloth. She hadn't gone barefoot since she was a little girl, but her feet still stung from their flight. Perhaps the cool grass would soothe them.

She was barely ready when Mildrith came in, Cynestan behind her.

'Cynestan! Thank God you're still alive!'

'And you, my lady, and you!' said Cynestan warmly.

They left the children with Mærwyn and Cenwyn, with a charge from Mildrith to kindle a fire and get something cooking, and stepped outside. Cynestan's face was hard and utterly weary, his gait more halting than ever.

'Who has fallen?' Edith asked once they were out. Her steadiness was wavering now. She *must* keep hold of herself.

'Not everyone is back yet, my lady, so it's hard to say. But as far as we know, Byrnhelm, young Ceola and—'

'But Ceola's only a boy!'

'Fifteen winters, my lady.'

Fifteen winters! *She* was only fifteen winters, so young. Yet she had to do the work of a woman, and Ceola had done the work of a man and died like one. Edith swallowed hard and nodded. Ceola wasn't the last. She saw it on Cynestan's face.

'Who else?' she asked.

'Ludan, my lady.'

Edith winced. She could almost feel his hand on her arm dragging her from her sleep, hear his hurried shouts, see his shadow steadfast in the doorway.

'He killed a Dane, my lady, the only Dane any of us killed last night, so far as we know. We found them lying dead together.'

'Where is he? I want to see him and after that I'll go to the kin of the others.'

'My lady, his wounds... I don't think you should see him.'

'He belongs to my father's household! Take me to him!'

If Ceola could die like a man at only fifteen winters, then she could do what she knew she must. She could do what her mother would have done, what her father and brother would do if they rode into Oakdene this morning—pray God they would. She wanted them so badly it hurt. She saw Cynestan glance at Mildrith but didn't let her eyes follow his, for fear of what she might see on Mildrith's face. Cynestan sighed and led her away from the house.

Ludan lay covered with a cloth, and Edith didn't know where the Dane was. Someone must have taken him away. The grass around where Ludan lay was dark and sticky with blood. She hadn't known that spilled blood was so dark, and she had to stand back a little so as not to get it on her feet.

'I want to see his face,' she whispered, though she didn't any more. All she wanted now was to run away somewhere and hide from it all.

Cynestan looked at her, half-pleadingly, then bent down and lifted the cloth.

She only had a glimpse before she shut her eyes. She couldn't help it. She tasted something bitter in her throat. Was this what her father and brother saw on the battlefield, yet not one man but scores of them lying dead all around them? Was this what they had to do to their foe, or what their foe might do to them? The bitterness was swelling and choking her, and she turned and retched onto the grass. She felt Cynestan's hand on her arm.

'Come now, my lady,' he said. He didn't say that he had warned her though she couldn't have chided him if he had. 'We all feel like that sometimes, and it's hardest of all the first time you see it. Come away now. Let me show you what's left of the hall. We did what we could but there was little left by the time we got to it. And don't worry. Ludan won't be left lying here. I'll make sure someone gets him ready for burial, and we do right by him.'

WEEPING

Brother Wilfred's face was whiter than Tidræd's, his hands less steady even than Brinin's own had been. The monk didn't speak as he tended Brinin's wound, and the salve smarted too much for Brinin to try to. He kept his eyes away from it and watched the smoke rising from what was left of the hall. He saw Edith talking to the men who had stopped the flames. There was no wild fearfulness with Edith, and if she had wept there was little to see of it now. She only watched and listened and said little, then left with Cynestan.

'I can't do any more with it now but I'll look at it again.' Brother Wilfred's words were a little too soft, almost hoarse, as though he was barely keeping hold of himself and no more. 'Keep the arm as still as you can.'

'Is it too much like before, sir, when they came to your minster?'

Brinin hadn't meant to ask, but wasn't it a kind of fellowship to show that he had not forgotten? Brother Wilfred lowered his head, strengthening himself to speak.

'Not so bad. Thank God not so bad. Yet too much like before all the same,' he said. 'But there is too much to be done to think of that now.'

The thinking would come later in the darkness when there was no work or daylight to drive the thoughts away. Brinin knew only too well how it would be.

There was no loud weeping coming from Daglæf's house as Edith and Cynestan made their way towards it. Baldred's house was gone. Edith caught sight of his widow, Osgyth, and her children poking through the blackened ashes with sticks, to see if anything was left worth saving.

And the cowshed was gone, and the horsehouse, and the new storehouse. But she thanked God that the harvest wasn't in yet and that the cows had all been out with the cowherd.

There was no loud weeping, but Daglæf's wife wept quietly and his two sons sniffled from time to time. Daglæf himself sat like a man stricken, but looked up when he heard them in the doorway and welcomed them in.

'I'm so sorry, Daglæf, so sad...' said Edith as she sat down. Daglæf's father lay on a bed in the corner, covered with a cloak. Edith shuddered.

'I don't know what he was thinking, my lady Edith,' said Daglæf with such aching sorrow in his voice that tears stung Edith's eyes. 'He was an old man. He couldn't see well and could hear worse. He'd been a fighting man once, but he was old. It was a bold way to die, a death any man would be proud of, but there was no need for it.'

'He went out to fight them?' It seemed almost unbelievable.

'You know how it was last night, my lady, everyone shouting and running here and there. I was trying to get Bægswyth and the boys out of the house. My father had his sword with him, and I was glad he did, for he was to go with them and it was a weight off my mind that someone would be with them with more than a fork or shovel as a weapon. And as they were leaving I heard my father say, "I'm not running away from any Danes!" But I paid no heed to that, for he said a lot of things, as old men do. So I said to him, "You get Bægswyth and the boys into the forest, Father, and you have your sword if you need it." And I told them all to be quick and I ran off to look for the Danes myself. And I did find a Dane and fought him and wounded him too. My sword arm is still strong at least. Then Cynestan came and the Dane saw that he couldn't fight two of us at once, wounded as he was. All that was later, you see, as they were leaving. The other Danes were calling him and he made off before we could bring him down.'

'It was a bad wound you gave him,' said Cynestan. 'He may not live, not if it goes foul.'

'And all the time I thought my father was in the forest. But Bægswyth had lost him almost as soon as they left the house.'

'I looked for him, my lady,' wept Bægswyth, 'but it was so dark and I had to get the boys away.'

'You did right, you did right,' said Daglæf, his good arm round Bægswyth's shoulders. 'I don't think he even tried to follow you. I think he meant what he said and went looking for the Danes to fight them as he had when he was younger. But I didn't know that, my lady, not until morning. And then… then…'

Daglæf dropped his head and gripped his wife's shoulder tightly. Edith wiped away the tears that were trickling down her cheeks; no loud weeping, only tears that she couldn't stop from coming. There was nothing she could say. Sharing sorrow was the best that she could do.

'I found him by your father's cowshed, and he *had* found the Danes, or they had found him. And I think perhaps he wounded the one who brought him down. He still had his sword and there was blood on the tip, and I don't think it could have been his own.' At this Daglæf turned to his older son, 'That sword will be yours now, Bealdwulf, so mind you grow strong enough to wield it. Your grandfather would be proud of that.'

Then both boys began to weep loudly. Bægswyth rose to take them into her arms, and Edith knew it was time to leave. Outside she leaned against the wall.

'I don't know how to do this,' she said, mostly to herself, though she didn't care whether Cynestan heard her or not.

All that morning Brinin worked one-armed, dragging away fallen beams, anything that might help. And as he worked he watched out for faces: Ebba, Eawig, Wynith, Wulfrich, all alive and unwounded. The cold dread grew less with the sight of each one of them, but it was a wretched day. This household was whole, with everyone spared; that one was full of weeping with dead to bury. There were lives lost, beasts lost, buildings lost. And something else was lost too. What happened once could easily happen again. They were all like the wide-eyed children who had learned in the night what their mothers and fathers had feared.

The living were found, and the dead were found. Tears of joy blended with tears of sorrow. But no one knew where Eanflæd was. No one knew where she had hidden. No one could remember seeing her. More than once that day Brinin saw her father and brothers looking for her. He heard Eadulf asking his neighbours where they had hidden and if they had seen her. He heard Eanfrith call his sister's name, his shouts growing more fevered as the day went on. Brinin was by his hut late in the afternoon when her mother's wail rose above the other sounds of the village. Piercing, long, anguished, it was like nothing Brinin had ever heard before or wished to hear again. He knew the truth in his gut by then and not long after heard the news. Her brother had found her at the far end of the meadow, hidden among the shrubs and long grass. And she was dead.

WELCOME

It was already well into the morning when Oswald woke, lying on his back with his shield arm bound to his chest. He was alone, and it was good to lie in the stillness and listen to the sounds outside. Birds were chirruping as they nested in the eaves. Folk were talking too far off to hear what they said, then nearby a woman called out, 'Wulfstan, run and give this to your father.' And there was a thudding, soft and steady. It seemed to match the dull, throbbing ache in his shoulder. Oswald knew that sound, but now he couldn't think what it was.

He sat up and looked around him—that hurt a little though not as badly as he feared it might. There was another bed, narrower than his own. A long bench lay against the wall, fleeces strewn along the length of it for others to sleep on. A smaller bench was beside his bed; he thought he could remember his father sitting on it. There had been a fire in the hearth in the middle of the room, but it was little more than glowing embers now.

Outside the door, the earth was brown and worn down by all the feet that had trodden over it to reach the threshold. But the grass beyond the mud was rich and green with all the brightness of summer and it stretched away as far as he could see. The sky was blue. From where he sat, Oswald could make out the corner of another house away to the right. As he watched, a small boy—no more than six or seven winters—ran past the doorway without stopping or staring inside. He was barefooted and barelegged, wearing only a shirt that reached his knees. And Oswald had never seen him before in his life. Was *he* Wulfstan? There wasn't any boy in Oakdene with that name.

A jug sat on the table, and beside it was something hidden by a cloth. Oswald felt a sudden gnawing emptiness inside. He stood up, a little taken aback at how stiff and shaky he was, and made his way slowly to the table. Leaning against it to steady himself, he lifted the cloth. There was bread and butter beneath it. That was what he could hear; someone was churning butter outside. He took some and crept back to the bed to eat it.

He was about to lie down and sleep again when a shadow darkened the doorway. A man was standing there, a man unknown yet somehow half-remembered. Had he been in the camp with Oswald's uncle? And somewhere else too, unless he had only dreamed of a man like him. A woman was with him and a girl about as old as Edith. The girl was leading a smaller girl—no more than two winters old—by the hand. Perhaps these folk owned the house. Likely they had given up their bed for him. Oswald, weak though he was, began to rise, but the man lifted his hand to stop him.

'I can't let an ailing guest be on his feet to greet me, however young he is,' smiled the man. 'It's good to see you with your eyes open and sitting up, no less! It even looks as though you have eaten. It's good to see!'

'If you are the one who has welcomed me here, sir, then let me thank you,' said Oswald. 'I don't know where I am nor how I got here nor who the house belongs to. But I can see that someone has kindly given up their bed for me and I'm more than thankful for that. I do know that I was wounded and that I've been sick, though I seem to have forgotten almost all of it but a little here and there.'

'You have given us a few sleepless nights, not least your father who would barely leave your bedside to rest. But the worst seems to be over now and the end wasn't what we feared it might be. And now, at last, your father *is* resting. But it isn't kind of me to leave so much unanswered. My name is Godweard and I am a kinsman of your uncle, or rather of his wife whose father was more of a father to me than any man I have ever known. This *is* my house, but no one has given you their bed. It's a house I had built for guests.'

And now Oswald saw that it had to be a guest house. There were benches and beds, but it was wholly bare of all the little things that folk keep in a home; no tools, no cooking pots, no stores for the winter.

'This is Selethryth, my wife,' went on Godweard, 'and these are my first and lastborn children. Leoba is my eldest, and this is little Leofgifu.'

Leofgifu was staring at him, still clutching her sister's hand and half-hidden by her kirtle. Selethryth's greeting was as warm as her husband's. Leoba smiled with the unspeaking meekness that she had doubtless been taught was fitting, but her eyes flashed with something that left meekness far behind. They were quick, the kind of eyes it would be hard to hide from; eyes that could scorn a fool, love a friend or quell a foe without even a word needing to be said. Oswald felt suddenly at their mercy. He had barely seen Leoba while he spoke to her father; but she had been watching him and likely settling on whether he was to be a friend or only a fool. Oswald didn't know if he liked it.

'I think a little broth would be good for you,' said Selethryth. 'And we must tell your father that you are sitting up. Don't sit for *too* long, though. Come, girls.'

Leoba stooped down and lifted her sister into her arms. With one last look that seemed to ask again what kind of man Oswald was, she followed Selethryth out into the sunshine.

'My wife is wiser than I am,' said Godweard after they had left. 'I have kept you sitting too long. I'll stay until your father comes, but you *must* lie down.'

Oswald, already weary from such slight work, was glad to heed him, though he wouldn't have done it unless bidden to. Godweard took a seat on the bench beside him.

'Sir,' said Oswald, 'is there any news of the Danes? The last I remember they were holding the field, and we thought Wessex was lost.'

'There is both news and no news,' said Godweard, and his kind face seemed to darken. 'We have no hope at all of driving them out. For myself, I think I've known that in my heart for some time. But all is not lost. Yet. We have heard that the King wants to make peace with them and that he is going with some of his ealdormen to speak to their kings. Perhaps they are already speaking even now. Our news is some days old. It is not how we hoped this whole thing would end—it's rather shameful that we have been so overwhelmed by them—but it could have been much worse. And this new king of ours is shrewd, they say. Who knows what he has in mind? With peace and time to strengthen ourselves we may yet beat them, but if we keep fighting now we will surely be overrun.'

'So they might… they might leave?' Oswald was shocked at the sudden unsteadiness in his voice. Had he been snatched from a flood after watching his friends being swept away? 'Are you saying it might be over, sir?'

'Perhaps. For a time, at least. Your father still has a man with what is left of the fyrd to call us should we be needed, but our king is shrewd, as I said. And if he *does* make peace with them, I very much hope that, once you are strong enough, you and your father can go home.'

Home. How he had longed for it! Home, perhaps within a week or so—surely he would be strong enough by then—when Oakdene would be abloom with full summer. Home where the meadow and the hills, the trees and the fields would be all rich loveliness. Home to eat and sleep and live under his own thatch, by his own hearth where he belonged. Home to kin and friend. It almost seemed too much to hope for. Home in time for harvest, in time to keep his oath to Beorn. If Beorn had only lived through one more battle, through one more day… Had he been in sight of the end without reaching it?

'I don't know what to say, sir,' said Oswald at last. 'I can hardly believe it.'

'No more can I, yet that is what we've been told. Likely we will hear more soon. But I am *still* leaving much of what you asked at first unanswered. Forgive me! We brought you here after you were wounded because my house was nearer than either your father's or your uncle's. Can't you remember any of that?'

'I remember my uncle telling me to follow him from the battlefield, and a sudden pain in my shoulder. And I remember not knowing if I was cold or hot, and shivering and aching all over. Though perhaps that was *before* I was wounded. I've forgotten. And I remember being so weary that I wanted to lie down by the road and sleep, but my father wouldn't let me though I could barely sit on my horse.'

'You begged us more than once to let you lie down, and had we listened I doubt you'd be alive now to talk about it. We thought we'd lose you as it was. You were feverish, and we were very much afraid for you. Your father even had a priest come from a nearby minster to make you ready for death.'

'There was a woman, sir. At least, I think there was. I may have dreamed her.'

'Yes. Ansith. I believe it is thanks to God and the knowledge he gave her that you *are* still living. She lives here and has some skill with healing. She was the one who got the arrow out and cleaned the wound and treated it with honey. She kept telling us that she didn't think the fever was from the wound. Likely she was right.'

Oswald remembered some of that, foggily like a half-lost dream. He hadn't wholly forgotten the wild struggle and burning pain. The fever must have clouded his wits. He knew how to keep still, how to stifle his groans and set his teeth when he needed to. This arrow had not dealt him his first wound. Had he shamed himself by struggling like a frightened beast? He didn't remember the priest at all.

Before Godweard could shed more light on all that had been bewildering Oswald, Edrich came in, followed by Leoba with a steaming bowl in her hands. The sight of his father was another jolt. His cheeks were sunken, with dark shadows under his eyes. And this was *after* he had rested. Oswald eased himself up again to show his father that he could do it and perhaps lighten the burden that way. Besides, he would need to sit to eat whatever Leoba had brought.

Godweard rose to meet Edrich with as much warmth as he had shown Oswald. However wearisome these needy guests had been, his welcome wasn't growing any colder. And while Edrich and Godweard talked, Leoba—still swift-eyed and unspeaking—tended to Oswald. She shifted the bench a little nearer to the bed, then set the bowl and what was left of the bread and butter before him.

'Thank you,' said Oswald.

'I'm glad you're sitting up now. We all thought you would die.' Leoba looked down at him, not unfriendly but too steadily to put him at his ease. 'You ought to eat that while it's warm.'

Without another word she left with her father. Edrich stood until they were out of sight, then sank onto the other bed.

'Thank God you're getting better!' he said.

ANGER

Folk were gathered near the wreckage of the hall when Brinin reached them. They all talked at once, loud and heated and too many for Brinin to understand what even one of them was saying. He didn't see Eanflæd's mother anywhere, nor many women. Perhaps they had taken Sæthryth back to her house to weep with her there and tend to her dead daughter.

The babble dwindled a little when Eadulf began to speak. It was painful to hear him, as anguish and anger gushed side by side from his mouth, tears and rage on his face together. Eanflæd was not like the others, all men—or almost men—who had died fighting. Ceola was young, though enough of a man to stay and fight. But why had Eanflæd been chosen to die? A girl, young and no threat to the raiders? Brinin didn't like to think of the answer.

'Why didn't we slay more of them? Why only that one? Were we so weak? They're beasts, all of them! Worse than beasts, not men at all! The King should—'

Eadulf stopped without warning. At first Brinin thought it was only the weakening of a stricken father. But then he saw, chilled with the knowledge of it, that Eadulf's eyes had fallen on him, that all their eyes had turned to him.

'He's one of them!' Eadulf came towards Brinin, pointing at him, the anger all hatred now. 'He's one of them! Why is he alive, a beast like the rest of them? Why should a dog like that stand there unharmed while my daughter lies dead?'

Brinin took a step back. He would have been wiser to stay at his hut, wiser to keep out of sight. They didn't fully trust him here—he knew that. They didn't see him as their own. But surely they wouldn't blame him for *this*? Not when he was wounded as some of them were; not when he had helped keep some of their kin alive; not when he felt the anger and sorrow as much as any of them. Now wasn't the time to say any of that. How could he say that to a man with a dead daughter? They were all too angry for wisdom, but when they were cooler surely they would see that such words were an injustice. Surely their mistrust wouldn't stretch so far. Brinin turned to leave. Let the shock dull a little and they would remember that he was only their neighbour. But men stood behind him, all around him, shoulder to shoulder, penning him in. And he saw, with a sickening coldness in his gut, that there was no way out.

'Come now, Eadulf.' It was Cynestan, slow and carefully spoken as ever. 'You're angry, rightly angry. We all are. Better go home to your wife and say nothing now that you'll rue afterwards. You know he had nothing to do with it. You'll see that when you're cooler. What happened is dreadful, a dreadful thing, but those who did it are gone and no one here in Oakdene is to blame for it.'

'I *don't* know that he had nothing to do with it!' Eadulf almost spat the words back at Cynestan. 'Why are you so quick to speak for him when your son is dead too because of muck like him, and Daglæf's father, and others? How do you know he didn't help them? It was too dark to see. But we know he's a Dane, one of them and not one of us.'

If it had been unwise to speak, it was becoming rank folly to hold his tongue. Brinin opened his mouth, dry suddenly, to give Eadulf some words of sorrow, something to show them all that he had wished for none of this, but Eadulf didn't let him say anything. He sprung at him, swinging his fist into Brinin's face. There was no time to step aside or block it, barely time to see it coming. Brinin staggered back and fell, landing on his wounded arm.

'Why should that dog live when my daughter is dead? She's dead! And he lives!'

Eadulf made another rush to kick him. Brinin was ready for it, scrambling to his feet; but Daglæf stepped forward and pulled Eadulf away, his good arm strong and his grip tight. Someone helped Brinin up; another took his arm and held him back as though fearing he might fling himself at Eadulf with his own fists. Brinin's mouth was bleeding, or his nose or both. His whole face throbbed so that he hardly knew where Eadulf's fist had landed, but he could taste the blood. He tried to wipe it away, but it was hard to lift his wounded arm to do it, and a tight grasp held his other one. He saw then that it was Cynestan holding him, not letting go though Brinin wasn't struggling to fight. Tidræd stood to his left, Mildrith was nearby and Garulf and Eawig had stepped up behind him. Brinin didn't know which of their hands had helped him to his feet.

'We don't need any of that, Eadulf,' said Daglæf, soothing but still sounding like he meant to be heeded. 'No need to be so ready with your fists. Cynestan's right. Brinin had nothing to do with what happened here last night. He fought them off like the rest of us. He's wounded. Can't you see the blood on his shirt? My father's dead too, but I don't blame the lad for that. Come away now. Let me walk home with you.'

'Get off me!' Eadulf struggled, but Daglæf didn't let go. 'Are you all blind fools? He's a Dane! He even speaks their tongue. Why should we let a Dane live here among us?'

'There's only one fool here,' muttered Tidræd softly by Brinin's side, but his mother heard and pushed him sharply away.

'You hold your tongue!' she said. 'Better still, fetch the priest and the lady Edith too if you can find her, but if they're with Sæthryth don't bother them.'

Aculf stepped forward as Tidræd dashed away. He came and stood beside Eadulf. Brinin hadn't seen Aculf among the others. His mind was spinning too much to know who was there beyond those few who had already spoken. But Aculf was his old foe, and too keen to wound him to hold back.

'That girl was my wife's kin,' he said, 'and I know this Dane better than any of you. I know how cunning he is, though he's blinded Oswald Child and Oswald Child his father in turn.'

'I think Edrich Thegn is wise enough to choose whom he trusts, now that he's learned to be more careful!' snapped Cynestan.

Cynestan seldom spoke so bitingly. A sharpness had crept into his voice. He still didn't let go of Brinin's arm, and there was a hand on his shoulder now too. Brinin glanced down at it; it was an old hand, Garulf's. Pain shot from the wound as he raised his hand again to wipe away more blood. So much for keeping the arm still.

'We all know how much you dislike the lad, Aculf,' Cynestan went on, still sharp. 'Likely we needn't listen to anything you have to say about him.'

'I'm not ashamed of disliking him! I know what he is, and you would dislike him too if you knew him as I do!'

'Enough of this!' Brinin had never heard Cynestan raise his voice before, but he was angry now. 'Have you all forgotten the lad's father? I haven't, though he wasn't long among us. He was no more a Dane than any of us. I liked him. He was no fool, though he was a slave, and his son is like him.'

Cynestan's grip grew tighter as he spoke, and something tightened in Brinin's throat along with it. It made everything a little better to have a few to stand with him, two to speak for him, one to remember his father kindly as no one had done before. It made it a little better, but it couldn't make it much better; not when most of the village hated him for being a Dane and wished him dead. He saw on all their faces that they were with Eadulf. How could he live among them after this?

'No fool? Fool enough to wed a Dane!' Eadulf, still held by Daglæf, couldn't swing his fists now, but he had words to throw. Brinin did try to struggle forward then, anger hot inside, but Cynestan and Garulf pulled him back.

'And fool enough to let his Danish wife teach his sons her Danish tongue,' said Aculf. 'I've often heard that Dane speak with his brother when they thought no one was nearby to hear them. They were cunning. They thought we'd forget what they were if they hid it. But we haven't forgotten, have we? I didn't forget when I heard he'd been seen talking to one of the raiders, standing as near to him as I am to any of you. And the raider didn't kill him. Why would he kill another Dane who was likely helping him?'

'He wasn't helping them!' Wulfrich ran almost screaming into their midst. 'He wasn't! He—'

But Aculf met him with a sharp blow to the head that sent Wulfrich staggering away.

'Hold your tongue and get away from here!' he bellowed, raising his hand to strike again.

Wulfrich, holding his head, stumbled away a little but he didn't leave. He stood staring at Brinin, frightened, wide-eyed and near to tears. Brinin shook his head, warning him to say no more. This was not for boys, and later when he was home Aculf would make Wulfrich pay for what he'd said already.

Aculf had said enough, and Wulfrich's outburst couldn't help. Brinin saw how they were all looking at him; saw those who were unsure before beginning to think as the rest did. Only those few still trusted him and there was little they could do against the others. He *had* spoken to the Danes, more than once, and saved lives by it. But no one would believe the truth if he told them. They all already knew what they wanted to believe.

'Let me go,' said Brinin to Cynestan in a low voice. 'Let me go now. Perhaps they'll not be so angry when I'm out of sight.'

The anger would be no less—he didn't believe that even as he said it—but he wasn't going to stay there any longer. Cynestan let him walk away. Brinin didn't know if the other, angrier men would, but they all stepped aside as though he were filthy or rotting. One of them spat as he walked past. Brinin didn't see who it was and walked on as though he hadn't felt it. Eadulf was still struggling and shouting, Daglæf still holding him back.

'Oh, are you sneaking away like the dog you are, worse than a dog? Do you think we won't find you? Do you think you can hide from us? Why is my daughter dead when that Danish scum still lives? He should be dead, not her! Why isn't *he* dead? Why should we let that Dane live here among us?'

DARKNESS

Brinin sat in the darkness of his hut, only scant light slipping in to brighten the gloom. He didn't even light a fire. The cloth around his arm was sticky now as his wound bled afresh. His nose and mouth had stopped bleeding, though they were throbbing and swollen and his jaw was sore and stiff. But Brinin hardly cared about any of that. Thraldom had taught him that the bruises a man could see were seldom the worst kind. They always came with other, hidden wounds that didn't heal so quickly if they ever healed at all. Eadulf's fist hadn't dealt the heaviest blow.

He had been a fool to think, a fool to hope that he could ever live among these folk as one of them. He could never be one of them. He had always been on the edge; a slave, unseen, and a little too Danish to be welcomed. He had been born in the hut he sat in, but that had never been enough and now he knew that it never would be. Oswald's friendship wasn't enough either, nor even Edrich Thegn's goodwill. The mistrust had always been there like dry kindling ready to burn, waiting for one spark to set it alight. It had only taken one night, one dreadful night of Danes and death and torches, and now the mistrust had flared up into great leaping flames of hatred. He had been such a fool to hope that it could ever be any other way.

A field did not make him one with them, yet how could he walk away from it, away from his harvest and everything he had never hoped to have? How could he walk away? How could he leave the little friendship he had, friendship that came near to kin in Garulf and Oswald? He didn't know how to walk away, yet how could he stay? Perhaps it was folly to stay; folly to find some fearless pride to keep him boldly in his field until someone put a knife in him to rid them all of the Danish scum. And he was far from fearless now in the darkness; a little proud perhaps, but not bold. How could he stay? How could he go?

Brinin didn't know how long he sat there. He hardly even knew when the sun set. He was shaky again, weak and trembling. He hadn't eaten. He didn't know where to fetch his food from now that the hall was gone. He didn't want to leave his hut to ask.

Outside in the night, a light was coming towards the hut, hovering like a glow-worm. Brinin almost reached for a weapon, but his strength of will was too broken for that. And surely a foe would come upon him more stealthily, without a lamp to warn him.

'Are you there, my boy?' The light was near the door now, flickering into the face of Brother Wilfred as he held it.

'Yes, sir,' said Brinin, standing unsteadily to meet him as he stepped inside.

Brother Wilfred raised his lamp, casting its light about until he found a stool in the gloom. He sat with his lamp beside him on the floor. It shone oddly into his face.

'I've come to look at your arm again,' he said. 'Come into the light. I have salve and another cloth to bind it with. The salve will smart a good deal, but it will help the wound heal.'

Brinin pulled his stool nearer to the monk's and sat without speaking while Brother Wilfred carefully unwound the old bloodied cloth.

'It isn't any better,' said Brother Wilfred, lifting his lamp to peer at Brinin's arm. 'Rather worse, I think.'

'I fell on it, sir.'

Brinin saw Brother Wilfred's eyes dart from his arm to his face. Likely that told its own tale.

'Yes, I heard about that, my boy. Tidræd fetched me, but you had already gone.'

If Brother Wilfred had been there, he must know it all by now. There was no need to say anything more.

Brother Wilfred knelt on the floor and set his lamp on the stool. He said nothing as he saw to the wound, and the salve did smart a good deal. It was only when it was over and Brinin's arm was tightly bound that Brother Wilfred spoke again.

'The church is gone,' he said, 'and I need somewhere to sleep tonight. Would you let me sleep here?'

'Here, sir? You see what I have. I sleep on the floor.' Brinin pointed to the fleece thrown over a heap of moss and straw in the corner. 'There are better houses, sir, better places for you to sleep and anyone would welcome you.'

'I have slept on the floor before, my boy. That's a small thing.'

'You are welcome, sir, if you wish it, but surely—'

'Surely it would be wiser for me to be here with you than for you to sleep alone tonight.'

So that was what the monk was thinking. He didn't need somewhere to lie down. He wanted to be a shield against what might come in the night. Perhaps he too feared that now all the anger had been set loose something worse might come than spit, shouted hatred and a fist in the face.

'Don't sleep alone, my boy, not tonight.'

But tonight wouldn't be the only night. The anger wouldn't leave with the darkness. He wouldn't be less Danish in the morning. The raid wouldn't be forgotten. Eanflæd would still be dead. And the hatred would only grow as everyone talked about it and spurred each other on.

'How can I stay here, sir?' Brinin whispered. It was too hard to say it louder, almost too hard to say it at all.

'I don't know. I don't know. Yet where else can you go? Not to the minster, with the kingdom broken by war. Such a journey would be folly. For now, I think, we can only be careful and pray. Perhaps in time—'

'Brinin.' Eawig stood suddenly in the doorway, a darker shape against the darkness of the night. 'Mother has something for you to eat, and... Oh, I'm sorry, sir. I didn't see you.'

Brother Wilfred nodded for Eawig to go on.

'My grandfather wants you to sleep by our hearth tonight. He sent me to fetch you.'

'That's wise, don't you think, my boy?' said Brother Wilfred to Brinin. He rose with his lamp. 'It's better even than me sleeping here. We will find ways for you to be seldom alone while all this anger is still fresh.'

It was better than sitting in the darkness waiting for what might come. Brinin was beyond speech now, and not only because of the sore stiffness of his jaw or the throbbing of his lip. Even if he had words, they couldn't have found a path through the tightness in his throat. If Brother Wilfred and Garulf thought it was wise, he would heed them. Brinin lifted his fleece and walked to the door, but Brother Wilfred stooped down and gathered up his tools, handing them to Eawig.

'We won't leave anything here that you wouldn't wish to lose,' he said.

Ebba had been weeping. Brinin could see what was left of the tears. She stared, frightened, at his bruised and swollen face. Garulf was burdened by frowning weariness and Eawig stood restlessly by the door and didn't sit down. None of them had anything to say. What *was* there to say? Brinin did what he could with the food Wynith gave him, but he felt too sick now to want it and eating hurt.

When he shut his eyes, sleep did not come. There was no stillness of night. He seemed to hear shouting and screaming and heated, bitter, angry words. Raiders with weapons, glowing flames and men full of hatred rushed at him out of the darkness.

FEAR

It was a long night, and Edith slept fitfully. Lying beside Cenwyn, she woke many times. The first time, she sat up suddenly, not knowing where she was. She almost cried out, but remembered just in time. Once, she thought she heard wailing, but it was only Sæthryth's anguish creeping into her dreams and blending itself somehow with Ludan's white and wounded face. When the night was well spent, Tidwine slipped between her and Cenwyn. His small body warmed Edith's back as he slept. And she heard weeping, not from Cenwyn or Tidwine who were near her, but from one of the others; soft weeping that didn't want to be heard. Mildrith? Mærwyn? Tidræd? Oswyn? It could have been any of them, but Edith didn't know which and she didn't sit up to ask.

Before dawn, before even a chink of light could be seen outside, she gave up trying to sleep and sat up carefully so as not to wake the others. With the old cloak Cenwyn had lent her wrapped around her shoulders, she stared into the darkness and straightened out her thoughts. Tidwine moaned and stirred a little, but she put her hand on him to settle him again. Once the others were awake it would be a long time before she had stillness enough to think.

They would bury the dead that morning. She still didn't know what had happened to the Dane's body and kept forgetting to ask Cynestan about it, but they would bury their own. Their kin had made them ready. Cynestan had taken Ludan's body into his own house because the hall was gone and, he said, as workreeve it was right for him to do it.

Edith had known many burials; every year brought them, from the newly born to the old and everything in between. But seldom had there been more than two together, seldom more than one. Never before had the sorrow belonged so much to all of them, with weeping in every house. At first Edith had thought that Ludan's death came nearest to her, and that Ceola's was the most bitter because he was young like she was, and poor. His kin would have one fewer mouth to feed but also fewer strong hands to do the work. But when she had wept by Daglæf's hearth that had felt near and bitter too.

Then the wailing had begun, and the word about Eanflæd had spread swiftly from mouth to mouth. For the Danes to kill a weaponed man, Edith understood. It was time of war, and they were foes, raiders who had come to sow a little fear and bear off whatever wealth and beasts they could. All the men had died knowingly, fighting for their neighbours and kin. They had known what they were risking. But to kill Eanflæd—to kill her as they had—was nothing more than wickedness. Little wonder the blazing anger had leapt from house to house, more raging and harder to quench than the flames the Danes had left behind. Edith was angry too, and frightened. The Danes hadn't *chosen* Eanflæd. They hadn't sought her out or killed her before she killed them. What harm could she have done them? She was only a girl they had found in the dark. Any girl would have done. Eanflæd's end could have been that of any of them.

Eanflæd. No one could say how the Danes had found her. The talk of the night was so tangled that together it made no sense, and one tale seemed to call another a lie. Eanflæd, not a near friend but hard to dislike. Always cheerful, even when she had little reason to be. Sometimes foolish but never unkind, though Edith didn't know where she had learned kindness, there was so little of it among her kin. Eanflæd would have wed as soon as her father would let her. Edith knew that there had been more than one young man with his eye on her, though she didn't know which of them Eanflæd would have taken. She would have grown from a plump, flush-faced girl into a plump, red-faced mother, raising her children in a happier house than she herself had grown up in; cheerful, hardworking, foolish, talkative, kind, just as she had always been. Then in one night it had all been lost, and the young men were left as angry as Eanflæd's kin, and all the men of Oakdene with them. Eanflæd could have been their daughter, their sister, their mother, their wife. And all the women were angry because she could have been any of them.

Tidwine wriggled in his sleep, and Edith settled him again. It would be morning soon, and she didn't want to lose this dark stillness before she had to. The anger frightened her the most. It was a right anger. Right that Eadulf should want to find those Danes; right that the reckoning should be meted out on their own heads; right that they should pay for their wickedness. But they were gone, unknown, never to be found or seen again. Only God could mete out wrath now, but that wasn't enough for Eadulf or most of the village.

Brinin was too easy for them to see and too easy for them to hate, one half-Dane to stand for all the others. Edith hadn't asked him if he had spoken to the Danes, as folk were saying he had. She wouldn't ask. She wouldn't hint at mistrust when in her heart she knew what the truth must be. Brinin had spoken to the Danes in Readingum and wielded his tongue to save her father. Why shouldn't he have wielded it as a weapon in Oakdene?

Tidwine groaned a little. Edith could make out his open eyes through the darkness. He sat up beside her, still too sleepy to talk. The others would be awake soon. Tidwine wouldn't sit still like this for long.

Edith didn't know how to shield Brinin, how to keep this blazing anger away from him. It scared her. She could only pray that the flames would burn out and dwindle without taking too much with them. If only her father were here. It would be hard for even angry men to leave a word from him unheeded.

Tidwine scrambled up and went to wake his mother. Edith heard his feet as they padded across the floor. Morning. And time for the burials and work. There was so much to build up again, so much to mend. Would work, hard work that made them all sweat, be enough to make everyone forget the one they wanted to harm?

They were almost ready to leave when Cynestan came, blocking the light as he stood in the doorway.

'We're coming now,' said Edith. 'Are folk already gathering at the church—at what *was* the church?'

Cynestan nodded.

'Are they still angry?' Edith knew they would be, but what would their anger look like in the cold light of morning?

'There's no shouting this morning, my lady Edith,' Cynestan said grimly. 'But I can't say how it will be when folk see that girl put in the ground and watch her mother weep.'

They might hold their anger back until the last of the prayers was said. They might bridle it until then. But what about when they all scattered? What then?

'Afterwards, Cynestan, can we ask everyone to get to work straightaway? Not the kin of those who fell, but everyone else. Would they do that? You could gather the men in threes and fours with their households to help them, some working on one house and others on another. Osgyth and Tibba's houses are both gone, and they're widows. And we'll need a storehouse soon, with harvest coming. The hall is the least of our worries. It can wait. Would they do all that? Would they put their anger into their work and not... not elsewhere?'

'It can't do any harm to ask,' said Cynestan, though Edith didn't think he believed it. There was too much doubt in his eyes. 'I'll speak to them, my lady, and see what I can do. Now let's go and bury our dead.'

CRACKS

Brinin lay awake for the whole night. He was weary by morning, but he had settled on pride rather than flight. Not a bold, fearless pride—he knew fear enough, cool in the daylight—only an unshifting one. He had done nothing to shame himself. Why flee and throw away his livelihood? Why lose it because others were too angry and frightened for wisdom? He would be unshifting and work as though he didn't see or hear them. And if they harmed him… He wouldn't need a field when he was dead. While he was alive he did.

It was a wretched morning of weeping as they buried the dead. Brinin kept away. He would have liked to have gone for Daglæf, for Ludan; to stand nearby and hear the prayers. But it was better to keep away while they buried Eanflæd.

There was little work he could do until his wounded arm had more strength in it, so Brinin took a basket from Wynith and went into the forest, making his way towards the river. He knew he could find mushrooms there, and bruisewort, even strawberries—Ebba would like those—all good things he seldom had time to look for. It was a way to thank those who had been kind to him. As he left the village something hit him sharply on the back. It felt like a stone, but he had chosen not to see or hear so he didn't look back.

It didn't take long to find enough to fill the basket, and Brinin sat under a tree to watch the summer light in the leaves: oak and beech, willow bending low over the water. It was dark and shadowy beneath the trees, bright where the sun burst through them. It was good to sit there. Brinin was so tired he could easily have slept in the green stillness. After a time he wondered if he had. The light had changed from morning sunshine to afternoon, and he hadn't seen it happen.

Brinin met Eawig outside Garulf's hut. He was walking stiffly, and when Brinin was near enough he saw that one of his eyes was half-shut, dark like the bruisewort, and his lip swollen much like Brinin's own.

'Eawig!' he said. 'What's happened to you?'

'Nothing much.' Eawig fingered his lip a little gingerly. 'I was fighting.'

'Fighting! Why? Who with? Your grandfather and Cynestan won't like that when they hear of it.'

'Æfich,' said Eawig grimly and not sounding at all sorry about it. 'Don't worry. He likely looks worse than I do, and my grandfather and Cynestan already know about it.'

'But why?'

'He said something I didn't like, so I knocked him down.' Eawig walked away, muttering to himself as he left: 'And I'd do it again too!'

Brinin watched him as he trudged away, kicking crossly from time to time at anything in his way: a tuft of grass, a loose stone. Had the anger spilled over to the children now? Eawig never fought, not only because that was folly in a slave and years with Aculf as workreeve had taught them all to make themselves as unseen as they could. Eawig was mild, like Row had been, and not easily angered.

Brinin ducked through the doorway of the hut. There was no one there but Ebba, sitting on a stool by the fire to watch the pot.

'Did you see Eawig?' she asked unhappily.

'He told me he'd been fighting.'

'He *was*. I saw him. Æfich threw a stone at you—didn't you feel it? Eawig dropped his bucket and ran after him, and I ran too. Eawig said, "Why did you throw that?" And Æfich said he could throw a stone at a Dane if he liked and Eawig said, "Are you so scared that you throw stones at a man's back?" And Æfich shoved him and said, "You're only a slave. You can't tell me what to do." Then Eawig said, "If you throw another stone at him, I'll knock you down!" But Æfich only laughed and said, "Are you a Dane too?" And he said he was glad there was only one Dane in the village now and not two and he'll be even gladder when there are none. And Eawig hit him and knocked him down.'

The anger had spilled over, spreading everywhere. Instead of standing together to strengthen each other in their sorrow and fear, everything was cracking and breaking apart.

'So they fought?' Brinin was stiff, the words tight in his throat. For a child to be glad that Row had fallen to his death, that he had lain broken on the rocks, that Brinin had been left alone in the world... But he didn't want Eawig to fight for him.

'Yes! I didn't know what to do. And then Æfich's father came with a whip and started beating Eawig. So then I ran to find Grandfather but I didn't know where he was. But someone told Cynestan and he went and took the whip away from Deorstan and asked what he thought he was doing, beating another man's slave and if Eawig had done wrong he should speak to him. And Deorstan said, "I won't have a slave striking my son." Then Cynestan was angry with Eawig and asked him what he'd been doing, and Eawig told him everything. Then Cynestan said, "Go to your work now and I'll talk to you later." And Eawig went away but I was still watching. Deorstan said that Edrich Thegn's slaves didn't do such things when Aculf was workreeve. And Cynestan said—Cynestan was *very* angry—he said, "You would do better to see to your son and teach him not to throw stones." And Deorstan said something about you being a Dane, but Eawig told me not to tell you that. He told me not to tell you about Æfich wishing there were no Danes in the village, but I forgot. Cynestan threw the whip onto the ground and walked away.'

Brinin set down the basket. Ebba wasn't the one to hear what was in his mind, though he had heard so much of hers.

'Give these to your mother,' he said, turning back again to the door. 'And you can have the strawberries if you like.'

Brinin found Eawig in Edrich Thegn's swine pen, shovelling dung like that was a fight too.

'Eawig,' he said, 'don't get yourself into trouble on my behalf. There's no need for that.'

Eawig didn't look round at him. He dropped another shovelful of dung into the barrow, banging the shovel hard on the side as he did it.

'Ebba talks too much!' he said gruffly.

'You know how things are. It will always be worse for you in the end, even if you are the stronger one in a fight. Forget Æfich and don't see or hear him next time.'

'Cynestan wasn't very angry, not after I told him what happened. He only said that if I was going to get into fights he would have to beat me for it and that he didn't want to. Aculf would have let Deorstan beat me, then beat me worse himself afterwards.'

'Cynestan's right. *You* can't fight, whatever anyone does or says. You know that, and I don't want you doing it on my behalf.'

'Deorstan didn't even say a word to Æfich. He said he'd heard him yelling and that he'd soon make me yell and that he kept the whip for the hounds so it would do well for me. But I didn't yell. I kicked him hard a few times, and *he* yelled. And I didn't keep still enough to make it easy for him, though he held on too tight for me to get away.'

'You can't do that, Eawig. Cynestan might be kind, but you're no less a slave than you were when Aculf was workreeve. Do you think Edrich Thegn would have let you off so lightly if he'd been here?'

'If Edrich Thegn had been here, maybe he would have stopped them yesterday! He would have stopped them from saying what they said and doing what they did.'

'Edrich Thegn can't change what folk think—'

'Why did no one stop them?'

'Cynestan and Daglæf did what they could.'

'They didn't stop them and they didn't make them sorry. Someone should make them sorry!'

'But you can't, Eawig. So many things are wrong that we can do nothing about. That's how it is. And if *you* try to do anything you'll only make it worse for yourself and likely for your kin too. Don't see them or hear them and perhaps in time, when they aren't so angry and frightened, things may be better.'

'I don't care,' said Eawig. 'Someone should make them all sorry. And if Æfich does anything like that again, I'll fight him again. And I don't care what his father does or Cynestan or even Edrich Thegn! I'm away to the dung heap.'

Eawig strode away with the barrow, still too angry to listen to wisdom. There were cracks everywhere. Any peace or goodwill between neighbours had been too thin and brittle to withstand the coming of the Danes. The Danes had shattered it with their axes, and now the village was seeing what had always been underneath.

As he walked to his hut Brinin saw and heard everything he had told Eawig not to, all the bitter looks and muttered words. If there was no true goodwill between neighbours, they had been drawn together by one thing: that he was a Dane who didn't belong among them.

Something was wrong. Brinin knew before he even reached his hut. He had left the door shut, but it was open now, a gaping darkness in the doorway. He didn't want to look inside. He almost turned back and walked away, because he knew in his gut that Brother Wilfred and Garulf had been right to warn him not to sleep there alone.

Inside, everything was broken. The stools were smashed beyond any mending. They had no great worth in themselves, those stools, but his father and mother and Row had once sat on them. The ashes from the hearth had been kicked across the floor with the moss and straw he lay on and the sticks and the kindling from the woodpile. Everything was scattered and broken, and if his tools had been there they would have been broken too. In the door was a great crack, low down where someone's foot had kicked through it.

Once he would have said that only Aculf hated him enough for this; that others didn't much care but didn't wish him any harm. Now it was no good wondering who had come and left this brokenness behind them. Now it could have been almost anyone.

SUNSHINE

A dreamless night, a still morning and Oswald felt stronger. He even left his bed and ate at the little table with his father and uncle, and learned more of what he had missed during those dark days when his mind had been clouded by sleep, ache and fever. Now that his wits were back again, the sunshine had burst in. He learned that Sigulf had been sent to Oakdene with word of Beorn—that was done at least—and had come back with the news that all was well there. He learned more of his fever and the bewildering things he had said, of the sleepless nights his father and uncle had had and how well Ansith had cared for him. Oswald would likely have learned none of this if hadn't been for Hildræd his uncle with his easy and ready speech. If it had been left to his father it would have been buried with all the other things that were too hard to talk about, like Oswald's mother and what the Danes had done to him in Readingum. Oswald understood one thing about his father now: the more deeply he felt something, the less likely he was to speak it aloud.

'Godweard has been more than good to us, Hildræd,' said Edrich as they ate together. 'I have seldom been more thankful for a man in my life. And I'm thankful to you for knowing him and to your wife for being his kin! We need such ties more than ever.'

'Godweard would give you the shirt off his back if he thought it would do you good. I've known him since he was a boy of ten winters and I wasn't much younger than Oswald here. His mother sent him to her brother—Cenræd, my wife's father—and I was there when he came. Cenræd was a friend of my father and kept a big and busy household. My father would send me there from time to time to learn from him.' Hildræd poured himself a cup of ale and sat turning it round in his hands before he spoke again. 'Nothing was ever said about it, then or since, but I always wondered if she sent him not so much to learn in the household of his wealthier kin, as we were told, but to get him away from his father. I never met the man myself, but there was talk about him back then. Godweard was a frightened little thing at first, though it's hard to believe now. I remember turning to speak to him one day, and he started away from me like I was about to strike him. Another time, Cenræd was chiding him for some small misdeed—mildly now, as Cenræd was never an overly stern man—and the fear on Godweard's face was a sorry sight. All that soon passed though. I can say this: Cenræd had no love for his sister's husband. I overheard him speaking of him once. Godweard didn't leave Cenræd's house until both his mother and father were dead and he came back to be lord here. I've never heard him so much as speak his father's name, but he often speaks warmly of Cenræd. He says he owes him everything. They're alike in many ways, both open-handed, giving men.'

Oswald remembered Godweard speaking of his kinsman. Then it had seemed like warm fondness only; now more like the scars left behind when a wound has healed. But if Cenræd had indeed taught Godweard everything he knew, then Oswald too could now be thankful for him.

'If what you say is true,' said Edrich, 'then I can't say that I blame him. Some things in this life are best forgotten and the less they are spoken of the better. Now, Oswald, what will you do this afternoon? Will you rest again? Or will you go outside for a little while? I think that might be good for you. It's a fine day today.'

'I *would* like to go outside, Father,' said Oswald. 'It's hard to see the sunshine and to keep away from it. And I'm a little better today.'

'Go now then,' said Edrich, 'while you have the strength. But don't walk too far. Find somewhere to sit for a while.'

Outside the sun was warm and lovely. The smell of freshly mown grass hung everywhere. They must be making the hay in the meadow, wherever that was. The houses here were more scattered than in Oakdene, spread further apart. The biggest of them lay behind the guest house. That must be Godweard's house. His father had said it was nearby, and though it was smaller than the hall in Oakdene, it was bigger than anything else he could see. Outside one house, a woman and her daughters were spinning. Two of the girls combed the wool while their mother and sister spun it into long strands of yarn with their spindles. Far off to Oswald's left a man walked along pushing a barrow. Somewhere nearby a dog was barking. It was all so much like Oakdene, and yet so unlike it, that Oswald ached to be there.

There was a beech tree ahead of him, just far enough to make the short walk worthwhile. Beyond it, some boys had gathered to work on their bowmanship. Why not sit under the tree and watch them for a while?

The woman and her daughters smiled at him as he passed. Likely they had all heard of the wounded stranger in their midst. He reached the tree just in time to see a little boy scrambling down from among its spreading boughs. He stared at Oswald unsmilingly. There was nothing odd about that—he himself had stared at strangers as a boy—but hadn't he seen this boy somewhere before? The spinning woman called him—'Wulfstan'—and the boy dashed away. Oswald settled himself down, his back against the tree and his legs stretched out in front of him. It would be easy to fall asleep there on a day like this.

'Are you stronger today?'

Oswald looked up and saw Leoba standing watching him, unhindered by her little sister now.

'I think so,' he said. 'It's good to be outside. I've never much liked being indoors.'

'Those are my brothers. The one shooting now is Leofstan, and the smaller one with the blue shirt and curly hair is Leofmær.'

'Your brother's a good shot,' said Oswald, 'but he needs to lift his bow a little more.'

'I'll tell him. I can shoot too, you know. I'm as good as Leofstan though he doesn't like that at all! Do you have any brothers or sisters?'

'One younger sister, that's all.'

'What's she like?'

'About as old as you, I should think. She doesn't look much like me or my father, though her hair has the same hue as mine, and her eyes are like my father's. She's good at knowing what folk need or what they might be thinking. I think she's likely wiser than I am about most things, though she is younger.'

'You're an odd kind of brother!' Leoba laughed. It made those quick eyes wrinkle around the edges. 'I don't think either of my brothers would ever say that about me, and I'm older.'

'I learned the hard way,' said Oswald, though he straightaway wished he hadn't. Words like those seemed to beg Leoba to ask him to say more and he didn't want to. But she didn't ask. She only looked at him.

'Leofstan! Leofmær! Come! Father wants you,' she called.

Neither boy was happy to be called away but they came nonetheless, the smaller one glancing over his shoulder at the friends he was leaving behind.

'This is Father's guest,' she said, 'the one who was wounded by the Danes. He says you need to hold your bow up more, Leofstan.'

Leofstan scowled at his sister, but he eyed Oswald in a not unfriendly way.

'They told me it was an arrow wound,' he said. 'Was there much shooting then?'

'Only at the end,' said Oswald. 'It was mostly swords, spears and axes.'

'The boy shooting now,' said Leofstan, 'that's Dudwine. The Danes killed his older brother, and he's worried they'll all leave before he's old enough to fight them himself and pay them back for it.'

'I hope they do,' said Oswald. 'If they don't, we'll be utterly overrun.'

Leofstan said nothing to this, but he gave Oswald a look much like one of those his sharp-eyed sister seemed to have such a hoard of. Leoba shoved the smaller of her brothers to spur him on.

'Don't keep Father waiting,' she said, and all three of them began to walk away, but Leoba turned back to Oswald as she left. 'If you're well enough tomorrow, we'll show you round the village.'

Oswald, alone again, leaned back to drink in the sunshine and the smell of the grass. Was the sun shining in Oakdene that afternoon?

FATHERS

Oswald didn't leave the guest house at all the following day. In the morning Ansith came to tend to his wound and by the time she was done with him he didn't feel like going anywhere. She was older than he had thought she would be, with few words and hard, unsparing fingers. She cleaned the wound and rubbed on some sticky, sweet-smelling, smarting salve. He had thought he felt better until she began her work, but her hands didn't rest and showed him no mercy until she had done all she wanted. Oswald stiffened under her touch but wouldn't let himself do more than that. This time there could be no writhing or groaning, barely even a gasp if he could help it. This woman must see that, in his right wits, he could bear a wound as well as any man. And this time he must spare his father whatever he had watched before.

When she left, Oswald's head matched his shoulder throb for throb; but when a new morning came he was all the better for it, stronger if not happier. With so many dead, with Beorn's grey face and unseeing eyes so fresh in his mind, there could be no happiness. So much death, but no great victory. Oswald woke before dawn with the loss sitting heavy in his chest, and lay waiting for first light and listening to the birds outside and to the breathing of his father and uncle nearby.

Once he had asked Beorn what everything might be like when it was all over. They would go back to Oakdene, but to what? To make sure Ælfwyn had all she needed. Yet what would she want or need from him when she and her daughters had been doing all the work alone for all these months? She might need help with the threshing or ploughing, but what good would he be with work like that? Even if there was enough strength in his shoulder to learn—and there might not be for some time—surely his time would be better spent in finding someone who could do the work well. It was hard to know what he was going back to. Would he go to Brother Wilfred to learn Latin as he had done as a boy, as he had done at eleven winters, at fourteen winters, until he had been thrust into manhood and war?

On the battlefield he and his father had been men together, side by side under the same king and against the same foe. But at home his father would be lord and he would only be his son. Not a boy, but not yet what he had been taught to be. He couldn't lead or offer wisdom unasked, and he had almost none of the work that other grown sons in Oakdene filled their days with, no tilling the land, no tending the beasts. What *was* he going back to?

Oswald heard his father stirring in the other bed and saw his shape in the gloom, stretching and sitting up. A strip of light seeped under the door, but it was still dim inside. Edrich stood up and made his way to the door, opening it a little and brightening the room. Oswald saw that his uncle too was already awake, leaning on his elbow as he lay on the bench by the wall.

'Well then, Oswald,' said Edrich, sitting down on his bed again and running his hands through his hair. 'How are you this morning?'

'Better, I think, Father,' said Oswald as he sat up. 'It was easier to sleep yesterday, but I think I'll go out this morning and walk about a little.'

'I think he *does* look better, much better,' said Hildræd. 'Don't you think so, Edrich?'

'Perhaps he does, perhaps he does,' said Edrich, looking at his son so carefully that Oswald lowered his eyes. 'But take care not to do too much too soon, Oswald.'

Was that his father's way? Hadn't he driven himself for months through pain that he never spoke of? Oswald had seen it and wondered at it and hoped that he too would have such strength of mind. Yet here was his father warning him *not* to do what he had done himself.

'Father, do we know yet if we will be needed for battle again, or might we go home soon? Are we far from Oakdene here? I don't even know where we are.'

'I shouldn't think we are as much as a full day's ride from Oakdene, but we won't be doing it in a day and we won't be going for at least another week, perhaps two. Once I'm sure that you're strong enough for the road we'll go first to your uncle's. If you will welcome us, Hildræd'—a nod from

Hildræd—'then when you have rested for a day or two, we can ride on to Oakdene from there. We'll break the journey so you don't spend all your strength at once. But not for a week or two, not until you're stronger. That will also give us time to hear if the King *has* made peace with the Danes.'

'Father, I'm sure I'll be ready to go sooner than that. I rode all the way to the minster when—' But Oswald cut the words down before they could do any harm. He'd sworn to himself that *that* was not to be spoken of. 'And won't Edith… I mean, we've been away so long. Would it be kind to her to linger here longer than we must? When we were last in Oakdene she seemed so…'

But there was nothing on his father's face that welcomed this speech. He could see that his father was in no mood to listen to any thoughts that did not match his own.

'I'll hear no more talk like that, Oswald,' said Edrich, more sternly than Oswald had heard him speak for months. 'You seem to be unaware of how ill you have been and how much worry we have had. I have already settled in my mind what we will do and have nothing further to say about it. As for Edith, I told Sigulf to say nothing that would worry her needlessly. She doesn't know you've been unwell, and he told her that the King is speaking to the Danes. That will ease her mind for a while until we go to Oakdene ourselves. She has no grounds to be fearful for us. I have thought about what is best for you, and that is what we will do.'

Behind his father and unseen by him, Oswald's uncle caught his eye, shaking his head and warning him to say nothing more. Perhaps he didn't know that Oswald had learned that as a young boy. Knowing when to speak had been harder to learn.

'I've been waiting for you,' called Leofmær, dashing towards Oswald as soon as he stepped outside. 'My sister said I was to tell her when you came out. Don't go anywhere while I fetch her and my brother. She says we're going to take you round the village and show you everything. I don't know why! There's nothing much to see.'

He was away before Oswald could say a word and before long was back with his sister and older brother, Leofstan straggling sullenly behind the others.

'I thought you were sick again when we didn't see you yesterday,' said Leoba, 'but your uncle told us you were only resting. Do you feel better today?'

'Yes,' said Oswald, glancing back at Leofstan, but saying nothing. 'There's nothing much wrong with me that a little time won't put right. I think I'm well enough to go home, but my father doesn't want to yet.'

Perhaps Leoba had seen the look he had cast at her brother. She lowered her voice.

'Don't worry about Leofstan,' she said. 'He's angry because he didn't want to come but Father said he had to be kind to you because you're our guest and have been ill. Leofstan wanted to work on his bowmanship. He'll cheer up soon enough.'

'I don't mind what I do or who goes with me.' Oswald couldn't blame Leofstan. At thirteen winters he wouldn't have wanted to walk about with guests of his father whom he barely knew. 'I hope your father didn't scold him because of me.'

Leoba burst into sudden laughter that wholly changed her thoughtful face, brightening her eyes.

'I can see that you *are* a guest here! I don't know when my father last scolded anyone! When we were small children my mother sometimes said that he ought to be sterner so we wouldn't grow wild, but it's not his way to be stern so he left all that to her. This is the way to the meadow—they've made all the hay now. Leofstan! Leofmær! Come quicker!' Leoba lowered her voice again. 'I think my father's own father was very harsh. I don't *know*— he never speaks of him, only of his mother and her brother whose house my father lived in for years—but I've heard things sometimes. I think my grandfather was a *wicked* man!'

Leoba looked suddenly very fierce. What would Edith think of this girl? Edith found a way to like most folk; he had always been quicker to loathe. Leoba was swift-eyed like his sister, but she was more forthright. Was she too outspoken for Edith?

'You can see the whole village from here,' said Oswald, because he didn't know how to talk about wicked grandfathers. That was too unlike his own kin to understand well. 'The land must be higher. Our meadow is low lying but there are hills to the west of our village where you can see everything. I often go there.'

'It is higher here. I like it. Off to the south, that way, there's a minster. It's a women's house, and one of my father's sisters is there. And that's where the priest came from when we thought you would die.'

Leofmær was running around, snatching at something Oswald couldn't see, but Leofstan sat on the grass with his back to them.

'Does your father have many kin? His house seems very busy.'

'He raised one of his brothers and his two sisters after their mother and father died. They were still young children. The other brother stayed with their uncle. I never feel like my father's firstborn because *his* brother and sisters have always felt like brother and sisters to me. The younger of his sisters and I always shared a bed until she wed two winters ago, and I miss her. His brother was wounded at Æscesdun and died from the wounds, and it's like it was *my* brother who died.'

So much loss. Who in Wessex didn't feel it? Perhaps only those in far-off places, away from other men and the things that harmed them all. For the rest, if they hadn't lost kin, they had lost lord or neighbour or friend.

'Does your father let your brothers shoot here?' said Oswald at last, glancing again at the sullen Leofstan. 'I'd like to see them at it again. Would they fetch their bows and let me watch them for a while?'

Leofstan still didn't turn round, but Oswald saw him stirring a little. Likely he had been listening to everything they had been saying.

'Oh, Father won't mind if it's what *you* want to do. Leofmær! Run and fetch bows and arrows for you and Leofstan, and mine too. Tell Father it's what his guest wants so he'll let you take them.'

'I'll help him,' muttered Leofstan, as he scrambled to his feet to run after his brother.

'That was good of you!' said Leoba. '*Do* you want to watch them shoot?'

Oswald didn't. He didn't care if he watched them shoot or not. But he hadn't forgotten what it was like to be thirteen winters and have everything he wanted flouted by his father's wishes.

'I don't mind,' he said. 'Your father and mother have been kind to me. It's easy for me to do something your brothers would like.'

But somehow that was the wrong thing to say. Leoba's face clouded over and something flashed into her quick eyes. It wasn't anger. Oswald didn't know what it was.

'She *isn't* my mother,' she said. 'My father wed her after my mother died—she was a widow—and only the littlest girl is my sister. The other two are her daughters from before. She's a kind woman and I don't mind her, but she isn't my mother. She isn't anything like my mother, and I don't like it when folk call her my mother!'

'I'm sorry,' said Oswald. 'I didn't know.'

'I know you didn't. Why should you? I knew a girl whose stepmother hated her and always told the girl's father things so he'd be angry and perhaps whip her. Often what she said wasn't even true. The girl's grown now. She wed a man from another village and doesn't live here now. My stepmother isn't like that at all. She's always been kind to me and my brothers, and she's never favoured her own daughters over us. She's just the kind of good woman my father *would* wed. But she's not my mother.'

'When did your mother die?' asked Oswald. It seemed bold, but he didn't think Leoba would be easily wounded.

'Five winters ago, about this time of year.'

'So did mine,' said Oswald. 'Five winters ago, just after the haymaking. But my father hasn't taken another wife.'

In the sunshine that morning, doing something he loved—or rather watching others do it—Oswald almost forgot lost friends, aching sorrow and his longing for home. Leoba was a better shot than either of her brothers. Oswald didn't say that, not with Leofstan standing by to hear. Likely she wouldn't be better for much longer. Leofstan would soon pass her in height and strength. Oswald praised him and shared some of Thurstan's ready wisdom; it was a strange and slightly painful thing to hear Thurstan's words on his own lips. Leofstan soon thawed towards him, and by the time they saw Hildræd coming across the meadow he seemed to think of Oswald as a friend. Oswald knew Leoba had seen it too and that it made her happy. He liked that.

'I should go now,' said Oswald, the sight of his uncle reminding him of his father's warning. 'But perhaps we can do this again before I go. Thank you for showing me your village.'

'Do you feel better for a little time outside?' said Hildræd, turning back towards the guest house when Oswald reached him.

'Much better, sir. I don't think I'm ill any more. Not as strong as before, but surely that will come.'

'In time, no doubt, in time.' Hildræd put his hand on Oswald's shoulder as they walked along and leaned a little towards him. 'Let me speak plainly to you, Oswald, while we're alone. I could see you were bristling a little earlier and that you think your father is being overcareful. I understand, my boy, truly I do. In your place I would bristle too. But give him what he wants and don't push back too much against it. Likely you weren't going to—you've never been wilful—but I thought there was no harm in speaking to you about it. There were a few days when we feared we might lose you, and your father was greatly distressed. Give him what he wants now, whether you think it's needful or not.'

Oswald had been doing what his father wanted all his life, yet it felt so wrong to do it now. Why let them all behave like he was weak? He hated it and wanted them to see how strong he could be. But his uncle was earnest, and he knew that heeding his father was the only thing his father would let him do.

'Was it bad then, sir?' he said. 'When I was ill?'

'You know your father has never been a man to speak his heart openly to anyone. Yet in these last few days I think I heard more than I have in all the years I have known him. And that's a long time. This care he is taking now, which seems so burdensome to you, is another way of him saying some of what he said to me while you knew nothing of what was happening around you. Remember that for days he thought he was going to lose his only son—for months, if the truth be told, for don't we ready ourselves for such things every time we go into battle? Remember that and bear the burden. That's also a kind of strength, you know.'

There was something in Hildræd's voice that stung Oswald's eyes a little, and he saw again his uncle's stricken face as Alrich died in his arms. Somehow his father had been spared all that while others—no worthier—must live with it.

'I do understand, sir,' he said. 'I was going to do what he asked and not say much about it. That's always been the only way with my father, you know.'

'Good lad,' said Hildræd, patting him on the back. 'I thought you would. Now Godweard has food for us at his table. Come and eat some of it.'

HOOVES

Godweard's house was busier than any other Oswald had known. It was a house without a still corner. Godweard might be lord in this village, richer than any other man who lived there, but his house was as full as his neighbours'. His many children all shared beds, keeping each other warm at night. His many guests found seats at his table, their elbows rubbing against those of the men beside them. The many men and women who worked for him—Oswald could barely tell if they were slaves or not—bustled in and out all day. And the hustle never seemed to stop.

There was a friendly warmth to the household, with as much happiness as any of them could hope for in such times. Oswald felt it all around him as he sat with his father and uncle, taking evening-meat at Godweard's table, much as he felt the heat of the fire, smelt the roasting meat and listened to the blend of work and speech everywhere. Godweard spoke to Edrich and Hildræd of what might come of the King talking to the Danes, but Oswald only half-heard them. Leoba, with the meekness that Oswald knew slipped away when her elders were out of sight, filled their cups so they never ran out of ale.

'Well, Edrich, my son tells me that young Oswald was a great help to him yesterday when he was working on his bowmanship,' said Godweard. 'And without so much as handling a bow himself. He must have a sharp eye.'

'He *is* a good bowman, and ought to be. He was taught by one of the best.' Oswald started a little at this sudden praise from his father. 'But you should see him throw a spear. That is what he's truly skilled at.'

'Perhaps another time, when his wound is fully healed. My son would like that too.' Godweard held out his cup to his daughter. 'Thank you, my dear. Do our guests need more to drink? I trust that—'

A pounding of hooves outside, near, very near, almost upon them, right at the threshold. Godweard leapt up and ran to the doorway. They were all on their feet. All work, all eating, all drinking stopped. Every tongue was stilled. Such a hush fell on the house that for the first time that evening Oswald could hear the crackle of the fire in the hearth. The pounding stopped. A man, dusty and windswept, burst into their midst.

'My lord!' he gasped. 'My lord! The King has made peace with the Danes. They're withdrawing to East Anglia or Lundenwic or some such place. Some have already gone.'

The hush was gone at once. A babble rose again even louder than before. Oswald's father and uncle gathered round the rider with Godweard, talking swiftly and earnestly and all at the same time. Leofstan was at his father's side, listening keenly to everything the men were saying. But Oswald stood by the table. His hands were shaking a little, and he didn't know why; his heart pounding as the hooves had pounded outside. Had hope, left crushed on the battlefield at Wiltun, risen from the dead and stridden in among them?

He saw suddenly that Leoba was beside him, still holding the jug she had been about to empty into her father's cup. She stood unspeaking, unshifting, staring straight ahead with tears streaming down her cheeks. Oswald took the jug and poured a cup of ale for her, thrusting it into her hands.

'Drink this,' he said.

She sat down and sipped the ale, wiping away her tears.

'I don't know why I'm weeping,' she said. 'I almost never weep—not when others are around to see—but I can't help it. I thought of my father's brother and how, when we were small children and he was a bigger boy, he would crawl around on the floor—just over there—and let us sit on his back like we were riding a horse. And of his widow and their little girl who won't even remember him when she's older. And of all those weeks when we were tending his wounds and he was in so much pain. Even Ansith could do nothing for him, and I don't think there's a leech in Wessex who's a better healer than she is. By the end he was so feverish he didn't know who we were. What was the good of him standing against the Danes and fighting them and dying for it, if all it took to make them leave was the King *talking* to them? What was the good of it all? There! I'm beginning all over again. I *hate* weeping!'

Leoba wiped her eyes again and took another drink. Was this what Edith would have asked if *he* had fallen? What was the good of it all? Was this what Mildrith would say when the news reached her? Was this what Ælfwyn and her daughters would say? What Osgyth and Tibba, Cynestan and Wynflæd would say? What *had* been the good of it all?

'Don't think like that,' he said, sitting down beside her. 'You'll drive yourself mad if you do. Think of Northumbria and East Anglia. There they were wholly overrun by the Danes. If we hadn't stood against them from the beginning perhaps they would have overrun us in Wessex too. When the Danes came there were twelve of us from our village to fight them, and only six of us are left alive, two of them too wounded ever to fight again. I watched my kinsman die—Hildræd my uncle's oldest son—and on the day I was wounded, a friend died in my arms while the Danes taunted us and drove us from the battlefield. His mother has lost both her husband and her only son. And we lost Thurstan, my father's friend since they were boys and one of the best men I've ever known. Was it all for nothing? I can't believe it was or that talk alone would have been enough to drive them out. I won't *let* myself believe that! We may not have won a great victory, but the King could never have made peace now if we hadn't withstood them all these months. If we hadn't withstood them, Wessex would have been utterly lost and the King likely murdered like Edmund the King of the East Angles. And isn't it a greater thing to keep fighting against a stronger foe when all seems lost? Isn't it when our strength grows weak that we need bolder hearts? So don't ask what the good of it all was. Instead thank God that he kept us strong enough to withstand them for so long; that he gave us these men, your kin and mine, and our friends who were ready to die fighting them; and that he gave us a king wise enough to make peace now before we *were* all lost.'

'Amen, my boy!'

Hildræd put a hand on Oswald's shoulder, and Oswald saw that his father, uncle and Godweard had all come back to the table and were standing beside them, listening. Leoba sprang up and scuttled away—perhaps she didn't want anyone else to see her tears—but she smiled at Oswald as she left.

'Your son's wisdom belies his youth, Edrich,' said Godweard as they took their seats again.

'Isn't wisdom what we all need in such times?' said Edrich. 'Well, Oswald. Perhaps now we may think of home. In a few more days we'll see if you're strong enough for the road.'

BROKEN

Early in the morning, Cynestan and Garulf came with the faces of men bearing news of the dead. Brinin's gut sickened a little when he saw them, he who had no more dead left to bury. It couldn't be Eawig or Ebba or Wynith, or Garulf would be mourning with his kin, not walking towards him ready to strengthen another man in his sorrow. Who then? Had word come from outside? Oswald, wounded or worse? That blow would wound him like the loss of a brother. He had toughened his mind for it these last months, but when was anyone ever ready? He didn't run to meet them and ask what it was all about. Bad news had a way of finding a man whether he ran to it or not. Perhaps the lady Edith was already weeping somewhere.

'You'd better come,' said Cynestan when they reached him. 'There's been bad work in the night.'

'What kind of bad work?'

'Easier to show you than to tell you.' Cynestan shook his head. 'It's a bad business.'

Garulf said nothing, but he walked beside Brinin with his hand on his shoulder like that night when Eanflæd had been found and all the hatred had simmered over. A bad business? But likely not a death. They were hardly leading him to show him a body.

There was a crowd by his field, already scattering. None of them met his eyes, and only Mildrith showed him any pity. She reached out, motherlike, and touched his arm as she passed him.

'I'll tell the lady Edith,' she said. 'You haven't spoken to her yet, have you, Cynestan?'

'Not yet,' said Cynestan. 'Bad work. I've never seen anything like it.'

The last few bystanders turned their backs and walked away as Brinin reached them, and he saw what the darkness had brought. Everything was broken, spread about like the dead on a battlefield. Not a stalk of wheat still stood. It lay everywhere, uprooted and crushed, headless and leafless, cut down too soon like boys who never learned to be men. The kernels, still green and unripe, were torn and flattened, and his hopes with them. All his dreams of gathering in a free harvest—his own harvest—of laying aside seed for another, of eating his own bread, all those dreams lay dead and rotting. Birds were already swooping down to feast on the pickings of his harvest and hopes. All around the edge of his field Edrich Thegn's wheat stood tall and unharmed, unbreachable like the Danes' earthen wall. And it rippled in the breeze, fresh and green in the morning light.

'You can see it was no mishap, lad,' said Garulf, his hand still on Brinin's shoulder.

Brinin nodded. A beast couldn't have done it. An unknown foe wouldn't have stopped before they cut down Edrich Thegn's wheat too. Better if it had been an unknown foe. The knowledge that others bore it too would have dulled the worst of the smart. War was war and it struck blindly. If one man was spared, another was not. But this foe had come in the night because he knew Brinin. He knew him and hated him.

'Listen, Brinin,' said Cynestan. Brinin dragged his gaze away from what had once been his crop. Cynestan's face was grim, angrier than Brinin had even seen it. 'Nothing is ever done here without someone knowing about it. Even if no one saw anything last night, someone might know who was out of their house. Someone might have heard something—even a stray word—that will tell us who did this. Folk have forgotten the little sense they had after all that has happened here this last week. But give it time. Give it time. I'll find the man out. I'll not rest until I do.'

Brinin's mouth was too dry for speech. He swallowed to find some spit to make the words with.

'It can't have been only one man,' he said at last. 'The nights are too short for one man to have done it alone. There's nothing left!'

'Mildrith told me!' Edith, with flushed cheeks, came running towards them. 'Who did this?'

'We don't know yet, my lady,' said Cynestan, 'but we'll find out.'

'We must! To do such a thing! If my father were here… They would never have dared if my father had been here!'

But he wasn't. Edrich Thegn with all his thankful kindness might never be among them again. And if this man—or men—had not been afraid to do such a wicked thing, had felt no shame at the thought of his neighbours knowing, would fear of his lord have stopped him? And how *were* they going to find out? Brinin had watched how the crowd had melted away with barely a look of friendship among them. Which of them would break trust with his neighbour for the sake of the Dane in their midst? And how would knowing help? His harvest was gone. Even if he picked through the whole field for a few ripe heads of grain, there would never be enough for even a day's bread. What would he eat? What would he plant?

Brinin looked at them again—at Cynestan, Garulf, Edith—with their pity, anger and friendship. The birds were still feasting on his field, but he had no will to drive them away. And the sky was dull. There would be rain that day. If anything was to be saved, it would need to be gathered quickly.

'Can you lend me a barrow, Cynestan?' he said, his mouth still dry. 'What's left might do for someone's beasts. No good letting it rot in the field.'

'Take anything of mine you need,' said Cynestan. 'No need to ask.'

Folk stared at him as he walked back to his hut, their faces all hard and unsmiling as though he had done the wrong himself. Two boys laughed, and one muttered something to the other, only to find himself leapt upon by Tidræd who knocked him to the ground. They rolled and pounded at each other in the dirt.

In his hut he hardly knew what tools he needed for so bleak a work. A bucket for anything worth keeping? A fork to scoop the rest into the barrow? He caught sight of the flail he had so carefully made, working on it each evening and lovingly smoothing the wood. All lost. Something heavy and hard and dead sat in his chest and throat, stuck and unshifting. How would he make it through the winter with no harvest? All lost.

He went back to his field the lonely way, along the western edge of the village away from the staring eyes. Kneeling in one corner he plucked up a kernel and ground it between his teeth. Much too soft to be worth saving and the rest would be the same. Even if he dried it by the fire or roasted it, he wouldn't get any bread from it. It was fit only for beasts. For birds to peck at and cows and swine to lie on.

Brinin took up his fork and began to toss his broken harvest into the barrow. A harvest fit for beasts and he had no beast to give it to. It was worthless to him. Cynestan could have it, and Edrich Thegn and Mildrith and Daglæf. Those few households had offered him a little friendship and they could split his worthless wheat between them.

He'd filled four or five barrowloads, tipping them into a heap at the edge of the field when the rain started. Unsparing, it drenched him and drowned any lingering hopes in mud. Brinin was leaning on his fork staring at Edrich Thegn's healthy green wheat, when he heard a sound from the barrow beside him. And there was Ebba, kneeling nearby as she gathered the bruised stalks in her arms to drop into the barrow. The sight of her stung Brinin's eyes somehow, he who never wept, who could only remember weeping once since he was a small boy. Strange how the kindness of a child could almost bring him to it.

'You shouldn't be here,' he said hoarsely. 'You'll be scolded if they find you away from your work.'

'Cynestan said I could help you.'

'But it's so wet. Better find some indoor work for now.'

Ebba only shrugged and dropped her little bundle into the barrow.

'I don't mind,' she said.

They worked side by side, odd-looking fellows at odd-looking work. But the clouds only grew darker, the rain heavier and the field muddier beneath their feet.

'It's no good,' sighed Brinin at last. 'There's nothing to save now it's all so wet. Go in and get yourself warm and dry again.'

Ebba said nothing. She stood with chattering teeth, clutching a bundle of wheat with muddy hands, her face tight and fierce as the rain dripped from her sodden hair and down her cheeks. Then suddenly she threw the bundle to the ground and flung her arms round Brinin.

'I hate them!' came her muffled voice from somewhere down by his chest. 'I hate them all! And if I was bigger, I'd find out who did it and make them pay you for it!'

Then she ran, stumbling away through the mud until other men's spared crops hid her from sight.

Back at his hut, Brinin tossed aside his fork and lit a fire. Shivering, he dropped onto the floor beside it. In the corner lay the broken stools that he couldn't mend but couldn't bring himself to burn. His face hidden in his hands, he sat unmoving while the rain from his clothes grew into a puddle around him.

UNFALTERING

Edith almost flung herself through Mildrith's doorway, too angry to walk or slow down or hold back. Mærwyn, as ever, sat at her loom, Cenwyn on a stool by the hearth shelling peas for the pot. But Mildrith was walking to and fro, neither working nor speaking. None of the children were in the house.

'Whoever did this…' gasped Edith, still breathless from her swift bolt from the fields. 'Whoever dared… When I know… I won't wait for my father to come back. I'll have the Moot called and I'll see Brinin is paid for every stalk. It's theft! Worse than theft as they've left his whole crop worthless! Would they have dared to do such a thing had my father been here? I'll see that the man is shamed for it! All his neighbours will know what a shameful man is living in their midst!'

'It's a wicked, wicked thing!' said Mildrith. 'Folk are losing their wits since the Danes came!'

Edith sat down near Cenwyn to help her with the peas, but she had only shelled a few before she was on her feet again. Her hands were trembling a little, and she folded her arms tightly across her chest to steady them.

'Doesn't anyone know who did it?' said Cenwyn. 'Surely someone must have seen something!'

'Cynestan says no one knows.' Edith began walking about like Mildrith, too driven by anger to stand still. 'I don't know what to do! And if someone would do this, what else might they do? What if someone—'

The door burst open and flew back against the wall, and Tidræd strode into the house. His shirt was muddy and torn. One of his cheeks was darkening, and a trickle of blood ran from his nose. More blood

197

was smeared across his face. He wiped his nose again as he stood there, scowling as though daring any of them to say a word.

'What have you been doing?' Mildrith, angry already, snapped now.

Tidræd didn't bow his head or step back. He met his mother's eye without the slightest shadow of shame or fear.

'Fighting,' he said.

A quick glance passed between Cenwyn and Mærwyn. Mærwyn had stopped weaving, though her hands were still raised to the loom. There was some old tale here, the unforgotten beginnings of something that Edith had missed but knew she didn't want to see the end of. She thought of slipping away to let it work out its end without her, but Tidræd was between her and the door.

'After the last time?' Mildrith's voice was low, slow and steady and the more frightening for it. Edith didn't know how Tidræd was still unfaltering before her. Why did he have to be troublesome on a morning when everyone was already angry? 'After I warned you? Did you forget what I said to you then?'

'No, Mother, I didn't forget,' said Tidræd, as steadily as Mildrith and with a bolder look than Edith had ever seen. 'I was thinking about what you said when I hit Æfæd, but I thought I'd better not heed you when *he* said that he'd never been happier to see a wrecked harvest and wished he'd thought of wrecking it himself.'

'I hope you hit him hard,' muttered Cenwyn, so softly as to be almost unheard. But Edith heard it and shocked herself by thinking the words after her, she who'd never even thought of striking anyone in her life.

'So I fought him and I won too, though he's bigger than me,' went on Tidræd. There was still no shame. He looked straight at his mother and barely even blinked. 'Shall I fetch you a stick then, Mother?'

Edith heard a small choking sound. Cenwyn's head was lowered, and her shoulders were shaking. Surely she wasn't laughing! At such a time! Mildrith seemed to be struggling with herself. She still glared at Tidræd, but her mouth was twitching.

'Oh, go and clean that blood off your face!' Mildrith threw up her hands. 'Then get to work! Must it wait all day while you fight and squabble?'

Tidræd did blink then. This didn't seem to be the answer he had readied himself for. He didn't smile but his scowl softened a little, and some of the boldness melted away from his eyes. A look of understanding passed between him and his mother, and he left the house without another word.

'I don't know what I'm going to do with that boy!' Mildrith sank onto a bench. 'I can't even scold him, much less beat him, though I did warn him before. Not when I'm as angry as he is. And if Æfæd were a son of mine…'

'I'd rather have ten Tidræds than Æfæd, for all his mother keeps saying how good he's always been and how she and his father have seldom had to scold him. He might be better if they'd scolded him a bit more! And he *is* bigger than Tidræd.' There was pride in Cenwyn's voice. 'Æfæd's not much younger than me. And had I been there to hear him, I'd have wanted to fight him too and I wouldn't have stopped Tidræd from doing it!'

Mildrith cast an unspoken chide at her daughter, but said nothing.

'What makes it worse,' said Mærwyn, 'is that it isn't only the children. The men and women might take more care over what they say aloud and who is nearby to hear them, but they're thinking it all the same. Did you see them this morning? Almost none of them were sorry, only a few. That's where the children are learning it. Don't blame Æfæd, Cenwyn. Blame his father and mother and every other man and woman in Oakdene who thinks what Æfæd said.'

'How can they all behave so to that boy?' Mildrith was on her feet again, too restless to keep sitting. 'Oh, I know he's more or less a man, but he's young and without father or mother or any other kin, all alone. And he's done no harm to any of them, and more than enough good to some. Whoever did this ought to be ashamed to lift their head or to set foot outside their house. And those that are happy it was done ought to be ashamed too!'

Their anger stilled Edith a little. She heard it in Mildrith and Cenwyn's swift and biting words, and even in Mærwyn's softly spoken wisdom. And as for Tidræd, his anger was all reckless boldness that cared little for what the end would be, least of all for himself. But Edith must care. Their anger bridled hers; she mustn't let it run wild. She must hold it back and think.

'This isn't the first fight among the children because of Brinin,' she said. 'On the day of the burials, Æfich threw a stone at him, and Deorstan didn't care. I heard about it from Cynestan because Eawig did the fighting that time. And now Æfich's older brother says this! Mærwyn's right. They're learning it from their mothers and fathers. There's no love for Brinin in Deorstan's house. I'll start there. But, Mildrith, is it wise to go from house to house or is there a better way?'

'Go from house to house,' said Mildrith, 'but don't let folk see that's what you're doing and don't see them all in one day. If they know why you're speaking to them they won't say a word. And talk mainly to the women because they'll speak to you more freely and may have seen or heard more. And I'll do the same. There's much you can learn from your neighbours if you say little and listen well.'

'Then I'll begin with Deorstan, or rather with Godflæd.' Edith sighed. 'But not yet. I need to be alone first.'

Mærwyn leant round the from her loom and peered outside through the open door.

'It's raining,' she said.

Edith had neither seen nor heard the rain before, but she heard it now and saw it dripping from the thatch above the doorway and gathering into a muddy puddle beyond the threshold.

'I'll find myself somewhere to sit,' she said.

Edith dashed away to the nearest tree, one of the many oaks of Oakdene with broad and spreading boughs. It grew only a little way up the hillside so she didn't have to make her way too far through the gathering mud. She huddled under it, her back against the bole, cold but dry enough in a still little haven while the lashing rain poured from the leaves just beyond her reach.

The swift wild anger was melting away now, but all it left behind was a kind of hopelessness. She had once thought that fear might draw them all nearer to one another in Oakdene, that folk might forget their little tussles and stand together against a shared foe. But now that the foe had come and they had all tasted the fear, sorrow and loss together, hatred had sprung up from what was left. That was what they shared now. There had always been some dislike between neighbours. Men had got into fights—sometimes bad ones—and women had turned away from one another and would not speak. Sometimes her father had stepped in before the troubles spread and grew into something worse. The children had always fought from time to time, though their battles had seldom had much to do with those of their elders. But there had been nothing like this before.

Edith had said that this unknown man would never have dared to do such a thing if her father had been among them. And she had believed it. But what could her father have done? He couldn't have looked into the man's mind and found out what he was plotting. He couldn't have seen what was done in the dark any more than she could. And why would the man fear his lord if he hadn't feared the shame he would bring on himself if his neighbours learned what he had done? Why should he fear her father who couldn't know hidden thoughts or see in the dark, when he hadn't feared God who could? She had only been saying what she wished for: that her father would come home and make it all stop. But what could he do if he did come? Could he know the truth or make Brinin's harvest spring up again overnight? What could he do that *she* couldn't?

Yet she was faltering and she hardly knew why. What was the worst that could come of it if she dug up the truth? Learning that someone she liked had done something she hated? And wasn't that better than not knowing at all, or wondering if everyone she spoke to was the guilty one? Folk wouldn't speak to her father freely about such things. He was their thegn and he wielded the law. Most folk thought that *she* was only a girl; her father's daughter but too young to be much of a threat. Yet she had eyes and ears that were better than most, and she would put them to work. She would meet the thing as Tidræd had met his mother: eye to eye and unfaltering.

HOUSEHOLDS

As soon as the rain had eased into a light sprinkling, Edith left the shelter of the tree and made her way to Deorstan's house. As she reached it, Godflæd came to the doorway with a bucket that she emptied outside onto the already sodden grass.

'Oh, my lady Edith!' she said, wiping her hands on her kirtle. 'I didn't see you! I hope I didn't get you wet!'

'No, no. Though it *is* hard to stay dry today.'

'Indeed, my lady, what a morning it's been! I haven't done even half of what I wanted to do.' Godflæd called sharply into the darkness of the house. 'Æffe! Didn't you hear me tell you to put more wood on the fire? Be quick about it! Then sweep the floor. Yes, what a morning it's been. And what a thing was done in the night! Here in Oakdene! Now I don't say I didn't think something of the kind might happen, my lady—folk are still angry about that poor girl—but to cut down a whole harvest like that! What a thing! All that wheat gone when there are those among us who worry every year if they'll have enough to get them through the winter. A dreadful thing! I said as much to Deorstan.'

Godflæd was careful. She said nothing on Brinin's behalf—there was none of Mildrith's angry pity—but she didn't say much against him either. Beyond speaking of Eanflæd's death in the same breath as the lost harvest, she said nothing about him at all. She stood, shaking her head, and seemed truly shocked that a whole crop should be left to rot. Yet it was almost as though she thought the wheat had sprung up on its own; as though the field was without an owner, as though no back had strained to plough it, no hands had tilled it, no brow sweated over it, as though no belly would now be left empty. There was shock, but no neighbourly feeling.

'You must have been shocked when you heard.' Edith could be careful too. There must be no blame, not if she wanted Godflæd to speak freely. Besides, could Godflæd have done it? It didn't seem like the work of a woman.

'Oh, so shocked, my lady! Deorstan, he looked at me and said, "Does this man not know"—it must have been a man, don't you think, my lady, never a *woman*—"does this man not know that there are those in Oakdene who sometimes go to bed hungry?" That's what he said, and isn't it the truth of it? Seldom in this house, I thank God, my lady, but sometimes I did when I was a little girl.'

This seemed to call Godflæd's own girl to mind, and she peered through the doorway again.

'Æffe! Do you want me to come in there to you? You'll be sorry if I do!' Godflæd turned back to Edith, shaking her head and speaking as though her daughter wasn't within earshot to hear her. 'I can do nothing with that girl, my lady, however stern I am—and I am stern with her, and her father is too. Always idling unless I keep a sharp eye on her. So wilful. Not like her brothers at all. They're both such good boys. But you'll find that, my lady, when you come to have children of your own. No two are the same, even the children of one household.'

As though he had heard his mother speaking of him, Æfæd, Godflæd's elder son, came round the side of the house. Tidræd had not lied. The marks of their fight were all over Æfæd's face.

'Æfæd! What happened?' gasped Godflæd. 'Who did this to you?'

'Oh, don't worry, Mother,' he said, fingering his cheek a little gingerly. 'I'm not much hurt.'

'But you are! Who did it? Your father will make sure the boy's father hears of it!'

'Well, it was Tidræd. He flung himself on me from nowhere. I don't know why, but you know how he is.' Æfæd glanced at Edith with a sly, simpering smile. 'Don't talk to Mildrith, Mother. Why worry her?'

Godflæd beamed at her son with unashamed pride, but before another word could be said she strode into the house. Edith heard fierce whispering and a few sharp slaps—though no cry from Æffe—and the girl dashed through the doorway with a basket. Æfæd, away from his mother's eye and either forgetting or not caring that Edith was watching, smirked at his younger sister and put out his foot to trip her as she passed him. Æffe stumbled but didn't fall, and ran on without looking back. Her untidy braids flew behind her as she ran, her bare feet growing dark with mud. Idle? Wilful? Or perhaps this girl could do no right because she wasn't one of her older brothers. Her brothers could do no wrong.

'Don't let me keep you from your work any longer,' called Edith through the doorway.

She didn't smile at Æfæd as she left.

'You shouldn't lie to your mother,' she said. 'She'll find out sooner or later.'

Was anyone guilty in this house? Not one of them cared about Brinin in the slightest, yet they seemed to know the worth of a harvest too well to do such a thing themselves.

Across the wounded village, without the cowshed, the old storehouse and Osgyth's house to hide it, Edith saw Aculf's house. Were his former sins enough for her to lay the blame on his shoulders now? Since the Danes had come, he wasn't the only man in Oakdene who hated Brinin. As she watched, she saw him leave his house and walk towards the fields, a rake over his shoulder. So much the better. It wasn't Aculf she wanted to speak to anyway.

Sægyth didn't see Edith at first, pulled as she was between a simmering pot of broth and her children. Her older daughter sat sobbing on the floor, not loudly but bitterly. The younger, with flushed cheeks and a growing frown, seemed to be about to follow her sister's lead. Edith almost withdrew before she stepped inside. A woman trying to cook with two weeping children at her heels did not also need a guest to see to. But Sægyth caught sight of her. There could be no leaving now, so Edith did the only thing she could think of doing. She walked into the house and scooped up the smaller girl into her arms. That was enough to halt her threatening tears; and even her sister, taken aback by the stranger suddenly in their midst—for this was a house that Edith had seldom been in—forgot to weep as she stared up at her.

'I thought I might see you this morning, my lady,' said Sægyth. She kept her eyes down, on her pot, but she reached out and stroked her older daughter's head, smoothing her hair away from her face. 'I thought you or Cynestan might come. I think Aculf did too, for he lingered in the house a long time. You want to know if he wrecked that boy's harvest, don't you, my lady?'

'I don't want to blame anyone until we know more,' said Edith. Hadn't Sægyth spoken the truth, though? Aculf was the first man she had even thought of blaming, though she had said it aloud to no one. But there was no hiding that from Sægyth.

'I do understand, my lady.' Sægyth spoke slowly and softly. She didn't seem to be angry or afraid, only weary. 'I know how things were between my husband and that boy. And I know my husband didn't always do what was right by him. I understand why folk might think he did this too. But he didn't, my lady. I know he didn't.'

'You know?' There wasn't only one kind of knowledge. A wife might *know* her husband to be guiltless because she hoped he was, yet he might be guilty all the same. Or she might know the truth of what her eyes and ears had told her. Which was it here?

'Yes, my lady. The little one has teeth coming through and she was fretful last night. I was up with her most of the night and even sat outside so she wouldn't wake Aculf with her weeping. He didn't leave the house all night. I don't even think he left his bed. I would have seen him if he had gone out. And I didn't see or hear anyone else either. It was too dark for that, and I was soothing my child.'

Not Aculf then. There were no lies in Sægyth's eyes, nothing that made Edith want to disbelieve her. Her daughter's red cheeks and her own weary eyes stood as her witnesses. Besides, she sounded like a woman who spoke the truth, much as Æfæd had sounded like a boy who didn't. Yet if not Aculf, who?

'I know folk haven't shown enough sorrow over what was done last night,' said Sægyth, when Edith didn't speak. 'But I wish the boy no ill, my lady. I don't think he's a bad boy, far from it. Though perhaps the man who did this even thought he was doing right, because of poor Eanflæd.'

Sægyth stroked her daughter's hair again. There were tears in her eyes now, unshed tears she knew how to hold back, like she knew how to hush a child who wept in the night.

'She was such a good girl. She would come and help me with the children whenever my sister could spare her. Such a good, kind girl. What a wicked thing! But…' Sægyth frowned a little, as though reaching for more careful words. 'My lady, on the night the Danes came—'

Outside, they suddenly heard Aculf's voice as he talked loudly with one of his neighbours. He wasn't by the doorway about to come in, but somewhere behind the house. Sægyth began to bustle about. The words she had been reaching for would be left unsaid for now. And Edith knew that it was time to leave Sægyth to busy herself with her house and children.

Edith listened all day. She listened to folk talk about their harvests, their work and their children. She swallowed back sharp words when some said a little too boldly what was truly in their minds. Few did that. Most seemed to know that, as it was her father who had freed Brinin, her father who had given him a field, her father who had shown him such open thanks before the whole village, that any bitterness must stay hidden. Some, like Godflæd, thought the work of the night had been a shameful waste. Others, though they were careful not to say it openly, seemed to think that Brinin had brought it upon himself by daring to be born to a Danish mother. Edith listened all day but she learned little.

In the evening, when the shadows were lengthening, and she couldn't bear to listen any more, she wearily made her way back to Mildrith's house. As she walked along, she caught sight of Tidræd with his bow and a hare, not long dead. He smiled at her shyly as they met.

'I shot this,' he said, somewhat gruffly. 'I thought my mother might like it for the pot. I can skin it for her.'

It was a peace offering, a little unspoken thanks for that sudden mercy when he had only foreseen wrath. Better ten Tidræds than one Æfæd.

Mildrith did like it. She took the hare in the peace Tidræd meant her to, then sent him outside to get it ready. He squatted by the door with his seax to begin his bloody work. Cenwyn wasn't in the house, but Mildrith and Mærwyn asked Edith everything with their eyes. She shrugged her shoulders.

'Nothing much,' she said. There wasn't much more she *could* say, not with the children in the house or with Tidræd listening nearby.

It wasn't long before Cenwyn came home, striding in with a bundle of sticks in her arms. She dropped them onto the woodpile and turned to her brother.

'Well, Tidræd! Æfæd didn't get off as lightly as you did today,' she said. Tidræd glowered at her, rather fierce with his seax and blood-smeared hands. 'I saw him just now with his father, halfway up the hill. Deorstan was very angry, though I couldn't hear what he was saying. He even struck him! More than once. I think what Æfæd said earlier has reached Deorstan's ears.'

'He struck him!' said Mærwyn. 'Godflæd won't like that!'

'Likely that's why he was scolding him away from the house, so he wouldn't have to listen to his wife telling him how their son can do no wrong. What do you think, Edith? Did you talk to Godflæd and Deorstan today? Do you think I'm right?'

'I only spoke to Godflæd, but they both think it was a dreadful waste of a harvest,' said Edith. 'Beyond that, I don't think they care. I don't know if you're right. Would Deorstan care about Æfæd when he didn't mind Æfich throwing stones? He may have been angry about something else.'

'Come now, girls,' said Mildrith, handing Tidræd a bowl to put the hare in. 'Talk like this won't put food in our bellies. There is still work to be done today. Tidræd, when you're done with that, clean your hands and go and find Brinin. Tell him that he's to eat here this evening. He and all our neighbours will soon see that *this* household still welcomes him.'

PRIDE

'My mother says you're to come and eat with us this evening.'

Brinin, still sitting listlessly on the floor, looked up as Tidræd leaned through the doorway. His face was rather bruised—perhaps the marks of that struggle Brinin had seen in the morning—and he was frowning.

'Listen,' Tidræd went on. 'I hear things all the time, things that folk likely don't want me to know. I'll find out who did this, and then... Come. My mother wants you, and it's no good not listening to her. If you don't come with me, she'll likely come and fetch you herself.'

Mildrith was kind. But to sit by her hearth and listen to kind and perhaps angry words... Brinin didn't know how he could bear that. It wasn't that he wasn't thankful. He was so thankful that it threatened to be his undoing. Yet how could he turn down her kindness? Slowly he rose and saw Tidræd's face brighten a little, but before he had even left the hut, Eawig came running up to them.

'The priest is asking for you.' Eawig's brow was furrowed. 'He's at... where the church was.'

'Thank your mother, Tidræd,' said Brinin, 'but tell her I have to go to see the priest.'

He had to heed Brother Wilfred and besides, seeing him would be easier. Tidræd and Eawig stared after him as he left, whispering to one another.

The sun skulked among the trees, ready to slip away, as Brinin made his way to what was left of the church. Those trees would have been hidden before, blocked out by the hall. Now only the blackened roof-posts stood among the ashes, and the village seemed ragged without it, like a poor man left almost naked.

There was even less of the church than there was of the hall. But the stone altar, cracked a little by fallen beams, was where it had always been. Brother Wilfred had tidied away the wood and ashes to leave the altar clean and now he stood by it, watching Brinin in the evening light.

'I heard about your harvest and want to talk to you, my boy,' he said, coming towards Brinin. 'I have some food. Let's go to your hut and we can eat there and see what's to be done.'

'You are welcome, sir, but there is nowhere to sit there. Only the floor.'

'What do you mean? You have stools. I have sat on them before.'

'Not now, sir.'

'What's happened?'

'Everything's broken, sir. That night you came and told me not to sleep alone. That night, after I'd left, someone came, broke in the door and smashed up the stools, and scattered all the straw and ashes everywhere. If I'd been there or if I'd left the tools… I'm glad I heeded you, sir. I've mended the door—not well, only patched it up until I have more time. But the stools… I can't… My father made them, sir.'

Eadulf's hatred had been bitter, but bearable because it was so understandable. The loss of the stools had been woundlike, deepening as the days had gone by. But now he had lost almost everything else. Now the hatred and the wound were so much worse than before. Brother Wilfred must have heard the choking that Brinin was trying to keep out of his voice. He put his hand on Brinin's shoulder.

'We'll sit on the floor then,' he said. 'Come. Who knows about this? I haven't heard anyone speak of it.'

'Someone knows, and not only the man who did it. He couldn't have done it without being heard, sir. But no one stopped him and no one has said anything to me.'

'And who have you told about it?'

'Who would I tell, sir? Garulf is already worried about me and can do nothing to help. Everyone who has ever shown me any friendship has their own troubles, worse than mine. And what's the good in talking, sir? Talking won't bring back my harvest or unbreak anything.'

'Nevertheless, we *will* talk.' They had reached the hut now and Brother Wilfred sat down on the damp grass outside. 'Sit here, my boy. Can't you even think who it might have been?'

'No, sir. You've seen how it is. More than one man is angry enough to have done it and plenty more are angry enough to have let him.'

'There will be a way to learn who it was. But tell me about your harvest. Could you save any of it?'

'Nothing, sir. There'll be nothing to eat and nothing for seed.'

Brinin had known that there was little good to be found in talking. Saying it aloud made him see more clearly what was coming: a dark, wretched and hungry winter with no hope of a new harvest beyond it. How little could a man live on? How hungry would he have to be before he sickened and died like that sister and brother he had never known?

'And have you nothing else?' asked Brother Wilfred.

'Some peas. I've gathered most of them in already. The man who wrecked my hut didn't find them. They're in the swine shelter. And I have some beans—not many—and some carrots and cabbages growing behind the hut.'

'It will be better to keep the peas and whatever else you have somewhere away from your hut. We will thank God for what has been spared and see what is to be done about the lack.'

'I will be hungry, sir,' said Brinin. What else could be done for lack of food? Even if he were to spend his days, sunrise to sunset, looking for what grew wild, he could never find enough to feed himself through the winter. Even if he could work for his bread, who would give work to the foe in their midst? How could he even ask for it, for anything from any of them?

'Yet you are not hungry now.'

'No, sir. Edrich Thegn bade me eat with his slaves until harvest, but—'

'And if our good Lord brings him back to us, will Edrich Thegn stop being kind because another man has been evil?'

'No, sir, but—'

'Then why would he let you go hungry now if he didn't before? If he helped you before would he not help you now, when you have lost so much, through no wrongdoing of your own? And Edrich Thegn is not the only one ready to help you. If there are some in this village who wish you ill, there are others who wish you well. You must know that. You won't be left starving and helpless.'

That got to the heart of it, to those deep things that were best left unsaid. Better to be free and hungry. Row had told him that he didn't know what he was talking about. Had he been a fool then? Was he a fool now? He knew there were a kind few, but he had spent so much of his life longing for freedom and there was no freedom in begging his bread from another man. That was shame and weakness so much like thraldom that it might as well be its near kin.

'I don't want to ask, sir,' he said.

'Ah,' said Brother Wilfred. 'Now I understand. That's not wisdom. It's pride.'

Brinin said nothing. He didn't need Brother Wilfred to tell him he was proud. For so long pride had been almost the only thing he could call his own, and he had thought of it as strength to keep him from sinking too low. He could not readily believe it was folly.

'Now, my boy, let me speak to you plainly. I have seen that you are kind and quick to help. You have been willing to give when all you had to offer was a stronger back to take blows earned by another. I know how things were. If someone needs your help, do you think less of them for asking?'

'No, sir. I don't mind but—'

'So you are happy to do what is right and good and kind, but you won't let another man do the same. Aren't a man's good deeds between him and his God? Would you stand in his way because you are too proud to ask for help?'

Surely Brother Wilfred wouldn't ask him to lay aside his strength? He had lost everything else. Pride and freedom were almost all he had left.

'To eat another man's bread, sir—'

'No one eats what did not come from another. Where does bread come from? You know your Paternoster: "Give us today our daily loaf." Do you make the sun shine and rain fall on your field? Do you make the seeds grow? If a man has bread it was given to him from heaven. Will you throw away God's good gifts because he sent another man to put them into your hand? Listen, my dear boy. I don't want to chide you, but take care. If you let pride lead you, it will take you where you do not want to go.'

The village was sinking into nightgloom now. It was better that way. If speech—hard and painful speech—was going to be thrust on him against his will, it was better to have a little darkness to hide in.

'My boy, please don't lose all hope. You are not alone and you are not without friends, even though they are few. I myself will see you do not go hungry, whether you want me to or not. Put all thoughts of hunger from your mind and let us think about what we will do about this dreadful thing.'

'That night when Eadulf was so angry—I don't blame him, sir, not after he lost his daughter—that night I asked myself if I should go back to the minster. I was happy there. The prior, everyone, was kind and no one asked me who my mother was. But I thought it would be wrong to walk away from my field when Edrich Thegn had been so good as to give it to me. I'll never have another. I thought that folk here might not hate me so much when the first anger had passed. Now I can see that I can never belong here, field or not. Perhaps I should go back to the minster after all. I once thought that this was home, or near to it, but I see now that it can't be.'

'Why not now, my boy? These are not the first troubles you have known.'

Brinin glanced at the monk. He could hardly see his face in the dusk. He sat beside him, shadowy and unmoving. Brinin remembered how once, when Brother Wilfred had not been long among them, Oswald had said that he was a man who made him speak his thoughts, that he could hardly think anything without telling the monk sooner or later. Brinin had thought then that it was because Oswald didn't know how to keep a still tongue. Not like him. *He* knew how to keep his mouth shut. The less he said the better he liked it. Yet here he was, finding words to say what he had never shared before. Perhaps Oswald, with his untamed tongue, had been right after all.

'May I ask you something, sir, if it isn't too bold? Were you ever beaten when you were a boy?'

'Hard and often. I had a master who believed that only a rod could drive knowledge into a boy.'

'Then you know, sir, that a beating is bad at the time but there is an end to it. However sore and angry I was, I knew that if I waited it would be over and even the bruises would be gone after a few days. It was harder to know that I would soon be beaten again and could do nothing about it; that I could never hope for anything better; and that there is no justice in the world and little kindness. I could bear it then because even when I was sorest and angriest, I was never alone. And I wasn't hated by everyone because I wasn't worth enough for them to see. But now I can't shut my eyes and wait for it to stop, and the bruises don't go away, and there's still no justice in the world. I've done nothing wrong, sir. I've done nothing to them but have the wrong mother! And I'm hated for what the Danes are doing. If I had wanted to be with the Danes, I could have stayed with them. I could have stayed but I walked away! And every night… every night when I come back to this hut…' Brinin could hear his voice, too shaken and anguished to sound like it truly belonged to him. Words were dangerous. Once let loose they couldn't be stopped. He couldn't steady his voice now or bridle the words. He could only trail off into a kind of whisper. 'When I come back, it's… it's empty.'

'Brinin, my dear, dear boy.' And as Brinin had heard anguish in his own voice, he thought—he was almost sure—he heard something near to tears in Brother Wilfred's. 'Your loss, your sorrow, is still fresh. It's too soon—much too soon—for you to feel anything but pain. But it won't always be like this. There *is* little justice in the world. When you have lived as long as I have, you will know that even better than you do now, though you have learned the truth of it younger than most. I won't lie to you. I can't swear to you that things will ever be any better here. But one day there will be an end to this too. Have you forgotten that prayer we read at the minster? The time is coming when there will be no trouble, no death, when everything will be right and the poor man will not weep. So don't lose heart, my boy, and don't lose hope.'

Hope had been a new thing for Brinin, blazing in when everything was at its darkest, and it was Brother Wilfred who had first offered it to him. But it was hard to see now, dimmer. He had to strain his eyes even to glimpse it. Was it still there, the same as before?

'So you don't think I should go back to the minster, sir?'

'I think you should be slow to leave.'

'So we do nothing, sir?'

'What I ought to do and what you ought to do are not the same. You must pray for strength to do what is right and not be afraid; and you must pray to be shielded from pride and bitterness, for those would be sin. As for me, yours is not the only soul here entrusted to me. Can I do nothing when some in my care are so ready to do evil? That would be sin indeed, a greater evil even than theirs. You pray for strength, and I will try to find out who has been doing these things, for their good as well as yours.'

LOSS

Oswald and his father were both wrong. The road home wasn't as easy as Oswald had hoped nor as hard as his father had feared. The first half-day's ride to his uncle's house left Oswald so weary that he barely heard the greetings of his kin or tasted the food they laid before him. Sleep threatened to take him while he sat eating, and his limbs seemed too weak and his body too heavy to leave the table and lie down.

The aching tiredness had passed by morning, but it was a painful day. Alrich's shadow was everywhere: on the seat where he had sat, on the bed where he had slept, by the hearth where he had warmed himself, in the green meadow where Oswald and his kinsmen had played as boys. Now the seat was empty, the bed empty and the stillness by the hearth loud above the voices still there. Oswald felt it keenly, but how much sharper was it for Alrich's father and mother, for his brothers and sister who had to see the empty seat, the empty bed, the empty hearthside and empty meadow every day?

On the third day, they took leave of their kin and began the last ride home. Oswald's father led them slowly, stopping often to sit and rest and feel the summer. They said little to one another, though it was the first time they had ridden together alone as men without others by their sides. Oswald's thoughts were far ahead of the horses, already home, but often that day they wandered back to Godweard and his household, to his daughter. Would he ever see these kind friends again?

They walked the last few miles, while away to their right in the far west the sun sank in a blaze of spreading fire, almost as though it could have set the whole earth alight. Not long now. Far ahead of them, Oswald could see the last little hill beyond which lay Oakdene, home,

Edith, Brinin, his old life and his new one. The sun would be set by the time they reached it, but not long set. Oswald could see it in his mind, the shapes and shadows of Oakdene in the dusk, the hall and the church and beyond them the other houses and the fields to the south. All beyond that one last hill.

'I wonder if Saxulf and Sigulf have reached home before us,' said Edrich.

'Eadswith will be glad to have them back.' Oswald kept his eyes on the hill ahead of them.

'And in time for harvest. That's a blessing I didn't foresee.'

Unforeseen blessings were all around them now, things which before had been too small to think of. And so much that had once been burdensome, like work or duty, had become blessings on the battlefield. Their lives had been spared for what was dull and wearisome, and it was a gift from heaven.

'Father,' said Oswald, 'what will it be like now that it's over?'

Not the same. Nothing would ever be the same again. Edrich didn't answer at first, but he looked at his son with some understanding.

'It will be what we make of it,' he said at last. 'Who knows what tomorrow may hold? We can only keep doing what we ought to as best we can.'

They reached the last hill in the half-darkness as night fell. Still on foot, they climbed it wearily, then stopped to gaze down over the houses of Oakdene through the gloaming. And something was amiss. Had they lost their way and climbed the wrong hill? Was this another, smaller village? How could they have strayed when they had known this land all their lives? The hill they stood on was the same. The line of trees to the east was the same, black against the darkening sky. Everything was the same. But the houses were wrong, too few, too scattered.

Edrich dropped his horse's bridle, gasping out a flow of words that Oswald missed as his father ran from him. Oswald stared after him as he stumbled down the hill and sped across the meadow.

Sudden understanding struck Oswald in the face. It *was* Oakdene, or rather what was left of it. The hall was gone, the church, more buildings than that even, though he couldn't see how many in the gloom. How could so much be so wholly gone? There was only one answer to that: they must have been set alight and blazed like the sunset. And where would such flames—eager, hungry flames—have come from but the hand of a foe? And what other foe but…?

Oswald was at the bottom of the hill now, his heart and head pounding together, and shaking a little as weakness, weariness and fear sprung on him all at once. He clambered onto his horse, fumbling as though he had never done it before and holding the bridle of his father's horse as well as his own. Edith had readied herself, had found places to hide. She had sworn to him that she had. He had asked her time and again. But fear can make even the most careful folk forget, and if there had been no time… Surely they would have sent someone if… In that other village, that forsaken village Beorn had spoken of, there had been no one left. Only a dog. And homecoming was suddenly a fearful, dreadful thing. He couldn't bring himself to drive the horses any faster than a trot.

Oswald found his father standing where his home had once been. Edrich didn't speak. He stood with his shoulders slumped and his head bowed. He was so still, almost lifeless, that he didn't seem to see Oswald. Oswald's throat was too tight for speech and his words too scattered. His father's shoulders heaved suddenly and he uttered a sound that was half-groan, half-gasp, almost beastlike. It stabbed Oswald. His father was weeping. When had he ever known him to weep before?

Oswald looked around wildly, straining his eyes and ears for anything that might help them. Surely someone still lived. Surely someone could tell them the truth of what they both feared. Oswald must be the one to learn it. His father, always so strong and swift to take the lead, was beyond all that now, too broken even for word or thought. It was for Oswald to be strong and swift now. He grasped his father's arm.

'Look, Father,' he said. 'That's hearthsmoke coming from Saxulf's house. Shall I go and ask them if…?'

But what was the good of waiting for an answer? Oswald ran to the house and pounded on the door.

'Open up! Open up!' he yelled. 'It's Oswald. Open the door!'

Shifting about and voices inside; heavy steps on the floor. The door swung open, and Saxulf himself stood before him.

'Oswald Child! You and your father are back, then? We only got back this afternoon. They've had a bad time here. Sigulf, run and tell Cynestan. Come in, Oswald Child. Where's your father? Come in, and we'll find you something to eat. You'll be tired from the road.'

'My sister…'

'Oh, yes! She's with Mildrith. She's been staying with her since—'

But Oswald didn't wait to hear more.

'Thank you,' he called over his shoulder as he ran.

Edrich hadn't moved. He still stood wordless and with bowed head.

'Father,' gasped Oswald. 'Edith is with Mildrith. Come, sir.'

Edrich stirred then. He ran his hand across his face but still said nothing.

'Come, Father,' said Oswald, laying his hand on his father's arm. 'Edith is in Mildrith's house.'

Edrich nodded. He strode away from Oswald, who had to run after him before he lost him in the twilight. They left the horses where they were.

Edith was alive, but was she wounded? Had the fire harmed her? Had the Danes harmed her? Saxulf had said they had had a bad time. Were others dead? What about Brinin?

A babble of voices came from Mildrith's house and a chink of soft light under the doorway.

'It's me, Oswald. Is my sister here?' he called, as he knocked. The talking inside stopped at once. A scuffle sounded inside, and Tidræd flung the door wide.

Edith was standing by the hearth, staring at them. She held a spindle but had dropped the yarn. All the others sat round the fire, little Tidwine on the floor by Edith's feet.

'Father? Oswald?' she said at last, almost steadily. 'I'm sorry. It… They came. We did what we could, but… everything's gone but my grandfather's spear. And… and we lost four. Byrnhelm, Ceola, Ludan and… and… Eanflæd. And… and we did what we could, but…'

Her steadiness melted away, and she sank onto a stool and wept. Edrich strode into the house and knelt beside her. He took her in his arms, pressing her head to his chest. Oswald leaned against the doorframe, suddenly and dreadfully weary.

'Tidræd,' he said, 'we left the horses by the hall, by where it was. Can you deal with them? I don't even know where we should put them.'

STONES

In the morning they walked round the village to see what the Danes had left of it. They heard over and over the tale of that dreadful night, what had been lost, who had been lost. By mid-morning, Edrich was looking grim and weary, and Oswald was feeling it.

'At least the harvest is unharmed,' sighed Edrich as they passed where the horsehouse had stood, the fields ahead of them golden in the morning light. 'We can be thankful for that. It seems it was only a small raid, only a few eager to take what they could. It could have been much worse. We could have had many more to bury, and a hungry winter ahead of us.'

Oswald saw Edith open her mouth to speak, then shut it again before the words were said. And he saw how heavily worry was weighing on her, and how much older she seemed than the young sister he had last seen a few short months before.

Eawig was ahead of them, pushing a dung-barrow. He was walking swiftly, throwing the odd glance behind him to be sure that his lord could see how hard he was working. Then suddenly he yelped and stumbled. The barrow shot forward, and he banged his face against it as he fell, almost toppling into the dung itself.

'I saw that!' shouted Edrich, breaking into a stride as Eawig scrambled to his feet, eyeing them fearfully and rubbing his head.

Oswald glanced wryly at Edith as they both quickened their step. Surely their father wasn't angry about that: a slight slip, a mistake, none of the dung even spilt. But Edrich didn't say a word to Eawig. He stopped under the old oak tree and glared up into it.

'I saw that! I saw the stone you threw. Get down now!' he snapped. 'Do you hear me, boy? Now!'

219

There was a rustle of leaves as the tree seemed to come alive. Two dirty legs dangled from one of the boughs, and Deorstan's son, Æfich, jumped down, looking round quickly for some way to flee. But Edrich Thegn grabbed his arm and pulled him over to Eawig, who stood uneasily with his hand on his head.

'Let me see your head, boy,' said Edrich to Eawig.

Eawig lowered his hand and started a little. It was red with blood. Edrich's frown deepened and Æfich, already sullen, began to look a little frightened.

'Do you see his head?' Edrich was very stern now. 'You did that with the stone you threw. What have you to say for yourself?'

'Please, my lord, I... I...' Æfich got no further than that. Anything he said would likely make everything worse, and the sight of Edrich Thegn wouldn't make words any easier. When Oswald was a boy, his father had sometimes looked at him like that and it had often dried up even words that might have helped.

'Where's your father?'

'In... in... the field, my lord,' stammered Æfich.

'Where you ought to be. We'll see what he has to say about this. Will he be pleased with you for throwing a stone at the head of a boy who had done nothing to you? For throwing a stone at all? I think not.' Edrich turned again to Eawig and said more kindly, 'You come too, boy. Leave the barrow here for now.'

Edrich strode away, still with a tight grip on Æfich's arm and with Eawig, rather dazed, trotting behind him. Oswald grimaced at Edith as they followed.

'There'll be trouble now,' he said.

'There's already been trouble, and this isn't the first time it's been between Æfich and Eawig. It's...' The worried look passed over Edith's face again. 'I'll tell you about it later. It's been bad here.'

'Bad? Because of the Danes?'

'More than that.'

Deorstan was coming away from the fields when they met him, frowning at the sight of his son, rather wretched now, being pulled along by his thegn.

'Ah, Deorstan, I was coming to find you,' said Edrich. 'Have a look at my slave here. Do you see his head and his cheek? Just now

I watched your son throw a stone at him. It cut his head and made him fall. Now, I am not the man to do another father's work for him, least of all when that father is nearby. So I've brought him to you.'

Deorstan glared at Æfich, but the scowl he threw at Eawig was fierce indeed. What *had* been happening here?

'My lord,' said Deorstan. 'My son was wrong to throw a stone, but I have no doubt that this slave was to blame and angered him. Perhaps there was nothing else my son could have done to—'

'My slave did nothing that I could see,' said Edrich coldly. 'He was going about his work while your son was hiding in a tree. Do you think I would blame your son without reason?'

'Forgive me, my lord, but this slave is cunning and dislikes my son. He has already been wholly to blame for a fight between the two of them—I had to pull him off my son to stop him from beating him. It was not much more than two weeks ago, my lord, and my son still bears the marks.'

Æfich looked up now and Oswald caught sight of the bruises, yellow and fading but still there. And that wasn't all he saw. There was something in the look that Æfich shot at Eawig. A taunt? Eawig was frightened now—Oswald saw that too. But surely he, a slave, hadn't started a fight with the son of a freeman. Cynestan was no Aculf, but he would have swiftly put a stop to anything like that. Yet would Deorstan dare to lie so boldly to his thegn?

'Did you do that, boy?' said Edrich, turning to Eawig. 'What did you mean by it?'

Eawig licked his lips and opened his mouth, but he said nothing. Oswald saw another unspoken taunt from Æfich, bolder this time.

'Answer me!'

But Eawig was scared beyond all answering now. Edith put a hand on her father's arm.

'Father,' she said. 'I heard about this from Cynestan. I don't think the blame was all Eawig's. Cynestan could tell you everything.'

'Very well,' said Edrich. 'Fetch Cynestan then.'

'My lord—' began Deorstan, as Edith left them.

'We will wait for Cynestan,' said Edrich Thegn. 'No need to speak until he comes.'

So they stood uneasily. Eawig, still with his hand on his head and with his hair matted with drying blood, looked round again and again to see if Cynestan was coming. *What* had been happening? Oswald saw that the taunt was wholly gone from Æfich's eyes.

Cynestan came, leaning on his stick and unsmiling as he walked at Edith's side. Edrich Thegn wasted no time.

'Cynestan, Deorstan tells me that this boy here'—a nod towards Eawig—'was wholly to blame—I think that's what you said, Deorstan—*wholly* to blame for a fight with Deorstan's son. I thought it best to ask you about it as you likely dealt with it at the time.'

'Well now, my lord, I did deal with it at the time,' said Cynestan, glancing scornfully at Deorstan. 'I took Deorstan's whip away. He was beating Eawig with it and more harshly than the thing called for to my mind; and then, Eawig is not his slave. As for blame, it seemed to me that much more of it lay with Deorstan's son than with Eawig here. I dealt with the boy for fighting, but it's little wonder that he was angry, my lord, when he had seen Æfich hit Brinin on the back with a stone and heard him say what should not have been said. The lad is fond of Brinin, who's kind to him.'

'Another stone!' said Edrich, grimly.

'I didn't!' said Æfich, half-sullen, half-pleading.

'You did!' muttered Eawig, so softly as to be almost unheard, but with a sudden gleam of battle in his eyes that melted away at once at the sight of his lord's frown.

'Enough!' said Edrich sharply. 'What did your son say, Deorstan?'

'My lord, I... I wasn't there to hear him say anything, and neither was Cynestan when it comes to it, and—'

'What did you say?'

Æfich looked helplessly at his father but didn't speak.

'Can no one answer me? Eawig, what did he say that made you so far forget yourself as to strike him?'

Eawig, with one last beseeching look at Cynestan, drew a deep breath.

'My lord, he... he said that Brinin was a Dane, my lord, and that he was glad there weren't two Danes in the village now and that it will be even better when there are none, and I... I hit him, my lord.'

'He said *that*? You little—'

But Edrich raised a hand to stop him and Oswald tailed off, glowering at Æfich and Deorstan alike.

'I'm… I'm sorry if I did wrong, my lord,' said Eawig meekly.

Was he sorry or only wise enough to say so? The meekness in his words was not in his eyes, and Oswald liked him the better for it. He would find something for this boy, some gift—if the Danes had left anything behind worth giving—some small thing to show Eawig that *he* thought he had done right, even if it had been something a slave should never do.

'So, Deorstan,' said Edrich. 'This is how your son is without blame: in throwing stones and speaking ill of one whom I welcome here—doubtless you have not forgotten why. Was he likewise blameless this morning? I'm not one to tell another man how to be a father, but it seems that you did not teach him well enough the first time. He has not yet learned. Eawig, find your mother and have her tend to your head. And take care that there is no more fighting. I will be very stern if I hear of you striking anyone again, whatever they may have said. But as Cynestan already dealt with it—and *only* because of that—I will say no more.'

Eawig slipped away, looking more than glad to be going, and Edrich turned to Cynestan again.

'I am beginning to wonder what other trouble there has been while I've been away. As I cannot ask you to sit by my hearth and talk, Cynestan, let us sit by yours. And, Deorstan, you should see to it that your son *does* learn this time.'

Oswald glanced behind him as he followed his father with Edith and Cynestan. Once more, Æfich was being pulled along by an angry man, his father this time. Yet had the stone-throwing made Deorstan angry? Oswald doubted it. Deorstan didn't seem to care much about that. No, it wasn't the stones he minded, but he didn't like being shamed before his thegn.

TELLING

At a nod from Cynestan, Wynflæd bustled the children from the house and busied herself outside. Cynestan was unsmiling, and Edith's face had taken on the worried look again. This time Edrich Thegn saw it. Oswald saw him frowning at her as he sat down on a bench and bade the others to do the same. Oswald stood restlessly by the doorway. Why couldn't Edith and Cynestan say what was wrong and be done with it? Why all the frowns and sideways glances?

'What's all this about, Cynestan?' asked Edrich.

'Well, my lord, I can't rightly say how it began, but for some months there has been talk, or at least an uneasiness—'

'Speak plainly, Cynestan! I know nothing about all this. Talk and uneasiness about what?'

Oswald saw Edith take another quick glance at him and he suddenly knew. It wasn't the Danes that were worrying her, or whatever had been happening. She was worried about him, dreading telling him whatever this trouble had been.

'Father,' she said. 'Some folk in the village don't think Brinin belongs here.'

'Doesn't belong here?' Oswald couldn't even wait for his father to speak before his anger burst out. 'He was *born* here! What more do they want?'

'Let her speak, Oswald!'

'It's because his mother was a Dane, Father. That's what they don't like.'

'My lord,' said Cynestan, 'folk are scared, and fear can make fools of them. That's the truth of it. At first I thought it was only talk and nothing to worry about. Some perhaps don't like a freedman having a field, but others are friendly enough—he's a helpful lad, and hardworking. But since the raid there's been more than talk, and even the talk has spread to the children. That's why those two boys were fighting.'

'What do you mean there's been more than talk? Has Brinin been harmed?'

Oswald's gut twisted a little. He had thought that if Brinin had been harmed or even killed in the raid that Edith would already have told him. But he hadn't seen Brinin yet, not even from far off. There had been no time. It had been dark when they reached the village, and his father had wanted him in the morning. And he hadn't even known to ask if someone other than a raider might have harmed Brinin.

'Well, what do you call harmed, my lord?' asked Cynestan. 'Nothing happened that he's likely to die from. As it was, he was only struck once before—'

'Struck! Who struck him?' Oswald's anger burst out again as the fear left him. Why was he even asking? It had to be Aculf. Aculf was the one behind all this. Who else could it have been?

'Let him speak, Oswald. Go on, Cynestan.'

'It could have been much worse, but Daglæf and I talked a bit of wisdom into them. Everyone was angry that day because of the raid and all the dead and wounded, but most of all because of Eadulf's daughter. I was angry too, my lord. But some wanted to blame Brinin because those who were to blame—those Danes who came—were already gone and couldn't be reached. After that evening not much more was said about it but… when was it done, my lady Edith?'

'About a week ago, I think,' said Edith, with another of those swift looks at Oswald.

'Yes, about a week ago, my lord, a man or men—it could even have been a woman for all we know—someone went to his field in the night and wrecked his harvest. There's almost nothing left of it. It was no mishap. No one else's field was touched. I've asked folk, listened in the hope of overhearing something, but no one seems to know anything. Or at least no one will *say* that they know anything.'

So that was why Edith had been so worried and Cynestan had taken so long to give the thing a name. Oswald saw his father looking at him now, but not with another warning to wait before speaking. It was with understanding and shared anger. There was only one man who could have done this, and if his neighbours were going to hide his guilt, he would have to be made to say it aloud himself.

'No one knows?' Oswald slammed his hand against the roof-post. 'Everyone knows, more likely! There's only one man who would do that. Who else hates Brinin enough to take everything? First the swine and now the harvest! Brinin has so little. Can't he be left with the little he has?'

'Swine?' said Edrich, slightly bewildered. 'What do you mean, Oswald?'

Oswald dropped his head. He had forgotten that the dead sow was never to be spoken of.

'Father,' said Edith quickly, almost as though she knew and was trying to save her brother from his folly. 'Once I would have thought the same as Oswald, but not now. After the Danes came and after what happened to Eanflæd... Eadulf was so angry, everyone was...'

'That's what I mean, my lord. I can't say who it was because there was more than one angry enough to do it—not all, mind, but too many for the blame to fall easily on one man. And as for the rest, those who didn't do it, many of them were angry enough to be glad about it and keep their mouths shut.'

'It's true, Father. I've spoken to almost everyone, some more than once. They were careful about what they said, but I don't think many were sorry about it. It could have been almost anyone.'

Edrich Thegn said nothing for a long time. Oswald, leaning on the doorframe, stood and watched his him. He saw that his father's face was stern and weary, but not if he was finding any wisdom. Oswald had no wisdom. He only knew that it must be put right, but not how to do it. Edith had taken her leave and slipped away long before Edrich said a word.

'Oswald,' said Edrich at last. 'Go and find Brinin and speak to him about this. He may know something that Cynestan and Edith don't.'

Outside in the morning sunlight, Oswald stood and gazed round the broken village, trying to tame his restless anger. There would be no good in going to Brinin breathing out threats against some hateful neighbour, known or unknown. Unbridled wrath had never been the way to coax Brinin into talking, even if it was wrath on his behalf. It was the meadow that stilled him a little, because he could see it. It stretched before him unhidden with no hall between it and where he stood. Oswald had thought he was coming home, but only the bones of home had been there to meet him, lying where they had fallen like a dead man. It was a loss, a bitter loss. Yet wasn't it easier to bear loss at the hands of a foe than at the hands of one who ought to be a friend? With a heavy sigh he trudged away to find Brinin.

He hadn't gone far when Edith stopped him, running to him from Thurstan's house. Mildrith's house—it was so easy to forget.

'Oswald, wait!' she said as she reached him. 'Are you going to find Brinin?'

'Yes. Father wants me to find out what he knows about all this.'

'I don't think he knows any more than Cynestan or I do. He likely knows less. He's been keeping away from folk.' Edith stopped, eying her brother keenly. 'What did you mean about Brinin losing his swine and why were you worried when Father asked you about it? I know Brinin had a swine and that he doesn't now. Were you saying that someone—well, I know you meant Aculf—took it or killed it?'

So Edith *had* been trying to save him but not because she had knowledge, only sharp eyes.

'Don't ask me. I shouldn't have said anything—I told Brinin I wouldn't—but I spoke without thinking. Hopefully Father will forget what I said.'

'Aculf did do something to Brinin's swine, didn't he? Father ought to know. He would make Aculf pay him for it.'

'I know, and I told Brinin that but… but I shouldn't be talking about this.'

'Don't start hiding things again, Oswald. Tell Brinin that Father *must* know.'

'It isn't as easy as that, Edith. You don't understand everything, and I can't talk about it. Let me go and find Brinin.'

Walking between the other houses, Oswald saw Brinin outside his hut. He sat shaving a long board, smoothing and flattening it. His eyes were on his work, and Oswald was almost at the hut before he looked up.

'I heard you were back,' he said with almost a smile.

'There were days I thought I never would be,' said Oswald, sitting down on the grass beside him. 'But here I am, not dead yet.'

UNEARTHING

Everything about Oswald was wrong. He was too thin, his cheeks hollow and a little too white, his eyes weary and a little too dark. He didn't walk as he always had, swiftly as though time was slipping away from him and he couldn't stop long to think. He walked slowly. And he had grown older, as though that same time he had always been chasing had snatched him up and driven him along its path, leaving his boyhood friend far behind. What had war done to him?

'I was wounded,' said Oswald, rubbing his shoulder and answering what Brinin had not yet asked. 'An arrow. Mostly healed now, though it still aches a little. And I was ill for a time.'

'How ill?'

In these last weeks Brinin had feared that Oswald and his father would *never* come back. And when the dreams—many each night and full of Row as they hadn't been for months—had dragged him from sleep, he had wondered if his friend was lost and if he himself would be driven from the village. Had those midnight fears been nearer to the truth than Brinin had known?

'Ill enough to remember barely anything about it. I was out of my wits for days. It was worse for my father, I think, having to watch me like that. But God spared me.' Oswald bit his lip, some thought darkening his face. 'Beorn died in my arms, with a spear in his side.'

There was nothing to say to that, nothing that Brinin could think of, but it was little wonder that Oswald was so changed. Perhaps he too would see the faces of the dead now in his sleep.

'How long before you have to fight again?' asked Brinin, still shaving the long board he was working at.

'Haven't you heard? The Danes are leaving. Most of them have already gone.'

'Driven out?' If news like that hadn't reached him, Brinin was shunned indeed. No one had stopped by his hut to share it.

'No,' Oswald grimaced. 'Paid to leave, I think. If the King *has* paid them, I can't blame him. There were so few of us by the end I don't think he could have done anything else.'

'It's hardly for us to blame the King.'

'No.'

Brinin watched as Oswald's eyes swept the village, resting from time to time not on what was left but on what was gone. The hut, sitting higher as it did, had always been a good place for watching the rest of Oakdene. He saw Oswald's lips tighten as he turned his eyes away from where the hall had been.

'Tell me about the night they came here,' he said.

'You can see most of what there is to tell. They came, they did all that and they left.'

'No warning?'

'Not much, but enough to stop it from being worse. Likely you already know who's dead.'

'Cynestan told us, though not if our folk killed any of them.'

'One. Ludan killed him.'

'Ludan?'

'Yes. Who would have thought a slave would bring down the foe while others were running?' Brinin stopped shaving the wood and looked up. He hadn't meant the words to sound so bitter. Better soften the others. After all, Oswald wasn't to blame for everything wrong in the world. 'He killed him with a fork, ran at him and died doing it. Tidræd saw it. If you want to know about that night, ask Tidræd. He will have heard everything. I can hardly put it all straight in my mind, much less tell you.'

'Likely he will tell me and ask me about the battles I've fought. I don't feel like talking about them now.' Oswald sighed. 'Listen, Brinin, Cynestan told us about your field. It must have been Aculf. Surely no one else could have done a thing like that.'

'Is that what Cynestan said?'

'No, but it must have been.'

'Must it?'

It was hard for Oswald to see beyond Aculf. How could Oswald, well-liked, the thegn's son, know what it was to have few friends? He had spent his whole life at the heart of the village. How could *he* know what it meant to live at the edge, where an otherwise friendly neighbour could swiftly become a foe?

'I can't think of anyone else,' said Oswald, 'though Cynestan—and Edith too—thought that more than one man could have done it. But who else could it have been?'

'I only know who didn't do it.'

'That's something! If you don't know who did it, tell me who didn't.'

'Cynestan didn't nor Daglæf nor Garulf nor anyone in their houses. And Brother Wilfred didn't nor anyone in Mildrith's house. And your sister didn't do it. On the night after the raid—likely Cynestan told you what happened then too—that night they were the ones who spoke wisdom and stood beside me. And if it worries them that I'm a Dane—'

'You're not a Dane! Your father was as much a Wessex man as—'

'I *am* a Dane, and don't ever say that I'm not! It may not be all I am, but I am a Dane and I'm not ashamed of it! Those folk don't care, and I know they didn't do it. But it could have been anyone else.'

Oswald got up and began to prowl about restlessly. His anger was understandable, though Brinin himself was too weary of it all for anger now. Oswald's anger wasn't the old kind that would spill out thoughtlessly with little to stop it. He was holding it back, though perhaps it was too hard to hold himself still at the same time.

'So none of those folk did it,' said Oswald at last. 'But someone did and they must pay for it. Can't you think of anyone?'

Brinin shrugged his shoulders. Why waste their time like this? It wouldn't bring his harvest back.

'If it wasn't Aculf,' Oswald went on, 'likely there are only one or two others it could have been.'

'Other than those I named, it could have been anyone.'

'How could it have been anyone? You can't believe that the village is full of men who would wreck your harvest? What harm have you ever done them?'

'Do I need to have done them any harm? After the raid and after Eanflæd died like she did, no one asked if I had done them any harm. All they wanted was someone to blame, and I'm the nearest Dane!'

This time Oswald didn't call him a Wessex man. He *was* a Wessex man too, though it was easier for his neighbours to forget that. Oswald stopped prowling and stood for a time frowning and tight-faced, his arms folded across his chest.

'So more than one man was angry,' he said at length, 'and more than one man might have been glad to see it done. But most didn't do it. Even if they might have wanted to, they likely wouldn't have dared. Have you never told yourself you would do something but then *not* done it when the time came?'

'No.'

'Well, I have and I'm sure others have too. Wanting to do something isn't the same as doing it. But someone did it, and I'm going to unearth who. Aculf killed your sow and hates you enough to wreck your harvest, so we'll say he *might* have done it. That's one man. Cynestan said someone struck you the day after the raid. Who was it?'

'Eadulf, but his daughter had been found not long before. To blame him for what he did then—'

'Eadulf then. He and Aculf are kin; their wives are sisters. Who knows what Aculf has said to him about you? And Eadulf is always squabbling with his neighbours. That's two men now, and their households.'

'Their households? Do you think Wulfrich or Ulf sneaked out to my field in the middle of the night? Or their little sister? Or their mother with a baby in her arms? You didn't see the field. A small child couldn't have done it.'

'They aren't all small children. Some of them aren't much younger than—'

'Oswald, what good is all this? It doesn't tell us anything.'

'This is my father's village and will one day be mine. Whoever did this will pay for it, and I will learn who it was. What about Deorstan? He's your nearest neighbour. Has he ever been friendly towards you?'

'Never,' said Brinin. Deorstan had been less than friendly, and Brinin knew that his household could not have slept while his door and stools were smashed.

'He didn't mind his son throwing a stone at you.'

'Oh, you heard about that?'

'Æfich threw a stone at Eawig earlier and my father saw him. He dragged him off to Deorstan and the tale came out, but only because Edith fetched Cynestan. My father would never have got the truth out of Deorstan.'

'I heard Deorstan beating Æfich this morning.'

'Not before time!' said Oswald, with an unfeeling grimness that was unlike him somehow. 'But not for throwing stones, only for my father learning about it. Deorstan—and his household—makes three.'

'None of this helps, Oswald. I don't know who did it. I can't tell you what you want to know, and knowing won't feed me in the winter.'

'Feed you? What does that have to do with it? You don't think my father—or I—will let you starve, do you?'

He wanted to feed himself! Brinin could almost have shouted it at Oswald, but he only leaned heavily on the wood and shaved it a little too deeply. He wanted to be free enough to feed himself. Yet Row had said that he didn't know what he was talking about, and Brother Wilfred had said that he was more proud than wise. It made him uneasy.

'We're going to need woodsmiths now to rebuild a new hall and church and all the other buildings,' went on Oswald. 'Think about whether you want to be paid in money or beasts.'

And he left without waiting for an answer.

WRONGS

Oswald spent the day in mourning. He heard how Daglæf's father had said he would never run from the Danes and had meant it enough to die. His eyes stung as Ceola's mother wept for her lost son. Tidræd told him about how Ludan had brought down a Dane with his fork; about how he himself had wounded one with an arrow, perhaps. He wanted to know about all the battles Oswald had seen and how he had been wounded, and Oswald only got away by giving Tidræd his word that they would work on some warcraft and talk about it all another day. It was the last thing he felt like doing, but Tidræd was Thurstan's son and Oswald would have done all that and more for Thurstan.

He had no sooner left Tidræd when he met Eanfrith walking along with a barrow. He drew a deep breath. Eanflæd had been no older than Edith, a girl, no danger to anyone.

'I… I heard about your sister,' he said.

Eanfrith stiffened and dropped his head, his lips shut tightly. He gripped the handles of his barrow, turning his hands around them.

'She… she was the best of us,' he said. 'And I still don't understand how we lost her that night.'

'Do you think she lost her way in the dark?' It could have happened to anyone. It could have been Edith they had buried. Oswald didn't know what to say to a boy whose sister had died like that.

'I don't know. We were well into the forest when I saw she wasn't with us. My father was so angry with me because he said she was meant to… meant to be with me, but…' Eanfrith looked up then. He wasn't weeping but his lips, his whole face was trembling. 'I swear, Oswald Child, I would never have left without her. I thought she was with him and my mother, and I never heard him tell me to watch her. I had Eanbald on my back but I would have waited for her. I would never have left her behind. I should've waited but I didn't know. My father and I looked for her for half the night, but we couldn't find her. He thought perhaps she was with Osgyth and Sifflæd, but she wasn't. We don't know what happened.'

Eanfrith rubbed his hand across his eyes, still trembling. Oswald was blinking back tears now too. Eanfrith was a brother, and he was a brother. She was no older than Edith.

'We looked for her all day and… and… when I found her I was with Eanwine but I didn't want him to… to see her so I sent him to find Father. I tried to wake her, but I knew… Why her? What could *she* have done to them? It was wicked! She never did anyone any harm. I hear my mother weeping every night now. Eanflæd was the best of us. She was the best of us! She was the only one in our house who was never unkind to anyone. It would've been better if it had been me. My mother and father could have spared me, but none of us could spare her. She was the best of us, Oswald Child! Why her?'

Sometimes there were no answers. Some wrongs were too deep for words to be enough. Oswald could only rub his eyes as Eanfrith had done, and squeeze his arm as they parted. He left with Eanfrith's anguished words ringing in his ears: *She was the best of us. She was the best of us.*

Late in the afternoon, Oswald made his way down to the fields to see what was left of Brinin's harvest, though he wasn't at all sure that it would do him any good to see it. But before he even reached them, he met his father coming back, weary and not a little stern. He smiled grimly when he saw Oswald and beckoned him to follow him.

'I was looking for you, Oswald,' he said. 'Let's find somewhere to sit and talk.'

It was strange to go to the old beech tree with his father and to sit there on its twisted roots as he had so often done with Brinin, but they needed to go somewhere now that they had no hearth to sit by.

'Well, Oswald,' said Edrich. 'What have you done this afternoon?'

'Mostly listened to folk talking about the Danes, Father, and how their kin died. But I did see Brinin. He doesn't know any more than we do. He said that it could have been almost anyone.'

'Anyone?'

'Yes, sir. Brinin said that folk want someone to blame for the raid, and he's the nearest Dane. When I first heard of it I thought Aculf must have done it, but now—'

'You were very quick to think that, a little too quick when we know so little. This morning you spoke of Brinin losing his swine—first the swine and now the harvest, you said. What did you mean by it?'

Oswald's heart sank. Now what was he to do? Anger his father by keeping his mouth shut? That didn't frighten him as it once would have done; he had been near death too often to fear stern words. But to come home battlescarred only to be scolded like a child, that was too belittling to think of. Yet if he answered his father, then he would have to go to Brinin and tell him that he'd done it. And Brinin's tongue could be sharper even than his father's.

'Oh, it's nothing, Father,' said Oswald. 'I was angry and spoke without thinking.'

'Likely you did speak without thinking—you do at times and you ought to tame it—but you meant something by it. Even when we are angry our words are not empty. What did you mean?'

'Please, Father, don't ask me.'

'I have already asked you. Speaking openly is better than hiding these things. I would have thought that we had both learned that by now.' Oswald couldn't help wincing a little at that. 'But if you have forgotten that, let me tell you what I think you meant. Brinin had a swine; you gave him a sow, didn't you? And now it seems that he no longer has one, either because it was lost or stolen or even killed. You believe that Aculf was to blame for the loss of the sow. Although you didn't speak his name, that was who you meant, wasn't it? As lord, it is for me to see that such things are put right. How can I do that if you hide them from me? And, what's more, Brinin is your friend, yet what you have done is not friendship.'

A bad son and a bad friend. So much for being toughened by battle. It only took a few words to thrust him back into boyhood. And if his father had learned all that from one unwary slip spoken in anger, then he did need to tame his tongue.

'I'm sorry, Father. I *thought* of speaking to you about it but...' Yet how could he say how it had truly been? How could he say that he had wanted to speak and that Brinin had begged him not to? It was no more than the truth, but it was too much like blameshifting now that his father was already chiding him.

'You did Brinin an injustice. Has Aculf paid him for the beast?'

'Not that I know of, sir.'

'If he is truly to blame, he will be made to pay. What were you thinking, Oswald? Why would you hide this from me? And why didn't Brinin come to me himself? You were both more than foolish!'

'It was because of Aculf's son, sir, Wulfrich.' Why hide the rest when his father already knew so much? 'We found him by the pen, very frightened. He said something about his father sending him with fodder and that he didn't know that the sow would die. And then he ran off. I looked in the trough and there were yew leaves in it. That's how we learned it was Aculf. He sent his son to kill the sow, but Wulfrich didn't know that's what he was doing. That's why we didn't speak of it, sir. Brin... *we* were worried that if Aculf was shamed before the village, and if he learned what Wulfrich said, then he would make Wulfrich suffer for it. Brinin says that Aculf is overharsh with him.'

Edrich rose and stood leaning against the tree, deep in thought. Oswald sat, hunched and unhappy, growing more uneasy as he waited for him to speak. His father was angry, but Brinin would be angrier still. There would be nothing he could say to make him understand, because Brinin would never have spoken unthinkingly to begin with. And he would have to tell Brinin himself, before he learned of it another way.

'When did this happen?' asked Edrich.

'When we were here after Easter, sir.'

'So he has been three months without the beast and without payment. I can understand Brinin not wanting to bring trouble on the boy when he likely knows only too well what that might mean. But from you, Oswald, it was badly done. You knew of the thing and, what's more, you're my son, one day to lead this place yourself. You ought to have seen that it was put right and you ought to have trusted me to deal with it carefully. Calling a man before the Moot isn't the only way of righting a wrong. We don't know if Aculf had a hand in wrecking Brinin's harvest, and we mustn't blame a man before we *do* know. But if he did, then who is to say that he didn't grow bolder when nothing was done about the sow?'

'Forgive me, sir,' said Oswald. If this chiding had gone beyond what Oswald thought he had truly earned, he understood how the thing must look. But Brinin had been so dogged. 'I *am* sorry, and I do want to put it right.'

'It will be, but let us speak no more of it now. I talked to Brother Wilfred at some length this afternoon. He is very good. He has spoken to everyone in the village about the loss of Brinin's harvest; he has listened and watched. And as he has slept in many houses since the church was lost, he has heard what folk have said by their own hearths. Yet beyond being sure that some *do* know, he has learned nothing. Perhaps I will learn nothing either, but I'm going to do what he has done and go from house to house. In the morning I will start with Aculf, and you will come with me. But, Oswald, while we're there you are to say nothing, not a word. It will be good for you to learn to take care with what you say; but even more, I want you to watch and listen. Watch how I deal with Aculf and learn from that. At times, you have seen what I have missed. Perhaps you'll see something while we are with him. Do you understand? Listen and watch, but don't speak.'

'Yes, sir.'

'Very well. I'll go now. There's so much to be done, and I've felt ready to sleep for much of the day.'

Oswald watched his father walk back down the hillside, but he himself sat on rather gloomily. If they wouldn't go to Aculf until the morning, then there was no need to speak to Brinin straightaway. He had heard enough from his father and wasn't ready to hear Brinin chide him as well. That could wait for another day. How could they right all the many wrongs?

WEAKNESS

As he left the hillside, Oswald saw Eawig trudging along wearily with an empty bucket swinging by his side. The bruise on his cheek had darkened since morning and, as Oswald watched, Eawig fingered it with a grimace. Was this boy to be left unthanked for the bold friendship he had shown? Not while Oswald was there to thank him.

'Eawig!' he called. 'Stop! I want to talk to you.'

Eawig looked up a little warily, but he stopped and waited for Oswald to reach him.

'Is your cheek sore?' asked Oswald, fumbling with the pouch he wore on his belt. Beyond money there wasn't much he could give Eawig now that almost everything he had ever owned was dust and ashes.

'More than my head, sir, though it was only my head that bled.'

'Was Cynestan angry with you? For fighting, I mean.' Oswald's fingers, inside the pouch, fastened onto a penny. That would say what he wanted as readily as anything else. Besides, it was likely more than Eawig had ever had in his life.

'Only a little, sir. He scolded me and warned me not to do it again, and even my grandfather didn't say much about it.' Eawig was shifting uneasily from foot to foot. 'I… I know I ought to have held my tongue, sir, and kept my fists to myself. I hope you'll forgive me, Oswald Child, sir, and my lord your father too. My mother and my grandfather would be so unhappy if—'

'Come now! You heard what my father said. He's going to overlook it. As for myself, let this be a token of how angry I am.'

Oswald reached out, took Eawig's hand and pressed the penny into it. Eawig stared at it before shutting his fingers round it. His bruised face was twitching with a struggle that Oswald saw and knew only too well, that battle he had often fought with himself when he had wanted to weep like a child but tears had seemed like a weakness he was too much of a man to give way to.

'Oh, sir,' said Eawig, his voice hoarser now, though Oswald saw that he would win the battle after all. 'Can't anything be done, sir? It's wicked what's happened here, sir! And Brinin has been so good to me. And you were always such a friend to him, sir, better than anyone. Can't anything be done?'

Oswald felt the weakness then, as Eawig's battle became his own.

'If anything can be done,' he said, 'it will be.'

Ælfwyn was outside her house, cooking over a fire, the steam from her pot drifting away into nothing. When they had shared sorrow in the winter, it was Oswald's breath that had drifted cloudlike. They had huddled around the fire in her house to keep warm, and Ælfwyn had soothed his short-lived sorrow more than he had soothed hers. Winter and summer. The sun had shone, the earth had bloomed and fathers, sons, brothers, friends and homes had all been swept away. How could so much have been lost in a few short months?

A few short months, but Ælfwyn seemed older by years as she greeted him with a smile that was nearer to weeping than anything Oswald had ever seen. Was it even more bitter to lose a son than a husband? She had held her son in her arms once, when he had been too little and weak to lift his own head and had needed a mother to shield him from harm. Beorn's life had ended as it had begun, in weakness, with the arms of another to hold him and lift his head for him. But perhaps loss couldn't be reckoned like that, where one sorrow was weighed against another to see which was the heavier; not when husbands or sons had been lost.

'What a thing for you and your father to come back to, Oswald Child,' said Ælfwyn. 'So much lost!'

'I almost didn't know what I was seeing when we came in sight of the village. My father understood before I did.'

'And they say you were ill. Are you stronger now, Oswald Child?'

'Nothing much wrong with me now that a little time won't put right.'

Through the steam, Oswald saw Ælfwyn weaken. She bowed her head and rubbed her hands down her kirtle.

'Sigulf told me that you were with Beorn when…' she said.

'He… he died in my arms.' Ælfwyn was making it easier for him. There was nothing wild about her sorrow. She stood with her arms wrapped tightly about her chest, holding herself as she had once held her lost son. 'I was with him until the end. Almost the last thing he said was… was "my mother," and I swore that I would see you had everything you needed, as much as if you were my own mother.'

Ælfwyn looked up again at him then. She wasn't sobbing. There was no gasping sorrow that shook her body or drove strange sounds from her mouth. She was still and quiet, but tears were snaking their way down her cheeks as though she barely knew they were there. She didn't speak.

'I won't wait until you ask me,' Oswald went on. 'I'll come and find out what you need. Perhaps you don't need much, and likely there's very little I *can* help with, but Beorn—you know, he saved my life once—Beorn wanted me to. He wanted to know that someone—'

Osgyth's son, Sibwine, came round the side of the house with a bucket of water. Ælfwyn bent down and scooped something up from the ground—Oswald didn't see what it was—then dashed inside. Sibwine, with a knowing glance at Oswald as he set down the bucket, looked after her sadly.

'It's good to see you back whole, Oswald Child,' said Sibwine. Had the Danes waited another winter before gushing into Wessex, Sibwine might have fought at Oswald's side, and might have been among those who hadn't come back whole. But his youth had spared him for now. 'Ælfwyn's been good to us, letting us stay with her until our own house is built again. She and my mother have always been friends. Without our neighbours, we wouldn't even have had the tools to build the house again, nor anyone to help us do it.'

'We can thank God for good neighbours,' said Oswald. They both stood homeless together and both needed others to welcome them under their roof. 'I don't know what my sister would have done without Mildrith. I wish everyone in Oakdene had found their neighbours so good.'

Oswald didn't say it to chide and he would never have thought that Sibwine would take it that way. Why would Sibwine, straightforward and likeable, be among Brinin's foes? But as soon as the words were uttered Sibwine flushed a deep red and dropped his eyes.

'Oswald Child,' he muttered. 'I need to—'

He needed to leave? To speak? To beg forgiveness for being a foe to one who had done him no harm? Though surely *he* couldn't have wrecked the harvest; Oswald couldn't readily think it of him. The words were cut down before they were fully grown. Oswald caught sight of Eanfrith and Ælfæd coming towards them and Sibwine did too. They were only boys, boys like Sibwine, boys like Oswald had been not so long ago. But they were enough to stop Sibwine's speech. He mumbled something Oswald couldn't make out, then walked away.

The evening shadows were long now, but there was no well-known threshold to cross, no table of his own to sit at, and Oswald couldn't bring himself to go back to Cynestan's house yet. He made his way slowly to where home had once been, wearied suddenly, and stood by what was left of his hearth. The hearthstone was still there, blackened like everything else around it. Scorched earth, charred wood, ashes, dust. Everything he had thought of as home, the good and the ill, all gone for ever. He stood by the hearthstone and remembered. After all those months of longing, they had come home to this.

There had been no time for weeping the night before. His father had wept gasping sobs, but Oswald had only thought of what to do, how to find his sister, how to learn what had happened and help his father learn it too. But as he cast his eyes around, almost seeing the shadows of what—and who—had once been there, he did weep. Not with heaving breaths as his father had done. If anyone had been watching from afar, they wouldn't have known. He wept like Ælfwyn and didn't even wipe the tears away.

It was a weakness. He knew it was. Weakness and folly. He had come back alive from war when others, better men than he was, were dead. He had come back alive to find his home gone, but his sister and friend unharmed. Why was he weeping? Surely he should be thankful. He *was* thankful, but the tears still came. Another shadow, long like his own, stretched out beside him.

'It's good to see you home, my boy.' Brother Wilfred, twice spared.

'I don't know why I'm weeping,' said Oswald, almost ashamed to say it aloud. And suddenly Leoba sprang to mind, as she wept in her father's house. But why hide his tears? Brother Wilfred had eyes, and sharp ones too.

'We have all wept,' said Brother Wilfred. 'It would be stranger if you weren't.'

LIES

Early in the morning, Oswald and his father found Aculf still with his beasts. Aculf didn't greet them with any great warmth but he wasn't so bold as to greet his lord with coolness either.

'I've come to talk to you, Aculf,' said Edrich.

'You're welcome, my lord,' said Aculf, though he didn't sound as though he meant it. 'I'll tell my wife to take the children out.'

'No, I want them to stay, your wife and the children. Come, let's sit together by your hearth.'

The three younger children were huddled together in one corner. They weren't playing, not even in whispers. They only sat, watchful and still, without a word passing between them. Wulfrich stood by one of the roof-posts and was more than watchful. He was frightened. He stared at his mother, wordlessly begging her for something, but she only shook her head slightly.

Oswald saw all this while his father and Aculf talked. Edrich Thegn did nothing quickly. He asked Aculf about his harvest, about his wheat and barley and beans. He asked about his beasts. He listened to Aculf talk and put him at his ease. He asked about the night the Danes had come, and Aculf told the tale. Sægyth, his wife, sat with her head lowered and said nothing. Her hands were clasped tightly together in her lap. Oswald saw that too. No one in this house was happy.

But Aculf was all smiles, those overbroad, overmeek, overslippery smiles that he had always kept for Edrich Thegn and which Oswald had loathed since he was a young boy. Yet even as he smiled, Aculf's eye kept falling on his son. He looked at him, then his eye darted towards Oswald. No, not towards him; above him, perhaps, or a little beyond him. Something unspoken was uttered, and Oswald saw

Wulfrich stiffen and put more of the roof-post between himself and his father.

Oswald looked over his shoulder to find the unspoken thing that the boy had understood—and feared—so swiftly. There on the roof-post behind him, the fellow of the one Wulfrich hid behind, hung a rod. It wasn't very long or thick, but it was sturdy. It hung proudly before the eyes of the whole house as a warning—a threat—about what it would do to them if they did not heed Aculf swiftly, if they did not keep him happy.

Aculf's eyes fell on his son again, on the rod, on the doorway. Wulfrich, as soundless as a shadow, slipped from the house, and Aculf's smile grew broader. He'd sent his son away, against his lord's wishes, and he was happy with his work. Why? Why did Aculf want Wulfrich gone? Why had he uttered that unspoken threat?

'Now, Aculf,' said Edrich. 'It has come to my knowledge that some months back you killed Brinin's swine by sending your son with fodder that had yew leaves in it.'

It was such a swift step, such a sudden dive that Oswald could have laughed aloud. He saw his father's wisdom. Aculf had been stiff as he had welcomed them, a little warlike and ready to be blamed. He was guilty of something; Oswald could see that. If his father hadn't forbidden him from speaking, Oswald would have rushed straight to blame and wrenched the truth from him. And it would have been folly. His father had taken the slow way and had softened Aculf with friendly speech, as though they had come in fellowship only to greet him after being away. Aculf's shield was lowered and now Edrich could throw the blame at him without warning and see what he did with it.

The swift blame hit Aculf hard and shock, fear and anger flickered over his face. But it was fleeting. He raised his shield again and met Edrich Thegn's eye.

'Yes, that was a bad business, my lord,' he said smoothly. 'I did send the boy with it, not to Brinin but to anyone who wanted it. I had more than I needed that day. The boy was careless with what he put in the bucket and took it to Brinin. He often troubles me with his carelessness. The sow died as you know, my lord. I beat the boy for it at the time.'

Was it a lie? Oswald's gut told him that it was. It sounded like it might be true, and Aculf was answering his father so boldly. Yet there had been that fleeting flicker of fear. Had his father seen it too?

'That might be so, Aculf, and *if* your son was careless'—that 'if', a little more weighted than the other words, sounded to Oswald much like disbelief—'*if* your son was careless, you must teach him to be more careful. But beating him still leaves Brinin without a sow. And you're the boy's father. Even if the blame was not yours, you still must pay for the lost beast.'

Did Sægyth know the truth of all this? Would her face share any of it? But she still sat a little too stiffly, her head down, her hands still clasped in her lap. The children still crouched watchful in the shadows. There was so much fear in this house that it was almost like a stench. Oswald longed to be outside where the air was fresher.

'My lord, I *did* try to pay for it. I sent the boy with one of my own beasts, but Brinin wouldn't take it. He brought it back himself and even threw the rope at me. Some of my neighbours saw it, my lord. You can ask any of them. I can't make him take the beast if he won't have it.'

Was it all lies? Could lies sound almost like truth? Would Aculf call upon his neighbours to be witnesses to a lie? Perhaps there was some truth in what Aculf said; he had always been skilled in twisting it. But Brinin had said nothing about Aculf offering to pay for his dead sow.

'Nevertheless, Aculf, you will pay him—eight pennies—and I will see that he takes it. He has no father to teach him wisdom in these things. And you cannot tell me, Aculf, that you have given him no grounds to dislike and mistrust you. Now, if you have the money, I'll take it to him myself.'

Aculf opened the leather pouch on his belt and dropped eight pennies into Edrich's outstretched hand. Aculf was not among the poorest in the village but neither was he among the richest, and eight pennies was a lot to spend in one day with nothing to show for it. His pouch would be lighter, and he might have to sell one of his beasts to fill it again. But if Aculf was angry, he had the wisdom not to show it. There had been no moot, no shame, no talk among the neighbours, none of what Brinin had warned Oswald against. If Edrich Thegn had been unshifting, he had not been unkind. That was wisdom instead of the folly that Oswald himself had wanted.

'Now tell me what you know about the loss of Brinin's harvest,' said Edrich.

It was another shift, but Aculf was ready this time.

'Nothing, my lord. No one I've spoken to knows anything about it.'

'Someone knows. Let me ask your son. Children often hear and see what the men and women miss.'

Edrich looked behind him to where Wulfrich had been standing. He turned back to Aculf with a frown.

'Where is he? Didn't I say that no one was to leave the house?'

'He must have slipped out against your bidding while we were talking, my lord. He's very wilful,' said Aculf, and Oswald saw Sægyth's hands clasp each other even more tightly. 'I'll see to him later, though I doubt he knows any more than I do.'

That *was* a lie. Aculf hadn't been ready for Edrich Thegn to ask him about the sow, but he'd been ready for this. He knew something. Wulfrich knew something, and Aculf didn't trust him to keep his mouth shut. And the lie was spoken as coolly as everything else. How much truth had there been in any of it?

'My lord, it was bad that he lost his harvest,' went on Aculf, still cool, still smooth, 'but I wasn't shocked to learn that someone had wrecked it. Given what happened that night, my lord, folk were angry.'

'Given what happened that night?' said Edrich. 'What does that have to do with Brinin?'

'No one thought it had anything to do with him, my lord, until we learned that he'd been seen speaking to one of them; not fighting, my lord, only speaking. Young Sibwine saw and heard them; he's old enough to be a witness to it. The Danes killed or wounded others that night, but the Dane *he* met only spoke to him. What were folk to think after that?'

Oswald almost forgot to heed his father then. A whole flood of angry words were ready to gush out, and it was hard to hold them back. His father caught his eye, and Oswald clenched his teeth to keep the words in. But his father hadn't forbidden him from speaking to Sibwine. Sibwine would hear what he had to say. Little wonder he had blushed with shame.

'You forget, Aculf,' said Edrich, icy cold now, 'that Brinin saved my life and that his knowledge of their tongue helped him do it.'

'No, my lord, none of us have forgotten that and we are all thankful that he did. But no one saw him helping anyone that night.' Sægyth lifted her head—Oswald saw her—but she dropped it again without speaking. 'No one saw him fighting anyone. No one knows how he was wounded. I don't say that this is what I think, my lord, only what folk are saying, and why one of them might have wrecked his harvest.'

'Well, Aculf,' said Edrich, still cold as he rose to his feet, 'a man cannot be found guilty of what no one has seen. And you would do well to spend less of your time in idle talk.'

And Edrich left without wasting any more time, Oswald still struggling to hold his tongue as he followed him. It was only when they were outside and a little way from the house that he said anything.

'He's lying, Father.'

'How do you know?'

'Aculf told Wulfrich to leave. He has a rod hanging up in the house. Twice I saw him look at Wulfrich, then at the rod, then at the door. Aculf threatened to beat him if he stayed in the house and then lied to you and blamed Wulfrich for it. And when he said that no one had seen Brinin helping anyone, his wife looked up at him. That was the only time she lifted her head. She's scared of him too, not only the children. And she knows something, and Wulfrich knows something, and Aculf doesn't want *us* to know.'

'We'll sift it out. Something like this can't stay hidden for long. Now, Oswald, see if you can find the boy. He may talk to you when he's away from his father.'

WEDGES

The afternoon was hot with the smell of rain in the air. Sweat trickled down Brinin's forehead and into his eyes, and he had to keep stopping to wipe it away. A heap of long boards lay beside him, green and ready for crafting. He had done work like this before but never the skilled kind, only the weary dragging which needed little care and less wisdom, when his hands had smarted from the splinters and Aculf had always been somewhere nearby to goad him. But Brother Cwichelm had taught him how to drive the wedges into the fresh wood and beat them down until it split cleanly along the whole length. So today he did the skilled work with Garulf while others did the dragging, and Aculf was nowhere in sight. It was free work; work that Cynestan had asked him to do but which he didn't *have* to do; work that he had been chosen for because he had a skill to offer; work that he would be paid for at the end. And he felt the first little sparks of hope and happiness he had known in weeks.

He worked swiftly. The more he did the less Garulf could do. He was uneasy about Garulf; there was something in his look that Brinin didn't like. It had been months since they had last worked side by side, and Garulf was tiring a little too quickly. He was slower and dropped things too easily and too often. Brinin hadn't forgotten that frightening swoon during the haymaking. He was glad when Cynestan called Garulf away. Perhaps Cynestan hadn't forgotten either.

When Oswald came, Brinin was sitting in the shade waiting for more newly felled boughs to be dragged in from the forest. He didn't mind a little fellowship while he waited and was happy to quench his thirst from the flask of ale that Oswald brought. The skin on his face and the back of his neck were burning where the sun had beaten down on them.

'So my father wants you to help with building, then?' asked Oswald, sitting down beside him on the grass. 'I thought he would.'

'Yes, Cynestan spoke to me about it yesterday evening and he says I'll be paid too.' It was strange to say something like that aloud. It was still too new, something that once he would never have dreamed of. 'Cynestan says that for two weeks' work your father will give me a swine or its worth in other things. And he says that there'll likely be more work after that.'

'So will you take the beast then?'

'I don't think so. Better to take it in wheat or barley or even oats if your father can spare me any, or money if he can't. I'll need to eat this winter and I'll need seed. Daglæf gave me a little wheat for some work I did for him, but it isn't nearly enough.'

'You were always going to eat this winter, one way or the other,' said Oswald doggedly, 'but you will need seed.'

Brinin took another long drink. The ale felt good, cooling his throat.

'Listen, Brinin,' said Oswald. 'I need to talk to you.'

'Then talk now. The men won't be back with the wood for a while.'

Oswald kept his eyes on the grass, pulling it out blade by blade.

'I… my father knows about your dead sow.'

Brinin froze with the flask halfway to his lips. Only he and Oswald had known the truth. Ludan had almost stumbled over it, but he was dead and could tell no one. So how else could Edrich Thegn know unless…

'How does he know?' But Brinin didn't want to know the answer. Why wasn't Oswald looking at him?

Oswald tugged up a handful of grass all at once.

'I told him.'

'You told him?' But how could Oswald have told him? He had said he wouldn't. How could a friend break his word? It made no sense.

'I… I didn't mean to.'

'I don't understand. You must have meant to or you wouldn't have done it.' Brinin knew his voice was cold—too cold for speaking to Oswald—but he couldn't help it.

'Brinin, please believe me. I didn't mean to. When I heard about your harvest, I was so angry. I wasn't thinking. I said, "first the swine and now the harvest". I wished I hadn't as soon as I'd said it, and then my father asked me about it afterwards.'

'But you told me you wouldn't.'

How could being angry make anyone say anything? Speaking something aloud meant a man had thought, otherwise how could he speak? Brinin didn't understand it. Even when he had called Aculf a fool he had thought about it first, not for very long perhaps, but he *had* thought.

'I'm sorry, Brinin. I... I knew you'd be angry, but I don't think it will be as bad as you feared. My father—'

'You told me you wouldn't. And you still answered your father when he asked you about it.'

'You know what my father's like. I had to answer him!'

'Did you?'

'Besides, what I'd said to begin with was enough for him to think it all out. He's no fool. I told him how Aculf is with Wulfrich because I knew he'd be careful then. He doesn't want to be unkind but—'

'What's he going to do about it?'

'He's already been to Aculf and he's made him pay for the sow. He's got the money to give you himself, but there'll be no moot, Brinin, no shame before the village, none of what you were worried about.'

Brinin stood up and walked away a little. He needed that money. He needed a sow for the dung, to give Eawig the beast he owed him from among the sow's young, to be free enough to feed himself. But he would have given it all up for Wulfrich, to make his life a little easier. He *had* given it all up for Wulfrich. And Oswald had given him his word, and Brinin would never have thought that he would break it. Brinin could see that Oswald was as sorry as he said he was, so unhappy as he sat there, but he had still done it.

'You gave me your word,' he said.

'I didn't. I didn't swear to anything. I only said—'

'Saying it is as good as swearing!'

'I'm sorry! I need to learn to keep my mouth shut. I know that. But it isn't as bad as you feared. You'll have the money, and there'll be no moot, so even if—'

'And what about Wulfrich?'

'What about him? Nothing's going to be any worse for him—it's likely as bad as it could be already. I was with my father when he spoke to Aculf this morning. He laid all the blame on Wulfrich—my father didn't believe him—and he said he'd already beaten him for it and offered you a sow that you wouldn't take. Aculf already knew that you thought he'd done it. Perhaps Wulfrich told him himself.'

'I told him.'

Now Oswald's face shifted from uneasy wretchedness to utter bewilderment. He gaped at Brinin.

'What do you mean?' he said.

'I told him that I knew and that I would overlook it instead of going to your father about it. And I asked him to be kinder to his son.'

'You said *that* to him?' The bewilderment grew into outright disbelief. 'Did he offer you a sow?'

'Yes, and I gave it back. I didn't want his beast. I wanted him to be kinder to Wulfrich. He only gave it to me so he wouldn't have to listen. And I asked Daglæf to tell me if he heard Aculf beating Wulfrich. And now that your father has spoken to him he'll do as he likes to him.'

'He's doing as he likes already! I've never seen a boy more frightened in my life! Don't be such a fool, Brinin, and don't look at me like that. You *are* being a fool, and I don't care if I say it! Daglæf would never tell you what Aculf was doing. He may be friendly towards you, but he's Aculf's kin, and you can't tell a man how to raise his son, even if he is a bad father. Why would you even think Aculf would listen to you? You know what he's like better than almost anyone else in the village. I'll tell you what he's likely been doing: he's been beating Wulfrich where the neighbours won't hear! And *you* got him that beating Aculf told my father about! Wulfrich doesn't look like a boy who hasn't been beaten in three months. Three days more likely, if it's even been as long as that!'

Brinin had been staring down at Oswald, angry and unshifting, blaming him for an unwitting mistake. But Oswald's words hit him like a hammer blow, driving a wedge into the anger, splitting it open to show the truth that lay inside. Brinin had never thought of himself as a fool. Foolishness was for other men. Aculf was a fool. Even Oswald had sometimes been foolish. But now, suddenly, he knew that he had been the biggest fool of all; too foolish even to see that he was one;

harming Wulfrich because he had been too sure of himself and too stuck in his thoughts to see what was before his eyes. That was far worse than a few unthinking words.

He heard the men coming back with more wood, heard himself muttering something to Oswald about needing to work, saw Oswald walking away. He drove in the wedges, beat them down, split the wood along its length, began again with another felled tree. But all of it seemed dim and far off. He had been a fool. Why had it taken him so long to see it?

STING

Oswald's forbearance was gone. He had spent most of it in Aculf's house that morning, Brinin had scattered the rest. He was restless as he left Brinin, his hold on himself slipping away. But that wouldn't help him much. He still had work to do that day, if it could be called work. Only after he had found Wulfrich could he brood over the wickedness and folly of the world.

Wulfrich wasn't easy to find, and Oswald soon tired of looking for him. What was the good of hunting for a boy who was likely playing or skulking in some hidden place, of which there were too many to name? Oswald had not been a man so long that he had forgotten what it was like to be a boy. And how often had his father scolded him for whiling away the day where he could not be found? It had been the one misdeed his father's sternness had never helped him to overcome. Wulfrich would be found when he was hungry enough to make his way home. What boy isn't led by his belly?

It was Sibwine he found, or perhaps Sibwine found him. Afterwards, Oswald was never sure which it had been. At the sight of him, all the anger of the morning simmered up again. He strode towards Sibwine, took him by the arm and pulled him away from the houses.

'So! Were *you* the one who spread that tale about Brinin talking to the Danes? And have you forgotten how he spoke to the Danes to save my father? Couldn't you have shown a little sense? What bond do you think he has to the Danes when he risked his life to get my father away from them?'

Oswald's words seemed to feed his anger. He would never have hoped for anything better from Aculf; but he had always liked Sibwine and that made it worse. He saw Sibwine wince as though his words were stinging him like so many thorns, saw him redden and bow his head as he had done the evening before.

'You're right, Oswald Child,' he mumbled. Then he lifted his head, clenching his teeth like a man readying himself for a wound to be tended. 'I... I did see it. Brinin warned my sister and me that the Danes were coming to the swine pen where we were hiding. He helped me get my sister away, and we ran to the forest. I hid her somewhere better. She was very frightened, and it took me a while to settle her. I thought I could hear a struggle and I went back to see if it was Brinin and if he needed any help. But when I got there, he wasn't fighting. He was standing, talking to someone, and in the Danish tongue too. I don't know what they were saying. Then the Dane ran off. I didn't understand it and I didn't know what to do, so I said nothing to him and went back to my sister. He didn't even know I'd seen him. I still don't understand. He helped *us*, and I didn't see him helping them, but why was he talking to one of them? I didn't see him fight but—'

'How does that make it any better? You had everyone thinking he'd helped the Danes, yet you've just told me he helped *you*!'

'I never told anyone he'd helped them! I swear it, Oswald Child! I told my mother what I'd seen—no one else, not even my sister—and she said I'd be wiser to keep it to myself so no harm came of it, and she wouldn't let me say another word about it. She said that if I didn't understand what I'd seen, how would others understand, and it would do no good to speak of it. I didn't even get to tell her about how Brinin had helped us. And my sister won't speak of that night at all. She's barely said a word since. Someone else must have overheard us, as before the day was out half the village knew about it. It wasn't my mother. She's always hated idle talk—says the world would be better if more folk knew how to keep a still tongue—and she was very angry with me when she thought I hadn't heeded her. I had a hard time making her believe me.'

Sibwine was so earnest, his words dripping with so much truth, that Oswald didn't think to doubt him. But he was still angry. Brinin had been left to the mob like a bone cast among hungry hounds. It was a mercy that nothing worse had happened.

'But couldn't you at least have said a word on his behalf? How could you keep your mouth shut after he helped you like that?'

'I *know* I did the wrong thing! I've hated myself for weeks because of it, more so after that wretch, whoever it was, wrecked Brinin's field. But I didn't understand what he'd been doing. You don't know what it's been like here! I was ready to fight the Danes but to stand alone against the village… I was scared. Perhaps you've never known fear, Oswald Child, but I have!'

Sibwine hadn't meant to chide, but Oswald felt the sting. His anger melted away at once, leaving him only with shame. He saw himself as he had been not so long ago. He remembered how he had said nothing to help Brinin with less to fear than Sibwine; how time and again he had stopped short of what he knew to be right until at last he had come up with a plan that had killed his best friend's brother. Who was he to blame Sibwine for being afraid?

'I have,' he said. 'And I've done worse than you because of it. I'm sorry. But please, you must put it right or, believe me, you'll never forgive yourself. I'll stand by you if anyone gives you any trouble.'

Sibwine set his jaw again and nodded. Oswald left him, his hand resting briefly on Sibwine's shoulder in friendship as he went. Aculf had been very swift to put Sibwine's name to this tale, but perhaps it had been Aculf, smooth-tongued, who had spread it after all. Would they never be rid of him?

The sun flung down its heat all afternoon. Most men were working shirtless now—it was too hot to do much else—though Brinin was already wishing he wasn't. Eawig, light-haired but darker-skinned, didn't seem to feel it. He sweated, but the sun poured off him like water and left no mark. Brinin, as speckled as a throstle's breast, could feel himself slowly roasting. His arms were already growing a deep red, and he knew his skin would keep burning long after the sun had set. But the sting of folly was a keener one.

The heap of boards was growing, and everyone was waiting for Cynestan to come to tell them if they could stop. Standing in the shade of the trees, Brinin watched as Wulfrich came round behind Aculf's house, then shrank away, cowering, as his father followed him. He had no time to dash away before Aculf grabbed his arm, lifting it so high that the boy's feet barely reached the ground. Brinin couldn't hear what Aculf was saying but he knew how he would be sounding. He knew the angry hiss. Aculf drove his words home with a parting blow to the back of his son's head then stalked round the side of his house and out of sight. Wulfrich, his hand on his head, watched after his father warily. Then he rubbed his arm across his eyes and trudged wretchedly away.

It was too easy for a man to shut his eyes to knowledge, whether it burst in on him without warning or grew up slowly like an unwelcome weed among his crops. And if that knowledge had a sting to it, who wanted to linger long to bear it? He had been angry with Oswald once for blundering in and making everything worse because he hadn't stopped long enough to think. And now was he, Brinin, the blunderer? Brinin knew he was no Thurstan with enough strength of will to make a man listen when he spoke. Aculf had heeded Thurstan, at least for a time. But who was he? Why would anyone listen to anything he said? He might be free, but he was young and alone, with few friends and no kin. Besides, Thurstan had warned Aculf to take care how he handled another man's slave, but Wulfrich was Aculf's son.

Brinin was still lost in such thoughts when Cynestan came to say that they were done for the day. He was still lost as he made his way through the trees to the stream in the clearing. He knelt beside it and bent low, shutting his eyes and splashing the icy water over his face. He scooped it up to his neck and let it spill down his back in long, cold trickles. Here in the shade the water was almost wintercold, soothing and cooling him for a time. But the coolness would be short-lived. He would feel the sting for a few days until his skin peeled away like birchbark. He'd be better to keep his shirt on in the morning, however much he sweated, and to pray for a cloudy day.

Brinin sat down on the grass and ran his hands through his wet hair. Years before, he and Oswald had come to this same clearing to play. That had been a golden day, the like of which Brinin had never known before nor since. It had been full of dragons and battles, and every tale they had told themselves had seemed to come alive before their eyes. They had eaten the food Oswald had brought with their feet in the stream, the cool water lapping around their toes. Afterwards, they had leapt about in the ripples, laughing and kicking the water at each other.

The day had ended badly. Even as a small boy, Brinin had known that it was folly for a slave to shirk his work for a whole day, had known even as he had played what the end of it must be. And although Oswald had never told him, Brinin had somehow known that the day had ended worse for his friend than it had for him. Aculf, eager to shame Oswald before his father, had left Brinin's beating to Row, and Row had spared him, settling instead for a few well-chosen words. Oswald's father was nothing like Row.

That was what Brinin had lost when Row had fallen. He had not only lost the fellowship of a brother, the sharing of everything—spoken and unspoken—that only a brother could truly understand. He had lost the wisdom of an older kinsman. He had lost someone near enough to tell him when he was wrong and when to stop being a fool. Ludan, Garulf and Brother Wilfred had offered him wisdom, and he had only half-listened to them, though he owed them all better than that. Besides, Oswald hadn't only played with him here. This was where he had hidden the horses on the night Brinin and Row had fled—Brinin knew almost everything about that time now, thanks to Tidræd. If anyone had earned the right to call him a fool, and if anyone had earned the right to have his mistakes overlooked or at least met with a little kindness, it was Oswald. Brinin was a fool, a proud fool and, what was worse, a thankless fool. Given who Oswald was and what he had done, that was almost unforgivable.

Brinin stood up and gingerly put on his shirt again. Things with Oswald could be put right. Neither of them had ever held on to anger with the other for long. The trouble was Wulfrich, and Brinin didn't know how that wrong could be undone.

Edith's father and brother were back with her again. The many tearful prayers she'd whispered in the darkness had been answered. They were back whole. But it wasn't the homecoming she had longed for and built up in her mind. They had come home to so much sorrow, so much wrong. Edith loved Mildrith and her household. Cenwyn was such a steady friend, and Mildrith had welcomed her like another daughter, had listened to her troubles and shared ready wisdom. Edith loved them all, even Tidræd, so unlike her own brother. But it was bitter to have her father and brother back, yet to eat and sleep scattered about the village and not together under one roof.

Her father seemed to have grown old in a few short months. His beard was streaked with grey that hadn't been there before. Even now that he had rested from the road, he still seemed weary. As for Oswald, it stung Edith to look at him. They had told her he had been wounded and then ill for a time. Her own eyes told her the rest, and she knew that they hadn't told her the worst of it. She understood now why Sigulf had kept his eyes from meeting hers when he had ridden home with news. He had been shielding her, as her father and brother shielded her now. Oswald had brushed aside her worries as a man drives away a fly. It was a kindness. Wasn't it better to know that her brother had felt death's fingers only after death had already withdrawn its hand? Yet for all their shielding, she knew. And it chilled her to learn how near she had come to that sorrow others were stumbling under.

Edith was with Osgyth that afternoon to see her almost rebuilt house. There was only the roof and doors to put on now. She stood with her between the four walls and looked at the sky, while Osgyth's daughter, Sifflæd, and two of Ælfwyn's daughters pushed mud into the cracks in the wood to keep out the wind in the winter. Sibwine sat outside making a stool, with Daglæf standing over him to guide him. Neighbours had come together to help one another, though it hadn't drawn them any nearer as she had hoped. Friends helped friends, and any mistrust still simmered unbridled.

When she left Osgyth, Edith caught sight of Sægyth under the eaves of Aculf's house, staring at her earnestly, almost beseechingly. Edith went to her at once. Her eyes were very red, though there were no tears on her face.

'May I speak to you, my lady Edith?' she whispered. 'Now, while Aculf is in the field?'

Without waiting for an answer, Sægyth leaned through the doorway and told Wulfrich to watch his little sisters and keep them away from the fire. Then she led Edith away from the house, her eyes darting everywhere to be sure her husband was truly out of sight.

'Something has been weighing on me, my lady,' she said. 'You know how folk have been talking, how they've been saying that Brinin helped the Danes that night, that he spoke to them and wasn't seen helping any of us. I don't know if he spoke to the Danes or not, my lady, but he did help my son.'

Edith almost asked why she had said nothing before, how Sægyth could keep quiet about such a thing while the village turned Brinin into a foe, but she stopped herself. Sægyth's watchfulness and Edith's knowledge of her husband were answer enough. Shouldn't she rather wonder how Sægyth had found the strength to speak now?

'Ulf got lost that night, my lady,' went on Sægyth, her eyes filling with tears at the thought of it. 'I thought he was with Aculf, but he wasn't, and then I couldn't find him in the dark, but Brinin found him and brought him to me. If he hadn't…'

Sægyth looked around again, almost fearfully now.

'Why are you telling me?' asked Edith. 'What do you want me to do?'

'Your father came to see us this morning, my lady. I don't want to… I can't say anything against my husband, but some of what he said might have misled your father. Please, my lady, tell him what I told you, but I beg you, ask him to say nothing of it to Aculf nor to anyone else. If folk were to start talking about it… But it will be enough that your father knows and I think… I think he'll understand.'

Without waiting for an answer, Sægyth walked away, but she stopped and turned back again.

'Brinin isn't a bad boy, my lady. He's been good to my Wulfrich too, though heaven knows I couldn't blame him if he wanted nothing to do with any of us.'

Then she left, dashing out of sight to her house and her children.

LORD

'Ah, my boy,' said Edrich Thegn, as Brinin stepped from the gloom of the trees into the bright sunshine. He spoke with a warmth that still seemed strange to Brinin on the lips of his lord. 'Cynestan showed me the work you did with the wood today. I am thankful for it. We will need many hands if we are to build this place again before winter.'

'Yes, my lord,' said Brinin.

'Now, I want to speak to you. Come. I'll go home with you.'

There was shame in having nothing but the floor for his lord to sit on, and in his eyes falling on the emptiness of Brinin's hut and the broken pieces of what had once stood there. Each step nearer had a sting to it. But the bench Brinin had been working on was done and stood outside the hut. Edrich Thegn sank onto it wearily, then beckoned Brinin to sit beside him.

'First, you're to take this as payment for your lost sow,' he said.

Edrich tipped a handful of pennies into Brinin's hand. Brinin stared at them. Was this what his sow had been worth? He had never held—or even seen—so much money before, cold and heavy in his hand. Aculf must have almost nothing left.

'Aculf ought to have given you this months ago,' went on Edrich Thegn. 'I must say, I am more than unhappy with my son for not bringing this business before me sooner. He did you a great wrong, and I have spoken to him most sternly about it. I very much fear that leaving this wrong unrighted has opened a door to other, greater wrongs.'

The truth flashed on Brinin like sunlight on an arrowhead. He saw how Oswald, penned in by a few unwary words and a stern father, had spoken unwillingly. He saw how he had let all the blame be heaped on his own head, when in truth it was Brinin who had browbeaten him into it. He had made Oswald choose between angering either his father or his friend. That he should have done this to Oswald of all men—Oswald whose marked back he could still see in his mind—and left Wulfrich no better off for it… He was a proud, thankless fool, and he didn't mind saying so.

'My lord,' he said. 'Oswald Child has taken upon himself blame that was rightly mine. If you must be stern, be stern with me. Oswald Child wanted to go to you straightaway, but I begged him to say nothing so as not to bring trouble on Wulfrich. As it is, I didn't help Wulfrich either. Blame me, my lord, not Oswald Child.'

'Well,' said Edrich Thegn, 'I think I understand things now. You grew up in my household so let me speak to you as your father might have done had he lived. Overlooking one wrong will not right another. All fathers make mistakes—I have made more than I care to remember—but some go far beyond mistakes. I don't mind telling you that I did not like what I saw in Aculf's house today, and it is worthy of you to wish to help the boy. But some wrongs cannot easily be righted and, if they can, only time and care and wisdom will do it. You cannot help the boy by overlooking his father's wrongdoing. And you are no longer a slave who must wait for his lord to say what is wrong and put it right. You are free. If you are wronged, you may ask for justice. Indeed, it is your *duty* to ask. Otherwise any man might kill his neighbour's beasts or flatten his neighbour's crops without fear. You will take this money and buy a new beast or whatever else you need. And if anything like it happens again you will come to me at once, for your neighbours' sake if not your own. Now that brings me to your harvest. My son tells me that you don't know who could have done this wicked deed. Is that so?'

'Yes, my lord. The way things have been, it could have been almost anyone.'

'That's what others have said to me.' Edrich was very grim now, truly stern as he hadn't been before. 'But listen, my boy, when I find the man who did it, this too will be put right, and he will wish that he had kept to his bed that night.

'Now, you are doubtless aware of the talk there has been, with folk saying that you were seen speaking to the Danes or even helping them.

I more than any man know what kind of weapon that tongue of yours can be and that speech need not mean friendship. If I am to put an end to the talking, I must ask you about it. Tell me everything about that night: what happened, what you saw, what you did, who you spoke to. Then perhaps we can put these fears to rest.'

Brinin drew a deep breath. No one had asked him anything about that night, no one but Oswald, whom he had brushed aside rather than speak of it. No one had asked, and he had offered no answers. But Edrich Thegn was the one man who would swiftly understand how Brinin could have spoken to a Dane and lived.

So he told him everything: how suddenly the Danes had come and the wild fear they had let loose; how he had seen that his few friends were safe, then had thought and watched in the darkness. He told him about stumbling over Ulf and helping him find his mother; of the Danish voices speaking of swift and easy takings; of the torchlit head that had fallen into darkness before he could shoot; of the fire that swept through the village; of the weeping in the swine pen.

'Sibwine and I dragged her out, my lord. We ran to the forest, but a Dane came after us. I hid in a tree while they ran on ahead. Then I fell on the Dane. We struggled for a long time, but he got the better of me in the end. The fire was bright then, and I saw him. It was Skorri, my lord.'

'Skorri?' asked Edrich Thegn, but without the ready understanding Brinin had hoped for.

'The Dane we left bound in Readingum, my lord. He said he ought to have killed me before, and I thought he would kill me then, but he only slashed my arm.' Brinin put his hand to his arm. The skin was tight round the wound now. Likely he would bear the scar to his grave. 'He said he would show me mercy because we had shown him mercy. Perhaps someone saw me speaking to *him*, my lord.'

'Someone did see: Sibwine. Though it was a shameful thing for him to spread that tale while saying nothing about how you had helped him and his sister. Shameful. I shall have something to say to him about it.'

Edrich Thegn was even grimmer now than before, his brow as furrowed as a freshly ploughed field. Brinin could almost have pitied Sibwine if he hadn't forsaken him to the hatred of the village. Everything about the world was twisted and wrong, when a foe showed more thanks than a neighbour.

Edrich Thegn rose and stood for a time looking down over the village without speaking. Brinin saw his eyes, as Oswald's had done, fall upon the burnt earth where the hall had been, saw his lips tighten as Oswald's had done, and saw him turn away.

'You are in no easy place,' said Edrich Thegn at last. 'Fear makes fools of most men. It seems to have made fools of half the village. But keep your head and your courage. You are not without friends here. Perhaps you have more than you think. Remember that. You are not without friends.'

With that, Edrich Thegn left him, Brinin suddenly as weary as his lord had looked.

～

Oswald caught no sight of Wulfrich until well into the afternoon. He was standing with Tidræd and Tidwine, watching the men who were rebuilding the storehouse. Tidræd, older and taller, seemed almost fatherlike as he pointed things out to the younger boys and bent over to speak to them. None of them saw Oswald coming towards them.

'Wulfrich!' Oswald called, with one last glance around for Aculf. 'Come here. I want to speak to you.'

Wulfrich started, his eyes wide with fright, as though Oswald, beastlike, might tear him limb from limb. Slowly he backed away.

'There's nothing to worry about,' said Oswald. 'I'm not going to—'

Wulfrich dashed away. Oswald looked at Tidræd in bewilderment, but Tidræd only shrugged his shoulders and turned back to the workmen. Was Oswald to wait all day to find this troublesome boy only to lose him again at once? He ran after him.

Ahead, Oswald saw Wulfrich dash behind Brinin's hut and heard him speak.

'Don't let him talk to me! I don't want him to talk to me!'

'Who?' Brinin now. 'What are you scared of?'

'Oswald Child! Don't let him talk to me! I won't talk to him!'

'Come now!' said Brinin. 'Oswald Child won't hurt you, and besides, he'll be your lord one day so you ought to listen to him. Let me go with you, and we'll hear what he has to say.'

Perhaps Brinin could settle Wulfrich. Oswald had little hope of getting near him without help now. He was about to go round the side of the hut when Wulfrich spoke again, almost screaming now, and Oswald stopped dead.

'No! I won't talk to him! I won't! I hate him!'

What had he ever done to this boy to earn hate? He'd barely even spoken to him before.

'You hate him? Don't say that. He's my friend, and so are you. I don't want you to be foes. What harm has he done you?'

'He said my father couldn't be workreeve any more, and now he's always at home and… and it's all Oswald Child's fault.'

Then Wulfrich saw Oswald. He dashed away again, and this time Oswald didn't follow. He sighed and looked down at Brinin, who sat on the grass with his tools around him.

'He hates me for that?' he said, sitting down.

'Likely he didn't see so much of Aculf when he was workreeve.'

'What could I have done? We had to find someone else.'

'And you were right to. Aculf isn't fit to be workreeve. But who can blame Wulfrich for wishing he still was?'

'There's never an easy answer to anything. My father told me to speak to him, but there's no good trying again today. What on earth did he think I was going to say?'

Brinin was sitting without even a shadow of coolness or anger, as though no hard words had passed between them that day. But Oswald could still hear his own words ringing in his head.

'Listen, Brinin,' he said. 'I'm sorry I spoke as I did. I need to learn to hold my tongue. I don't think you're a fool and I shouldn't have said you were, even if I don't think you should have—'

'I *am* a fool!' Brinin cut Oswald short. 'The only thing you did wrong was not to say more. If you had kicked me a few times, I couldn't have blamed you!'

'Kicked you? What do you mean? I'm sorry. That's all I want to say.'

'Don't be sorry. If either of us needs to be sorry it's me.' Brinin began to gather his tools. 'I'm too quick to think I'm right. You weren't the only one to tell me to have Aculf dealt with swiftly, and what I did likely brought Wulfrich more harm than good.'

This was as near to asking for forgiveness as Oswald had ever known Brinin to come. How had calling him a fool brought it about?

Didn't harsh words from a friend wound most folk? Yet Brinin was speaking so straightforwardly, as a man might speak of his farm or the weather, without even any awkwardness to hinder him.

'We all make mistakes,' said Oswald.

'True, but some mistakes shouldn't be made. Oh, and while I think of it, there was no need to leave your father thinking that you were to blame for what I wanted. I've told him how it was. Call me a fool as much as you like, Oswald, and stubborn, and proud too. It'll do me no harm to hear it, and heaven knows you've earned the right to say it more than anyone.'

'Then let me ask you about the money my father got from Aculf. What are you going to do with it? My father wants to go to market to buy some more beasts to make up for what the Danes took. He could get another sow for you while he's there. He's going to take Eawig with him, and Eawig has a good eye for swine.'

'I ought to buy another sow. I told Eawig I'd give him one of the young—he's been a good help to me—and I don't want to break my word.' Brinin fingered the pouch on his belt, weighing it in his hand. 'I've never felt so rich in my life! And to think that a few days ago I didn't know how I was going to make it through the winter.'

'You were always going to make it through the winter! How many times do I need to tell you that?'

Brinin stiffened a little at this but he said nothing. Was this the pride he had spoken of, too prickly to handle carelessly? And hadn't Edith once said that she thought Brinin wanted to *feel* free, feeding and clothing himself? But even though he had given Oswald leave to say them, there had been too many truths for one day.

'You know, I longed to be here for months,' said Oswald. 'But since I got back, I've barely looked at the place. Come for a walk with me. Then perhaps I might feel like I'm home, even if I am sleeping under another man's roof.'

LIGHT

'Tomorrow I will put an end to all this talk,' said Edrich Thegn. 'Better to bring it into the light and deal with it there. Gather everyone in the meadow at midday, Cynestan.'

Oswald and his father sat with Cynestan by his hearthside that evening. Wynflæd sewed by the firelight and the children were either already asleep or near to it, lying in the darkness beyond the glow of the flames.

'As you wish, my lord,' said Cynestan. His wounded leg was stretched out in front of him while he slowly rubbed it. Oswald could see that it still troubled him after all these months, and it likely hadn't helped that he had given Oswald and Edrich Thegn his bed while he and Wynflæd slept with the children. 'I had wondered what you might do about it. It has worried me.'

'Some of it will be easily dealt with,' said Edrich. 'The Dane Brinin spoke to was one we met in Readingum, whose life we spared the night we left. It was mercy for mercy, that was all. Nothing for folk to worry about.'

'Well now,' said Cynestan. 'That does throw some light on the thing, my lord. I couldn't understand where the tale had come from, beyond being some wicked talk spread about by those who wished him harm.'

'It *was* wicked talk to bring him harm,' said Edrich, 'but there was truth in it, all the same.'

'I wish he had said something to me about it,' sighed Cynestan. 'Then we might have put a stop to the talk sooner and perhaps saved his harvest.'

'He wouldn't say anything,' said Oswald. 'The worse things are, the less he says. He's always been like that.'

'And perhaps he thought it wouldn't do much good without me here to speak to the truth of it. It seems an unlikely tale.' Edrich took a long drink of ale. 'It was spread about by young Sibwine, and after Brinin had got him and his sister to safety too! But he shall answer to me for that. I shall ask him about it tomorrow when we gather. And I shall ask Aculf why he said nothing about Brinin finding his son in the dark. Everyone will see what harm their talk—or lack of it—has done, and we will have no more whispering.'

Oswald didn't care if his father shamed Aculf—likely most of the talk *had* begun with him, even if others had helped it grow—but Sibwine? He had seen, somewhat unwillingly, how alike he and Sibwine were and now Sibwine's coming shame felt like his own. He had given Sibwine his word to stand by him, though he hadn't thought the trouble would come from his father.

'Sibwine spoke to me about this, Father,' he said. 'He thinks someone overheard him speaking to his mother, but neither of them said anything about it to anyone else. Please don't be too harsh with him, sir. I don't think he's as much to blame as it looks.'

It was a wonder what battle could do to a man, that Oswald should now be telling his father what he thought he should do. His time among the fyrd had left him with boldness as well as scars.

'And you believed him?' Edrich snorted in disbelief. 'It sounds like blameshifting to me. And why didn't he tell folk how Brinin had helped him? No, I'm going to put a stop to all this talk once and for all, and I owe it to Brinin and to Sibwine's father to deal with it. *He* would have made the boy put it right.'

'I did believe him, sir,' said Oswald earnestly. How far could he go before his father would think he had gone too far? 'And I think you would have believed him too had you seen him. It's been worrying him, and he does want to put it right.'

'Well then,' said Edrich, still unshifting, 'he can put it right tomorrow when the village is gathered, and perhaps that will also teach him to take more care about what he says and be quicker to do what he ought to do another time.'

Oswald drew a deep breath. Wouldn't he have wanted someone to speak for him in Sibwine's place?

'But, sir, isn't it easy to do wrong or to be too slow to do right? I know I've found it so! He's young, and it hasn't been long since he lost his father and now they've lost their house too. Perhaps he was afraid of what further trouble he'd bring on his mother if he spoke. I would never speak on his behalf if I didn't believe him, but I don't think he wanted to harm Brinin, truly, Father. Please, sir, if you must speak to him about it, speak to him alone. Don't shame him before the village. He's already ashamed.'

Edrich Thegn looked from Oswald to Cynestan without speaking. One of Cynestan's children stirred, turning over in their sleep.

'Well now, my lord,' said Cynestan. 'What Oswald Child says sounds more like what I know of the boy. And things haven't been easy here. I think it's more likely that other men made the mischief, my lord.'

'Very well then,' said Edrich at last. 'I will speak to him myself in the morning and leave it at that. We ought to sleep now. If we speak for much longer we might wake your children, Cynestan.'

∾

Edrich Thegn found Sibwine as soon as it was light. Oswald watched as they stood alone together a little way from Sibwine's half-built house. His father didn't raise his voice or frown much. He didn't even do all the talking himself. Oswald saw Sibwine answering him from time to time though he couldn't hear what either of them was saying. But the longer Edrich talked the more slumped Sibwine's shoulders became and the lower his head drooped. By the time Edrich beckoned Oswald over to them, Sibwine looked utterly wretched.

'Oswald,' said Edrich. 'I have bidden Sibwine to beg Brinin's forgiveness for not giving him the help he owed him. I want you to see that it's done.'

Sibwine bristled a little to learn that his word wasn't deemed to be enough, but he had the wisdom to say nothing. Edrich put his hand on his arm in a fatherlike way.

'Then we'll lay the thing aside and say no more about it,' he said kindly.

As they walked away together, Sibwine turned to Oswald with such a wry smile that it was almost a grimace.

'Is your father often like that?'

Sibwine didn't seem to know what a near miss he had had, that however sternly Edrich had spoken it had been a kindness that Oswald had had to beg for.

'Often enough. You boys would laugh at me when I wouldn't do things I knew he wouldn't like. Now you know why! And it could have been much worse, you know. My father wanted to have you up before the village and talk to you there. He said the best way to stop the whispering was to speak of the thing aloud. But I begged him not to.'

Oswald had thought Sibwine might be chilled at the thought of even greater wretchedness or glad that he had been spared. But he only looked at Oswald rather thoughtfully.

'And how do you think Brinin will be, Oswald Child?' he said. 'Will he even want to listen to me? I couldn't blame him if he didn't.'

'I don't know. You can never tell with Brinin. But I don't think you have too much to worry about.'

Brinin was still splitting wood for the new buildings. They waited until he was done with the long bough he was working on—Sibwine growing a little restless—then Oswald nodded to Brinin to follow them.

Sibwine stammered out what he had to say while Brinin listened without a word, neither smiling nor frowning.

'Say no more about it,' he said when Sibwine was done. 'You didn't make all the trouble on your own.'

Sibwine mumbled out something like thanks then trudged away.

'He meant what he said,' said Oswald. 'It's been weighing on him for weeks.'

'That's why I listened to him. I could see he meant it, even if it came a few weeks too late.'

Under the bright midday sun, Edrich Thegn gathered the village and shed light on what had been done in the darkness. He spoke of their fear, their loss. For a long time he sorrowed with them, speaking kindly of the dead and the kin and friends they had left behind. He urged them all to work together to rebuild the village. He brought the whispers out into the sunshine and spoke of them aloud. He told the tale of the Dane he had met in Readingum and why he had spared Brinin, but he said nothing about Brinin finding Ulf. Oswald wondered at that. He had known that his father would be as good as his word and would not speak of Sibwine, but why shield Aculf?

As his father spoke, Oswald watched those listening to him. Brinin stood at the back, away from everyone else, barely heeding his lord's bidding. Oswald passed his eyes over the crowd to see if there was any softening among them, any understanding or even shame. But, other than on the faces of those Oswald knew were already friendly, there was none. As soon as Brinin's name was spoken, a stiffness settled on the crowd, and Oswald saw no more feeling among them than if they had been stones.

Edrich Thegn seemed to see this too. Oswald saw his face change as his eyes darted from man to man. His words were still slow and carefully meted out as he spoke of Brinin's harvest, but they were no longer so steady. They were shaking a little. Surely his father wasn't going to weep, not here before everyone! Edrich's words dwindled into nothing. Oswald stared at him, inwardly begging him not to give way to tears. He could see him struggling with himself. But then Oswald saw what the fight was. It wasn't sorrow he was battling. It was anger.

'Are we to become beasts?' Edrich thundered suddenly. 'Is anyone to rush headlong into whatever wickedness he chooses with nothing to stop him? Is every man to do as he likes because he knows his neighbours will stand aside and hold their tongues, because he knows that no wrong will be righted and no misdeed punished? Is that what we are to become? Not while I am lord here!'

The stoniness crumbled a little. Men and women shifted awkwardly. Some lowered their eyes. Cynestan stood grimly, leaning on his stick. Brother Wilfred was frowning deeply, as stern as Oswald had ever seen him. Brinin had withdrawn even further, a few more steps between himself and the back of the crowd. Who among them had seen their lord like this before? Oswald hadn't. He'd only once seen his father's wrath get the better of him. Then it had been sudden, swift and shocking, but short-lived before his father had bridled it again into the quiet and careful anger that Oswald had always feared. Some of the children wept. Oswald saw Ebba and Wulfrich with heaving shoulders and red, tear-streaked faces.

'Is such a thing to be done here?' Edrich roared. There was to be no bridling that day. 'To one who was born here, who grew up here, who saved my life, who is *one of us*! Am I to believe that none of you knows anything about it? That none of you has eyes nor ears? That none of you did this himself? I do *not* believe it. Rather I believe that some of you have lied to my daughter, have lied to Cynestan, have lied to the priest and have lied to me. But I *will* learn the truth!'

Not even the angriest man can shout for ever. With that one last bellow, Edrich's strength seemed to run out. He shut his eyes and breathed deeply. No one stirred. In the stillness Oswald heard birdsong, rustling leaves and the stifled sob of a child. Edrich opened his eyes.

'If any of you know anything about this, come forward now and tell me,' he said more quietly, the thunder wholly spent. 'Come and speak now, while you can still do it freely with the hope of mercy. Don't wait until you have been found out another way.'

But no one said a word. They were still stiff, still sullen, with anger on their faces now though not outright boldness. Had such speech truly been wisdom? Every word had been true, but Oswald could see that folk were already forgetting that their lord had sorrowed with them first.

'No one?' said Edrich wearily. 'No one has anything at all to say?'

There was a sudden murmuring, and Oswald saw stirring in the middle of the crowd. Someone was pushing their way forward, others shifting aside to let them through. Flushed but with that set jaw Oswald had seen the day before, Sibwine stepped out from the crowd. Without meeting anyone's eyes, he went straight to Edrich Thegn and stood before him.

'My… my lord.' But Sibwine's voice was choked. He coughed, swallowed and this time found words loud enough for everyone to hear. 'My lord, may I speak? Not… not about the lost harvest—I don't know anything about that—but… but about something else, my lord, something that everyone ought to know.'

Edrich nodded. Sibwine swallowed again and began. He only looked at Edrich Thegn and spoke as though only to him, as though telling him something he didn't already know. And as he spoke of the raid, of how Brinin had warned him they were in danger and helped him get his sister to safety, his face grew redder and his words faster, but they didn't falter and they didn't trail off to a whisper. Everyone heard him.

'No one… no one ought to say he only helped *them* that night, my lord,' said Sibwine, his words almost tumbling over each other now in their rush to get out. 'He helped *us*, which is more than some did, who only hid and… and I don't only mean the women and children, my lord. He helped *us*. And… and I wanted to tell you, my lord, because it's wrong what folk have been saying. It's wrong, my lord.'

And with that, Sibwine was done. He dropped his head. There was another long bird-filled, wind-filled stillness, but no one was weeping this time. Much of the crowd was still cold. Oswald couldn't see Brinin anywhere.

'Do you see?' said Edrich. 'Do you see how it was that night? This is the one whose harvest one of you so shamefully wrecked. Let that man be sure that I *will* find him out.'

Oswald, slightly bewildered by it all, watched as his father put his hand on Sibwine's shoulder and spoke to him. Sibwine looked up and nodded. Had his father *asked* Sibwine to come forward or had Sibwine done it himself? He saw his father stride away through the crowd, speaking to no one. By his side, Edith's eyes were glistening with unshed tears, but she wasn't weeping.

'I've never seen Father like that before!' said Oswald.

'He was wonderful!' said Edith, almost fiercely. 'He said everything I've wanted to say for weeks!'

Oswald went to Sibwine then. He saw how coldly men and women were turning their backs on him. He saw how some of the boys—Æfæd, Eanfrith and others whom Oswald had thought of as Sibwine's friends—were glaring at him with utter scorn and hatred, as though by speaking up for Brinin he had somehow broken their trust. And Oswald could see that Sibwine felt it.

'Did my father ask you to do that?' he asked.

'No.' Sibwine's words were not so steady or unfaltering now, though they still came quickly. And now his flush had faded he was rather pale. 'This morning your father scolded me like I was a small boy, Oswald Child. I didn't like it, though he was right to do it. But it didn't do

Brinin any good, did it? How could my begging for his forgiveness change anything? And when your father said nothing about him helping us, I remembered what you said about how he wanted to call me before everyone and that you'd begged him not to. Thank you for that, Oswald Child. It was good of you, but your father was right. The only thing I could do to put things right was to tell everyone the truth. They know the truth now, though some of them don't seem to like it much.'

'Yes, they do, and those who said otherwise ought to be ashamed of themselves.'

'Perhaps some will be, Oswald Child, but likely others won't.' The other boys were walking away now, in a pack, shoulder to shoulder. Sibwine watched them and sighed. 'Well, I have work to do. We're putting the roof on today. It's already half-done.'

Oswald left the meadow then too, but he didn't know whether to look for Brinin or his father first.

TIDINGS

Harvest burst golden upon them. Loafmas and bread-blessing, thanksgiving for another winter, another summer, another harvest. And how much more heartfelt the thanksgiving was when so much could easily have been lost. Long days of reaping, from dawn until the low evening sun cast long shadows and richly gilded the wheat and barley. Never had they been happier to see bundled sheaves. Never had storing them for the winter seemed like such a blessing. A few short weeks earlier there had been nowhere to put them, and only by sweat and swift work had the storehouses been raised on time.

Oswald kept his oath to Beorn, wearying himself in Ælfwyn's field in the mornings and in his father's in the afternoons. Still weakened from his illness, he did it more by strength of will than strength of body. He ached each day as he trudged home in the evening light, while the wind turned the wheat from one golden hue to another, rippling through it like water in a stream. Only Brinin's field was wrong, a bruise on a pale and otherwise unwounded face. Already weeds had sprung up where his harvest should have been. Untilled, unploughed, unharvested, utterly forsaken. They had failed Brinin. The man who had done this to him was still unfound.

The harvest in, they raised the hall, snatching a few dry days to build it before the full strength of winter was upon them. Posts, lintel, walls, roofbeams, thatch. When it was done Oswald and Edith stood inside and looked at their new home. Their voices were as hollow and empty as the hall was, their feet too loud on the floorboards. It was a little bigger than the old hall, standing where it had stood yet stretching beyond it. But there were no skilfully woven curtains, no bright shields hanging from the walls, no benches, no seats, no table, no loom in the light by the doorway. The roof-posts were plain, without the fine carvings that had adorned the old ones. Only the blackened hearthstone stood in the middle where it had always been, too strong to be harmed by the blaze that had swallowed up everything else.

Beside Oswald, Edith's quick eyes darted about her as she learned what this new home would be like. Then, without warning she left, striding into the pale sunlight outside. As she passed him, Oswald saw that she was weeping. Home, yet not home. Home without any of the things that came to mind when he thought of home. Not what home had been, yet the only home they had. It was waiting for them to make it home. Besides, was home only four walls, a roof and whatever they put beneath it? Wasn't it also trees and hills and fields, neighbours and kin? All those—most of them—were still there. One day this new, hollow hall would feel like home too.

Between Michaelmas and Winter's Day, Edrich Thegn took Cynestan and Eawig to market before the days grew too short and cold to risk the journey. Eawig, who had never left the village, was overawed beyond all speech. He could barely sit still in the back of the cart as they left, Cynestan driving and Edrich on his horse beside them. And so for seven nights, Oswald was lord of Oakdene in his father's stead.

Oswald had fallen back into his old ways, as things had been when he had still thought of himself as a boy all those months before. The mornings he gave to warcraft, as much to strengthen his wounded shoulder as anything else. If he was alone he worked on his bowmanship, with Leoba and her brothers springing strangely often to mind. She had been good with her bow, Leoba. Would he ever see her again?

If Mildrith would spare Tidræd he worked on swordcraft with him. There were days when Oswald didn't fully believe that she *had* spared him, though he left that for Tidræd to work out with his mother. Tidræd had always been the kind of boy who would rather do as he liked first then suffer for it later if he must, much like his father had been. When Oswald asked Tidræd one morning if his mother had given him leave to come, the boy had said that he had once heard his father say that sometimes it was better to ask for forgiveness than to ask for leave.

'Did you ever try that with him?' asked Oswald.

'Once or twice.'

'And how did it go?'

'Not well!' grinned Tidræd.

Oswald was in the new church when his father came home, sitting with Brother Wilfred while the monk helped him drag from his mind one of the Latin psalms he had learned at the minster the winter before. That was another of his old ways Oswald had taken up again, because it was something to do and he didn't want to forget what he had once known.

'That sounds like it might be your father,' said Brother Wilfred, glancing towards the door.

'Yes. May we stop, sir? I'm sorry I've been so slow today. I seem to have forgotten at least half of everything I ever learned. I don't know how *you* remember so much.'

'Ah! It's easier for me. I started much younger, had more to fear if I made a mistake and sang these psalms every day for most of my life. If you have time, learn as far as *Domine, in caelo misericordia tua*, but if your father needs you don't worry about it. We can take it up again tomorrow.'

Oswald found his father by the newly built horsehouse, the bridle of his horse still in his hand. Edith was beside him, stroking the nose of a brown mare. A little way off he saw Cynestan driving four or five swine towards the swine pen and caught sight of Eawig as he led a sow round Deorstan's house.

'Welcome home, Father,' said Oswald. 'How was the road?'

'Good, though I am always happier to be home than I am to be away. But as you see, I bought this mare. She seems a steady beast, good for Edith. And I heard her last foal was strong, so we might think about breeding her when the warmer weather comes. And we got all the swine for good money—one for Brinin too. And plenty of cloth.' Edrich smiled at Edith. 'See what you think of it, my dear. Some will do well for clothes, I think, and some to hang by our beds. That might make the place seem a little more like home. Oh and, Oswald, who do you think we met on the road?'

'I can't think, sir.'

'Godweard! And two of his men and his older boy too. I can't remember his name.'

'Leofstan, sir. I wish now I'd been with you. Are they all well? Did he give you any news of Leo… of his household?'

Oswald saw Edith looking at him and felt his cheeks burn. Why shouldn't he ask after the kind friends who had given them such a warm welcome? What was wrong with that? It was nothing for Edith to stare about. He didn't understand her sometimes.

'Very well. And he had good tidings to share: his wife has borne a son—a week before Michaelmas—and when he left home both she and the baby were well. I can't remember what he said they'd called the boy. He took us to spend the night with a kinsman of his wife—wouldn't let me say no—and we spent a most happy evening together before we parted in the morning. He hoped that *you* were getting stronger. I told him you were.'

'I truly wish I had been with you, Father,' said Oswald. This time he didn't look at Edith.

'Godweard wished you had too, as did his boy.' Edrich turned to Edith. 'Is there anything to eat, my dear? We've been on the road since early morning. Oswald, go and see how Brinin likes his new sow and send Eawig back to me. I want him to see to the beasts and then he should eat too.'

Oswald made his way rather thoughtfully to Brinin's hut. It was odd that these tidings should only leave him wanting more. He hadn't known he'd been thirsting for them until his father spoke Godweard's name. Yet this unforeseen news had left the thirst unquenched, as though his father had put something that he longed for to his lips, then snatched it away just as he tasted it. And news of a baby wasn't at all what he had hoped to hear, glad though he was that he and the mother were well. Wasn't bearing a child as fraught with danger as rushing into battle? But he didn't know what he *had* hoped to hear. And he was a little cross with Edith, though she hadn't said a word. That was odd too.

'She was the best of all the sows we saw. I made sure of it!' Oswald heard Eawig's swift chatter before he saw him. 'You should have seen that place, Brinin! So many beasts, and other things too, so many men, all talking at once. I hardly knew where to look, there was so much to see. And would you believe it? Edrich Thegn even asked me what I thought of one or two of the swine. And he asked me to choose one for you. He got a good price for her as he was buying other beasts too and he has some of your money to give back to you. You can breed her soon. She's already had one brood. I saw one of the young, and he was fat and strong. Thank heaven the Danes didn't get Mildrith's big boar!'

Oswald rounded the corner of Brinin's hut and saw Brinin and Eawig by the swine pen, leaning on the fence, Brinin reaching in and rubbing his hand along the sow's bristly back.

'She seems a good beast,' said Oswald. 'Are you happy with her?'

'I take Eawig as my guide on swine,' said Brinin. 'If he says she's a good beast, then she must be.'

Eawig blushed. He didn't look like a boy who had been on the road since dawn. Oswald could see that going to market had been the most thrilling thing in his life.

'My father wants you, Eawig,' he said. 'He says you're to see to the beasts now and then eat something. You must be hungry.'

'Yes, Oswald Child, sir, I am. Though I hadn't thought about it until you said so, sir.'

Eawig leaned into the pen to pat the sow's back, shot a parting grin at Brinin, then left them.

'If you breed her soon as Eawig said, you could have your own bacon by next winter,' said Oswald. He nodded to the green rows growing near the pen. 'But until you have bacon, those leeks would taste good. Have you eaten any of them yet?'

'I pulled up a neep the other day.' Brinin laughed awkwardly. 'But I don't know how to cook! I've never cooked anything in my life. Once it was out of the ground I didn't know what to do with it, so I put it on a stick and held it over the fire like I've seen folk do with meat. It went black on the outside but was still hard in the middle. I ate it anyway. I might ask Wynith to show me what to do with them. They need to go in a broth or something, but I don't know what else to put in the pot. I don't think it's only water and neeps.'

'I couldn't tell you,' laughed Oswald. 'The only thing I can cook is what we ate in the camp, roast meat and the like. What you need is a wife.'

Oswald had meant it in jest, or perhaps only half in jest. Didn't most men wed? All but priests and monks. And weren't he and Brinin almost old enough to be thinking about it? Beorn had, and he had only been a few winters older than they were. Yet Brinin was staring at him as though he had told him that he needed a dragon or a buried hoard or to learn how to fly.

'A wife!' Brinin gaped at Oswald in disbelief.

'Why not?' said Oswald. There was nothing even slightly foolish about it. 'Don't men find wives all the time? My father wasn't much older than us when he wed my mother.'

'But what man would let his daughter wed a Dane and live here?' Brinin swept his hand towards his hut. Oswald, as though for the first time, saw how small it was and how the door had been broken and patched up. 'What woman would want to?'

'You could build a bigger house,' said Oswald stoutly. 'My father would let you have the wood for it.'

'And even if there was such a woman, I'd need to feed her and find cloth for clothes and everything else she'd need. And where there was a wife there would likely be children, and I'd have to feed them too. And I haven't even gathered in a harvest yet. Let me first see if I can feed myself before I find a wife to feed too.'

Had all this fear sprung up from Brinin's wrecked harvest? It *was* fear, though Brinin tried to make it sound like wisdom. Did he think that all his harvests would be wrecked? That he would never eat his own bread? Yet there was good food growing beside them even as they spoke.

'Ask me again when I've gathered in a few harvests.' Then, perhaps seeing Oswald's bewilderment, Brinin said: 'What about you? Are you thinking of finding a wife? There's nothing to stop *you*.'

Had Brinin asked Oswald a day earlier, Oswald would have said that he wasn't; that he only wanted to be at home and rest after war; that he wasn't old enough. But now he saw that he *was* old enough, or at least would be by the time things could be settled. He did want to find a wife and he knew who he wanted to find.

'I might be. Godweard—the man who welcomed us when I was ill—has a daughter. She… I like her,' said Oswald. Godweard's house was so busy, always so full of guests. Wasn't it likely that some other young man would like her too? And Oswald knew *that* was a thought he didn't like. Better make sure she knew what he was thinking before it was too late. 'I think I'll speak to my father about it.'

MIDWINTER

I t was settled. Oswald spoke to his father the next evening, sitting by the fire after everyone else in the hall was asleep. Long before it was over, he was smarting with such awkwardness that he began to wish he had never begun. But he somehow found the words and drove them out without too much stammering, and if his father saw his struggle he sparingly looked away.

'If I'm truthful with you, Oswald, the thought had come to my mind too,' he said. 'Godweard's a good man. This is one of the few times in life we get to choose our kin, and he is a man anyone would want. If he doesn't seem as wealthy as we are, I believe that's because he has spread what he has more thinly. He's trustworthy, brave, wise and good-hearted. He has more than made up for anything that was lacking in his own father. Your uncle speaks most highly of Godweard, as you know, and he is a man whose thoughts and wisdom I would trust on anything. As for his daughter, I liked what I saw of her. She speaks meekly and fondly to her father and stepmother, behaves as she ought and is good to the younger ones, her stepmother's daughters too. Indeed, her stepmother spoke well of her to me, and I place more weight on that than on anything Godweard might have said. A father or mother can often be blind as to the true worth of their children and think of them more highly than they ought.'

'And you don't think I'm too young, Father?'

'You are young, and so is Godweard's daughter, but the business won't be settled tomorrow. We will need to go and see Godweard and tell him what we've been thinking and ask for his own thoughts, and that won't be until after midwinter. And likely he will want to come here to stay with us, and perhaps his daughter too. And there will be money to think about and the morning-gift and many other things to make ready. Nothing will be fully settled until next harvest at the earliest, perhaps not until the following Easter. And by then you will both be older.

'Yes, I am glad you raised this, Oswald. It had been in my mind and I didn't know how best to speak to you about it. It's a long time since my father talked to me about such things. With me, we did not at first have a girl in mind and had to think carefully. I knew your uncle before I knew your mother, and it was he who thought of his sister. I was thankful that he did. And here's another thing to think of, Oswald. When taking a wife too many think only of the bonds they are making with the kin or of wealth and that kind of thing. Perhaps for some men that's enough. But think how worthy a woman your mother was. Ask yourself if Leoba is such a woman. Can she be wise? Can you learn to be fond of her? Many men would be ashamed to own it, but I don't mind telling you, Oswald, that I often spoke to your mother about the many burdens that come from being lord here, and she was wise and often brought before me things I had not seen myself. I can truly say that there has seldom been a day since… since we lost her that I have not felt her lack. And I cannot think of seeking another wife, as many have told me I ought to. Your uncle is the only man who understands as he knows what his sister was. Find a woman who is wise and of whom you can become fond and you will do well. And from what I have seen of her, Leoba is such a woman. A foolish woman whom you could not like would not make for a happy home, however much wealth or strong kinsfolk she brought with her. Would you want such a woman to be mother to your children? Now, many think otherwise, but it is what I have often thought and I cannot say it strongly enough.'

When had his father spoken to him so freely, or opened up his mind to let Oswald see inside? They had only fumbled at such things before, like workmen who didn't know their own tools. Before sleeping that night, they settled the thing: when they would go and who should go with them. And while they waited for the darkness of midwinter, they would have time to think about how they should speak to Godweard.

'Me?' Brinin leaned on his shovel and stared at Oswald. 'What do you want *me* to go for?'

'That's what folk do, isn't it?' Oswald just stopped himself from sighing. Why couldn't Brinin make things a little easier for once? 'They go with their fellows so the woman's kin can see what kind of friends they keep, and the friends can speak to their good name. My father wants to stop at my uncle's house on the way and ask him and one of his sons to come with us. You're my best friend and you saved both my life and my father's. Why wouldn't I take you?'

'When this girl's kin see that you have a half-Danish freedman as a friend, it may not help you. Friend or not, you'd be better off leaving me behind for something like this.'

'I'm not leaving you behind. Besides, they already know all about you and how you got my father out of Readingum. They'll be more than happy to welcome you.'

Brinin bent down and scraped up another shovelful of dung, dropping it into his bucket.

'There's work here that I can't easily leave, and the sow—'

'My father says that he'll have Cynestan see that all your work is done and that Eawig can look after your sow. He wants to leave soon after Twelfth Eve.'

'Then there'll be the ploughing and—'

'We'll be back before the ploughing. We'll be back before Candlemas. If the ground is soft enough to plough before we're back—which isn't likely—my Father says he'll have Cynestan see that ploughing is begun in your field and Mildrith's. You see! There's nothing to stop you from going!'

Why did Brinin want to find all the hindrances that lay across their path? Was it easier for him to see everything that might go wrong than what might go well? But Oswald—or rather his father—had thought of them all before even speaking to Brinin about it and he had ready answers to everything.

'It's good of your father to think of all that,' said Brinin slowly. 'But how will I get there? You'll be on horseback, and I'll be on foot, slowing you down. Even if I knew how to ride, there's no horse for me. That new mare your father bought wouldn't take my weight.'

'No need to worry about that,' said Oswald cheerfully. 'My father's already spoken to Mildrith. She's happy to lend us Thurstan's horse—you remember we brought it back to her after Basing. Thank heaven the Danes didn't get it! You can ride mine, and I'll ride Thurstan's. Mine's steadier, so it will be easier for you.'

'But I don't know how to ride a horse!'

'You can learn! There's more than enough time before Twelfth Eve.'

'For one journey? When would I ever need to ride again? Even if I had enough money for a horse, I'd spend it on something else.'

'You need to know so you can come with me to Godweard's house. My father says I'm to start teaching you tomorrow. I'll come and find you in the morning.'

Midwinter, with its dark days; midwinter, with its long nights and holy feasts, quickened its steps towards them. And on those short, cold days, Brinin learned to ride.

Oswald was a far sterner teacher than Brinin would ever have foreseen. He didn't so much teach as drive Brinin to learn. No weather was too harsh to go out in. There could be no slacking, no resting, no giving up too soon. He was going to make Brinin learn, and learn well and swiftly. Brinin could see something of Edrich Thegn in his friend; or perhaps it was Thurstan, who after all had taught Oswald so much. Neither man would settle for work half-done, and neither, Brinin learned, would Oswald.

It wasn't that he disliked horses. They were beautiful beasts, with their sleek hides and thoughtful eyes. Everything about them had a loveliness to it. He had never had much to do with them before and hadn't at all liked his two days of clinging to Oswald's back on the way to the minster. But as Oswald taught him how to sit, how to move with the beast, what to do with his hands, knees and feet, he began to like it much more than he would ever have told Oswald—once his body learned to stop aching. He only fell off once, early on, though that was a day when Tidræd was there to laugh at him, only to find himself scolded by Oswald. Tidræd didn't mind the scolding any more than Brinin had minded the laughter. The day they first galloped, the icy winter wind in their faces, was more thrilling than anything Brinin could have put into words. Even if he never rode again, he could die knowing that he had once felt that speed.

Midwinter, *Adventus Domini*, the monks had called it—the Coming of the Lord—Yuletide, Childermas, Twelfth Eve. On the evening after Twelfth Eve, Brinin stood by his pen stroking his sow's back. He didn't love her as he had loved his first sow—he wouldn't make the same mistake twice—but she was a good beast, and Eawig was hopeful that she would have her brood before Easter.

Edrich Thegn wanted them on the road by sunrise, and Brinin was ready to go. He had bundled up his better clothes to take with him—he didn't want to dirty them on the road. He had got some socks from Daglæf's wife for some leeks and a little work. They were itchy but warm. And Edrich Thegn had given him some new shoes and a thick, heavy cloak. It was awkward to take them, but he did not dare say no. Besides, he would be glad of them on the road in winter, and they would make him a more fitting friend for Oswald. With his new shoes and cloak, his better shirt, a quiver of arrows across his back, his seax on his belt and a little money in his pouch, he would ride into this other village looking nothing like the slave he had once been. What a thought!

'Well, lad! Who would have thought that one day Edrich Thegn would choose you to go with him on such a journey? We didn't see this coming, did we?' It was Garulf, coming up and leaning on the fence beside him. 'Don't worry about your sow. We'll see to her for you, and to everything else too.'

'Thank you. There's none better with swine than Eawig.'

'That's the truth!' said Garulf warmly, with not a little pride in his voice. 'I hear Edrich Thegn wants to set off early tomorrow.'

'At first light.'

'Best to make the most of the daylight at this time of year. We'll miss you, lad. I've often thought of what a friend you've been to us. You always were a friend, but many would have forgotten friendship once things changed for them. Not you. I know Edrich Thegn will see that Wynith and the children are clothed and fed, and Cynestan is no Aculf, but none of that is the same as friendship. I'm old now, and it does me good to know that there's one around to keep an eye on them.'

Garulf put his hand on Brinin's shoulder and squeezed it a little. Brinin could feel the old man's hand trembling.

'You should sleep, lad,' said Garulf. 'It will be a long day for you tomorrow.'

Garulf left him, and Brinin slept, curled up by the glowing embers of the fire. And in the morning as the pale, cold sun rose, they rode out of the village.

GUEST

They were on the road for most of the day, sometimes riding swiftly, sometimes only walking. None of them spoke much. Their breath and the hot breath of the horses drifted away from them in wispy clouds. It was a bitterly cold morning, the grass white and crisp with frost. The trees, black and bare, were half-shrouded with a cold mist. Even the sky was white. They hadn't been going for long before Brinin was chilled to the bone, even with his warm cloak and itchy socks.

They ate their food standing, stamping and walking about to keep warm. The midday sun, low and weary, did little to thaw them, and Brinin wondered if his own face was as red with cold as Oswald's and Edrich Thegn's. It felt raw enough. Before they set off again, Edrich Thegn pointed far ahead to a dark line of trees. His kin lived a little beyond them and, God willing, they would reach them before nightfall.

They reached Hildræd's village with only a little daylight to spare. As they rode in among the houses a young boy of perhaps ten winters—whom Brinin could see at once was Oswald's kin—ran out of the hall. He ran inside again as soon as he saw them. They could hear him calling his father. That boy looked more like Edith's brother than Oswald did.

'Edrich! Oswald!' called Hildræd as he strode from the hall. 'What delight is this? Surely you haven't ridden here in this weather only to see us! Aldulf, run and find someone to take care of the horses. Oswald, my boy, how well you are looking! It does me good to see you. And surely, Edrich, this is our bold friend who walked into Readingum to walk *you* out! That's a face I can't forget! Come in, come in. You all look frozen half to death. What a day to be on the road! Look who's here, my dear! What a gift on a cold winter's day!'

Long afterwards it was the warmth of the fire, the glow of the lamps and the taste of the ale that Brinin remembered most. The ale was like nothing he had ever drunk before. It had been mixed with mint and other things he could not name, and it was hot. He remembered the smell of the feast they had eaten together while Edrich told Hildræd why they had come. He remembered how, rather longingly, he had watched the easy fellowship that Edrich Thegn and Oswald had with their kin.

It was settled that Hildræd and his older son, Aldred, would go with them in the morning, and they bundled up everything they would need. That night Brinin slept on a bench heaped with soft fleeces. He was warmly wrapped in his new cloak, and his feet almost touched Oswald's. As he drifted off to sleep, he seemed to feel the thundering of the horse and the chill wind as he was borne along swiftly through the winter day.

The road was easier and shorter in the morning, and it wasn't even midday when Oswald rode up beside Brinin and pointed to some trees sloping up a little hill, ahead of them and a little to their left.

'Beyond those trees—I'm not sure how far beyond—there's a minster,' he said. 'I haven't been there, but Leoba told me about it. It's a woman's house. One of her father's sisters is there. They were raised together, so she's like a sister to her. We're almost there now. We'll turn north soon and shortly after that we'll see the village.'

Oswald wanted to ride faster, but Edrich Thegn wouldn't let them. Why hurry so early in the day and when the horses had worked so hard the day before? Besides, wouldn't hard-driven horses only frighten everyone and make them fear bad news or worse? There was little Oswald could say to that—it was the truth—but Brinin could see that he was growing restless. Little wonder, given what they had come for.

But they *were* almost there. They turned north. A little after that Brinin saw long, snaking clouds of smoke rising into the winter sky, hearthsmoke from the fires scattered through a village. And then ahead he saw the houses, not so many as in Oakdene and spread further apart. Three children came out from behind a little clutch of trees. The youngest, a boy, was dashing here and there, slashing at the air with a stick. The other boy and the girl—or perhaps more of a woman—were walking behind him.

The children stopped as soon as they saw the riders. The younger boy dropped his stick and pointed at them. He spoke swiftly to the others. Oswald was already off his horse, and something about his face made Brinin wonder if this might be the very girl—or woman—who had brought them here. Brinin climbed down too.

'I hope we find you all well,' said Edrich Thegn, 'and that your father is at home.'

'Yes, sir,' said the girl. She *was* the girl then, and now Brinin couldn't remember what Oswald had said her name was. She turned to the younger boy, her brother surely. 'Leofmær, run and tell Father who has come. I hope, sir, that you have met with no trouble on the road.'

'Nothing that a good fire won't put to rights,' laughed Hildræd, 'and I know that your father always has a good fire.'

The girl was watching Oswald. She had very quick eyes, like Edith.

'You look stronger,' she said. 'Are you better now?'

'I'm as well now as I ever was,' said Oswald. 'This is the friend I told you about.'

The girl nodded, but the boy gave Brinin a sharp look that made him think of Tidræd. Would Readingum follow him to his grave? Oswald had told him that they all knew the tale here.

'Forgive me, but I must go ahead now to help make everything ready for you,' said the girl. 'My brother will help you with the horses.'

So both boys were her brothers. This one was nothing like her at all. The girl dashed ahead of them to the houses, lifting her kirtle away from her feet. It was blue.

'My dear friends!' Godweard ran to meet them as they neared his house. 'I could barely believe what my son was telling me. How glad I am to see you! Oswald, you are not the man who left us in the summer! And Aldred, my boy, you have grown tall! He will pass you soon, Hildræd, and I fear he has passed me already.'

Upon seeing Brinin, Godweard patted him warmly on the back.

'Any friend of theirs must see themselves as a friend of mine,' he said. 'Welcome to my home.'

Godweard beckoned to a man standing a little way off, a slave most likely. He wore no seax on his belt.

'Oslaf, have someone help you put another bed in the guesthouse. Make sure that all the beds are ready and that the house has been swept, and kindle a fire there. And send someone to tend to the horses.'

Oslaf hurried away, and Godweard flung his arms wide.

'Come into my home,' he said.

After that, it was much as it had been at Hildræd's house: fire, food, fellowship. They met Godweard's wife. They met his new son. They met all his children—Oswald hadn't told Brinin how many there were. They gave their gifts. Brinin learned that the girl was called Leoba; he remembered as soon as someone spoke her name. Edrich Thegn, Hildræd and Godweard spoke freely with one another, though nothing was said about why they had come. Oswald said very little. Aldred and the older of Leoba's brothers sat a little apart, speaking earnestly with one another and taking no heed of the grown men.

Brinin sat and watched them all. Godweard's hall was filled with so many men and women. He watched what they were doing. He listened to snatches of their speech. His eyes grew heavy in the heat. He began to fear that Edrich Thegn and the others would talk all night. But almost as soon as he had thought it, the talk was over and they were led through the cold night to the guesthouse to sleep.

TALK

In the morning Edrich Thegn went away with Godweard to talk. Brinin didn't know where Hildræd was. Aldred soon went off with Leoba's brothers, and Brinin and Oswald were left alone.

He watched as Oswald picked at his food, barely eating any of it. Oswald got up and walked to the door. He stood on the threshold looking out for a while, before walking back to the bench. He leaned back against the wall, his legs stretched out in front of him, drumming on the bench with his fingers.

'We wait now,' said Oswald.

'Yes.'

'We haven't seen anything of Leoba this morning.'

'We haven't been outside.'

'No, but her brothers came.' Oswald got up and walked back to the door.

'Her mother likely has work for her, given how many younger ones there are,' said Brinin.

Oswald sat down again, leaning forward with his arms resting on his knees. Then he got up and threw some sticks onto the fire, which was burning brightly and didn't need more wood. Then he went to the door, back to the fire, to the door again.

'Is it raining?' asked Brinin at last. 'Or snowing?'

'No!' Oswald stared at him in bewilderment. 'You can see it isn't!'

'Has your father forbidden you from going outside?'

'No! You heard everything he said. What are you talking about?'

'Then why are we sitting in here? We've slept and eaten. Let's go out! Why don't we go and find your kinsman and Leoba's brothers? Or see how the horses are doing? Did they show you round the village the last time you were here? Why don't you show *me* round? Anything but sitting in here!'

'Sorry!' laughed Oswald. 'I must be very tiresome to watch. I wonder what my father and Godweard are saying.'

'Walking between the bench and the door won't make them say it any faster. If you must walk, let's walk outside.'

'I want to be sure my father can find me when he's done.'

'He'll find you.'

Brinin stood up, fastened his cloak around his shoulders and strode to the door.

'I'll wait for you outside,' he said.

It was a bright morning. Brinin looked around, breathing in the chilly air. It tasted clean. Better to be outside than sitting by a smoky fire, however cold it was. At the nearest house, a woman stood on the threshold watching him. Other houses lay behind it. Oswald came outside and shut the door behind him.

'Where do you want to go?' asked Brinin.

They walked towards the other house. Oswald smiled at the woman as they passed her.

'I remember her from before,' he whispered when they were out of earshot. 'She and her daughters often sat outside the house spinning, but I've never spoken to her.'

Brinin glanced behind them. A girl—likely one of the woman's daughters—came round the side of their house with a heavy bucket. The woman was still watching them.

They went wherever Oswald led them. They didn't see Leoba or her brothers or Oswald's kinsmen. But other folk smiled or nodded or spoke a few words to them. An old woman in a green kirtle left the stool outside her house and came over to speak to them. She walked swiftly for one so old.

'Are you well?' she asked Oswald. She didn't look at Brinin.

'Yes,' said Oswald, 'thanks to you.'

'You look stronger,' said the women, eyeing Oswald up and down. 'Have you had much pain in the wound?'

'Very little,' said Oswald. 'Weakness, mostly, but I worked a lot with my bow to strengthen it.'

'Good,' said the woman, then walked back to her stool as swiftly as she had come.

'That's the woman who saw to my wound. She's a good healer, but'— Oswald grimaced—'what she did stung like you wouldn't believe, what I can remember of it anyway. I wish I could remember less.'

'It worked,' said Brinin.

As they walked towards Godweard's hall, they saw Edrich Thegn coming towards them. He beckoned to Oswald.

'I'll see you back at the guesthouse,' said Brinin. Perhaps now the waiting would be over, and Oswald might remember how to sit still.

The first woman they had seen was still in her doorway, this time speaking earnestly to a man. They stopped talking as Brinin drew nearer. Brinin smiled at them as Oswald had. The man smiled back. The woman, rather startled, almost did. Likely they didn't see as many strangers here as Oswald had said, even though Godweard was so welcoming.

The guesthouse door was ajar, and inside Brinin found Aldred and Leoba's brothers.

'You're the one who got Oswald's father away from the Danes, aren't you?' asked the older brother, before Brinin could even sit down. 'Will you tell us about it? What were they like? How many did you have to kill?'

Brinin had seen this coming. It was warm inside. He took off his cloak. Better to get it over with. He sat down on a bench and began the tale.

'Well, my boy,' said Edrich. 'You will be glad to hear that Godweard will think about it.'

'Think about it?' said Oswald. 'He didn't say "yes" then, sir?'

'He hasn't spoken to his daughter yet. Let him talk to her before he says "yes" or "no" but, on the whole, he seemed to think it could work very well. He was of the same mind as me that, although you are both young now, you will not stay young. He's a much more careful man than you might think and—understandably, given the little we know of his father—unwilling to give his daughter to a man whose moods and way of life he knows little about. But Godweard knows much more about you than perhaps you might have thought.'

Edrich spoke so slowly and with such care, not looking at Oswald, but straight ahead as they walked, that Oswald, with a sudden rush of shame, knew what his father had stopped short of saying.

'Surely he doesn't know about...' But Oswald couldn't bring himself to say 'the Moot'. This was a place where he and his father dared not lurk for long, a path too full of snares to be safe or easy.

'Oswald,' said Edrich, 'you cannot think that Godweard stood by while your wounded shoulder was tended without seeing that... that it was not the first wound you had ever had. Let me say this, Oswald, and then we will put it aside. He said nothing to me at the time. Indeed, I was so overcome with fear for your life that that other time was the last thing on my mind. But he did speak to your uncle about it. I don't know what your uncle said—I knew nothing about any of this until this morning—but whatever it was it seems to have been rather to your good than anything else. Godweard said to me—and this is what I want you to remember, Oswald—he said that a man who is more ready to bear pain than to give it—except in war—is the kind of man he likes. And he said that he would rather see his daughter as the wife of such a man than a much wealthier man who found it easy to be harsh. But enough of that for now.'

'So... so are you hopeful, Father?' he asked, eager to step swiftly away from the Moot and everything to do with it.

'More hopeful than not. But Godweard won't thrust her into it against her will. I like him better for that. I wouldn't do it to Edith either. He wants us to go back to the guesthouse early this evening and he'll speak to her then. We also spoke of money and how I will settle on you the rents from my mother's lands. That will give you some freedom even though you will still live at home. It's what my own father—or rather, my mother—did with me and there was wisdom in it. But no more for now. We will see what Leoba herself says and then we will talk more.'

Leoba said she would think about it, and for the next few days they did little else but talk and sleep. Edrich spoke to Godweard again. Hildræd spoke to him. Oswald himself spoke to him. Edrich and Oswald sat and talked with Leoba and her father and stepmother. And fairly often

Oswald asked Aldred or Brinin or both to take their bows to the meadow with Leoba's brothers and shoot while he and Leoba watched and talked.

Leoba had a lot she wanted to ask him—perhaps it was her way of thinking about it—though very little of it seemed to have anything to do with being wed.

'You know,' she said on the third morning, 'it's hard to think of leaving home.'

Oswald almost said, as his father had to him, that it wouldn't be tomorrow, that there would be time to get ready for it. He almost said that she could come back from time to time, that her kin could go to Oakdene and stay with her sometimes. He even built a guesthouse for them in his mind. But now he saw that he would give up nothing to wed her. All the giving up would be on her side. Little wonder she wanted to think about it.

'It would be hard,' he said.

Leoba said nothing. She stood for a while gazing at something far off, beyond where the others were shooting.

'They could come and see me sometimes,' she said at last. 'Or I could come here. I like riding in good weather.'

The next afternoon, Oswald and Brinin were alone in the meadow after Leoba and her brothers had gone inside.

'You're a good bowman,' said Oswald.

'I'm not quick enough for battle,' said Brinin. 'I could have shot one of the raiders if I hadn't spent too long thinking about it.'

'You're still good, though.'

'Good enough to help you, anyway,' said Brinin dryly.

'And I'm thankful for it!' laughed Oswald. 'Leoba has a lot she wants to talk about. Today she asked me what kind of father I would be, if I would be stern or not. I'd never even thought about it before and I didn't know what she wanted me to say!'

'You must have thought about it before! You're about to take a wife, and the two do mostly go together!'

'But I hadn't! How should I know what kind of father I'll be?'

'Much like your own father, I should think. Stern at times. I've seen how you teach a man to ride a horse! What did you say?'

'I went for something in the middle: that I might be a little stern sometimes if I needed to be.'

'Did she like that?'

'It was what she wanted! She said she loves her father more than anyone else on earth, but that he isn't stern at all. She said it was always her mother who dealt with them if they were wilful, and since she died it hasn't been good for her brothers to be without someone stern, and that there's only so much a sister can do.'

A man was coming towards them, smiling, a fork over his shoulder. Oswald knew his face, but he couldn't have said which was his house or if he had spoken to him before. There were so many faces.

'It's been another good dry day,' said the man. 'You're the one who was here during the haymaking, aren't you? The one who wounded?'

'Yes,' said Oswald.

'You look stronger now. I helped lift you into the guesthouse the night you came, though you were in no fit shape then to mind anything of it now. Is this your friend?'

'Yes,' said Oswald.

'What's your name, son?' said the man, turning now to Brinin.

'Bruni,' said Brinin. 'Or Brinin. I mean, folk call me Brinin from Brynefæx, because of the hair. But my name's Bruni.'

It was a long answer for Brinin, an odd answer. Had Oswald been calling him by the wrong name for all these years? Had Brinin disliked it? Oswald had known that Row had called him 'Bruni' but he had never thought much about it.

'You're from the same village?' asked the man to Oswald this time.

'Yes,' said Oswald.

'And are your kin there, son'—to Brinin again—'your father and mother?'

'My father and mother are dead. I have no kin,' said Brinin.

'Forgive me for asking, son, but what was your father's name?'

Something worrying was on Brinin's face, but Oswald didn't know what it was. Why must this man keep talking? Why must he ask so much? Oswald almost told him to stop, but Brinin spoke first.

'Wulfstan,' he said.

'And your mother?'

Brinin licked his lips. Oswald saw him swallow. Was he going to speak a Danish name to a man they knew nothing about? After everything that had happened?

'Hallveig,' said Brinin.

'We have been poor neighbours to you during your stay here,' said the man. 'Please come and have a drink of ale by my hearth.'

They followed him. Oswald hardly knew why. Brinin didn't speak. He didn't look at Oswald. The man led them to the house nearest the guesthouse. The woman who had spun with her daughters was sitting on a stool outside. She stood up as they came towards her. She looked at Brinin and Oswald and then at her husband. The man nodded. The woman sat down again and began to weep.

KIN

The woman was still weeping but she lifted the hem of her headcloth and dabbed her eyes with it. Oswald shot another glance at Brinin. He was staring down at the woman unmoving, barely blinking, frowning a little. No, it wasn't a frown. It was a battle, some struggle with himself. It was how he had often looked in the old days when Aculf was at his worst.

'Didn't I say so?' said the woman.

'You did, my dear,' said the man.

'I told him,' said the woman to Oswald and Brinin, as though they already knew what she was talking about. Oswald didn't know if Brinin did, but *he* felt like he was in some bewildering fog.

'My dear,' said the man. 'Let's give our guests a cup of ale and talk. Where are the children?'

'I sent them out when you said you were going to speak to him.'

'All the better,' said the man. He turned to Oswald and Brinin. 'Please come inside.'

Inside a fire glowed in the hearth in the middle of the room. A pot of broth simmered over it and the house smelt of woodsmoke and boiling parsnips. Round the fire were stools and benches. Oswald sat on a stool, Brinin on a bench beside him.

The woman lifted a flask to pour some ale into a cup, but she spilled it. Shaking her head, she handed the flask and cup to her husband and sat down on the bench across from Oswald and Brinin. The man poured ale for Brinin, for Oswald, for the woman, for himself, then sat down beside his wife. Oswald watched as Brinin looked down at his cup, then set it on the bench without raising it to his lips. He gripped the edge of the bench. He kept swallowing. What on earth was going on?

297

'Friend,' said Oswald, 'we don't know your names. And I don't understand…'

But Oswald wasn't sure *what* he didn't understand. He didn't know what to ask, and Brinin seemed to have frozen beyond all speech.

'Forgive me,' said the man. 'My name is Bald, and this is Wulfswith, my wife. His name's Bruni, my dear.'

Brinin was still staring at them, still clutching the bench, his ale still undrunk beside him. But now he spoke.

'You knew my father and mother,' he said, steadily but very quietly.

Wulfswith opened her mouth to speak but said nothing. She looked at her husband.

'Son,' said Bald, 'I believe your father was my wife's brother.'

Brinin shifted a little on the bench, as though steadying himself after a blow. Wulfswith let out a little gasp, almost more of a sob, and turned again to Bald.

'Both dead now, my dear,' he said.

'I knew,' said Wulfswith, nodding and wiping her eyes again. 'They had to be after so long, and them both older than me, but I hoped… What about Row? He'd be a man now, but not an old man.'

But Brinin didn't seem to hear her. Oswald wasn't sure if it *was* Wulfswith and Bald he was staring at any more.

'My father's *sister*,' he said, almost whispering now.

Oswald didn't truly belong here, any more than an outsider, a man peering through his neighbour's door. He didn't understand how this woman had known that Brinin was her kin, or how his father and mother had ended up in Oakdene if they had once been here. He had never asked, had never even thought of asking. He had thought of them only as slaves, belonging first to his grandfather and then to his father. There was a tale here that these folk and perhaps even Brinin knew, but that he did not. He ought to leave Brinin alone with his kin, but Wulfswith was looking at Brinin so hungrily. No one had spoken of Row, yet this woman had asked of him. Had she known him as a little boy? She wanted to know—she *ought* to know—and Brinin hadn't answered her. He hadn't even heard her.

'Row died two harvests ago,' said Oswald, wishing then more than ever that he'd never thought of sending them to the minster or had even heard of it.

Wulfswith lifted her hand to her mouth, but then she straightened herself and took a sip of her ale. Bald put his hand on her arm. Brinin seemed to wake up then. He shut his eyes and took a long breath, then looked at the woman.

'You've been watching me for days,' he said. 'I saw you. How did you know who I was? I wasn't born here.'

'By looking at you! I saw you standing outside the guesthouse the day after you came and I said to myself, "If Gyrich had lived, he'd have looked much like that young lad." And then—perhaps because I'd been thinking of little Gyrich—when you walked towards me it put me in mind of my brother. But I said to myself, "You're a foolish old woman! Your brother never had hair like that, though his wife did." But I couldn't put it from my mind. I told Bald here and, would you believe it, while we were talking about you, along you came. And you smiled at us and it gave me such a shock, for it was like my brother's eyes were looking at me after all these years. Bald said that thinking of him had made me see what wasn't there. But I was right!'

'You were right, my dear,' said Bald. 'You were quick to see it, but I took longer. I can see it now though. No mistaking it.'

'The more I watched you, the more I saw,' went on Wulfswith. 'You walk like he did, and there were other things. And yet you're like your mother too, more even than you look like him. I said to myself, "Could this lad be so much like my brother and so much like his wife and not be their son?" And then there was the baby. A little before they left, your mother told me she thought she was going to have another baby, but that it was too early to be sure. And I thought, "If that baby lived, he'd be about as old as this lad is now." And then last night… last night… You tell him, Bald.'

'Last night,' said Bald, 'our Bægloc—that's our oldest—came in and said that young Beadheard had told him the best tale he'd ever heard. He said that one of the lads in the guesthouse was the one who had gone into a Danish camp to get his lord out. Now we'd heard something of that tale, but not how it had been done. "He didn't even fight them," says Bægloc, "just walked in, bold as day, and talked his way out. Seems he can speak the Danish tongue." "How can he speak the Danish tongue?" says I. Says Bægloc, "Seems his mother was a Dane." That settled it for me. After the children were all asleep—for we'd said nothing of what their mother was thinking so as not to raise their hopes—after they were asleep, I says to my wife, "It would be an odd thing for him to look as he does *and* have a Danish mother, yet not be who you think he is. The only thing we can do now is ask him. I'll do it tomorrow." '

'I knew,' said Wulfswith. 'I knew before he asked you, and when I saw him coming with you to the house, I knew I'd been right.'

'Didn't you think, son,' said Bald, 'that you might find some kin still living when you came here to this village?'

'I thought I had no kin and I didn't know where my father had come from. I was so young when he died—no more than five winters—and my mother died when I was nine. I think I remember her speaking of a sister of my father, but not often. We were slaves. It was easier not to talk about what had gone before.'

At the word 'slaves', Oswald saw Bald and Wulfswith glance at one another. Bald nodded slowly.

'We did wonder about slavery,' he said, 'but we'll speak of that later. You don't seem to be a slave now, though, son.'

'I'm not,' said Brinin.

'Listen, Bruni,' said Wulfswith. 'You do have kin. It breaks my heart to think of you without your father and mother so young and thinking you had no kin, and we were all here. We have five children, all your kin. And there's Ætte—her grandmother was my father's sister. She's your kin too. And there are things in this house that were your father's that are rightfully yours. Where's that chest, Bald?'

Bald went to a darker corner of the house. Oswald heard him scuffling about but couldn't see what he was doing. He came back with a seax and handed it to Brinin. Brinin sat and stared at it. He didn't say a word. He didn't even turn it over in his hands. He only held it and looked at it. It was nothing like the skilfully carved seax he had on his belt. It had a plain blade and a plain bone handle, smooth and yellowed by many winters.

'This was your father's, son,' said Bald, 'and his father's before that and perhaps even *his* father's before that. We found it in their house after your father and mother and Row had gone. That's when we first wondered about slavery.'

'You must eat here with us tonight, Bruni,' said Wulfswith earnestly. She turned to Oswald. 'Don't you think he ought to eat here tonight? We have so much to ask and to tell him—I can't even think of it all now—and he'll have things he wants to know too. And the children will be back soon—they're mostly grown now, none of them children but the last two—and he has to meet them too. Godweard will understand.'

'He must stay,' said Oswald, rising from the stool. 'I'll speak to Godweard and my father. I'll see you later, Brinin.'

Bald and Wulfswith smiled as he left, but Brinin didn't look at him. It was getting dark outside. Oswald glanced back into the house. Brinin was still staring at the seax.

WICKEDNESS

The guesthouse door was open, and smoke rose darkly from the roof hole. Oswald was rather dazed. There was so much he didn't understand. Who was the little boy that first made Wulfswith look at Brinin? Gyrich, she had called him. Why had Brinin's father and mother left and how had they ended up as slaves? They hadn't always been slaves; that much was clear. And how had Brinin's father taken a Danish wife? That was something he'd never thought of before. It was bewildering, all of it, but he understood enough. His father and Godweard would have to be told everything. Perhaps they would understand more than he did.

His father and Hildræd were sitting by the fire when he went inside and looked up as they heard him. His father was frowning.

'Where on earth have you been, Oswald? Godweard sent someone to find you,' he began but stopped short. 'What's wrong?'

'It's the strangest thing, sir,' said Oswald. Where should he even begin? He pointed back through the doorway. 'The woman in that house—the nearest one—Brinin's father was her brother. I've just come from there. Brinin's still with them.'

'But how could she learn such a thing?' asked Edrich. 'Sit down, Oswald. I'm not saying it isn't the truth, but I can't see how—'

They heard a sound from the threshold and saw Godweard coming in. Even if he had sent someone out to find Oswald, he wasn't frowning about it as Oswald's father had been.

'Ah, there you are, Oswald,' he said. 'I'm glad we found you. We'll be eating soon. Where's your friend?'

'Come and sit with us, Godweard,' said Hildræd. 'There's something you ought to hear. Tell us from the beginning, Oswald.'

So Oswald told them how Bald had come to find them and asked who Brinin's father and mother had been; how he had taken them to his house and everything that had been said there.

'And what does Brinin say to all this?' asked Edrich, when he was done.

'Very little, sir,' said Oswald. 'He seemed too overwhelmed to speak. He thought he had no kin and now suddenly he does. But they're telling the truth, Father. I'm sure of it. The woman asked about Row, and neither Brinin nor I had spoken his name. I don't understand it but I don't think they're lying.'

'They aren't lying,' said Godweard. 'Bald and Wulfswith are good, trustworthy folk. They wouldn't lie about it. Besides, I know something of this man, Wulfstan, Brinin's father. But surely, Edrich, so do you. If he was your slave, you must have known where he had come from.'

'I remember the man well. He was much like his son: worked hard and said little. But Wulfstan was my father's slave first, and I was away when he brought him home. When I came home, my wife was unwell. She was with child—with you, Oswald—and I was worried about her. All my father said to me was that he had stopped in a village somewhere to rest his horse for a few days. While he was there, Wulfstan had come to him and said that he had become so poor that he had to choose between slavery or watching his wife and son starve, and begged my father to help him. My father took him out of kindness and because—forgive me for saying this, Godweard, he didn't much like the little he had seen of the lord of the place. My father thought that if things had become so bad, they'd be better off in Oakdene, even if they were slaves. There was something odd about what was done with the money Wulfstan got for selling himself and his wife and son. I meant to ask my father more about it but, as I said, I had other worries on my mind, and my father didn't live long after Oswald was born. I ought to have asked Wulfstan himself but I didn't. He didn't live long either, not for more than four winters after he came. But, Godweard, you said that *you* knew something about him.'

Godweard had been listening to Edrich very carefully, leaning towards him as he spoke. He had stiffened like a man in pain, like one bearing a wound that his fellows couldn't see. He sat up straight, frowned a little, and looked at Hildræd.

'You know I never speak of my father, Hildræd,' he said.

'I've never heard you say a word about him,' said Hildræd.

'It's better that way,' Godweard sighed. 'But if I'm to speak of Brinin's father, I must also speak of my own. My father was... was not a good man. He was unkind to my mother. He was harsh with his children; more than harsh, if I'm truthful. As his eldest son, that harshness fell on me somewhat more often than the others, but we all suffered, boys and girls alike. No free man in this village could hope for justice while he was their lord. His anger came without warning and often with such fierceness that I have sometimes wondered if he had a devil. We could not know where it would come from or what path it would take. For those of us in his household—even my mother, it shames me to say—it almost always ended in blows. My mother was as good as my father was not. My father's wickedness began slowly and grew with the years. By the time my mother and her kin knew what he was, it was too late. She was wed and had children and she would not leave them with such a man.

'To be his son was a dreadful thing, but to be his slave... I will leave you to think for yourselves what that was like. He had many slaves, far more than he needed. Now, don't forget that in my tenth winter my mother sent me to her brother. To this day, I don't know how she brought it about, but I am thankful that she did. What I am about to tell you happened before then. I can't have been more than seven winters, though it was so unlike anything I had ever seen that I've never forgotten it.

'My father had got himself a new slave woman—little more than a girl. She was a Dane. I don't know where he got her. Very swiftly, he turned his anger on her more than on the others. I don't know why; we seldom understood anything that he did. One day, he was whipping her, outside with half the village looking on. I was among them. He had thrown her to the ground. Every time the whip fell, she screamed. And so it went on. Then suddenly, I heard a man say, "Stop!" I couldn't believe my ears! My father did not stop. He struck her again. She screamed again. Then Wulfstan came forward from somewhere behind me, walked up to my father, grabbed his arm and again said, "Stop." He wasn't shouting; he didn't even seem to be angry, though likely he was or he wouldn't have done it. I thought it was the bravest or else the maddest thing I had ever seen. My father snatched his arm away and slashed his whip across Wulfstan's face. He yelled at him to step back and mind his own business. Wulfstan didn't step back even an inch. He didn't even raise his hand to his face though it was bleeding. I remember it all as though it were yesterday because I was so stunned. He only reached out, took the whip and flung it away. I'll never forget how he looked at my father, with utter scorn and not the slightest fear, nor what he said to him. "You're a wicked man," he said. "But one day God will bring your sins down upon your own head." I remember thinking, "My father will kill him!" But my father seemed too shocked to do anything. Wulfstan bent down and lifted the woman to her feet, then told one of the other women to take her away and help her. Then he turned and walked away. I know a man may whip his slave if he so chooses, but my father was not like other men. Nothing he did was like what other men did. And I'd never seen anyone try to stop him before.'

All those months before, Leoba had told Oswald that her grandfather was a wicked man. She had likely known nothing of what Godweard was telling them now but she had been right.

'I thought my father would beat her again later with the door locked so Wulfstan couldn't stop him. But he didn't. Not many weeks later, Wulfstan came to my father, bought her freedom and made her his wife. Many years later I learned that he had parted with almost half his land to do it, which may have been foolish but I could never bring myself to blame him for it. For years, I remembered him as the bravest man I had ever seen.'

Did Brinin know *any* of this? He'd never spoken of it, but then there had always been so much he didn't say. Little wonder that Wulfstan had begged Oswald's grandfather, a stranger, for help rather than go to his lord. What kind of man had he been? Much like his son, as Oswald's father had said: rather fearless in a quiet, stubborn kind of way. There was a jug of ale on the table. Godweard poured himself some, drank it and went on with his tale.

'Now perhaps you wonder why we should make ourselves unhappy with this wretched tale from so long ago. Please bear with me a little longer, my friends. You will understand. One thing that frightened me most about my father was a way he had of seeming to overlook or even forget a misdeed, only to mete out his wrath without warning days or even weeks later. I believe this may have happened to Wulfstan and led to him leaving this place.

'I was sent to my kinsman, as you know. There I stayed until my eighteenth winter when my father died and I came back to be lord here. My mother had died a few years before. I had long sworn—since I was a small boy—that if I ever became lord in my father's stead I would put right the many wrongs he had done. This I set about doing. I freed all his slaves. To my mind, they had bought their freedom many times over with the wounds he had given them. To most, I gave money and helped them find work elsewhere. A few stayed here. All the slaves I have now are new. There were many other wrongs that I need not weary you with. Here is what you need to know:

'Bald and Wulfswith came to me. Wulfswith, almost overcome with weeping, told me how her brother's harvest had failed—like many in the village that year—how his two younger children, weakened by hunger, had sickened and died. Then one day, only a few months before my father had died, Wulfstan had left with his wife and son. He had told Bald that there was work for him elsewhere and that he was taking it to feed his household. Bald and Wulfswith did not at first think of slavery. They only feared that when they found Wulfstan's bow and seax and many other things left behind in the house, things that a freeman would have taken with him. They believed he had gone with a stranger who had been staying in the village—your father, Edrich, as we now know. They begged my father to tell them who the stranger was and where he was from. He wouldn't. No one else knew. I asked everyone.

'I gave them back the land Wulfstan had paid for his wife—I would have freed her anyway so I did not feel I could do otherwise. They have kept it in the hope that he might come back; sometimes they have tilled it and other times they have left it fallow. And they kept his house good, though empty. I have even seen Wulfswith going in to sweep it. I pitied them because in my heart I knew that none of us would ever see Wulfstan again.

'I learned one more thing that Bald and Wulfswith did not know. One of my father's slaves told me that he had overheard my father threatening Wulfstan a few weeks before he left. He said that unless Wulfstan paid for some misdeed or other, he would have him taken before a moot not in the village but before the ealdorman. Wulfstan had called my father a liar, said that he had done no such deed and asked where he was to get that kind of money. My father said he had men who would swear that they had seen the deed done. The slave knew no more, but I wonder, Edrich, if that was the odd thing you thought had been done with the money. I believe my father waited for years until Wulfstan was weakened by hunger and the loss of his children, then took his revenge. It's a hard thing to say of one's own father, but that's the kind of man he was.'

Godweard's tale was weighing down on them all. No one spoke. Oswald followed Godweard's lead and got up to pour himself a cup of ale. A drink might stop him from weeping; tears were creeping shamefully near. Was Gyrich, whom Wulfswith had thought Brinin looked like, one of the children who had died, a brother whom Brinin had never met? Most men buried at least one child—his father had—but burying two and falling into slavery in a few short months was more than Oswald liked to think about. He sat down again and tried to keep the tears at bay.

'This land you spoke of, Godweard, this house,' said Hildræd. 'Surely they are rightfully Brinin's. He's Wulfstan's son.'

'They *are* his!' said Godweard. 'And his kin will want him to have them. He belongs here. His kin are here. The land was his father's and grandfather's. I don't know how things are for him in your village, Edrich. Folk know him there, and he has lived there all his life, so he likely thinks of it as home. But he belongs here. Folk here would welcome him. His father was highly thought-of, and there was great sorrow when he left.'

Oswald caught his father's eye. The land was Brinin's. It must rightfully pass from grandfather to father to son. But would he leave Oakdene?

'Will you tell him all this, Godweard?' Edrich said. 'I don't know how much he knows.'

'I will,' said Godweard, 'but not tonight. Leave him with his kin. I'll never forget how Wulfswith wept when she and Bald came to me for help. And I couldn't help them. Come, let's go and eat. My wife will be wondering why we are lingering.'

BROTHER

Brinin didn't know how long he stared at the seax. He tried to gather his thoughts and straighten them out. There were too many for him to tell one from the other. He knew he needed to talk, but none of the words he wanted seemed to come readily to hand. As for the feelings—which could be hard enough to understand at the best of times—he wasn't even trying to untangle those. The urge to weep, to laugh in disbelief, even to retch were all jumbled up together with other things he could not name. He had woken up that morning kinless and now he sat in the home of his father's sister—not some far-off kin, but his father's *sister*, as near to him as Hildræd was to Oswald, with the same blood and bone. He was sitting in the home of his father's sister, holding a seax which had been his father's and his grandfather's—he didn't even know his grandfather's name—and now they said it was his. He was beginning to think that he did want to be sick. He somehow needed to settle whatever was happening in his gut. Hadn't there been some ale somewhere? He had forgotten about it.

'I had some ale,' he said, 'but...'

'It's beside you on the bench, son,' said Bald.

It *was*, though he couldn't remember putting it there. He set the seax down carefully, half-afraid that it might melt away. His hands were shaking as he lifted the cup to his lips, but he took a drink and then another. He couldn't sit here wordless all night. These folk—his kin—were waiting for him to say something.

'I'm sorry,' he said. They were his blood and bone. Wulfswith had seen that he looked like her kin. Perhaps he wasn't the first among them to find speech slow in coming. Likely she would understand. 'I've never been good at talking and now I don't know where to begin.'

'There's no need for us to say everything in one evening,' said Bald. 'We'll all take our time over it. Tomorrow will be as good as today, better perhaps as then we'll have had the night to think of it. Is the food ready, my dear? I think I can hear the children coming. We'll tell them who Bruni is and eat together and speak of whatever comes to mind. There are things we need to tell you, son, but it doesn't have to be tonight.'

Wulfswith began bustling about, cutting hunks of bread and scooping the broth into bowls. She wasn't done before a little boy, no older than six winters, dashed in. He stopped dead, staring wide-eyed at Brinin, then crept over to his father.

'Father, that's the one who went into the Danish camp,' he whispered loudly. 'What's he doing here?'

'Sit down, Wulfstan, and hold your tongue,' said Wulfswith. She put her hand on her son's shoulder and pushed him down onto the bench. She thrust a bowl of broth into one of his hands and a hunk of bread into the other. 'Eat that and don't spill it. Your father and I will tell you everything you need to know in good time.'

She had called him Wulfstan. She had lost her brother years before, but her son bore his name. Brinin smiled at Wulfstan, this small kinsman with his father's name. The boy was still staring at him, not eating.

Everything happened at once then. Three girls came in, two of them old enough now to be called women. Brinin couldn't tell which was the older of the two. The youngest was a little older than Ebba, but a little younger than Eawig. Twelve winters? No more than that, surely. None of the girls had such a wayward tongue as their younger brother. They asked nothing more than a glance could say and began to help their mother. One handed food to Brinin, another to Bald. The youngest poured them both more ale.

But it was the sight of Bald and Wulfswith's son, their firstborn, coming in behind his sisters, that wounded Brinin. He could easily have walked past the girls or little Wulfstan without stopping to look at them. But this man, standing now in the doorway, the light of the fire on his face, was like Row, much as Hildræd's son had seemed more like Edith's brother than Oswald did. Blood and bone. He was taller than Row. His hair was a darker hue. But his eyes were the same and the shape of his jaw and the way he leaned his head to one side wordlessly to ask his father, with half-raised eyebrows, why this guest was sitting among them.

'Sit down and eat, Bægloc,' said Bald.

Bægloc took a seat beside Brinin, on the stool where Oswald had sat. Wulfswith, her bustling done, was rather tearful again as she looked at them all. Little Wulfstan still wasn't eating.

'This is Bruni,' she said, a little quiver coming into her voice. 'Your kinsman.'

'Kinsman!' Bægloc looked from his father and mother to Brinin, to his mother again, back to his father.

'A Danish mother, that's it! I should have thought of it myself,' he muttered, half to himself. Then he turned to Brinin. 'Are you the son of my mother's brother?'

'He is!' cried Bald before Brinin could answer. 'And it's what you said about him having a Danish mother that made us think to ask him.'

Bægloc turned back to Brinin with a warm smile, a smile that was almost Row, yet not Row. He set his bowl down on the floor and took Brinin's free hand tightly in both his own.

'Then welcome home, brother,' he said. His voice was rather choked. 'Welcome home. We had almost lost all hope.'

That threatened to be Brinin's undoing on this day of near undoing. His throat, his mind, his heart were all too swollen for any words to come. All he could do was tighten his grip on Bægloc's hands. He had called him brother. Bald had called him son. But before he was wholly undone, Wulfswith pointed out her other children.

'Bægloc's our eldest. He was born before they left though was too young to remember. And this is Frigyth.' Wulfswith pointed to one of the older girls, though not the taller one. 'She must be about as old as you. She was born not long after they... How old are you, Bruni?'

'Seventeen winters,' said Brinin.

'That's what I thought,' said Wulfswith. 'We called her Frigyth after my mother. And this is Mildgyth, and our youngest daughter is Deorswith. And this is our little Wulfstan. Don't sit staring, Wulfstan. You haven't touched your food! Eat it now before it goes cold.'

'So my grandmother was called Frigyth,' said Brinin. Let him speak now while the words were there to utter. 'I've never known anything about my grandfather or grandmother, not their names nor what kind of man and woman they were, nor what children they had. And I barely remember my father.'

'That's where we'll begin then,' said Wulfswith. 'My father was called Osfrith. I don't remember him well as he died when I was only a little older than Wulfstan here. But I remember a little. He was a hardworking man, stern—we had to jump quick to heed him whenever he spoke and there could be no lingering. Not so much with me, though, as I was the only girl and much younger than the boys. I remember how, sometimes, if he thought my mother was scolding me too much he would take me to sit with him and tell her that I was still young and would learn wisdom as I grew. But he was much sterner with my brothers. My mother once said that my father and your father were both too stubborn to live easily in the same house. But I believe they were fond of one another, all the same.'

'Brothers?' said Brinin. 'More than one, then?'

'Two. Your father was the eldest and Wulfræd a little younger. They were as good friends as two brothers could be. Our father died suddenly. He was well one day, feverish the next and dead two days after that. Wulfræd sickened at the same time. He didn't die then but was never the same afterwards. He always coughed after that and died the following winter.

'My mother was a busy woman, never standing still for long. I was a little scared of her at times, but she was never unkind to me. She died in about my tenth winter, a little before your father and mother were wed, and then they raised me like I was their own daughter. Your… your… say what Wulfstan was like, Bald. Let me eat my food now.'

'He was a good man, son,' said Bald, 'a good and trustworthy man. He was well liked here. He was a good brother, a good husband and father and a good friend to me.'

'He was all that!' broke in Wulfswith. 'He wasn't so stern as our own father, though all the children knew they had to heed him. There could be no folly in his house, no idling, no lying. Everyone had to learn to keep their word. I loved those children. I helped bring all of them into this world and to think that now…'

Wulfswith began to weep again and her daughter—Frigyth, Brinin thought it was—put her arm around her. They loved each other in this house. And Bægloc had called him brother.

'If your father had a fault, son—and we all do—' said Bald, 'it was that he could be stubborn. And he kept his thoughts too much to himself. If he had only told us more, we would have gone looking for him. Godweard wanted to, that's the truth of it. And when we feared slavery, we were worried about him. Your father wasn't the right kind of man to be a slave.'

'Is anyone the right kind of man to be a slave, Father?' said Bægloc. Brinin glanced at him. That was one of his own thoughts, and he'd never before heard another speak it aloud.

'But it falls to some to be slaves, and it's easier for some than for others,' said Bald. 'It worried us. Was he good to him—to all of you—this lord? No beating or chaining or starving or any of the things you hear about?'

And so it went on throughout the evening. Brinin laid their fears to rest as much as he could. He told them that they had never been hungry, that they had always been clothed and had their own place to sleep. He told them he had never seen a chain in Oakdene and that Edrich Thegn was a good lord who had given him his freedom and a field of his own. He said nothing of Aculf and his many blows; they hadn't fallen on his father or mother, and only once on Row, so they didn't need to be spoken of. He told them that Row had died swiftly and without much pain, but did not speak of the flight nor the mist nor of burying him alone, laying him in a hole he had made with his own hands. He didn't tell them that his mother had been shunned for being a Dane nor of how his harvest had been wrecked. He told them that Oswald was the best friend a man could ever have.

Things were remembered. Things were learned for the first time. Wulfswith and all her daughters wept, and Brinin came so near to it that his eyes grew dim. There was sorrow, there was gladness, there was fellowship, there was kinship. But at last, the words Brinin had somehow found were all spent, and he couldn't even bear to listen any more. Bald saw it. He said Brinin ought to sleep, that he was welcome under their roof but that his lord might want him in the guesthouse. There was still weightier business to speak of, much more that they needed to give him, but it could wait until the morning. He put Brinin's father's seax into its sheath and sent him away with it. Wulfswith flung her arms around him as though he were her own son and not her brother's.

It was cold outside. Brinin stood alone in the stillness and looked up at the sky. Clear and starry. Row had died too soon to know this day. He himself had almost missed it. He had forgotten why he hadn't wanted to come but thanked God that Edrich Thegn and Oswald had been stubborn enough to make him, and for softening him enough to listen.

The guesthouse was empty, and Brinin was glad of it. He threw more wood onto the fire, then lay on his bench, wrapped in his cloak and turned towards the wall. The others came in a little later, but he kept his eyes shut so they would think he was asleep. He had woken up that morning kinless. Now night had fallen and Wulfswith had known him, Bald had called him son and Bægloc had called him brother.

FOREFATHERS

From his bench, Oswald could hear low voices and scattered words. The words were too few and his mind too full of sleep for him to catch any meaning. Was it morning already? His body felt too heavy to believe it. He drew his cloak tighter around him. If he kept his eyes shut and lay still perhaps the night would linger a little longer. The voices were fainter now, drifting away. He was dreaming them.

'It must have come as a shock to you, my boy, though not an unhappy one. None of us had even thought of such a thing.'

The voice of Oswald's father tore him from his sleep. The fire was crackling and birds were singing outside. Oswald opened his eyes. It was still dark, but the fire burned well and lit the room a little. His uncle was sitting on the edge of his bed, running his hands through his hair, his face still heavy with sleep. Aldred lay on his bench, both arms hiding his face to shield him from the coming morning. Oswald's father and Brinin sat on a bench by the hearth, empty cups on the ground by their feet. Oswald's father held a stick that he waved a little as he spoke; its end was blackened where he had been poking it into the fire. Even as Oswald watched, he drove it in again and the tip of the stick glowed before fading into blackness again. If Oswald hadn't seen Brinin asleep the night before he would have wondered if he had slept at all. He still looked rather dazed but not so stunned. Now at least he seemed to know what was happening. Oswald stretched, stifled a groan and sat up.

'Godweard wants to speak to you about it all, early he said,' Edrich said to Brinin. 'There are things he wants you to know. He asks you to wait here for him. Your kin won't mind if you don't go to them straightaway.'

'Yes, my lord,' said Brinin. 'Whatever he wishes.'

Hildræd got up and walked over to Aldred. He shook his son's arm. Aldred groaned.

'Time to get up, my boy,' said Hildræd heartily. 'You're not going to lie there until the day's half-gone.'

Oswald grinned. The day was hardly half-gone. It had barely begun. There wasn't even any light showing under the door yet. Once Aldred had dragged himself up, Edrich and Hildræd soon left with him. Oswald followed them to the door, not to leave with them but to ask his father if he might stay. Edrich Thegn had already thought of this.

'Stay here until Godweard comes,' he said.

Outside the sky was beginning to brighten. Oswald turned back to Brinin.

'I don't know what to say,' he said.

Brinin lifted his hands almost helplessly.

'Neither do I.'

'Did you talk for long last night?'

'Until we were too tired to talk any more.'

'What did you talk about?' asked Oswald, sitting with him by the fire.

'I met their children,' said Brinin. 'I learned who my grandfather and grandmother were and what they were like, and that my father had a brother who died young. They talked about my father.'

But not about the land or the house, it seemed. Not even Brinin could have known that and said nothing about it. And perhaps learning he had kin and hearing his grandfather's name for the first time had been enough for one day. Oswald knew the name of his grandfather and his grandfather's father. He had walked their land and one day it would be his. He couldn't remember a time when he hadn't known. He knew his mother's kin. He knew who his father's brothers and sister had been and when and how they had died. But Brinin hadn't only been left without a father, mother and brother. He'd somehow been left untethered.

'Godweard spoke about your father yesterday,' said Oswald.

'He remembered him?'

'From when he was a boy.'

'Row once told me that the lord here was the worst kind of man, but Godweard…'

'He's nothing like his father.'

'My kin…' Brinin stopped as though to see how the word tasted. 'My kin were worried about us when they feared we were slaves. They wanted to know about that.'

'What did you tell them?'

'That we were always fed, clothed and housed. And that your father freed me and gave me a field.'

'Nothing about Aculf? Wasn't Aculf every bit as bad as they feared?'

'Row said Godweard's father was worse. That's what they feared. But Aculf did nothing to my father. My mother's life was hard because she was a widow and a Dane, not because she was a slave. Aculf only ever beat Row once, and we were never hungry.'

'But what about you?'

'They weren't worried about me. They didn't even know I was alive.'

Perhaps there was wisdom in saying little. Brinin wasn't a slave now, and Aculf wasn't workreeve. Oswald got up and went back to the door. He saw Godweard talking to Bald and Wulfswith outside their house.

'He's coming now,' he said. 'I'll go and find my father.'

Brinin found Godweard easy to like but hard to listen to that morning. Everything he said was both a gift and a wound, a kindness and an onslaught. He saw his mother as a girl, felt her fear and every blow that had fallen on her. But Godweard put words into his father's mouth and gave him a face, albeit a bleeding one. He gave him boldness when everyone else had cowered in fear. 'He must have lost all hope,' Row had once said. Perhaps sorrow *had* brought him that low, but he had still had enough fight left to put his wife and son beyond the reach of a wicked man.

Brinin heard what Godweard said about the land and house that were now his, but such things seemed small beside everything else he learned. His mother had always loomed large in his mind, no smaller after eight winters without her. His father had been too shadowy to know, but that morning he stepped out of the shadows and joined his wife, and Brinin loved him because *he* had loved her.

Brinin didn't know how long he sat there after Godweard had left. He stared at the fire but didn't see it. His mind was still where Godweard had brought it, watching his father and mother as they had been all those years before. A shadow stretched long from the doorway; not his father's shadow but still that of a kinsman.

'Your friend said you'd likely still be here,' said Bægloc. 'Did Godweard tell you about the land?'

'Yes,' said Brinin. 'It wasn't something I'd even thought of. I knew my father once had land, but I'd never asked myself what became of it.'

'Likely there would have been no good in asking before now,' said Bægloc. 'I can take you to see it, if you like.'

It was more land than he had in Oakdene, south of the village, well-scarred by many years of ploughing. It was good land. Brinin squatted down and touched the earth as he had done when Edrich Thegn had given him his field. This must have been where Row first learned to plough, walking alongside their father who would let no one in his household be idle. Brinin stood up and looked around. He wanted to see what they had seen. The little hills far off to the south, behind which lay a minster. The coppice where folk here seemed to get their wood; in the evening their shadows would have stretched towards it. The scattered houses behind them with their rising hearthsmoke. Which one had they gone home to? Beyond those lay the meadow, a little higher than everywhere else.

'Our grandfather wasn't the first to farm here,' said Bægloc. That 'our' sounded as welcoming as 'brother' had done. 'I believe his grandfather was the first, or perhaps his grandfather's father. My mother would know.'

'Does she know their names?' asked Brinin. Now suddenly it wasn't only his brother and father and grandfather whose eyes had seen what his saw now. It was forefather after forefather. It was all so strange.

'Some of them, I think,' said Bægloc. 'Our grandfather's father was called Tycca.'

Row, Wulfstan, Osfrith, Tycca and forefathers beyond them. Tycca, Osfrith, Wulfstan, Bruni.

'Do you want to see the house now?' asked Bægloc.

The house was nearer to the meadow and further west than Bald and Wulfswith's house. As Bægloc led Brinin there, a man met them. He was older than Edrich Thegn, though perhaps not as old as Garulf. He was walking slowly, and they stopped to wait for him.

'They tell me you're Wulfstan's son,' he said, taking Brinin's hand. 'Welcome home, lad. I'm Mærheard. Your father and his brother and I were friends when we were boys. Come and sit with me some evening. I like talking about the old times, and I have a tale or two I could tell you. Bægloc will show you the house.'

Home. Was *this* home? Here, where his father and forefathers had lived and worked, but of which he knew so little? Where he had land now, but needed a kinsman to show him around? Or Oakdene, where he had been born and lived and knew even in the dark? Where he had no kin, some friends and many who wished him gone from among them? Bægloc and this man had both welcomed him home. Godweard had told him he belonged here. But it was bewildering.

'I spoke to your friend's father this morning to thank him for being a good lord to my kin,' said Bægloc. He was watching Brinin, sidelong and Rowlike, as they walked. 'And he said that he hadn't been as good a lord as he ought to have been.'

Bægloc stopped and stood in front of Brinin.

'He said that his workreeve was overharsh with you, but that he found a better man to take his place. Yet you said nothing about this workreeve to us.'

'I wanted to spare your mother more tears,' said Brinin. 'My father died before he was made workreeve. He wasn't nearly as bad as Godweard's father and he wasn't harsh with my mother or Row. Only with me.'

'Only with you. Yet he was harsh enough to drive you into running away, which surely no slave does unless what is being done to him is worse than what might be done when they catch him.'

Bægloc was more dogged than Row had been. And what had Edrich Thegn been saying? Did he think Bægloc was a priest he needed to speak his sins to? Yet how could Brinin come to know this kinsman, this brother, unless he spoke to him?

'What did he do to you?' asked Bægloc.

'Cursed me most days, said my mother had been a dog. That was the one time I didn't hold my tongue—I paid for it though. Beat me often, not perhaps as badly as some slaves are beaten but hard enough at times to feel it for days afterwards. And he asked Edrich Thegn to sell me and send me away from Row. Everything else I could bear, but not that. It was folly to go, and we should have stayed where we were. What we feared might never have happened. But we ran away to stay together.'

'And then you lost him anyway.'

Brinin looked down. Bægloc was as much like Row in sorrow as when he smiled, Row whose face he would never see again. All this talk, everything that had been said at Bald's hearthside, everything Godweard had told him, this man who called him brother and sorrowed with a kinsman he barely knew; all these bewildering feelings were making him lose his grip on himself. If it went on much longer he'd be utterly undone.

'And you *still* went to get your lord from the Danes? After all that?'

'Oswald—my friend—helped us flee. They found out what he'd done and… and when he wouldn't tell them where we'd gone he got the flogging that would have been ours.'

'But he's a freeman!'

'And a thegn's son.' It *was* hard to believe, even after all these months. 'What was I to do after that? I was with him when he heard his father had been taken. I didn't much care if I died and I had no kin left to weep if I did.'

Bægloc put his hand on Brinin's shoulder. His grip was strong.

'You have kin now, brother, so think of that the next time you want to walk into a Danish camp.' He pointed to a house that lay ahead of them. 'That's the house. Do you want me to go with you or will you go alone?'

'Alone,' said Brinin. Alone was the only way he *could* go now.

The house was bigger than he had thought it would be. The door was unlocked. Brinin pushed it open and sunlight flooded the floor. He stepped inside. The floorboards creaked under his feet. It smelt damp and dust had settled, but it was the dust of months, not years. Light came from a hole in the roof and some fallen thatch lay beneath it on the floor. But it wasn't a big hole. It could easily be mended.

A bench and two stools stood by the hearthstone. One of the stools was so small that only a child could have sat on it, the other so like his broken ones that it must have been made by the same hand. The roofshelves were almost empty, a shovel and fork on one, a pot on the other. On one side of the house was the sleeping bench and on the other a bed. The bed was empty too, bare wood with no straw to lie on. A chest sat on the floor at the end of it. The roof-posts were smooth and shiny, worn by many hands. He didn't know which of his forefathers had first put them there.

Brinin sat on the bench and looked around. He had never learned how to weep. Or perhaps he had forgotten how to; there had been so many times when he had been too stubborn to give way to it. But now… He lifted his hand to his face and felt tears there. And he wept. He sat and sobbed like a child. He wept because his mother had been young and scared and alone, had been snatched from her kin and had fallen into the hands of a wicked man. He wept because his bold father—how he loved that man now that he was learning enough about him to love—had been so broken and brought so low that he had lost almost everything. He wept for the children who had been born here, had played here, had sat on the little stool and had been buried before he could know them. He wept because Row had died too soon to come home. So much had been lost.

Those tears somehow brought others with them, all the tears that he hadn't wept before. He wept for every blow, every bruise, for the burning, helpless anger, for his lost sow, his lost stools, his lost harvest, for every stinging injustice after stinging, smarting injustice. He had been so alone. He wept for every small kindness, every deed of friendship, for stars on a clear night. He wept for how it had felt to be worthless and how it felt to be welcomed, for how it had felt to be hopeless and how it felt to hope for that day when the poor man would not weep. So much had been lost—so much—and he had only ached that heavy, unshifting ache, and no tears would come. Now so much had been found, and they wouldn't stop.

THOUGHT

'My daughter and I have spoken to one another at some length,' said Godweard. There had been so many days of talk and thought that Oswald had wondered if the answer would ever come. 'We both think it would be a good match and I must say, Edrich, that I'm delighted at the thought of strengthening my friendship with you and binding our households in this way. And we are both happy with the morning-gift you are offering. Over the coming days, we will talk more about what I myself will settle on my daughter. I will want a scribe to write everything down. However, that need not be straightaway. My daughter is young. One more summer here, one more winter. After that will be the time for the wedding. When the weather is warmer and the days longer I hope to take her with me to see you. And perhaps you will come back to us again.'

Now that the 'yes' had come, it wasn't relief Oswald felt, though he was glad. It was more like fear. There could be no going back now, without bringing dreadful shame on himself and his kin. It wasn't that he didn't want to. He wanted her to be his wife. But what if he made a bad husband? What if he made a poor father, either too stern or not stern enough? What if leaving her kin made her so wretched that there was nothing he could do to make her happy? What if bearing a child killed her as it had killed his mother? But it was too late now. He could only swallow his fears and pray for strength and blessing.

Later in the meadow, Leoba herself didn't seem to be afraid in the slightest. She spoke with as much ease as ever, asking him more about Edith, about Oakdene, about the folk who lived there and what they were like.

'And what about your friend?' she asked at last. 'Will he stay here with his kin when you go home?'

'I don't know. I haven't dared to ask him,' said Oswald.

He had barely dared to think about it. Brinin had shown him the land. He had pointed out the house, though not yet taken him into it. It was a good house, big enough to live in and raise children in. Brinin's father and mother had sunk low indeed to die where they had. And not even freedom in Oakdene had made Brinin happy. The friendship of a few had not outweighed the hatred of others. The goodwill of his lord had not softened the hearts of his neighbours. Neither Oswald nor his father nor Edith had brought him justice. Every wise thought Oswald could gather told him that Brinin should stay and farm that land that had come to him from his forefathers. Everything in his gut wished he wouldn't.

'Why?' asked Leoba. She had her cloak wrapped tightly round her, holding it from the inside so that not even her hands were showing. It was cold that day.

'I think I'm afraid of what he'll say or of what I'll say,' said Oswald.

'What _you'll_ say? What do you mean? Don't you want him to stay?'

'I do and I don't. I hate the thought of Oakdene without him. I think he ought to stay, but we've been friends for so long and things can happen that bind you to a man.'

'Like Brinin going to get your father from the Danes?'

'Not only that,' said Oswald. It wasn't a tale he wanted to tell, but Leoba would learn it sooner or later and it was better that she heard it from him and not from someone else.

So he told the tale but kept it short. He spoke about what had been done and said nothing of how it had felt. He could speak of it all steadily now if he kept his words few: Aculf, the flight, the Moot, Row's death, the Danes.

'And you forgave your father after that?' asked Leoba. Oswald knew Leoba wasn't a weeper—she had told him that herself—but he had seen her face change as he spoke, even with his few, steady words.

'As he forgave me for hiding what was my duty to tell him, and as Brinin forgave me for sending him on a journey that killed his brother. And truthfully, it was worse when I _hadn't_ forgiven him. We understand each other better now.'

'He wept by your bedside when we thought you were dying. I was sent with food for him because he wouldn't leave you to eat. I found him weeping there but I left again before he could see me. I don't know why I'm telling you that.'

'Perhaps to show me that he doesn't hate me after all,' said Oswald. 'Don't worry. I know.'

'And *do* you think Brinin will stay here?'

'I think he ought to,' said Oswald.

Brinin had never liked to rush into anything. Thought—slow thought—had always been better. But sometimes a man could know what to do before there had been time for thought. Brinin had known as he had wept in his father's house. He had known that there was only one thing he could do. He had known that it would be hard. The knowledge had come first, and the thought had come after. It was one thing knowing *what* to do, another altogether knowing how to do it well.

A few days' thought was enough. It was a cold, wet, wretched day. Oswald didn't go to the meadow, and Brinin, dashing through the rain from Bald's house, found him with his father and uncle in the guesthouse. Perhaps Edrich Thegn had been thinking too, as he was the first to speak. Likely it was better that way. Brinin, for all his thought, didn't know how to begin.

'Come and sit with us,' said Edrich. 'I have some things to speak to you about.'

The fire stung Brinin's eyes. It seemed smokier that morning.

'We will go home the day after tomorrow,' said Edrich. 'I don't want to be away any longer, and our business here is done. But you, my boy…'

Edrich left the words unborn, waiting for Brinin to bring them into being. And Brinin could do that.

'You are my lord,' he said. It was easier not to look at Oswald. 'Everything I have I owe to you, my lord: my freedom, my field. Even coming here and finding my… my kin, my lord, was because of the friendship that you and… and your son have shown me. I had never even hoped for a field and I can't easily walk away from it without seeming thankless. And no man can seek another lord without leave. I will do nothing without your leave, my lord. But I think of my father. I ask myself what he would have thought if he could have known that one day I would be sitting here, free and choosing between tilling his land or going back to the place that sorrow and trouble drove him to. It isn't easy because you are my lord, and he was my father.'

Brinin saw Edrich Thegn glance at Oswald, but he didn't let his own eyes follow.

'It seems to me, my boy, that the owing goes both ways,' said Edrich Thegn. 'We could even say that it is not you who are asking leave to seek another lord, but your father who sought another lord without leave. As for your field, I have put some thought into that. The field is still yours. As to what a man owes to his lord and what he owes to his father, that has never been easy. But let us be wise. It would seem wise for you to take up your father's land. You are always welcome in Oakdene, but we cannot lie to ourselves and say that you have had no trouble there. If I were in your place—and as your lord, this is what I think you ought to do—I would find someone to rent the field in Oakdene and take up what is yours. I can think of a few poorer folk who might be glad of a little land to rent. And when I gather my own rents four times a year, I will gather yours and send it to you. Now that my household will be bound to Godweard's, there will be folk who come and go, if not as often as four times a year, at least once or twice.'

And so it was done. Edrich Thegn gave Brinin leave. He had given him his blessing. And he had gone further than that: he had bidden him to take up the land of his forefathers. It was only now that Brinin turned to Oswald. His face was hard to understand. This was the right thing to do, the only thing to do, a hard thing to do.

'Oswald, you know I would do almost anything for you,' he said suddenly. 'I haven't forgotten... I haven't forgotten anything you've done but—'

'You heard what my father said.' Oswald kept blinking; likely the smoke was stinging his eyes too. 'If you do anything else I'll say you're a fool, and you told me I could call you one as much as I like. So... so will you stay here when we go back?'

'I can't. I told Mildrith I would plough her land again. And my sow will have her young soon. And there are folk I need to speak to. Bald and Bægloc say they'll plough for me here, and get the sowing done. Then after Easter, they'll come to Oakdene with an oxcart and help me bring my sow and her young back here.'

'Easter then. I'm glad you don't want to be a fool.' Oswald stood. He was smiling, yet it wasn't the smile that Brinin knew. 'Godweard wanted to speak to me this afternoon. Let me go and find him.'

Oswald left them, running away through the rain and out of sight. They had settled on it. Edrich Thegn and Oswald were of one mind, and Brinin knew they were right. In Oakdene, he was his mother's son to be shunned. Here he was his father's son to be welcomed. There was only one thing to do, and yet it was so hard.

SHIVERING

Edith knew how to wait, and it wasn't a fearful waiting now. She didn't wake up each morning wondering if a sorrowbearing horseman would ride into the village. She only waited for one of two words—a yes or a no—and to learn if everything would change for ever. She wished she could slow the seasons, bridle the months, stop the weeks and tether the days to keep them where they were a little longer. She knew it was folly. So much was already gone. Oswald had come back from war older, her father wearier, and not even the hall felt like home any more. She could no longer see her mother there in her mind. It drove her outside into the cold, where she had to keep walking to stop herself from shivering, and where the meadow, trees and hillside were the same.

Edith was in the meadow when she found him. She heard him first, a little stifled sob from somewhere nearby. Then she saw Wulfrich, huddled under a tree. He was hugging his knees to keep warm but shivering all the same. His eyes were red and swollen. When he saw Edith he hastily wiped them but he had been weeping for too long and too bitterly for it to do any good. All he could do was to turn away. Edith crouched down beside him.

'Wulfrich, you can't sit here on a day like this.' She touched his hand. 'You're so cold. Come, let me sit beside you and put my cloak over you. Tell me what's wrong.'

He looked at her a little warily, though he didn't pull away. But he said nothing.

'Did your father beat you?' That was surely the likeliest trouble. Even Aculf's wife seemed frightened of him.

Wulfrich shook his head.

'Were some of the other children unkind? Or did you hurt yourself?'

Another shake of the head.

'I can't help you if you won't tell me. Oh, you're still so cold.' Edith wrapped her cloak round him more tightly. 'That's better. Come now, tell me about it. Perhaps there's something I can do.'

'My lady,' he whispered, 'if someone knows about a bad thing and tells no one, is it the same as doing it himself?'

'*Do* you know about a bad thing?'

Wulfrich didn't speak, but he didn't shake his head either. He sat sniffling for a while.

'I don't *want* them to do it!' he burst out at last with another sob. 'But I can't stop them!'

'Why don't you tell me what it is?'

'I can't! My father said if I told anyone who… He said he'd… I can't!'

'Your father knows about the bad thing too?'

'No, he didn't mean that. He meant Brinin's harv—' Wulfrich stopped sharply and gasped, his eyes wide at the thought of what had slipped from his lips, rushing out before he could stop it. He started sobbing again. 'Oh please, lady Edith, don't tell him what I said.'

'Did your father wreck Brinin's harvest, Wulfrich? I won't tell him you told me.'

'No! No! It wasn't him!'

But Aculf knew who had done it. Edith was sure of it. And so did Wulfrich. And he was too scared of his father to tell anyone and was wretched with the knowledge of it.

'Does the man who wrecked Brinin's harvest want to do something else? Is that the bad thing you want to stop?'

A nod from Wulfrich this time, and with it a burst of wisdom. Edith had sworn that she would put this wrong right and now she knew how to do it.

'I know you have to heed your father, but you said he didn't know about *this* bad thing, so he hasn't forbidden you to speak of it. Tell me what it is. Even if you don't tell me *who* wants to do it, if I know *what* they're going to do, I can watch out for it and stop them.'

Wulfrich was still wary, still tearful, but she could see his frightened stiffness softening as he understood what she was saying. He even shifted nearer to her. She could feel his little trembling body beside her.

'I'll catch them,' she said. 'But it will be *you* who stopped them by telling me.'

Wulfrich glanced fearfully towards the village, then put his mouth to Edith's ear.

'They're going to burn Brinin's house,' he whispered, 'and kill his swine. I heard them talking.'

And Edith thanked God for this frightened child. How could she have told Brinin that he'd lost everything he had while he was away? She would stop them, even if it meant watching every night.

'When?' she said.

'Tonight. Because he's still away. They said he might come back soon, and they have to do it quick. They don't want to do it while he's here, so the fire doesn't kill him.'

At least they wanted to stop short of murder! And *she* would catch them before they did anything else. She would put it right. After all these months, it would all be put right.

'How many are they?'

'Two.'

'I'll stop them. I'll find someone to help me. Brinin would be happy if he knew how much you'd helped him today. It was you, not me.'

'Will you tell him?'

'Do you want me to?'

'I like him. He made me a wooden shield and sword and tells me tales sometimes, good ones about dragons. Please tell him, but nobody else.'

'Nobody else.' Edith hadn't even known that Brinin *could* tell tales. And if ever a child needed a tale and a wooden sword, it was Wulfrich. 'Now, run home before your father or mother come looking for you.'

'And you'll make it right, my lady?'

'I have already thought of a way to do it,' said Edith.

Wulfrich let out a long sigh. He wiped his eyes again. The tears had mostly stopped now, though his lips were still quivering.

'They said they were going to burn his house like the Danes burned folks' houses,' he said, 'and kill his swine because they stole beasts. But Brinin didn't do those things, lady Edith.'

'No! *We* know he didn't, but some folk are foolish and wicked. We'll put it to rights. Don't worry about it any more. Now, you ought to go home, but first go and wash your face so your father and mother don't ask why you were weeping.'

Wulfrich scrambled to his feet, leaving a sudden coolness as the cloak fell away from where he had been sitting.

'They won't ask. My father will only say that I weep more than the baby and smack my head. And my mother will think I was weeping because of him. She'll be kind to me, but she won't ask.' He began to trudge away, but stopped and turned back to her. 'You won't tell anyone I told you?'

'Not even my father when he comes back.'

'Only Brinin?'

'Only Brinin.'

And that seemed to be enough for him. Edith watched him as he walked back towards the village. She shivered. She had known that Aculf was stern and that his children were afraid of him, but so were many other fathers. She had seen that his wife feared him too and had wondered if he watched over his household in much the same way as he had overseen her father's slaves. But he wasn't only harsh, foolish, blustering and unkind. He was utterly wicked. He had known all along who had wrecked the harvest, and he had frightened his son into saying nothing. She could almost hear the threats he must have breathed out. What kind of burden had that been for Wulfrich to bear? Wicked, wicked man!

Cynestan would help her. She would tell him what she had learned but not how she had learned it. Were they going to watch for men or women? How many would be enough to stop them? Cynestan would know. And he would know who was best to help them do it. Why did these things always have to happen when her father was away?

NIGHTWORK

'Rest for a few days, and then we'll see how you are,' said Cynestan. 'We'll get along easily enough without you. Go home now, and I'll come and see you tomorrow.'

Edith found Cynestan near his house, speaking to Garulf, and when Garulf left them he walked away so slowly that it seemed a wonder that he was walking at all. He was growing older and wearier every day, and Edith didn't like it. Nothing seemed to help, not lighter work nor rest. The winter was slowly stripping him away, as it stripped the leaves from the trees. Perhaps summer, with its warmer days, would be kinder. Or perhaps his days of work needed to be over. She would speak to her father about it.

'Can I talk to you alone, Cynestan?' said Edith when Garulf had left them. 'There's something we need to do.'

When she was sure that no one would overhear them, Edith wasted neither time nor words. She said nothing about Wulfrich, only that she had learned everything from a child who had been too frightened to tell anyone else, and even that much she begged Cynestan to say nothing about.

'No need to bring a child into it, my lady Edith,' said Cynestan. 'If we can catch them while the deed is being done, then *we'll* be the witnesses. It will be hard to prove that they also wrecked the harvest, as this child says, but once we've caught them, a bit of stern talking might bring it out of them. Some folk will weep and tell you everything as soon as they're caught in a wrongdoing. Others get stubborn and won't say a word. I've seen that in my children; we have both kinds in our house. Grown men and women are much the same at times. If we're dealing with the first kind here, we might get somewhere. But if not, I don't have much hope.'

'We'll need to catch them first,' said Edith.

'Oh, we will, my lady. Nothing easier. They've grown too bold. Let me speak to Saxulf. He and Sigulf will help us. And Daglæf. Now we don't know when they'll go out. But if it were me, I'd want to wait until everyone in my house was asleep. If the children got to know, it would be hard to keep everyone from knowing. And they'll want to be back in their beds well before anyone might wake. But we'll hide ourselves earlier and be ready for them. Will we take them to the hall after we've got them? Will you want to see them then or wait until morning?'

'I'm going with you,' said Edith. She wouldn't sleep whether she went with them or not. Better to wait where she knew what was happening.

'It'll be cold tonight, my lady,' said Cynestan, 'and we don't know how long we'll be sitting there for. You'd be better off inside. We'll take them to you when we've got them.'

'I swore that I'd find out who wrecked Brinin's harvest,' said Edith. 'I don't mind the cold, not even if we have to wait all night.'

It was a long, slow day. Edith sat at her loom but wove little. She took a meal but only picked at the food. She talked to Cenwyn and afterwards couldn't remember anything they had said. But night came at last. She put on another pair of socks and took a pair of gloves and another cloak. Then she sat on a stool by the fire, the cloak and gloves on her lap, her elbows on her knees, her chin in her hands. She didn't know how long she waited, but she must have half-drifted into sleep. She jumped as Cynestan touched her shoulder. She hadn't heard him coming.

'It's time now, my lady,' he whispered. 'The others are outside. Saxulf has a stout stick with him in case there's trouble. And I always have my stick with me these days. I've told everyone to stay in hiding until I give the word.'

'Do you think there *will* be trouble?'

'Does no harm to be ready for it, my lady. But we four have all fought the Danes in our time, and who in Oakdene will be a tougher foe than that? Let's go, my lady, and keep as quiet as we can.'

No one said a word as they crept through the darkness to Brinin's hut. Saxulf stood in the shadows under the eaves of Deorstan's house, at the back away from the door. Cynestan hid behind Brinin's hut. Daglæf was bolder. He opened the door and went inside.

'But what if they *do* set fire to it, and you're stuck inside?' whispered Edith.

'Unlikely to come to that,' said Daglæf. 'The thatch is still too damp from the rain yesterday to light quickly, and if they open the door to throw in the fire, I'll be ready for them. If they do light the thatch, shout and I'll come out quick.'

Daglæf shut the door behind him, and Edith crept out of sight behind the swine pen. Her heart was beating rather quickly. She didn't know where Sigulf had gone.

They waited until Edith was more than cold, even with her socks and gloves and two cloaks. She squatted, leaning against the pen until her legs ached. She clenched her teeth to stop them from chattering and was beginning to think that they *weren't* coming, that they'd taken fright or had somehow learned that Edith and the others were waiting for them when she heard something.

It was a door opening and shutting softly. She heard it creak. She shouldn't have heard such a thing, but she had been straining her ears for so long that night that she might have heard a feather drop. She waited. Nothing. Had it been Daglæf, coming outside after all?

A snakelike hiss somewhere nearby. A whisper. Soundlessly Edith dropped to her knees, the cold of the damp grass seeping through her kirtle. She crawled to the corner of the pen and peered round the side. There was a light, a candle or a lamp, already near and drawing nearer. Another whisper. They were coming. Edith crept back against the pen.

'But what if someone comes?' came a whisper, right beside Edith now. Only the swine pen was between them.

'Who's going to come at this time of night?'

'We might wake someone. The fields are far enough away, but this is right by my house.'

Who was it? Deorstan? It didn't sound like him, but it was hard to tell from a whisper. Yet who else lived so near?

'Do you want to do this or not, Æfæd? If you're scared, go home and I'll do it on my own!'

Æfæd! Brinin's nearest neighbour, but not a man. A boy. And Tidræd had fought him because he'd said he wished he'd wrecked the harvest. But he didn't need to wish it. He'd done it. Who was the other? Another boy? And why hadn't Cynestan given the word?

'I do want to but—'

'Then let's do it quickly and be away from here. I'll light the straw inside the hut. You see to the beast.'

'But I can't without the lamp.'

'It would've been easier to do this myself!'

The door of Brinin's hut opened. The sound was unmistakable this time. Stillness. A yell, swiftly muffled. Then sudden bewilderment. Scuffling, short-lived yelps, swift-moving shadows and it was all over. Edith stood. She made out the shape of one boy, already limp, with a man at his side. The other was writhing and struggling. She could hear strange sounds. The man who held him seemed to have his hand over his mouth.

'Get them to the hall before one of them yells and wakes half the village!' hissed Cynestan.

The limp boy—Edith thought *that* was Æfæd—went without a struggle. He seemed to know that he had no hope at all against four men and to have already given up. But the other boy fought like a wild cat all the way to the hall. Edith heard him trying to shout, but only smothered sounds came from his covered mouth.

She ran ahead and opened the door. Even in the dim light of the fire, the hall seemed bright after the darkness outside. She swiftly lit lamps and set them on the table. One was still in her hand when she heard a sound from the doorway. She turned, and the light from her lamp fell on Saxulf as he dragged the struggling boy into the hall by the neck of his shirt. Saxulf took his hand away from the boy's mouth, and Edith saw who it was.

That was when victory first tasted bitter. It was Eanfrith. Æfæd was full of sneaking ways. He lied to his doting mother and was unkind to his little sister. But Edith liked Eanfrith. She had wept with him after he had found his sister's body. She remembered how Eanflæd had told her that he had once begged their father to spare his slave and had taken a beating for it. She knew he could be brave and good-hearted. How had he come to this?

'Let go!' he yelled, still trying to writhe his way out of Saxulf's grasp. 'Why should you care about some filthy Dane and his filthy hut? Let go!'

'One more yell out of you and I'll give you something to yell about!' growled Saxulf, giving Eanfrith a shake.

'Let go!' yelled Eanfrith, louder this time.

Saxulf cuffed him sharply on the head and Eanfrith yelped, but he did let go of the boy's shirt to do it. He took Eanfrith's arm, pulled him over to a bench and shoved him down to sit on it. Eanfrith tried to get up, but Saxulf pushed him down again.

'Sit there!' he snapped, 'and don't let me hear another word from you.'

Perhaps Eanfrith knew he was beaten then. He didn't stand again. He didn't yell or speak. He only sat and glowered at them all. Æfæd hadn't struggled when he had been caught and he didn't struggle now. He stood and sobbed like a little boy.

'I didn't want to do it!' he wept. '*He* thought of it.'

Edith didn't miss the look of utter scorn that Eanfrith threw at Æfæd then. If they had been friends enough to do such work together, they likely wouldn't be after the night was over.

'Now you can hold your tongue too,' said Cynestan sternly. 'And there's no need for any weeping yet. Sigulf, shut and fasten the door.'

Sigulf laid the heavy wooden beam across the door and stood with his back against it.

'Now, my lady, I think we have a few things we need to ask these two,' went on Cynestan. 'How would you like it done?'

Edith looked from the scowling Eanfrith to the weeping Æfæd then back to Cynestan again. Cynestan had said that there were two kinds of children and two kinds of men: those who would weep and tell all and those who would be stubborn. That night they seemed to have caught both. Saxulf had already brought Eanfrith to stillness if not yet meekness, but he might be *too* frightening for Æfæd.

'We ought to keep them away from each other and talk to them alone,' said Edith. 'Cynestan, can you and Sigulf take Æfæd to the far end of the hall? Saxulf, Daglæf and I can speak to Eanfrith. But let me talk to you first.'

Edith and Cynestan walked a little away from the others.

'I think Æfæd might tell you everything if you press him a little, but don't let Eanfrith hear what you're all saying,' she whispered. 'When they first came to the hut I heard Æfæd say that he was afraid someone would hear them as the fields were far from the houses but the hut wasn't.'

'An odd thing to say if they *weren't* the ones who wrecked the harvest,' said Cynestan. 'Very well, my lady. I'll soon have the whole tale out of him, and without speaking too sternly either. Saxulf will have a harder time.'

Saxulf did have a hard time. At first, Eanfrith would say nothing at all, but stared stonily ahead. Then when Saxulf's forbearance was almost gone, Eanfrith shrugged his shoulders.

'You *told* me you didn't want to hear another word from me,' he said boldly.

That almost earned him another cuff, but Daglæf shook his head at Saxulf and sat down on the bench beside Eanfrith.

'You're a near neighbour of mine, Eanfrith,' he said, 'and I know you aren't a bad lad. I must say, I was sorry to find you throwing fire into another man's house. I wouldn't have thought it of you.'

'Why should a Dane's house still stand when better folk had theirs burned?' asked Eanfrith bitterly. 'And what are you going to do about it? Nothing happened. You stamped out the fire before anything *could* happen. Are you going to call the Moot and make me pay for a few bits of straw that got burned up?'

'How old are you?' asked Saxulf.

'Fourteen winters,' muttered Eanfrith sullenly.

'Fourteen winters and you talk to Daglæf and me like that! And you creep about at night to burn down another man's house! I don't know what the lady Edith will do, or her father when he gets back, but I know what I'm going to do. I'm going to your father in the morning to tell him to give you a good thrashing to teach you to watch your tongue and stick to your bed at night! I've half a mind to thrash you now myself and spare him the trouble!'

Edith thought she saw a little crack open up in Eanfrith's boldness then. Eadulf was even more frightening than Saxulf. But before Eanfrith had any time to patch up the crack, they heard a shout from the other end of the hall.

'Æfæd just told us that he and Eanfrith wrecked Brinin's harvest in the summer!' called Cynestan.

Eanfrith was white now with anger or fear or both. His fists were clenched, and his lips trembling. But he wasn't going to weep or beg.

'Well, if Æfæd has been such a fool,' he said loudly, 'what good is there in hiding it? We did wreck his harvest, and I'm not ashamed of it. He's a Dane, and it's because of the Danes that folk lie dead who never did anyone any harm.'

Edith could have wept then. It was all about Eanflæd. If Eanflæd had lived, Eanfrith would never have done what he did, however many houses the Danes had burned or beasts they had stolen. If Eanflæd had been spared, her brother would never have sunk into the shame he could not claw his way out of.

'That's enough for tonight,' said Cynestan, walking towards them, with Sigulf leading Æfæd wretchedly after him. 'They've both said they did it, and we've all heard them and can be witnesses to it. Your father will want to gather the Moot, my lady Edith, and I think we should wait until he comes before we do much more. Let's keep them here tonight and speak to them some more in the morning, and one of us will have to talk to their fathers. You should all get some sleep now. I'll stay awake and see that neither of them sneaks out.'

They sent Eanfrith to a sleeping bench at one side of the hall, where he lay, utterly still and facing the wall. From a bench on the other side, Edith could hear Æfæd weeping. That was all she wanted to do herself now.

'Thank you,' she said to Cynestan and the others, then left them and walked away to her own bed.

PAYMENT

They had parted with Hildræd and Aldred on the road from Godweard's house and had ridden home another, shorter way. Edrich Thegn drove them hard the whole day, so they were near Oakdene by nightfall. They spent the night with a man Edrich knew and were in the saddle again by dawn. By mid-morning, they were almost home.

They had slowed to a walk now, though Edrich was still ahead of them in his eagerness to be by his own hearth. Brinin and Oswald were riding side by side. All Oswald could think of was that in a few short months Brinin would be gone from Oakdene and nothing would be the same again. Those months would come and go swiftly, too swiftly.

'Oswald,' said Brinin at last, 'please don't tell anyone that I'm leaving. Once a few folk hear the whole village will learn of it before the day is out. With most folk I don't care how they hear or what they think. They can think they've driven me away if they like. I don't care. But there are some I want to talk to myself—Garulf and Brother Wilfred and one or two others. I don't want them to hear from someone else what they haven't heard from me. You can tell your sister, if you like. She won't speak of it if you ask her not to. And please, would you tell your father what I've said?'

'Very well,' said Oswald. 'Look. There's the last hill. That's where my father and I were standing when we first saw that the Danes had burnt down half the village. I'll never forget it.'

Something was wrong in Oakdene that morning. They were halfway across the meadow when they heard raised voices and when they went round the church they saw a crowd outside the hall. Edrich

KIN

was already striding towards them. Oswald swung himself to the ground.

'What on earth's happening here? Can you see to the horses?' he said to Brinin, then ran after his father.

Cynestan, Daglæf and Eadulf were in the middle of it all, Eadulf red with anger while the other two tried to settle him. Edrich Thegn and Oswald thrust their way past the others who were standing round them.

'My lord!' said Cynestan. 'Welc—'

'My lord,' cut in Eadulf. 'Cynestan has my son and Deorstan's shut in the hall and won't let them out nor let me and Deorstan in to speak to them.'

'What's this, Cynestan? Is he speaking the truth?' said Edrich.

'Last night, my lord, we caught young Eanfrith and Æfæd trying to burn down Brinin's hut. We took them to the hall to speak to them about it and—'

'Anyone can see that the hut is standing where it always has!' cut in Eadulf again. 'There's nothing wrong with it.'

'Will you let me speak?' snapped Cynestan.

'Enough!' said Edrich. He swung round to the crowd. 'Have none of you any work to do? Cynestan, Daglæf, Deorstan, Eadulf! Come into the hall, and we'll talk about it there.'

The crowd began to scatter, and Oswald followed his father and the others. Eanfrith and Æfæd trying to burn down Brinin's hut? Couldn't he and his father leave even for a short time without something going wrong? And where was Edith?

Inside Saxulf was walking along the length of the table. Eanfrith and Æfæd sat on a bench with Sigulf in between them. Æfæd was wretched and Eanfrith sullen. All four were weary. They jumped up when they saw Edrich Thegn striding in.

'Shut the door, or most of the village will gather outside to listen,' said Edrich. 'What's all this about? And don't say a word until he's done, Eadulf. You'll have your time to speak. Go on, Cynestan.'

'Well, as I said, my lord,' said Cynestan, 'we found these two trying to burn down Brinin's hut and brought them back to the hall. Æfæd came quietly enough, but Eanfrith put up a bit of a fight.'

'And spoke to his elders as no boy of fourteen winters ought to speak,' said Saxulf. 'I don't know how you raise your children, Eadulf, but I can tell you no son of mine would dare speak to a grown man the way your son does.'

Eadulf, glaring at Saxulf and Eanfrith alike, opened his mouth to speak but Edrich Thegn got there first.

'Keep going, Cynestan.'

'They told us that they wrecked Brinin's harvest in the summer. We thought we ought to—'

'They told you what?' Eadulf could hold his tongue no longer. He glared at Cynestan with such outrage that Oswald wondered if he might strike him. 'It's a lie! Why would they tell you that? I've seen how you and Daglæf favour that Dane. How do we know Cynestan's speaking the truth, my lord? They had them here all night! How do we know they didn't beat them into saying it? That's more likely! It's a lie, my lord!'

'You think Cynestan and the others *beat* these boys into saying that they wrecked the harvest,' said Edrich. 'Here, in the hall in the middle of the night? Did they also drag them from their beds and take them to Brinin's hut so they could say they had *caught* them there?'

'My son didn't wreck that harvest, my lord,' said Eadulf. 'I'm not like some fathers who let their children do as they like!'

Oswald glanced at Deorstan. There were two sons and two fathers here, yet only one father was talking. Deorstan shared none of Eadulf's outrage. He stood wordless, awkward, even ashamed. What was going on? Had they truly wrecked the harvest? It was hard to believe it of Eanfrith, yet Cynestan was a man he trusted.

'My son knows what will happen if he does wrong,' went on Eadulf, still simmering with rage. 'And Cynestan here—'

'Very well,' said Edrich. He turned to Eanfrith. 'Take off your shirt.'

'My… my lord?' stammered Eanfrith in bewilderment.

'You heard what your father said,' said Edrich. 'He thinks Cynestan and the others beat a lie out of you. It's easily proven. Take off your shirt. Let's see the bruises.'

'But… but there are no bruises, my lord,' said Eanfrith. 'They didn't beat us.'

'And *did* you wreck the harvest?' asked Edrich, in his stern, quiet way that left no room for anything but an answer.

339

Eanfrith looked fearfully at his father, biting his lip. Oswald saw his throat quiver as he swallowed.

'Yes, my lord,' he mumbled.

'You young—' began Oswald but cut the words short as his father shot him a warning frown. How could they have done such a thing? Two boys! Two boys whom Brinin had never harmed!

Eanfrith backed away as Eadulf strode angrily towards him, but Edrich stepped in between them.

'Now, Eadulf,' he said. 'I know this must be a shock to you after believing your son to be guiltless. And you will no doubt have much to say to him about it. But say it when you are cooler. He will hear it better that way.'

Oswald turned his back on them all and walked away. He stood and watched the fire. Two boys. Eanfrith! Perhaps he would find it in himself to be truly glad that Brinin was going to be rid of them all. Behind him, he heard Æfæd.

'It wasn't my fault,' he wept. 'I only went with him. He thought of it all.'

'Enough now,' Oswald heard his father say sternly. 'Cynestan, we'll have to gather the Moot, but let my son and me eat first. We'll keep the boys here for now. The rest of you may go. And, please, would one of you find my daughter?'

≈

The whole village seemed to know everything before the Moot had come together. Perhaps Eadulf's loud voice had seen to that. As they all stood waiting for it to begin, Edith heard him grumbling to his wife. Sæthryth herself was tearful. Her sister stood beside her, with her two little girls clinging to her kirtle. Wulfrich stood behind his mother, half-hidden from Edith's sight. He looked round warily but wasn't weeping. When he saw Edith watching him he gave her a tight little frightened smile. She didn't see Æfæd's mother anywhere and even his father stood well back.

Oswald stood near their father, very stiff and grim. Edith hadn't even had time to speak to him yet. Brinin was beside him. Was he happy that justice would at last be done, or only sad that someone had hated him so much?

Beside her father stood Cynestan, Daglæf, Saxulf and Sigulf, all weary after their long night. Edith was beyond weary. She hadn't slept at all. Æfæd and Eanfrith stood between Oswald and her father. Æfæd didn't lift his head, but Eanfrith was bolder than ever. He glared at anyone who met his eye as though daring them to say a word against him. Was he so unashamed? Or did he think that the best way to bear shame was to tell himself and everyone else that he didn't feel it?

Edrich stepped forward and raised his hand to still the babble of the crowd.

'Listen, all of you,' he said. 'By now you all know why we are here, and I need not keep you long. Let Cynestan first say what happened in the night.'

Cynestan told them all that it had come to his knowledge that someone was going to burn Brinin's hut in the night and kill his beast. He didn't say how he had learned it; he didn't even name Edith, let alone say that she had heard it from a child. Surely Wulfrich could stop worrying now. Cynestan told how they had caught Æfæd and Eanfrith and learned that they had also wrecked Brinin's harvest. There was a stir at this, but only a slight one. What had been said in the hall at night was known by most folk in the village by noon.

'They told us freely,' said Cynestan, 'and we four are witnesses to what they said. What's more, Eanfrith here said it again to Edrich Thegn this morning with Oswald Child, Eadulf and Deorstan there to hear it too.'

'And will you boys say again before everyone that you did it and that last night you were going to burn his house and kill his beast?' asked Edrich, turning to Æfæd and Eanfrith.

'Yes, my lord,' muttered Eanfrith.

'But only because he made me go—' began Æfæd.

'Enough, boy!' snapped Edrich. 'You did it and you may not shift the blame now.'

Eanfrith's scorn had become outright hatred of Æfæd now. He shifted away a little as though Æfæd smelt bad and he didn't want to stand too near.

'Cynestan and the others did you both a kindness by stopping you last night,' went on Edrich. 'But now what is to be done? Cynestan and I believe that Brinin would have had as many as eight ambers of wheat from that land. Neither of these boys has done such a thing before, so we will overlook what they wanted to do. We will leave it to their fathers to speak to them about that, and hope that the shame of standing here will be enough to keep them from such wrongdoing again. But the lost harvest cannot be overlooked. Brinin must be paid for it. Nor will we ask ourselves which of these boys was more to blame. They did it together and must pay together. They and their kin must each pay Brinin for half of what he lost. That will settle it. Deorstan! Eadulf! Tell us now how your households are going to pay what your sons owe. In wheat? Barley? Beasts? What do you say?'

'Deorstan knew about this all along,' whispered Cenwyn to Edith.

'What do you mean?' said Edith.

'He isn't shocked. When Eadulf was shouting outside the hall this morning and calling Cynestan a liar, Deorstan didn't say a word. He knew it was true. Do you remember how I saw him strike Æfæd the day the harvest was wrecked? That's when he found out, and he's kept his mouth shut all this time. I'm sure of it. Look at him. He knew.'

It was true. Deorstan was more than unhappy, but it was the unhappiness of a man who was bearing what he had known might come and had readied himself for, not some burden that had dropped on him without warning. Eadulf looked ill. All his loud, blustering anger had melted away. His wife was weeping on her sister's shoulder. Deorstan spoke first.

'If he were to take most of my sheep, my lord, and leave me with a few to build up my flock again, that might be enough. And if it isn't, I have a bushel of barley I could give him.'

'Very well,' said Edrich. 'Cynestan and I will look at your sheep and say if they will be enough. And you, Eadulf?'

'I will be ruined, my lord,' said Eadulf, dazed and unsteady, like a man staggering after a blow or staring death in the eye. 'We're hungry now. We always are by the end of the winter. If I give him the little we have left, what will we eat? The Danes took all my swine but one, and even if I gave him *all* my sheep they still wouldn't be enough and there would be none to give *you* for rent. It will ruin us, my lord.'

'You would have a full year to pay, Eadulf,' said Edrich. 'That's how these things are done.'

'But, my lord, a year won't make me a wealthy man,' said Eadulf. 'I have a bigger household than Deorstan. I rent less land and have fewer beasts. A year won't give me a large flock, and if I pay him out of my next harvest my children will be starving before midwinter.'

No one spoke. The only sound was that of Sæthryth weeping. Edith watched as Eanfrith's boldness, which he had been clinging to so tightly, slipped from his grasp. His face was white. He stared at his weeping mother and seemed to feel now for the first time the overwhelming weight of what he had done.

'Please let me speak, my lord.'

Brinin stepped forward. A murmur rippled through the crowd. Edith saw Eadulf glare at Brinin with sudden hatred, as though it were he and not Eanfrith who had brought about all the trouble.

'Very well,' said Edrich.

'As I was the one wronged, let me be the one to ask for mercy, my lord,' said Brinin. Another louder murmur, men and women turning to their neighbour. 'It was a blow to lose my harvest, but the winter is almost over and I have not been hungry. I have no wife or children to feed. Even if I get nothing of what I am owed, I won't worry about what will become of me. Eadulf's wife and young children have done nothing to me. Please, my lord, don't let them starve because of their brother. These boys have been shamed. Have mercy, my lord, and let that be enough. Or if they must pay, let it be less, my lord.'

Tears pricked Edith's eyes. She couldn't speak, not even in a whisper to Cenwyn. No one did. The crowd had fallen into stillness again. Not even Edrich Thegn seemed to know what to say. How could Brinin beg for mercy? He'd lost his whole harvest. He'd known little but hatred from his neighbours for months. Eanfrith seemed to have forgotten his mother and father. He was staring at Brinin now in utter amazement, in bewilderment as though forgiveness was a riddle he couldn't begin to understand. Even when Brinin stopped speaking, Eanfrith couldn't drag his eyes away from him.

'But, my boy, when a wrong—a great wrong—of this kind has been done…' began Edrich but he trailed off.

The first shock over, a stir passed through the crowd. Edith caught sight of Oswald speaking very quickly to Brinin. Brinin shrugged his shoulders. Eanfrith was still gazing at Brinin, white-faced.

'No one need starve, and Brinin need not go without, my lord.' Daglæf spoke up suddenly, his voice clear above the stirring of the crowd. 'Eadulf has a slave. He doesn't *need* a slave. Let him sell him and pay Brinin out of whatever he gets.'

'You're right, Daglæf!' said Edrich. 'I had forgotten Eadulf's slave. Where is he, Eadulf? I don't see him here.'

'In the field, my lord,' said Eadulf, but too stiffly, without nearly as much thanks as a man spared hunger ought to show.

'Go and fetch him, Daglæf,' said Edrich.

As Daglæf walked away, Edith saw Brinin watching him, frowning slightly. Oswald whispered something to him. Brinin shook his head.

'This is a much better way to settle things,' said Edrich. 'I have fewer slaves now than before and had been asking myself if I needed one or two more. I will buy your slave from you, Eadulf. Daglæf's right. If your household grows hungry each winter, then you'll be better off without a slave to feed as well. And you have four sons to help you with your work.'

Somehow this didn't seem to help Eadulf. Edith could see him bristling, almost choking on words he didn't dare to say.

Daglæf was soon back with Deormod at his side; watchful, wary, fearful, beyond frightened.

'Now,' said Edrich Thegn, 'let's settle the thing. Deormod, you will now be *my* slave. Deorstan, Eadulf, Brinin. Come with me into the hall and we'll talk more about the payment.'

As Eadulf passed Eanfrith, he grabbed his arm roughly and hissed something into his ear. But it was Brinin and not his father whom Eanfrith's eyes followed as they walked into the hall. Deormod was smiling. Or weeping. No, it was both. Cynestan went over to speak to him. The crowd thinned as folk drifted away. Æfæd and Eanfrith still stood awkwardly, side by side. They had neither been given leave to go nor told they must stay. Edith saw Æfæd speak to Eanfrith, but Eanfrith turned his back and took another step away. That friendship was dead now, smothered by blameshifting.

Deorstan came out again first, beckoning Æfæd to follow him. Deorstan didn't seem very angry, nor Æfæd very afraid, though who knew what would be said when they reached home? But perhaps

Cenwyn had been right. Perhaps Deorstan had known all along and had already said everything he needed to.

Eadulf strode from the hall, followed by Brinin and Edrich Thegn. He made straight for his son and took him by the neck of his shirt, much as Saxulf had done the night before. But this time, Eanfrith didn't try to fight his way free. He went without a struggle, stumbling a little as his father dragged him along. Eadulf stopped once to speak to his weeping wife. Eanfrith stared back, still bewildered, at Brinin. And the look he gave his mother as Eadulf hauled him away was as near to a plea for forgiveness as anyone could utter without words. Sæthryth didn't follow them.

It was over, wrong put right, Brinin given what he was owed, Wulfrich's burden lifted without his father's knowledge. Edith saw Oswald talking to Brinin again, but Brinin wasn't looking at him. He was watching Deormod. Deormod was still smiling, still weeping.

FORGIVENESS

Brinin had learned young not to dream. He had learned not to hope for justice. Yet he had left behind in Godweard's village what he had never dreamed of and had come back to what he had not hoped for. He had been given justice. Those who had done a shameful deed had been shamed before everyone. He had been given what he was owed, and it had left him feeling like a wealthy man. Those who had wronged him would bear the sting of their wrongdoing, though they wouldn't starve. But a man had been bought and sold to do it.

'What's wrong?' asked Oswald. Brinin had almost forgotten that he was there. 'What are you frowning about?'

'I was thinking about Deormod,' said Brinin.

'Deormod! That's hardly something to frown about. Look at him. I don't think I've ever seen him smile before.'

'Is he smiling? I thought he was weeping,' said Brinin.

'He's doing both! Eadulf's kinder to his beasts than he ever was to Deormod.'

'I know,' said Brinin.

'Then what's wrong? Be happy that you got what you were owed, and that Deormod is rid of Eadulf too.'

Everything *would* be better for Deormod now. He would be rid of Eadulf, as Oswald said. He would eat more, sleep better, be beaten less—likely not at all, Cynestan was so mild. There was everything to be happy about. But they had stood in the hall while Edrich Thegn asked the worth of the sheep, the worth of an amber of wheat, the worth of a man. How many sheep for an amber of wheat? How many ambers of wheat for a man? They had reckoned it up: so many sheep from Deorstan, so many of Edrich Thegn's sheep for Eadulf's slave. And Brinin had got what he was owed. He had a flock for his lost harvest. It was justice. No one need starve. Oswald was right: Deormod *was* smiling as well as weeping, with the stunned joy of a man snatched from a pit he'd been left to rot in. It had all been well settled. Why then had the reckoning felt no better than an ill-fitting shoe?

'I *am* glad,' said Brinin. Likely things had always been this way, when a man could pass from hand to hand like sheep or swine or wheat. Likely they always would be.

'I wonder how Cynestan learned what those two were doing. If I wasn't so angry with him myself, I could almost have pitied Eanfrith. My father told Eadulf to wait until he was cooler before speaking to him—that was always his way, you know, though the waiting mostly made it worse. But Eadulf didn't seem any cooler to me and it didn't look like there was going to be much *speaking*.'

But Brinin's eyes had been so much on Deormod that he hadn't even thought of Eadulf or his son. Could he pity Eanfrith? He didn't know yet. It was his mother he had pitied.

'Let me go and find Edith,' said Oswald. 'She doesn't know about Leoba yet. I can't believe we had to have a moot as soon as we got home, but I'm glad things are coming right.'

Brinin hadn't had time to speak to anyone either. He had shared a few words with Eawig. He hadn't seen Garulf at the moot—perhaps Cynestan had left him with work to do elsewhere—but before Brinin could leave to find him he saw Brother Wilfred coming towards him.

'Welcome home, my boy,' he said. 'Come with me to the church. I want to talk to you.'

Home. It was an odd thing. All his life, for good or for ill, Oakdene had been the only home he had known; stuck there like a beast in a pen, bearing whatever was thrown at him, with no way out. Now the gate had been flung open, a new meadow beckoned, and there was so much in Oakdene he didn't want to lose. How could he leave such friends behind?

'You brought tears to my eyes today, my boy,' went on Brother Wilfred as they walked together.

'Sir?'

Brinin had understood Sæthryth's tears. He had understood Æfæd's tears of shame. Since speaking to Oswald, he understood Deormod's tears a little better. Eanfrith might shed tears before his angry father was done with him. But he hadn't seen anyone else weeping and didn't know why they should.

'You don't understand that? Come inside and sit with me. Do you remember how we sat together when you lost your harvest? You said today that the loss had been a blow. But I remember how you were that evening, how low you had been brought, and how worried I was for you. It was rather more than a blow, wasn't it? Do you remember what you said to me then? You said that there is no justice in the world and little kindness. Yet what have we seen today? Wrong has been put right. Justice. But, my boy, the kindness today was yours. I have sometimes feared that you would become so embittered that kindness might become something you could neither give nor take. Yet today *you* asked Edrich Thegn for mercy, even if that had meant losing what you were owed. And it brought me near to weeping. I knew what the loss of your harvest had been. I knew what it might mean for you to do without payment. And, my dear boy, isn't forgiveness at the heart of what the Gospels teach us? What do we pray? *Forgive us our sins as we forgive those who sin against us.* We are bidden to ask for forgiveness and we are bidden to offer it. And to see you, who cannot offer forgiveness cheaply, do so this morning… I was proud of you, my boy, though I'm glad that Edrich Thegn settled the thing without loss to you.'

'I don't know if I *was* thinking of forgiveness, sir. I was thinking of Eanfrith's mother.' Brinin hadn't asked himself if he would forgive anyone. But he had seen Eadulf's angry pride give way to fear. He had seen Sæthryth weeping and knew that some of her children were young. He hadn't wanted them to sink as low as his own kin had sunk, or to be the one who drove them to that. Was that forgiveness? 'I was thinking of my own mother.'

'Asking for mercy for the one who has wronged you is surely a kind of forgiveness. But why were you thinking of your own mother?'

Brinin knew that if he were to say goodbye to anyone, he would also need to tell them why there had to be a goodbye. And he knew that it would be a harder tale to tell than Bruni—or Wulfrich—slaying a dragon. But he told it, and Brother Wilfred listened without a word.

'And what does Edrich Thegn say to all this?' said Brother Wilfred at last.

'He gave me leave to go. He told me I ought to,' said Brinin. 'And Oswald Child did too.'

'Oswald too,' Brother Wilfred said thoughtfully. 'Let me ask you something, or perhaps not so much ask as warn you of something. Do you think that this other village will be altogether without the troubles you have known here?'

'It was trouble there that drove my father and mother here, sir,' said Brinin.

Had he thought he would leave trouble behind in Oakdene? He had been welcomed in Godweard's village. He had been told that he belonged there. Wulfswith had wept when he left. No one had called him a filthy Dane, though they all knew of his mother. Yet trouble had a way of following a man. He and Row had fled trouble in Oakdene only to find worse on the road.

'And trouble that's driving you away from here?'

'I once thought that I would be better off elsewhere, better off anywhere else,' began Brinin.

'I remember you did, my boy.'

'But there was no good in thinking that. Where was I to go? But now, sir, I'm thinking of my father and mother, of my father's sister, who was so unhappy to lose him. I think it's as much for their sake as my own that I must go now, but…'

'But perhaps it will be harder to leave than you had thought?'

'Yes, sir. They have no church there, only a priest who comes from a nearby minster from time to time. I don't want to forget everything I've learned.'

Brother Wilfred said nothing for a while. The stillness had a heaviness to it. Brinin could almost feel the weight of the monk's thoughts.

'Perhaps Edrich Thegn is right,' Brother Wilfred said at last. 'It does seem wise that you go, though for some of us here the loss will be keen. How long do we have with you? Until after Easter? Isn't that what you said? That gives us a little time. Come to me every day if you can, like Oswald Child does, and we will see what you can learn in that time. Can you do that?'

'Edrich Thegn has someone in mind to rent my field, sir. Likely I won't even plough it or sow it myself, only Mildrith's. I can come.'

'Good. Come tomorrow, my boy. Find me whenever you're ready.'

As Brinin left, Brother Wilfred called him back.

'You *will* think of Oakdene when you have left, you know,' he said, 'of both the hard and, in time, the good. But remember: forgive us our sins as we forgive those who sin against us. When you think of this place, think of it with forgiveness. You don't need to lie to yourself and say that nothing was ever wrong, but think of it with forgiveness. You have begun on that path—I saw that today, even if you did not—and I will pray that you don't stray from it.'

Brinin went to find Garulf when he left the church, but he didn't see him anywhere. He wasn't in the fields, or with any of Edrich Thegn's beasts. He didn't see him with Eawig or Cynestan. At last he went to Garulf's hut, though he knew he was unlikely to be there in the middle of the day.

But he *was* there. A fire was burning in the hearth. Garulf—too grey, too still—lay in the corner on his bed of straw, leaning wearily against the wall. He brightened at once when he saw Brinin in the doorway.

'Brinin, lad,' he said, but his voice was thin with little of its former strength. 'Eawig told me you were back, and I hear that bad business with your harvest has been put right at last. Come and sit with me for a while. Cynestan wanted me to rest for a day or two, but it's lonely here on my own.'

Had Garulf been so sunken when Brinin had left Oakdene? Had his voice been so weak? Had something happened while he had been away or was he only seeing him with fresh eyes? Brinin knew Garulf was old, without the strength he had once had. He hadn't liked how easily tired Garulf was becoming. But now he saw the truth. He was dying.

SHOULDERS

'**C**ome quick,' panted Eawig, running after Brinin as he was on his way to see Mildrith. 'Your sow's farrowing!'

Eawig had watched such things many times before and had made everything ready, filling the shelter with good straw to keep the sow and her young warm. By the time Brinin got there she was lying on her side, her swollen belly quivering and her breath coming quickly. One small dark piglet had already found a teat to suckle on.

'There's no need to worry,' said Eawig with a laugh at Brinin. 'She's done it before, and this is only the beginning. I can't stay now but I'll come back whenever I can. Watch she doesn't lie on any of them. And don't worry!'

Brinin couldn't have found it harder to leave if he'd been tethered to the pen. He stayed with the sow and her growing brood all morning, with Eawig coming back from time to time. There were seven by the end—and another born dead. Some were dark, others lighter. Eawig was happy with them, so Brinin was too. And although the sow had done all the work he was tired by the end. Half the day had passed with no thought of ploughing, but he went to Mildrith in the evening and it was settled that he and Tidræd would start in the morning.

Tidræd came to find Brinin a little after sunrise, whistling so tunelessly that it was like no song Brinin had ever heard from bird or bard. They passed Deorstan and Æfæd on their way to fetch the oxen. Deorstan turned away. The knowledge of how his son had wronged Brinin had not made him a better neighbour. If anything he was even colder than before. He might have paid what he owed without grumbling, but there was no sorrow now. Æfæd's tearful shame had ended once he wasn't standing before the village. He glowered at Brinin with unblushing hatred. But Tidræd, muttering something to Æfæd that Brinin didn't catch, gave him a look that was an outright taunt, as sharp as the oxgoad over Tidræd's shoulder and meant to prick Æfæd in much the same way. Æfæd flushed and started after Tidræd but he stopped before he got very far. Perhaps he didn't dare while his father was with him, or perhaps Tidræd wasn't a foe he wanted.

'I'll fight you any time you like, Æfæd,' called Tidræd over his shoulder. 'You know who'll win!'

When they were in the fields and had yoked the oxen to the plough, Brinin took the oxgoad from Tidræd.

'Go on,' he said. 'Let's see you plough a furrow. I'll drive the oxen.'

'Me? I thought I was helping *you* plough!'

'Last year, yes,' said Brinin, 'but not this year. I'll help you. I'll teach you to do it well, but I'm not doing it for you.'

'But isn't that why mother lends you our oxen? You plough our land then borrow the oxen for yours.'

'Never mind about my land. You're the only man in your house—or near enough a man anyway—and this is your work. You don't need me to do it for you. You need to do it yourself. You know what has to be done and you can do it without waiting for your mother to tell you to. And who else is going to teach your brother how to plough and sow and the rest? It's down to you. I was younger than you when I first learned, and you're strong. Your shoulders will ache a bit at first, but you'll soon get into the way of it.'

'I've done it before,' said Tidræd. 'My father showed me.'

'Well then, what are we waiting for? Keep your eye on that taller tree to keep the furrow straight. I'll tell you when you're swerving off. When you get too tired, I'll do it for a while.'

Tidræd looked at him as though he had dared him to prove himself in battle, then squared his shoulders and put his hands to the plough. It would be a long time before this boy would own to being tired. So much the better. Brinin would soon see to it that Mildrith no longer had any need of him.

~

In the evening Brinin sat in his hut watching the wood glow and blacken as the fire swallowed it up. He drew out his father's seax and turned it over in his hands. He hadn't yet told Garulf about his new-found kin. He didn't know how to begin. Brinin had sat with him more than once—Garulf was still not out of his bed—but the words wouldn't come. He had known that there were folk in Oakdene it would be hard to leave behind, but would Garulf leave them all first? That made it harder still.

A sound from the doorway dragged him from his thoughts, and Brinin saw Eanfrith standing there, awkward and a little fearful, as though Brinin might take up a weapon to drive him away. Brother Wilfred had spoken of mercy and forgiveness. Brinin hadn't wanted Eanfrith and his kin to starve but nor did he much want to talk to him or welcome him into his hut. Hadn't he tried to burn it down only a few days before? Yet likely Eanfrith hadn't come for nothing. Why send him away without hearing him first? He looked as though he might go even without being sent, shifting uneasily as he stood there.

'I… I'm sorry,' said Eanfrith at last. That wasn't something Brinin had thought he would hear. It was much more than he had heard from Æfæd or either of the boys' fathers.

'You came here to say that?'

'Yes, I—'

'Did your father send you?'

'No, no. I came by myself. My father doesn't know. He wouldn't like it.'

'Likely you mean it then,' said Brinin. Eadulf wasn't a man to anger lightly. 'It's a bit late now for sorrow to keep you from trouble.'

'I *do* mean it. I'm not only saying it to… I mean… I… I wasn't sorry before but I am now.'

'Why?'

'I… you didn't want us to be hungry. I thought you'd be glad. I didn't care if *you* went hungry. Even when they caught us I wasn't at all sorry, but when you said what you did I wished I hadn't done it. Not only because I'd been caught or because of my father…'

'He was very angry with you.' Angry, but not about Brinin's field. Since the raid Eadulf had only ever looked at him with open hatred, but he didn't like his son shaming him before the village.

'Because I lost him the slave. He almost took the skin off my back afterwards—I can still feel it. We don't have much but we had that slave. We'll never have the money for another.'

That was a mercy at least: no more slaves falling into Eadulf's hands. He thought Eanfrith would leave after that, that he would creep home a little less fearful. But he stayed where he was, shoulders slumped, even more awkward than before.

'I... I broke the things in here too,' said Eanfrith.

'With Æfæd?'

'No. By myself.'

'My father made those stools, and I couldn't mend them.'

'I'm sorry. I... I was so angry after... after what the Danes did. And you are a Dane, aren't you?'

'Unless I disown my mother.'

'But you're not what I thought. You didn't want us to be hungry. I wanted to give you something for the things I broke. I thought about it all day yesterday and today, but I don't have anything and I can't ask my father. So I came to say I'm sorry.'

'That will be enough then,' said Brinin.

'Do you mean that? You don't want to go to Edrich Thegn about it?'

'I wouldn't have said it unless I meant it.'

Eanfrith seemed to breathe again then and he almost smiled.

'Thank you. If Edrich Thegn were to speak to my father...'

'He won't. Better forget about it now.'

But still Eanfrith didn't leave. Surely he couldn't be shouldering any more wrongdoing. Hadn't he unburdened himself of everything by now? Why this wavering on the threshold?

'Can I ask you something?' he said.

'Go on.'

'Your brother died, didn't he?' Eanfrith's face was twitching a little. Where was he going with this? 'They say he died while you were away.'

'He fell when the path we were walking on broke away. It was very steep and rocky there.'

'So you were there. You saw him after he was dead.'

'I found him and buried him myself. There was no one else there to help me.'

The easier breathing had gone now, and the twitching was growing.

'Have you... have you stopped seeing it? I mean... *can* someone stop seeing something like that, again and again?'

So that was what was weighing him down, and there was nothing Brinin could do to lift that burden from his shoulders. How could he take the sight of a dead sister out of Eanfrith's mind?

'I don't know. I haven't stopped seeing it. Not yet.' He could see it now, Row lying all wrong on the rocks. 'You should talk to the priest.'

'He won't want to talk to me,' said Eanfrith bitterly, 'not after—'

'He will. He knows about such things. He understands it all. Talk to him.'

'I should go,' muttered Eanfrith a little huskily. 'I told my father that I was going to the cackhouse, and I'd better not stay out too long.'

Then he was gone, a little unburdened, but still with the heaviest one to bear.

KITH

The seax gave Brinin words in the end. The few days' rest Cynestan had given Garulf stretched into many days. Brinin sat with him often as he asked about the ploughing and his beasts. Garulf was so weary that he didn't seem to remember that he'd asked the same thing the day before and the day before that, or that Brinin had given him the same answers. Sometimes he drifted into sleep as they talked. But the worst days were when Eawig would come in and say he hoped his grandfather would be out of his bed soon. Eawig didn't see the truth. Neither did Ebba, and Brinin didn't know how to tell them. Their mother knew; he saw it in her eyes.

After some days of this, Brinin began to fear they would soon hear of his new-found kin another way, and as he still didn't know how to begin he did the only thing he could think of. He drew his father's seax from its sheath and handed it to Garulf.

'What's this, lad?' asked Garulf.

'My father's seax.'

'Your father's? I haven't seen you with it before, lad. Where did you get it?'

'In the village I went to with Oswald Child. I met my father's sister there.'

The tale came out haltingly and turned back on itself many times as Garulf asked Brinin to say things again. But it came to an end at last and Garulf handed the seax back to Brinin.

'It'll be a loss to us, lad, when you go,' he said. 'Eawig will take it hard. He'll miss you. We all will.'

Brinin waited for Garulf to tell him he ought to go, to give him leave or blessing as Edrich Thegn had done. But he didn't. He didn't say he ought to stay either. He only lay back and shut his eyes, and it wasn't long before Brinin saw that he was asleep. He left Garulf's hut with an aching heaviness he barely understood.

Brinin went back to his hut the long way, by the hillside, deep in thought. Garulf and his household were no kin of his, but they had eaten by the same hearth and slept under the same roof. They had worked with him, sorrowed with him, lifted him to his feet, stood around him like a shield against the hatred of the village. They had shared their bread, their home and their hearts. Now Brinin had new kin to share bread with. How could he go without forsaking these kinlike friends?

'Brinin,' called a voice from behind. 'Stop. I want to talk to you.'

Brinin turned. Edith was running after him.

'Yes, my lady,' he said.

Edith reached him a little breathless, one last glance over her shoulder before she spoke, lowering her voice.

'I've waited until the Moot was well over and out of folk's minds a little, but I swore to Wulfrich I'd tell you.'

'Wulfrich, my lady?' asked Brinin.

'It was Wulfrich who found out that Æfæd and Eanfrith were going to set fire to your hut. He overheard them talking. And he already knew they had wrecked the harvest. Aculf knew all along, and Wulfrich too, though Aculf had forbidden him to tell anyone. But he told me. He wanted to stop them. He was so frightened. He begged me to tell no one that he'd told me—not even my father or Oswald or Cynestan know it came from him. But he wanted me to tell you.'

'Wulfrich did that, my lady, even though Aculf had warned him not to?' There were many kinds of courage in the world, and Wulfrich had never seemed like a boy who had any of them. But this had almost been like going to meet a wolf in its den. Little wonder he had been frightened. If Aculf were ever to learn of it...

'He didn't tell me that Æfæd and Eanfrith had wrecked your harvest. That's what Aculf had warned him not to do. But Aculf didn't know about them wanting to burn down your hut. So he told me about that. He didn't speak their names, but I warned Cynestan so he and the others could catch them at it.'

'Thank you, my lady. I can hardly believe it! He's so small and...'
Brinin trailed off. Wulfrich, defying his father to help a friend? Forget
the fyrd! Here was boldness, though no one would ever sing of it.

'He *was* very frightened, but he wanted to stop them so much.
Remember, no one is to know about it, not even my father or Oswald.
I swore to him I would tell no one but you.'

Later when it was already dark, Eawig came. Brinin knew before he
even opened his mouth that he had spoken to his grandfather. He was
very solemn as he stood in the doorway, the light from the fire
flickering on his face.

'Is it true?' he said.

'Come in and sit down,' said Brinin. He had a bench now, though
the broken stools still lay in the corner. Eawig sat down beside him.

'Is it true?' he said again. 'My grandfather told me you're leaving.'

'Yes,' said Brinin, 'but not until after Easter.'

'Easter will be here soon enough.'

Eawig wasn't looking at him. He leaned forward, his chin in his
hands, and stared at the fire.

'I might come back from time to time,' said Brinin. That was what
he'd been telling himself.

'You'd need a fast horse to come as often as we would want to see
you.' There was wounding scorn in Eawig's voice and with it came that
heavy ache again. 'They drove you out, didn't they? Everything folk did
here has driven you out. I didn't think—'

'It wasn't that,' said Brinin, though he knew that it would have been
even harder if there hadn't been so much hatred to help him along.
'I have kin there and none here, and my father's land and his father's
before him. Trouble drove my father to Oakdene. He would never have
been here without it, and neither would I. How can I turn my back on
all that?'

'But these kin don't know you like we do,' said Eawig.

And that was more hard truth. Kith, friends, might feel like kin after
a time, and for his whole life his true kin had been strangers. Brinin was
running out of answers for Eawig. He had no more to offer.

'Ebba will weep, you know,' said Eawig huskily. Ebba might not be the only one to weep. 'We… we haven't told her yet. Mother says it's better not to.'

And still there was nothing for Brinin to say. Eawig spoke only truth to him. Coming back from time to time would never be the same as living there. He had friends who knew him and kin who didn't. And Ebba would weep, Ebba who had helped him gather his broken harvest in the rain.

'I know why you're going,' said Eawig. 'But I don't like it. I don't want to talk about it any more. I had a look at your piglets earlier. They're growing well.'

'Which are the best?' asked Brinin.

'That big dark one,' said Eawig, brightening a little at talk of swine. 'She's bigger than the others and strong too. And the smaller of the two light ones.'

'They're yours,' said Brinin.

'What do you mean?'

'What I say,' said Brinin. 'I told you I'd give you a swine.'

'That was with the other sow, and you said nothing about two.'

'Listen,' said Brinin, 'you've earned those swine ten times over. Take them and keep them with Edrich Thegn's swine and fatten them up in the forest along with his. They're both sows so when they farrow you'll have more and you can build yourself a herd. You'll have to give some of the young to Edrich Thegn to pay him for keeping them on his woodland, but you'll still have enough for yourself. I'll ask Oswald Child to speak to his father about letting you do it. Then when you have a big enough herd, buy your way out of slavery with them.'

'Do you think I could?' asked Eawig. He was sitting straight now, staring at Brinin. 'What would I do if I were free? I'd have to feed myself, for one thing.'

'That's why you need to be slow about it. Don't wait until you have enough swine and buy your freedom straightaway. Wait until you have more than enough. Buy your freedom and have some of your herd left over. As for what you would do, you'd be a swineherd, but a free one and not a slave.'

'I'd never thought of that,' said Eawig, and there was wonder in his voice now. 'And I thought that when your other sow died, my swine had died with her.'

But the wonder was short-lived and his smile fell away.

'I'm going to miss you when you're gone,' he said.

That stung like a wound and left Brinin choked and wordless. Kith that he knew, kin that he didn't. Nothing in this life was ever easy.

TROUBLE

'The ploughing seems to be going well,' said Mildrith the next morning. She was standing under the old oak tree and beckoned to Brinin when she saw him.

'Tidræd's done most of it,' said Brinin. 'He's very strong.'

'I sent him to give something to Osgyth this morning, but he'll be back soon and ready to begin.'

Even as they spoke, they saw Tidræd grim-faced and walking swiftly towards them. Aculf was behind him, breathless and filthy and as angry as Brinin had ever seen him. What was this?

'Mildrith, your s—' began Aculf.

'Mother, he—' cut in Tidræd, but Mildrith stopped him sharply.

'You'll wait until your elders have spoken before you say anything,' she said sternly. She turned back to Aculf, though with no friendliness. What on earth had Aculf been doing? Muck—or who knew what—was smeared all over him. And he stank!

'You need to keep a better watch on your son, Mildrith!' Aculf spluttered. 'He drove my swine out of their pen and when I stopped him, he bit me. Look!'

Aculf held out his hand, reddened with the unmistakable marks of teeth. There was even a spot of blood. But surely that was more trouble than even Tidræd would fling himself into. There was a tale here, and likely Aculf wasn't telling all of it.

'Is that the truth, Tidræd?' said Mildrith, her words heavy with quiet threat. 'Did you do that?'

'Yes, Mother, but *he*—' began Tidræd.

'I don't care what he did! What *you* did is enough for me!' Mildrith pointed towards her house. 'Go home. And you can fetch a stick on your way there.'

'But, Mother, he——' He was dogged, this boy.

'Not another word! Go home now! And don't you dare stir from the house before I get there.'

Tidræd didn't speak again, though he looked like he might like to give Aculf another bite. He glared at him then strode away, his head high. Brinin caught the whiff of Aculf's work. Truth, half-truth and outright lies were tossed into the pot together and well stirred until it was hard to tell the meat from what was already rotten. Perhaps Mildrith would scoop out some truth when she had Tidræd alone—if she didn't let the stick do all the talking first.

'Mildrith, your son is——' But Aculf, ever hungry for the last word, wasn't going to get it from Mildrith.

'And you can hold your tongue too and mind your own business!' she snapped. She turned to Brinin. 'I'll send Tidræd to the field when I'm done with him. He won't be long.'

Then she walked away with strides not unlike her son's. Brinin watched her. Perhaps he'd better fetch the oxen himself.

Tidræd wasn't long. Brinin had barely yoked the oxen when he saw him coming, stiffer and slower now, but still with pride in his step. Whatever had passed between him and his mother had been swift but it hadn't left him any meeker. Brinin had seen Tidræd in many moods. He'd listened to his cheerful chatter. He'd seen him angry and bold, sullen and gloomy, but now he was thunderous. He cast a bitter look at Brinin, took the plough in his hands, set his teeth and his shoulders and pushed. They had ploughed half a furrow before he even spoke.

'She wouldn't listen,' he growled. 'She wouldn't let me say a word, not even one word! Ashamed that a son of hers should do such a thing, she said. But she knows nothing about it! She wasn't there and she didn't ask!'

They ploughed on. At the end of the row they turned the oxen.

'She thinks I'm still a small boy like Tidwine! I told her I'm not, and she said then I shouldn't behave like one. Behave like one? What does she think I do all day? This is a man's work we're at here! And I'm almost as tall as she is! Next time I might tell her that I'm not going home and if she wants a stick she can fetch it herself.'

There was another wordless row. They turned the oxen again. Back again for half a row. Brinin heard a sudden snort. He looked back at Tidræd. The boy's mouth was twitching.

'Did you see him?' Tidræd gasped with a burst of laughter. 'Did you *smell* him? He stank like a dung heap!'

'What on earth happened, Tidræd?' asked Brinin. His own lips were twitching a bit too. Now that the anger was passing, the sight of Aculf caked with dung was one he didn't mind smiling about. 'There must have been more to it than Aculf said.'

'There was,' frowned Tidræd, his laughter gone as swiftly as it had come. 'I was coming back from Osgyth's house when I saw Aculf with Wulfrich. You know how he is with him. He kept saying over and over, "What did you say? What did you say?" But he didn't give Wulfrich time to answer him before he hit him or shook him and asked him again. Then he said, "I'll soon have it out of you!" And he began to drag Wulfrich to the house. I knew what *that* meant! So I opened up his pen and drove the swine out. Those young ones scattered quickly. I shouted to Aculf that his beasts were out. He knew I'd done it. I was still standing in the pen and, besides, Eadulf had seen me. But he let go of Wulfrich. Eadulf helped him catch the swine. I didn't. I told Wulfrich to hide somewhere until his father wasn't so angry. When Aculf was getting one of them back in, another ran in front of him and he fell into the muck. That *did* make him angry. He grabbed me and hit me a few times, so I bit him hard. He tasted foul but he let go! And I said, "You're not *my* father! You can take me to my mother if you like, but you'll keep your hands off me." And you know the rest.'

It had been well meant, one of those bold, good-hearted deeds that Tidræd was so full of. But it had been anything but helpful.

'What's going to happen when night comes and Wulfrich has to go home?' asked Brinin. 'Do you think Aculf will have forgotten whatever he was angry about and that you drove his beasts out and landed him in dung?'

Tidræd's face fell, and his shoulders seemed to droop.

'Do you think I made it worse?' he said.

'I know you did,' said Brinin.

Little was said after that. They ploughed throughout the morning and into the afternoon, with Tidræd sunk in deep gloom. Brinin was uneasy too. There was something about Tidræd's tale that he didn't like, but he wasn't sure what it was. Tidræd barely spoke again until the afternoon, when they had already unyoked the oxen and penned them up in their stall.

'Forget what I said about my mother this morning,' he muttered. 'I don't mind her. I'm going to find Wulfrich.'

Brinin, still uneasy, went and sat with Garulf for a while. Again he told Garulf about the ploughing and his beasts. Garulf didn't speak of Brinin's new kin or him leaving Oakdene, and when he tired Brinin left him to sleep.

He didn't see Wulfrich or Tidræd, but he met Oswald coming away from the church, waxboard in hand. As they stood together, Tidræd came running up to them.

'I can't find Wulfrich anywhere,' he said. 'I've looked everywhere he goes to hide, and he isn't in any of them.'

'He'll come home when he's hungry enough,' said Oswald, but *he* didn't know the tale that Tidræd and Brinin knew. Why was Wulfrich still hiding after so long? What *had* Aculf been angry about?

'He won't,' said Tidræd. 'Ulf told me that Wulfrich asked him to sneak a cloak and a loaf of bread from the house. And it's even worse than that. Ulf says Æfæd went to Aculf this morning and told him that Wulfrich told Cynestan about him and Eanfrith wrecking your harvest. Aculf's very angry and he's out looking for him. I wanted to find him first but I can't. I'm going to knock Æfæd flat when I see him!'

What did you say? I'll soon have it out of you! Now Brinin understood why he had been so uneasy. Æfæd must have overheard Edith talking to him. How else could he know? And Æfæd, stirring trouble to pay Wulfrich back for the shame that had fallen on him at the Moot, had done the worst thing he could think of. What good would it do to find Wulfrich first? Aculf wouldn't have forgotten. Brinin left Oswald and Tidræd to walk back to his hut. Behind him, he could still hear the others talking.

'Keep looking for him,' Oswald was saying, 'and keep out of fights.'

Likely Oswald spoke wisdom, but it wasn't Brinin's mind. Brinin hoped Tidræd *would* knock Æfæd flat. Besides, it was wisdom Tidræd was unlikely to listen to.

'I *will* fight him!' Tidræd called after them stubbornly.

'What are you going to do?' said Oswald, running up beside Brinin.
'I don't know.'

'There's not much we can do. He's hardly likely to stay out all night.
He'll be scared and cold once it's dark. I'll ask my father to speak to
Aculf. He can't beat his son for doing the right thing!'

'Can't he?' Didn't Oswald know Aculf? Had he even met the man?

They had reached the hut now. Brinin stopped dead, suddenly sick.
Scratched in the dirt, shaped out of stones lying side by side, rubbed
onto the door with a blackened stick, was the same shape again and
again so Brinin couldn't miss it. Axelike shapes, as though a bundle of
weapons had been thrown to the ground. Wyns, many of them, the
only wordcraft that Wulfrich had ever learned. Wuh. Wyn. Wuh.
Weapon. Wuh. Wulfrich. Wuh. Wintanceaster.

'He won't be back by nightfall,' said Brinin. 'He's run away to
Wintanceaster.'

SWIFTNESS

'How on earth could you know that?' Oswald could find no meaning in what they saw. The markings looked a little like writing—and not very good writing—but that was all. Brinin was making a leap that Oswald couldn't understand.

'I tried to teach him how to read once,' said Brinin, 'but I was a poor teacher and he never learned any more than wyn. I wrote it in the dirt like this and told him you need it to write Wintanceaster. And sometimes when he was unhappy he talked about running away there.'

'But we don't even know Wulfrich wrote this, if it even is writing.' It seemed so unlikely. How would a boy like Wulfrich even have thought of such a thing?

'It *is* writing and Wulfrich wrote it. Who else could it be? I didn't write it, and it was hardly you or Brother Wilfred.'

'But he's too young to do such a thing! How would he even know the way to Wintanceaster?' said Oswald. Brinin was so sure, yet it seemed so unbelievable.

'He does know,' came a voice from behind them.

Oswald turned and saw Tidræd standing nearby, more than solemn, frightened.

'I told him which way it was,' went on Tidræd. 'He was talking one day about wanting to go there when he's older but said he didn't know where it was. My father went once, and I asked him how he would get there, so I told Wulfrich what I knew. I didn't think he would go himself, truly I didn't! And it was only the beginning of the way. He'll... he'll get lost soon, even if he remembers what I said.'

Oswald was ready to scold Tidræd, to ask him why he hadn't stopped to think what Wulfrich might do with this knowledge, but as he

366

wavered—Tidræd seemed more than unhappy already—Brinin walked away from them into his hut. The door clattered as he swung it open.

'What are you doing?' asked Oswald.

'He can't have got far,' said Brinin. His cloak was already round his shoulders, and he was fastening the neckpin. 'When did Ulf give him the bread?'

'I don't know,' said Tidræd.

'Find out,' said Brinin. 'Quickly.'

Tidræd knew how to be quick. He dashed away from them. Brinin took his bow and quiver from where they hung inside the door.

'Perhaps I can catch him if I hurry,' he said.

'We'll be quicker on horseback,' said Oswald. Brinin had said nothing of 'we', but Oswald knew it was the only way to do it. 'Find out which way Tidræd told him to go. I'll run and tell my father. I'll see you at the horsehouse soon.'

Oswald found his father in the hall, talking to Edith as they sat by the fire. The food for evening-meat was almost ready, and the smell made his belly feel empty.

'Father,' he said breathlessly. 'Wulfrich has run away to Wintanceaster. I can't tell you everything now—there's no time—but may I take two horses and go after him with Brinin? The light won't last much longer, but if we're quick we may find him before he goes too far.'

'Yes, if you're sure that's where he's gone. Ebba, run and tell your brother to get two horses ready,' said Edrich, standing now and frowning a little. Ebba left her mother and ran from the hall. 'But I don't understand why he *should* have run away.'

'That wretch Æfæd heard someone say that Wulfrich told Cynestan that he and Eanfrith had wrecked the harvest,' said Oswald. Edith gasped, lifting her hand to her mouth. 'Æfæd told Aculf, who's very angry about it. Wulfrich is running away from *him*. I don't understand it all, but that's what I know.'

'Likely that's enough for now,' said Edrich grimly. 'He may not have got far, as you say. I'll see if I can learn more about this business with Aculf.'

Oswald made his way to the door, but as a last thought he ran back for his sword. A weapon was never a bad thing to have on the road. As he left, he saw that Edith was weeping.

Brinin was already by the horsehouse. His thoughts seemed to have taken the same turn as Oswald's; besides his bow he had tucked an axe into his belt. Tidræd was beside him, talking quickly, and Brinin frowned as he listened to him. Eawig had been swift. He had the horses ready and was leading them from the horsehouse.

'Tell him that *I* ought to go too,' said Tidræd as Oswald reached them.

'No,' said Oswald, taking the bridle of his horse from Eawig. 'You'll slow us down.'

'I can sit behind one of you,' said Tidræd. 'I've thought it all out.'

'No,' said Oswald again, swinging himself onto his father's horse. Brinin was already on Oswald's.

'But you only know about—' began Tidræd.

'Go home, Tidræd,' said Brinin. 'You still have work to do today, and your mother won't want you to come with us. Haven't you already given her enough worry for one day?'

'Not as much as she gave me! She won't be worried. I told Oswyn to tell her where I've gone, but not until it's almost dark so it's too late for Mother to stop me. Besides, I don't mind a little trouble so long as it comes *after* we've found Wulfrich and not before.'

'You can't bring your little sister into it!' Tidræd was becoming tiresome, and Oswald was in no mood to listen. 'You're wasting our time! Do as you're told or, I swear, I'll get down from this horse and drag you home!'

'I'd like to see you try it!' said Tidræd boldly, and Oswald did begin to get down. 'You wouldn't even know he'd gone if it hadn't been for me. It's only right that I—'

'Do you dare to speak to Oswald Child like that? Have you forgotten that he will be your lord one day?' said a stern voice from behind them.

Oswald saw his father eyeing Tidræd with his most forbidding look. If Tidræd wanted to wrangle, let him wrangle with *him* and see how that turned out. Edrich nodded to Oswald to go.

They began to trot away. Oswald glanced back. His father was still talking to Tidræd, his arms folded across his chest. Tidræd wasn't saying anything.

'I've never met a more troublesome boy in my life!' said Oswald.

'He means well,' said Brinin. 'He likes Wulfrich and wanted to help.'

'I don't doubt it, but he needs a good thrashing to teach him to do what he's told!'

'He's already had one today, and I don't think it taught him anything.'

'He's too much like his father!' And perhaps Oswald was growing too much like *his*. He could hear his father's words in his own mouth. Thurstan had been stubborn and bold and troublesome at times, and Oswald had loved him for all of it. 'Did he tell you which way Wulfrich might have gone?'

'Yes,' said Brinin, 'and it was after midday when he asked Ulf for the bread.'

'Let's be quick and find him before dark,' said Oswald. 'But not too quick. We don't want to miss him.'

BLAME

E dith felt sick. She had sworn to Wulfrich that she would shield him and had failed to keep her word. Æfæd must have heard *her* talking. Who else could it have been? Wulfrich had trusted her. He had been so scared but he had trusted her, and she had let him down. She hadn't taken enough care. She had spoken too loudly and said too much. She should have whispered the least that Brinin needed to know and been on her way. And what if Oswald and Brinin didn't find him? He was so small. He could so easily lose his way or meet with danger. And it would soon be dark. A cold night was no time for a little boy to be out alone. He had trusted her. What had she done?

Edith was too lost in her thoughts to see Cenwyn coming into the hall and stopping beside her.

'Oh, Edith! Tidræd says that Wulfrich has run away and that your brother's gone after him. What's wrong? Have you been weeping?'

'It's my fault he's run away!'

'That can't be right,' said Cenwyn, sitting down beside her. 'Tidræd's blaming Æfæd. He's off looking for him to fight him, though I told him he'd better not. He's already been in enough trouble today. He drove Aculf's swine out this morning. It's a long time since I've seen Mother so angry.'

'It *was* my fault,' said Edith.

Now that Aculf knew, what harm was there in telling Cenwyn? And she needed to talk to *someone*. Cenwyn's eyes grew wider and her face grimmer as Edith told her, and by the time the tale was over she was glowering with anger.

'*You're* not to blame, Edith!' she said. 'Aculf is. What kind of man keeps his mouth shut about something like that? I'm glad Tidræd drove

370

his beasts out—I've a good mind to do it again myself. As for that sneaking Æfæd, I hope Tidræd does fight him. *He's* to blame too! He's not at all sorry, for all his head-hanging at the Moot. Eanfrith was bolder then but he's the one who seems sorry now.'

'What if they can't find him, Cenwyn?'

'I don't know. Surely he can't have got far.'

'I don't know when he left.'

'Has someone spoken to his mother?'

'My father might have,' said Edith. 'He went to find Aculf.'

'Why don't *you* speak to her?' said Cenwyn, standing up. 'What good is there in sitting here and worrying? You'd be better off doing something. I'm going to do something too.'

'What?'

'I'm going to tell Tidræd to forget what I said. If he doesn't fight Æfæd, I'll do it myself!'

Aculf's house was empty, and the fire had burned low. Edith knew that Aculf was out looking for his son—and not, it seemed, in the right place—but had Sægyth gone too? It would be hard with such young children who seldom dared to leave her side. But if she *had* been told that Wulfrich had run away, she would be frightened and likely weeping. Perhaps with her sister?

Eanfrith was kneeling outside Eadulf's house, digging a little furrow for some planting. He lowered his head when he saw Edith coming. Since the night he and Æfæd had been caught, Eanfrith hadn't met her eyes. It *was* an odd thing, as Cenwyn had said. Æfæd had wept when they were caught. Eanfrith had been angry and shameless but now was the only one who showed any shame at all.

Sæthryth was by her hearth, mending a shirt. She looked up when she saw Edith in the doorway.

'Come in, my lady,' she said, but Edith stayed where she was.

'I wondered if your sister was here,' she said.

'I was looking for her myself not long ago, my lady, but she wasn't at home. I wonder if she's gone out to find that boy. He does go off and hide sometimes which is not something Eadulf and I have ever let *our* children do. His father will have something to say to him when he finds him, I can tell you. Eadulf's helping Aculf look for him. It's a wicked thing to put his mother through, my lady. I heard folk say that he'd run away, but I don't think that can be right. He's a little too young for such a thing and he does often hide. If he's not found soon, he'll likely come home by himself when it gets dark, and I hope his father teaches him not to worry my sister like that again.'

There was no good in staying any longer. Edith hadn't come to see Sæthryth and didn't want to listen to her talking with so little pity for her own kin. As she walked away from the house Eanfrith came after her, his awkwardness gone.

'My lady,' he said in a low voice, 'do you think Wulfrich *has* run away?'

'Yes,' said Edith. 'My brother and Brinin have gone after him.'

'Should I look for him too, my lady?' he said, so worried that Edith couldn't help warming to him, whatever he had done. 'Perhaps he hasn't gone where they think. My father wanted this work done before he got back but surely the more folk who look the better.'

'I don't know,' said Edith. 'My brother thought they knew where he'd gone, but I don't know.'

'Well, I will look then, my lady,' said Eanfrith. 'I hope my father won't mind too much when I tell him why I stopped. And if he does, well… I'd rather know I tried.'

And that was the proof that Eanfrith and Æfæd were as unlike as two boys could be. There was no bitterness towards a child here. How had they ever been friends?

Edith began to make her way back to the hall, but she caught sight of Ulf standing forlornly with the elder of his little sisters. She ran over to him.

'Where's your mother, Ulf?'

Ulf pointed to Daglæf's house.

'With Bægswyth,' he said.

Bægswyth and Sægyth sat by the fire. Sægyth's eyes were swollen with weeping though she almost seemed beyond tears now. She held a cup but wasn't drinking from it. On a bed under the roofshelf, Sægyth's younger daughter lay curled up, fast asleep.

'I was looking for Sægyth,' said Edith. 'Ulf said she was here.'

'Well, here she is, my lady,' said Bægswyth. 'I said it was no good her sitting on her own. Daglæf and the boys are out looking for Wulfrich. Come and sit with us, my lady.'

'I don't know if you've heard,' said Edith as she sat down, 'but my brother thinks he knows where Wulfrich has gone and he and Brinin have gone after him.'

'Yes, my lady,' said Bægswyth. 'Young Tidræd told us. I thought his mother had sent him, but he said he came by himself. He's a good boy, and thoughtful, for all he can be a bit wild at times.'

'I'll never sleep another night under the same roof as that man after this!' Sægyth's tears gave way to fevered anger. 'He's to blame for this. He drove him to it. If you had seen him this morning, my lady, when that Æfæd came… What a wicked boy, stirring up trouble for my son for telling the truth when *he* was the one who had done wrong! And now my son's run off and if any harm comes to him…'

The thought of that brought about another flood of weeping and stung Edith's eyes too. Bægswyth put her arm round Sægyth. The little one stirred on the bed.

'I've told myself so many times that it wasn't so bad. He works hard and he's seldom drunk and doesn't strike *me* often. But the way he is with the children and Wulfrich more than the others… He has him so frightened, but he's such a good boy. He always heeds me and helps with the little ones. My sister says I wed him and I have to live with him. And that all fathers need to be stern and that if the children and I didn't anger him he'd have nothing to be stern about. But our own father was never like Aculf. He finds fault where there is none. I've learned to live with it, but he's not doing it to my children any more! I'll not spend another night in the same house as him. And when Wulfrich is found, I'm taking the children to my brother and I don't care what anyone says or what they think of me. My brother will take us in. He never much liked Aculf, nor Eadulf either when it comes to it. I should have listened to him at the time. I still have my morning-gift to help us. And if they don't find him… he'll have murdered him! He drove him to it. His own son! I've forgiven him so many times, but I'll never forgive him for this!'

As Sægyth raised her voice her little daughter whimpered. She went and sat on the bed with her, cradling her in her arms, rocking and weeping. Edith looked helplessly at Bægswyth then took her leave.

She had to talk to her father. He needed to know everything. The sun was low now. It would be dark soon.

NIGHTFALL

They barely spoke. Whatever Oswald said, Brinin answered with one or two words only and after a while Oswald gave up. They strained their eyes ahead for any Wulfrich-like shadows, but all they saw were bare trees with the first beginnings of new leaves, dark ploughed fields and scattered sheep. Brinin's eyes and ears never seemed to rest. Sometimes he stopped and listened. He got down from his horse and looked among trees or behind hedges or in ditches, anywhere a small boy might hide or might have stumbled into. And he called out again and again, never going far without another shout. His voice was louder than Oswald had ever heard it. It was borne into the sky, over the hedges, along the muddy path, across the fields to be met with nothing but the flutter of startled birds. And still the sun sank lower.

Oswald's heart sank with it. He had hoped to meet with Wulfrich sooner and be at least some of the way back by nightfall. What would they do if darkness came before they found him? What if they didn't find him at all? How long would they go on before they gave up and turned back? How *could* they give up? How could they go back and tell his mother that they hadn't found him?

At last they saw a man ahead of them, driving a small flock of sheep. He was the first man they had seen since they had left Oakdene. Brinin drove his horse on to meet him.

'Have you seen a boy?' he asked. 'No older than ten winters?'

'I've seen no one,' said the man. 'Lost, is he? There's a house nearby. You can't see it for the trees, but it's at the foot of that small hill, not more than half a mile off. You could ask them. Tell them Eadbald sent you. They know me there.'

Brinin rode off, making swiftly for the little hill. Oswald followed, but the man called after him.

'What should I do if I see him?' he said. 'What's the lad's name?'

'Wulfrich,' said Oswald and told the man the way to Oakdene. 'Ask for my father, Edrich Thegn. He's lord there.'

By the time Oswald reached Brinin, he was already coming away from the house. He said nothing but only shook his head and kept riding. They went on. More calling. More straining of the eyes and ears. They asked another man if he had seen a boy. He hadn't. The daylight faded and in the gathering gloom it became harder to see far. They couldn't ride on for much longer, but Oswald didn't know how to tell Brinin that.

They came to a little copse of trees at the edge of some woodland where it was thinning out. Again Brinin got down to look—Oswald didn't know how many times he'd done it now. It was dark and shadowy among the trees as night fell. There was little to see. Brinin cupped his hands to his mouth.

'Wulfrich!' he shouted.

A flapping of roosting birds frightened from their nests. Then nothing. Brinin stood, shoulders slumped, his head lowered. He began to walk back to the horse. Surely there was little more they could do that day.

Somewhere from among the trees came the scuffling of some small beast. But then Oswald heard a whimper.

'Wait,' he whispered. 'Listen.'

∾

It was almost dark when Edith's father came back to the hall. He sat down at the table with a sigh. Edith gave him some food and a cup of ale, but he barely touched them.

'I haven't seen Aculf yet,' he said. 'I've come from Deorstan's house. I had a long talk with him and made sure that his whole household was there to hear it. I even told them what I would have done had my own son wilfully harmed another as Æfæd did. I fear he has no understanding of the wrong he has done, either now or in the summer. But now I ought to find Aculf. I can't understand why his son should be so frightened. I know Aculf is overstern with the boy, but he's done nothing wrong.'

'I know why, Father,' said Edith.

So she told him everything she knew from when she had first seen Wulfrich weeping in the meadow to Sægyth's angry sorrow in Bægswyth's house. He was looking very stern before she was done, and Edith readied herself to be chided for not taking more care. She couldn't remember the last time her father had chided her for anything, but she didn't mind how much he scolded her so long as he put things right. If they *could* be put right.

'Your brother and I once went to Aculf's house to talk to him about Brinin's harvest,' said Edrich. 'He sent Wulfrich out of the house against my bidding, and Oswald thought he was hiding something. I understand that now. He will answer to me. As for his wife, she knows best what she and her children have borne with behind shut doors. No one likes to see a household broken up, but it does happen. I knew a man—a thegn no less—whose wife went back to her kin after he took another woman. She may be wise to take her children to her brother, even if it's only for a time. He threatened his son into wrongdoing that would have had him before the Moot if he'd been a little older. And had we not already dealt with Æfæd and Eanfrith, Aculf himself could have been made to pay. What would that have done to his wife and children? I won't stand in her way if she wishes to go, and by the time I am done speaking to Aculf I doubt he will either. If that boy should be lost…'

That was the great fear. Here father did not say it aloud, and Edith hardly dared to think it. What if they hadn't found him? It was so dark now. Edrich rose from the table.

'Let me find Aculf now,' he said. 'I have much to say to him. Don't wait up for me. I may be some time.'

Edith knew that she wouldn't sleep much that night whether she waited for her father or not.

~

Brinin froze. Oswald heard the whimper again. More scuffling, soft, almost unheard. If they'd been talking they wouldn't have heard it at all. Oswald got down from his horse. Brinin—or his shape, which was all Oswald could make out in the darkness now—turned and made his way back to the edge of the trees.

'Is that you, Wulfrich?' he said, not shouting now. 'It's Brinin. I saw your writing and came after you.'

A sob and another scuffle. A twig snapped.

'Come out from wherever you're hiding and we'll talk,' said Brinin. 'It's too dark and cold for you to be alone. Oswald Child is with me, but don't be scared. We're not angry with you.'

More stirring, and the shape of a boy formed beside the trees. Oswald saw Brinin's shape squatting down beside him. He could hear Wulfrich weeping—for surely it *was* Wulfrich and not some other lost boy.

'No need to weep now we're here,' said Brinin. 'We'll take you home to your mother.'

'No!' cried Wulfrich starting away, though Brinin had taken his arm and he didn't get far. 'I can't ever go home again. My father said he'd—'

'Never mind about your father for now,' said Brinin. 'Think of your mother. She doesn't know where you are and is worried. *We* were worried too. I was afraid we wouldn't find you or that you'd met with danger on the road. I've been praying all the way from Oakdene that we'd find you alive and not dead. And thank God we did.'

'Can't you tell my mother I'm not dead without taking me home?' said Wulfrich.

'That won't be enough for her. She wants *you*.'

'My father knows why you ran away, Wulfrich,' said Oswald. 'Perhaps he can talk to *your* father about it and tell him not to be angry. You did nothing wrong.'

'But my father—' began Wulfrich.

'We'll worry about him in the morning,' said Brinin. 'We can't go anywhere tonight. Should we stop here, Oswald? I wish I'd thought to bring something to kindle a fire.'

'I have something,' said Oswald. 'Here's as good a place as any. Let's get a fire going before it's too dark to do it.'

When the fire was lit and the horses tethered, they shared a scant meal of half of Wulfrich's loaf and some sips from a flask Brinin had. Oswald tried not to think of what he had smelled from the simmering pot in the hall. Wulfrich was tired and tearful. He kept coming back to his father, and Brinin kept steering him onto other things.

'You need to sleep,' said Brinin at last. 'What about a tale first?'

'Tell me the one about the dragon,' yawned Wulfrich.

Brinin leaned back against a tree, his legs stretched out in front of him. Oswald watched him in the firelight. Was Brinin, whose words had always been so few, going to tell a tale to a child?

'Far away from here there lies a great mountain,' began Brinin.

Oswald listened in wonder. It was a good tale, and he almost felt like a child himself as he heard it. He could never have foreseen such a tale coming from Brinin's lips. Wulfrich was asleep before it was over, his head on Brinin's lap, but Brinin kept going until the end. And there was another wonder: this boy, Aculf's son, loved Brinin and trusted him.

'I didn't know you could tell a tale like that,' said Oswald.

'Neither did I until I cheered Wulfrich up with it one day. It's one of my mother's.'

'About a man called Wulfrich slaying a dragon?'

'When she told it, he was called Bruni,' said Brinin. He shifted the sleeping boy a little, straightening his head. 'What are we going to do about Aculf?'

'What *can* we do? Wulfrich is his son.'

'Perhaps we should take Wulfrich to your father first and let him deal with it.'

'Aculf ought to be ashamed of himself!'

'He won't be,' said Brinin. He reached out and tossed a few more sticks onto the fire, carefully so as not to wake Wulfrich. 'We ought to sleep a little too.'

It was a broken sleep. Oswald didn't know how many times he awoke cold and stiff and stirred up the fire. The fire was on his mind all night, searing into his sleep. He dreamed that it had gone out altogether and that the horses were snorting and whinnying and stamping. The dream woke him. The deep darkness of night had passed, and the sky was already grey. The fire was out. The horses *were* whinnying and stamping. Very near he heard a low growl.

TEETH

'**G**et him away quick!'

Bewildered, Brinin woke to noise: the horses snorting and stamping with fear, shouting, something else he couldn't name. He opened his eyes to the first grey light of morning. Wulfrich was sitting up beside him, white-faced, wide-eyed and shivering. Where was Oswald?

'Hurry up and get Wulfrich away from here!' Oswald shouted, almost screamed from somewhere nearby. Where was he? Brinin sat up.

'For heaven's sake, don't sit there! Get him away!'

Brinin scrambled up, grabbing Wulfrich's arm and pulling him to his feet too. The fire was out. Oswald's sword lay beside the patch of crushed grass where he had slept. Where was he?

'Hurry up!'

And then he saw him a little away from them. He was walking backwards, stumbling, bent over with his seax stretched before him, gripped with both hands. It shook as his hands trembled. And in front of him, getting nearer by the inch, crouched low and ready to leap upon its prey, growling and baring its teeth, was a huge grey wolf.

'Brinin! Quick!'

Brinin looked around wildly. He couldn't ride off with Wulfrich—or even run—and leave Oswald behind. He couldn't leave Wulfrich to help Oswald. The wolf was nearer now, only a few feet from Oswald's seax. Why didn't Oswald strike? A tree. Brinin half-dragged, half-lifted Wulfrich to a tall tree with spreading boughs.

'Climb it! Quick!' He thrust Wulfrich up among the branches. 'Keep your feet well up and don't come down until I tell you.'

Yelping and snarling. Oswald yelled. Wulfrich screamed and almost fell, but Brinin shoved him back up again. Where was his bow? He ran, almost diving onto the grass to snatch it up. Oswald was scrambling up another tree, the wrong tree, far too small. His seax lay on the ground, and the wolf was at his heels. He couldn't go much higher. The tree was swaying under his weight. He would slip. Oswald yelled again. But Brinin could only fumble. His hands were cold and shaky. He couldn't fit the arrow to the bow. The wolf leapt and clawed at the tree, its teeth only inches from Oswald's feet. The arrow wouldn't stay steady. What if he hit Oswald by mistake?

'Shoot! Shoot!'

Oswald was straining to raise himself higher, grasping at anything that might hold him. A branch cracked and fell on the wolf's head. And still it snarled and scratched at the tree. Wulfrich was sobbing. Brinin shot. The arrow missed, flying past the tree into the shrubs behind it.

He was a fumbling fool, good for nothing, and his father had been a hunter! His hands wouldn't keep steady. Another snapped branch. Another yell from Oswald. Another arrow. It grazed the wolf's back. Oswald slipped a little lower. The wolf yelped and growled but it didn't fall.

'Here! Here! Come here! Here!'

Brinin stumbled nearer to the beast, shouting as though it could understand speech. The wolf turned. It took a few steps towards Brinin. Another branch cracked under Oswald's weight. But the arrow was ready and somehow it flew from the bow, striking the wolf's shoulder. The wolf fell. It writhed on the ground, whining like a whipped hound. But it didn't die. Still whining and growling it rose to its feet.

Oswald slid from the tree and staggered past Brinin, heading back towards the fire. The wolf crept nearer. Its eyes were yellow, yellow as the morning, yellow as Bruni's dragon's eyes. But there was no fire, no great tail, no wings; no iron shield or spear. Only teeth and claws and piercing yellow eyes and… Brinin tossed away his bow, his hands suddenly steady, and drew his axe from his belt. He took a step towards the wolf.

'Come, then!' said Brinin.

Rustling leaves, a scream, a crash. Pouncing, claws, teeth and yellow eyes, the wolf's breath hot on his face as they fell together. And it was over. Warm blood trickled along the axe handle onto his hand. Brinin shoved the wolf's body away and sat up just as Oswald reached him with his sword. Brinin looked at his bloodied axe and bloodied hand, then up at Oswald. Oswald stared down, white and breathless.

'It's dead,' said Brinin.

Oswald nodded. He drew a deep breath.

'I... I...' he began, then stopped and rubbed his hand across his face. 'You spoke to it in Danish!'

'Did I?'

Brinin heard a stifled sob. Wulfrich was sitting under the tree where he'd fallen, both hands over his mouth as he stared at them.

'We'd better get you home to your mother,' said Brinin.

They reached Oakdene by mid-morning. Tidræd ran from the fields to meet them, his eyes wide when he saw the dead wolf slung over the back of Oswald's horse.

'You killed a *wolf*!' he said, awe-struck. 'I wish you'd let me go too.'

'Brinin did,' said Oswald grimly. 'The wolf nearly killed me.'

Tidræd stared at Brinin in wonder, then frowned at Wulfrich who was sitting wretchedly on the horse in front of him.

'You shouldn't run off like that,' he said sternly. 'We were worried about you. That wolf could have eaten you!'

That was sickening truth from the mouth of a child. If Wulfrich had spent the night alone... Oswald leapt down from his horse.

'Let me take Wulfrich straight to the hall,' he said. 'I'll go to my father first and let him speak to Aculf before Wulfrich goes home. Can you deal with the other horse? And the wolf?'

When Oswald and Wulfrich had left them, Tidræd stood prodding the wolf, opening its mouth and running his finger along its teeth while Brinin watched him. His lip was swollen, and one of his eyes was rather dark.

'You've been fighting,' said Brinin.

'Æfæd. I said I'd fight him and I was winning too, but Edrich Thegn came and pulled us apart and sent us home. Well, he *took* Æfæd home—said he wanted to talk to his father.' Tidræd grimaced. 'My mother wasn't happy. I don't know why she hates me fighting. My father didn't mind it so much; he only said to keep it for something worthwhile. And this *was* worthwhile, and I'll have to be good at it if I'm going to be in the fyrd one day. Mother almost took a stick to me again, but Cenwyn came in and said if she was going to beat me for fighting she'd have to beat her too as she told me to do it. Mother was never going to do *that*! Not now that Cenwyn's a grown woman and taller than she is. And Cenwyn knew it too! So Mother tossed the stick onto the fire and only scolded us both a bit. But later when Cenwyn told her everything about Æfæd and Aculf and Wulfrich, she didn't seem to mind me fighting and she wasn't even so angry about Aculf's swine any more. I don't understand her sometimes. What are you going to do with the wolf? You should turn the skin into a cloak and then when you wear it everyone will know that you're a wolf-slayer. I wish it had been me! Can I have one of the teeth?'

Brinin couldn't help laughing at this, though he couldn't see himself strutting about in a wolfskin cloak. It might be good for sleeping on in the winter.

'Let's get the horse to the horsehouse,' he said, 'and then we can get some ploughing done. Who was helping you this morning?'

'My little sister. We've been ploughing without you all morning. I showed her how to drive the oxen. I left her watching them. They needed to stop for a while.'

They hadn't even reached the horsehouse when Oswald came running to meet them.

'You won't believe this! Aculf's wife is leaving and taking the children with her. Daglæf is taking her to her brother. They're leaving straightaway. They're already loading the cart.'

'But Aculf will never let them go,' said Brinin. Surely he would do everything he could to stop them, whether Daglæf was helping them or not. Surely he would go after them and bring them back.

'He isn't stopping them,' said Oswald. 'Edith says my father was talking to Aculf long into the night, though she doesn't know what he said to him. It was almost morning before he came back to the hall. My father says it's not something he likes to see, but that a wife is free to go and that Sægyth is likely wise to. And listen to this: he's made

Aculf send her away with some of his sheep so she has some way to keep herself and the children. You should have seen Wulfrich when his mother told him. He looked like I felt this morning when I knew that wolf wasn't going to sink its teeth into me after all.'

'They're leaving *now*?' asked Tidræd.

'That's what I said,' said Oswald. 'They're by Daglæf's house loading the cart.'

Tidræd muttered something and dashed away, but not towards Daglæf's house. He was going the other way. Brinin pulled the wolf from the horse. It landed at his feet with a thud. He knelt beside it and drew out his seax.

'Can you help me get a few of these teeth out?' he said.

Wulfrich sat on a chest in the back of the cart, rather stunned. His brother was beside him, and he held his baby sister on his lap. His other sister sat at the front beside Daglæf's older son. The cart was already full of sheep. They pressed against the children's knees. Sægyth was talking to Daglæf and Bægswyth in the doorway. Brinin didn't see Aculf anywhere.

'We're going away,' said Wulfrich in a small voice. 'My mother's taking us to her brother.'

'Oswald Child told me,' said Brinin.

'I don't know what my mother's brother is like,' said Wulfrich. 'I've never seen him.'

'But your mother has,' said Brinin. '*She* knows what he's like. Look. I have something for you.'

Brinin took Wulfrich's hand and tipped two of the wolf's teeth into it. They were sharp and curved and yellowed.

'Are these from the wolf?' Wulfrich whispered. Ulf bent over his brother's open hand, and even Daglæf's son leaned back to see them.

'Yes,' said Brinin. 'They're for you.'

Wulfrich shut his fingers round the teeth, squeezing them tightly.

'You almost forgot these. You were going to leave without them.'

It was Tidræd. He was speaking rather gruffly, but perhaps it was easier to sound gruff than it was to say goodbye to one he had come to think of as a friend. He handed Wulfrich the wooden sword and shield that Brinin had made all those months before.

'I'm leaving too,' said Brinin. He didn't mind if Tidræd heard him now, even if it did mean that half the village knew by sunset. He and Oswald had already given them enough to talk about that day, coming back as they had with a lost boy and a dead wolf. 'I met my father's kin when I was away and I'm going to live there with them. So we'll both be with new kin in a new place.'

Daglæf and Sægyth came to the cart and climbed up beside the children.

'Thank you,' said Sægyth. Her face was drawn, her eyes red and beyond weary. What kind of night had she had? 'That's twice now you've brought back one of my sons to me.'

'I'll see you when I get back,' said Daglæf. He prodded the oxen and the cart moved away.

Wulfrich didn't wave or call out as he left. He only watched. His sword and shield were tucked under one arm, and the other was round his baby sister. And in his hand he still clutched the wolf's teeth.

'You didn't tell me you were going away,' said Tidræd. 'That's why you wanted me to do the ploughing and why we haven't begun on your field yet, isn't it?'

'My father and grandfather's house is there for me, and their land,' said Brinin.

Tidræd nodded slowly, then walked away. When Brinin turned he caught sight of Aculf watching the oxcart as it left. And for perhaps the first time in his life he truly pitied him. He couldn't think of anything that Aculf had ever done to earn his pity or any kindness or goodwill. But once Aculf too had been a small boy like Wulfrich and Ulf. He had likely looked much as they did and had somehow grown up into the kind of man he now was, and everything had gone so very wrong.

LIVING

From a dead wolf, something new began to grow. Neighbours who had not met his eye since the raid bade Brinin a good day. Some asked after his beasts. Children even dared to come to his hut to see the wolfskin. Ceola's mother and brothers, who had been too sorrow-stricken to speak to him since Ceola had fallen to the Danes, were not unfriendly when they met with him and Edrich Thegn, and it was settled that they would rent his field.

'That business with Wulfrich and that wretched wolf has helped you no end,' said Oswald one evening. Winter had truly passed. Everything was greener and warmer, and they sat on the roots of the old beech tree as though the old times were not swiftly rushing to their end.

'How?' asked Brinin.

'I think folk have learned at last that you aren't going to help the Danes kill them in their beds.'

'Perhaps,' said Brinin. All he had learned himself was that folk are fickle. 'Until the Danes come back. And if they do, I'll trust those who didn't need me to kill a wolf to prove which side I was on, folk like Garulf and Mildrith and Cynestan.'

'Cynestan says Garulf isn't getting any stronger,' said Oswald.

'He's dying,' said Brinin, 'and he's taking a long time to do it. He won't get stronger.'

~

But in the morning Garulf was sitting up, better than Brinin had seen him for weeks. Wynith and the children were out. Brinin stirred up the fire and sat down on a stool beside him.

'Well, lad,' said Garulf, 'I was hoping I might see you today. How are your beasts?'

'All doing well. Eawig says my sow's young are almost ready to leave their mother.'

'He says you gave him two of them. I always said you were a good lad.'

'He's more than earned them,' said Brinin.

'He's a good lad too. Couldn't have asked for a better grandson. He's good to his mother and his sister. It's a weight off my mind.'

If Eawig and Ebba didn't know what was coming, Garulf did, like a man on a long journey who knows the end is ahead of him, beyond the next hill. Perhaps he'd known longer than anyone. They didn't speak for a time. The fire crackled. Brinin heard Cynestan talking to Deormod somewhere near the hut. Further away, he heard Eadulf loudly scolding Eanfrith.

'How long do we have left with you, lad?' said Garulf. This was the first time the old man had spoken to him of it. Brinin had even wondered if Garulf had forgotten.

'Not long,' said Brinin. 'My kin will come with an oxcart after Easter.'

'When's Easter, lad? The days are all one to me now, though it seems the weather is warmer than it was.'

'Soon,' said Brinin. 'Palm Sunday was yesterday.'

For a time Garulf said nothing. He lay with his eyes shut, and Brinin began to think he had fallen asleep. But just as Brinin was about to slip away, he opened them again.

'It was a blow to your father to lose his freedom. He never spoke of it to me, but he wasn't a happy man. I could see that. Little did he know that his son would one day have everything he lost. I understand why you're going. I was worried that everything they did to you here had driven you away. But it isn't only that, is it?'

'No,' said Brinin. 'It isn't only that.'

'And you won't forget us when you're with these kin of yours?'

'How could I forget you?'

Would he forget to eat and drink, to breathe and work and sleep? Would he forget that he had once had a father, a mother, a brother?

Would he forget that he had such friends? Garulf reached out and patted Brinin's knee. There was almost no weight to his touch.

'You're a good lad. I always said you were,' he said. 'I want Eawig. Can you ask Cynestan to spare him for a while?'

Garulf shut his eyes again, and Brinin left to find Cynestan and Eawig.

$\sim$

'This is a psalm they sang at evensong when you were in the minster,' said Brother Wilfred, handing Brinin a waxboard as they sat together in the church that afternoon. 'But it's only sung once a week. Can you read it to me?'

Reading had become almost easy now. Perhaps, for those who did it every day—like monks—it was a little like breathing: something they did without thinking, something they couldn't help doing. If he, unlearned, found it so, how much more for those like Brother Wilfred?

'I love the Lord because he heard the voice of my prayer,' read Brinin. 'He turned his ear to me when I called in my days. The sorrows of death were all around me, and the dangers of hell came upon me. I found trouble and sorrow. The Lord is merciful and just. Our God shows pity. The Lord guards the little ones. I was shamed, and he freed me. Turn, my soul, to your rest, since the Lord has blessed you; since he has snatched my soul from death, my eyes from tears, my feet from falling. I will please the Lord in the land of the living.'

'Now, my boy,' said Brother Wilfred. 'This psalm has been much on my mind lately. Look at it again and see how it tells the tale of your life. It's never good for us to dwell too long on old troubles, but neither should we forget them altogether. Think of what your life once was. Think of the daily shame you had to bear. Think of the troubles and sorrows you have known, the sorrows of death. And think of how our God showed you pity, how he blessed you with friendship, freedom, a field of your own. Now, some might say you *earned* those things by saving your lord, but you and I know better than that, don't we? We know that a slave can't earn anything. Edrich Thegn didn't have to free you or give you a field, but our Lord put it on his heart to do those things. And what man could have given you back kin when you thought you were without them in this world? The Lord has given you more than any of us could have hoped for.'

'I never thought I would have anything, sir,' said Brinin.

There had been a time when hope had seemed not so much a blessing as a curse, to be kept well out of reach. Brinin had mistrusted it. He had feared it would lie to him, then forsake him to a deeper despair. But in the end it had been a friend.

'Yet the psalm is not about your own life, but teaches us how our Lord is with his children: merciful, lifting us from death and from the troubles and sorrows of this world; bearing us in his arms to where we need not fear death nor tears nor falling. Wait here, my boy.'

Brother Wilfred left Brinin with the waxboard and went to some hidden part of the church. When he came back he was holding something flat and wooden, though Brinin couldn't see what it was.

'Look at this, my boy,' said Brother Wilfred as he sat down again.

It *was* wood, two thin boards fastened with leather thongs on one side so they opened and shut like a door. It was bigger than a waxboard and without any wax. And it was full of very straight and very small black writing.

'Is it a book, sir?' asked Brinin. He had never seen one, only the scroll that Oswald had read from in the minster.

'Well, it's near enough to one. Without bookskin we must do what we can. You told me you didn't want to forget what you'd learned, and I asked myself how I could help you. This is what I thought of. All the psalms and prayers you have already learned are written here, and some others too. Look. Do you remember Oswald reading this for us at the minster? I have put it into English for you.'

The words seemed to bear Brinin to the minster. He could almost hear Oswald reading them. *Where throngs of saints are glad, singing to the Lord with strong peace in the land of the living. Where there is happiness, where the poor man does not weep, where there is gladness, where there is no trouble, where there is no bitter death.*

'You've been more than kind to me, sir,' said Brinin. 'I don't know what to say.'

Brother Wilfred had been all kindness, since the day he had first seen a slave who was unseen to almost everyone else; since the day he had first taught him that a slave too could call God Father.

'I want to write some more before you leave,' he said, taking the book back again. 'You need not say anything. I only ask that you read it and learn it and understand it and do not forget. You have known trouble here and, though you are welcomed where you are going, you will know trouble there too. Even in our gladness, sorrow is never far from us in this world and it never will be until the day we read of here.'

After Brinin had left the church and tended to his beasts, he went back to see Garulf. Eawig was by the door, and Brinin knew something was wrong before he even said a word.

'I don't understand,' said Eawig. 'He was much better this morning.'

Garulf's eyes were open. They moved from one face to another and there was still knowledge in them. But his breathing, his hue, everything else about him seemed to have been touched by the hand of death.

'I'm going to fetch the priest,' said Brinin.

He ran all the way to the church, bursting in upon Oswald sitting by Brother Wilfred's side with his waxboard.

'Forgive me, sir,' he said. 'It's Garulf. He…'

He didn't need to say any more. Brother Wilfred rose and left the church at once.

'Is… is he dying?' asked Oswald.

Brinin opened his mouth to answer him, but any words he had seemed to be stuck somewhere deep in his throat, a hard, tangled lump that wouldn't shift.

'I'll tell my father,' said Oswald.

It was already dark when the end came. Brother Wilfred sat at Garulf's side. Brinin stood in the doorway, not kin enough to go further in, too much of a friend to leave. Eawig pushed past him and went out in the night. Ebba laid her head on her mother's lap and wept. Wynith, with heavy, weary eyes, stroked her daughter's hair and listened as Brother Wilfred spoke softly to them.

Outside, Brinin heard a strangled sob from Eawig. It was a dreadful thing to sorrow alone. Edith had sat with him. Oswald had flung his arms around him and wept on his shoulder. Brother Wilfred had spoken to him in the firelight of a stranger's house. And somehow they had all lightened the burden a little.

Brinin didn't know what to do, so he did something a little like what they had done for him. He went outside to Eawig, took the boy's head and held it to his shoulder. Let him do his weeping there. The sorrows of death were all around, never far away in this world until they reached the land of the living.

OXCART

No more than two weeks after Easter, Oswald and Tidræd were in the meadow working on some warcraft. Oswald drove Tidræd hard, as Thurstan had once driven him. Tidræd—already bold, strong and nimble—would one day be as good a swordsman as his father, perhaps even a better one. At only thirteen winters he was already a worthy foe, and Oswald had to work hard when he fought him, with only his greater height on his side. Thurstan would have been proud to see it, and Oswald praised Tidræd as he would have done, and not so sparingly as his own father.

'You've made me hot today,' said Oswald, tossing his sword and shield aside. 'And you had some good shield work too. I wouldn't like to come against you with a real sword in your hand.'

'My father's is still too heavy for me,' said Tidræd.

'You'll grow into it. You should fight some of the other boys too though, and not only me. It would be good for them as well as you.'

'I'd like to, but half the time they won't fight me.'

'That's because you gloat too much when you win. Keep your gloating for the Danes!' laughed Oswald. 'What now? Spears?'

'I wouldn't,' said Tidræd, peering at something behind Oswald. 'Someone's coming and they'd think we wanted to kill them. Looks like an oxcart. Danes don't come that way.'

Oswald turned and saw the shape of what was very much like an oxcart at the far end of the meadow. His heart sank. Easter had passed and, true to their word, Brinin's kin were here for him. Brinin would soon be gone.

'Run and find Brinin, Tidræd,' he said. 'I think that's his kin come to fetch him.'

'I don't see what that other place has that Oakdene doesn't,' frowned Tidræd.

'It has his father's house and land and his kinsfolk,' said Oswald. 'Would you walk away from all that?'

'I wouldn't walk away from my friends either,' muttered Tidræd, but he heeded him nonetheless.

Oswald shot another glance at the far-off oxcart, then gathered up the weapons and trudged back to the hall.

Summer was coming. Edith felt the smallest beginnings of its heat as she wove in the sunshine outside the hall and watched the life of the village pass by. Children ran barefoot again for the first time in months, and men and women lingered longer to talk when they met. She caught sight of Eanfrith and Deormod sharing a few words. Edith often saw them speaking, though never when Eadulf was in sight. She had seen Eadulf glare at Deormod, but she had also seen Deormod look back a little boldly. That was easier now that the wolf had no teeth. Edith shuddered. She didn't like to think of wolves—even toothless ones—since one had come altogether too near her brother.

Oswald came round the side of the hall, his arms full of weapons and his face grim. He stopped beside her before crossing the threshold.

'There's an oxcart in the meadow,' he said. 'I think it's Brinin's kin. Is Father inside?'

'No,' said Edith. 'He's with Cynestan.'

Oswald went inside to put away the weapons. He was soon out again without them and began to walk away, but Edith called him back.

'Oswald, wait,' she said. Oswald stopped on the other side of the loom. Edith looked at him through the warp threads. 'Oswald, you've never spoken about this since you told me Brinin was leaving. Don't you *mind*?'

'Mind?' said Oswald, eying his sister in disbelief. 'I hate it! But he'd be a fool not to go, and that's what I've told him. I swore to myself that I'd say nothing more than that. It's better not to say anything about it to anyone.'

'Because you're afraid he wouldn't go if you did?'

'Because I don't know. He can be stubborn once he's settled on a thing and he's settled on this. But he's loyal too, more so since that whole business with the Moot—the one I was before, not the other one. There! That's another thing I said I wouldn't talk about. I'm breaking oaths every time I open my mouth today. I think the Moot was in his mind when he went to Readingum to find Father, but I don't see why he thinks he owes me anything. Even if he did, wasn't finding Father and killing that wolf enough? If there's any owing, I owe him! And if you had been there when we sat in his kin's house... it was one of the happiest and one of the saddest things I've ever seen, somehow both at the same time. Brinin was so overwhelmed he could barely speak. He has to go.'

'And what will you do when he does?'

'Oh, I've thought about that. I'll ride out with them some of the way, then after a bit I'll smile, say goodbye and ride home.' Oswald smiled then, but it wasn't a true smile. It was only a tightening of his lips that was a little like one. 'When I sent Brinin and Row away, I told myself—and them—that it would keep them together and that one day I would bring them back and they would never have to leave again. And Row died, and Brinin's leaving anyway—it's right that he should. But my back will bear the scars for the rest of my life, and it was all for nothing. It was all folly. Let me find Father. They'll be here soon.'

Edith watched him go, walking slowly with his head down. He couldn't say with one breath that the Moot had sent Brinin to Readingum and with the next that it had all been for nothing. Besides, Oswald hadn't seen Brinin's shock as he first heard about it. He hadn't seen how it had been for him to learn, at his lowest, that he had such a friend; or how it had plucked him from reckless despair into wisdom. And who was to say what was for good and what was for nothing in this world, or which deeds led to others? Only God knew that.

Brinin went to meet them. Bald and Bægloc were almost at the church by the time he reached them. They climbed down from the oxcart and greeted him warmly, with arms around him and pats on the back, truly kinlike.

'This is a fine place, son,' said Bald. 'Good woodland. I like the look of it. It's bigger than I thought it would be. Now, what should we do with the oxen?'

'I'll ask Edrich Thegn,' said Brinin. 'How long before you want us to set out again?'

'Tomorrow if we can, the day after if we must. I don't want to be away for too long.'

That meant a day, two at most. And although he had readied himself for months and had nothing left to do, it now seemed a little *too* soon. Edrich Thegn was already coming round the side of the hall towards them, with Oswald and Edith beside him.

'You are welcome, friends,' said Edrich Thegn. 'I hope you met with no trouble on the road.'

'None worth speaking of, sir. Mild weather all the way,' said Bald. 'I was just saying to our kinsman what good land you have here. I'd be sorry to leave it if I were him.'

And that was when Brinin knew that he *was* sorry to leave; that Oakdene was all he knew; that the folk here, good and bad, were folk he understood. He knew enough of their ways, of their friendships and hatreds, of their strengths and weaknesses, their sorrows and joys, their wisdom and folly to truly know them. And when he left he'd be like a child learning to walk again, or like a man groping his way in the dark. He had thought it all out. He had settled on it. It was the only thing he could do. Or was it? Perhaps in forgiving and overlooking some of the wickedness of Oakdene, he had begun to see more good. But it was too late to do anything else now. His land was let, and his kin had come.

'He'll always be welcome here,' said Edrich Thegn. 'As will any of his kin. And I hope you will eat at my table during your stay. How long will we have you?'

'I thank you for your kindness, sir,' said Bald. 'Only until tomorrow.'

Brinin saw a quick glance pass between Oswald and Edith, and on Oswald's face the tight look of a man set on winning a battle. It was too soon.

Edrich Thegn led them into the hall to rest from the road, leaving Deormod to see to the oxen and cart. While Edith fetched them meat and drink, Oswald greeted them as warmly as his father had done.

Brinin saw Ebba staring at Bald and Bægloc warily but when he smiled at her she flushed and turned away.

'Will you show us round, Bruni,' said Bægloc when they had eaten. 'My legs could do with a walk.'

The walk became a kind of farewell: seeing things for the first time, looking at them for the last time. Brinin took them to see his field. On the way there, they met Mildrith outside her house and stopped to talk to her. She spoke so warmly of all the help Brinin had been with her ploughing that he felt a little awkward. Surely *she* had been the one helping him. Tidræd was with her, cold and sullen. He said little to begin with—and Brinin hadn't missed a warning look Mildrith had given him—but he seemed to thaw as they talked.

'Did Brinin tell you that he's a wolf-slayer?' he asked Bald and Bægloc.

'A wolf-slayer!' Bægloc turned to Brinin with raised eyebrows.

'Yes! He shot it and hit it with an axe. It was a big one too, almost as big as a horse! I saw the body. It nearly ate Oswald Child. I have one of the teeth.'

Tidræd fumbled with the pouch on his belt. He took out the wolf's tooth and dropped it into Bægloc's hand. Bægloc turned it over, his lips twitching with half-hidden mirth.

'A wolf as big as a horse!' he said, handing the tooth back to Tidræd. 'That's a tale I'd like to hear.'

'It was as big as a wolf, *not* a horse,' said Brinin as they left Mildrith's house.

'But still a wolf,' said Bægloc. 'With teeth.'

They saw the fields and the forest. They spoke to Cynestan and Daglæf. They stopped at Garulf's—Wynith's—hut, but it was empty. They went to the church and talked to Brother Wilfred for a long time. Before they left, he gave Brinin the book he had made for him, wrapped in cloth to keep it good.

'What's that then, son?' asked Bald as they walked from the church to Brinin's hut. The sun was low now.

'It's a book,' said Brinin. 'Only made with wood, though, not with bookskin.'

'Can you read, then?' asked Bægloc, with a hint of mild wonder in his voice. He looked so much like Row when he said it.

'Only in English,' said Brinin. 'And I can't write well. I learned at the minster I went to, and woodcraft too.'

'Woodcraft is a craft worth having,' said Bald, much as Garulf had once done. 'Your father was good with wood. As for reading, I can't say I rightly understand it, nor what the good of it is, though they say our new king is fond of booklore. Perhaps you can show us how it's done sometime, son.'

~

In the hall that evening, the fire was warm and the food was good. Brinin said little and let the others speak around him. He barely heard what they were saying. Last things came too soon. The night before he had eaten alone by his hearth and hadn't known it was for the last time. The night before that, he had eaten with Wynith, Eawig and Ebba and hadn't known that was for the last time either. Oswald, at his side, leaned a little towards him.

'Edith thinks your kinsman is like Row,' he whispered.

'He is,' said Brinin. The others round the table were deep in speech and not listening to anything he and Oswald might be saying. 'Oswald, you said I'd be a fool not to go with them. Is that what you truly think? You don't mind?'

'Why would I have said it if it wasn't what I thought?' said Oswald. Brinin couldn't see his face well; he took another drink as soon as he had spoken. 'And it's what my father thinks too. You can't walk away from all that. Listen. I think my father is speaking to you.'

'Your kinsmen and I have settled on the best way to do it, my boy,' said Edrich Thegn. 'You have more beasts now. We think you should only take the sheep with you in the morning. I'm hoping to see Godweard later in the year. I was thinking of taking a cart for some gifts I want to give him. I'll have Eawig care for your swine and I'll bring them to you then.'

Edrich Thegn didn't want to keep Bald and Bægloc from their rest. Not long after that, he urged them to sleep and they left the hall. Before he stepped into his hut, Brinin stopped by the threshold and looked up at the sky. It was a cloudy night. There weren't any stars to see.

~

In the morning, while Bald and Bægloc got Brinin's little flock onto the cart, Brinin talked to Eawig by the swine pen. Eawig hadn't chided Brinin about leaving since the day he heard of it, but he was so wretched that morning—barely mustering any words let alone a smile —that watching him was woundlike.

'Did Edrich Thegn tell you about me leaving the swine here for now?' asked Brinin.

Eawig nodded.

'And I want you to take another of them—a sow—for Ebba.'

Another nod.

'And you can look after them all and help your mother and sister that way. It's what your grandfather would have wanted.'

'I know,' said Eawig. 'He told me.'

Then they stood and watched the swine for a while without speaking. The young were strong now, the beginnings of a fine herd. There were so many beginnings in the world. And so many endings.

'And you'll come back and see us if you can?' said Eawig.

'If I can,' said Brinin.

Eawig nodded. He lifted his shovel and rested it on his shoulder.

'I have work to do now,' he said hoarsely. 'I hope… I hope you meet with no trouble on the road.'

Then he walked round Deorstan's house and was gone.

Everything Brinin owned was already in the cart. The hut was empty but for the ashes in the hearth, the straw he lay on and the broken stools in the corner. He didn't know why he left the stools there. He shut the door and went to find his kin.

The oxcart was loaded, and Oswald on his horse beside it.

'I'll ride out with you for a bit,' he said.

A little crowd stood round the oxcart; not everyone in the village, but some. A few folk spoke to him, and perhaps he answered them. He didn't truly hear what he or they said.

Ebba flung her arms round him and wept. Brinin didn't know what to say or what to do with his hands. In the end, her mother had to lead her away. That was another wound, sharper even than Eawig's wretchedness.

He set one foot on the cart, but then he remembered the last thing he had wanted to do. Aculf was standing alone, a little way off. Brinin left the cart and walked over to him.

'I bear you no ill will,' he said.

Forgive us our sins as we forgive those who sin against us. It was the nearest thing to forgiveness that he could find in himself to offer. There had been too many blows and too much hatred for friendship to be something Brinin could easily give. But at least he could leave well. Aculf looked at him, unsmilingly but with little of his old warlike glare. Then he walked away. Forgiveness was a good way of knowing a man. Some couldn't give it; others couldn't take it. Aculf could do neither. Brinin watched him as he left, then went back to the oxcart and they set off.

They went past the hall and past the church and across the meadow. It seemed to take a long time. The sheep were bleating. It was better not to look back.

Round midday they stopped to rest and when they were ready to go again, Oswald said his farewells. He took each of them by the hand—lingering a little longer with Brinin—and wished them a good journey.

'God willing, I'll see you later in the year when I come to see Godweard,' he said.

Then he swung himself onto his horse and rode away. Bægloc prodded the oxen, and the cart rolled on. The sheep bleated. Brinin looked back. Oswald wasn't riding hard, only at a trot.

'Wait,' said Brinin.

He jumped from the cart and ran after Oswald.

'Wait,' he shouted.

Oswald turned round, bewildered. He leapt down.

'What is it?'

Oswald had always been better with words. He was warm and knew how to make a man feel like he had a friend. Brinin didn't know how to do any of that.

He threw his arms round Oswald and held him tightly. And when he let go, he made himself speak, driving the words out.

'God willing, I'll see you when you come,' he said, his voice even hoarser than Eawig's. It wasn't everything he wanted to say, only what he *could* say.

He walked back to the oxcart, and perhaps Oswald started riding again too, though this time Brinin didn't dare look back. He climbed up beside his kinsmen.

'Shall we go then, son?' said Bald.

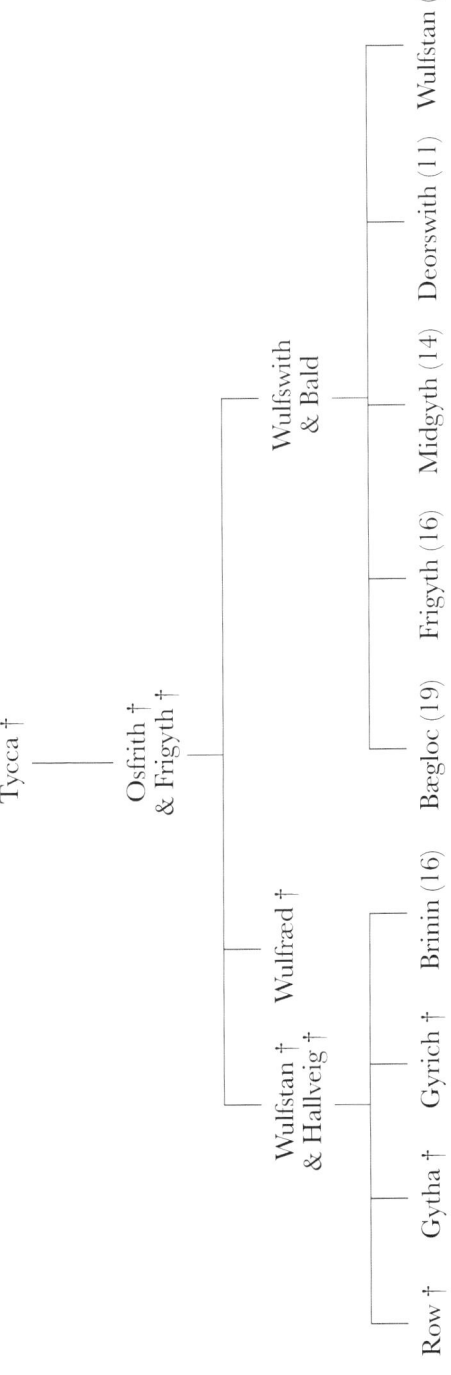

Tycca †

Osfrith †
& Frigyth †

Wulfræd †

Wulfstan †
& Hallveig †

Row † Gytha † Gyrich † Brinin (16)

Wulfswith
& Bald

Bægloc (19) Frigyth (16) Midgyth (14) Deorswith (11) Wulfstan (5)

AFTERWORD

I was surprised how much harder it was to write a sequel, than a first novel. How would the characters developed in *Kith*, continue to mature and behave in *Kin*? With *Kith* I had the luxury of timing the action so that the Danes arrived just as Oswald and Brinin's own story reached its peak. But by the following year the Danes were already in Wessex and would withdraw well before *Kin* was over, so I could not rely solely on them to add interest to the plot. And yet their devastating impact would surely linger on.

As in *Kith*, fictional events take place in the fictional village of Oakdene. Kings, battles and many locations are real.

Historical Events

It is difficult to overestimate how desperate and precarious the position of Wessex was in 871. After defeating the Danes several times early in the year, Wessex grew weaker as they lost more and more men. *Kin* opens with the Battle of Meretun, fought on 22 March 871. The exact location of this battle is unknown, but it seems possible that it may have been near Wimborne Minster in Dorset, as that was where King Æthelred was buried, dying from wounds likely sustained at Meretun. After Æthelred's death, the Witan passed over his two very small sons in favour of his younger brother. And so Ælfred—in his early twenties and possibly suffering from a chronic illness—became king. He would reign for another twenty-eight years, becoming the only British king to be called 'the Great', but he had to survive to the end of 871 first. On the very day of Æthelred's funeral there was another battle at Reading ('Swarms'). However, the Battle of Wilton in May decided the immediate future of Wessex. As portrayed in 'Scythes' and

'Paternoster', Ælfred simply didn't have enough men to keep fighting. In the aftermath of Wilton, he negotiated the Danes' withdrawal.

Much of my historical information was drawn from sources like the *Anglo-Saxon Chronicle* and Asser's *Life of Ælfred*. As with *Kith*, I had to exercise a little creative licence to fill out the lack of detail in these sources. We know of raids like the one portrayed in *Kin*, but I have not found any detailed contemporary descriptions. However, for over a decade, I have lived in an area of West Africa where village raids have tragically become widespread during times of inter-ethnic tension. The raid on Oakdene and its aftermath, and the fear and destruction the Danes left in their wake were all too easy to imagine. I know people who have lived through such events, those who have lost loved ones and homes, and those who have been falsely accused of helping the raiders, facing hatred, threats and ostracism as a result.

Language and Culture
As with *Kith*, I tried where possible to avoid using words that have come into English from Latin or French. This helped to create a style that depended more on Old English, I hope evoking an atmosphere in keeping with the story.

This just touches on some of the background to *Kin*. If you are interested in finding out more, come to my website **julierowbory.com** where I'm adding more detailed information about some of the historical background and linguistic choices I made while writing it.

Julie Rowbory grew up in Northern Ireland and obtained an MA and an MPhil in history from the University of Cambridge. She has worked as a Latin and history teacher, taught English in Asia and lived in East Africa. She is married to David, with whom she has four daughters. They divide their time between Scotland and West Africa.

Made in the USA
Columbia, SC
30 November 2024

48039531R00252